SOMNIUM

Also by Steve Moore:
The Trigrams of Han: Inner Structures of the I Ching
(Aquarian Press 1989)

And, available from Strange Attractor Press:
Tales of Telguuth (2016)
Selene (2018)

First published by Somnium Press in 2011, in association with Strange Attractor Press, in a signed and numbered edition of 250 copies and a standard edition of 250 copies.

This expanded edition, published 2017, contains *Sketches of Shooters Hill*, originally published by Somnium Press in 2012, in an edition of 30. Photographs by Mark Pilkington.

Cover by John Coulthart.
Frontispiece by Steve Moore: The Old Bull Inn, Shooters Hill, 1749–1881.

ISBN: 978-1-907222-51-1

Strange Attractor Press
BM SAP, London, WC1N 3XX, UK
www.strangeattractor.co.uk

Distributed by The MIT Press, Cambridge, Massachusetts.
And London, England.
Printed and bound in the UK by TJ International, Padstow.

SOMNIUM

A Fantastic Romance

STEVE MOORE

Afterword by
ALAN MOORE

Strange Attractor Press
MMXVII

For certain ladies of my acquaintance.
And, of course, for Selene.

Steve Moore

Always, O Moon, you hold my heart in thrall:
Delightful at the full, all golden light,
Or silver-sickled new, in early night;
Red-faced and grim, eclipsed, when witches call
And down from out the sky they cause your fall,
Belaboured into shedding foam, so white,
Lest they destroy you with their sorc'rous might.
Each phase that differs: same my love for all.

Since time began, the Moon was more than this.
Exquisite Goddess, sparkle-eyed with love,
Latmos called, and so you swift descended:
Endymion received your doting kiss.
Now once again you come down from above,
Endless joy to bring, so long portended.

Christopher Morley, 1803

For sweet Elizabeth and the radiant Moon, my lovely Muses both.

Wednesday, 19th September 1803

So all the world is changed, and here I am alone. I'm not sure I can bear it.

I wrote the dedication here above, and how my hand it shook; I'd thought to start my journal with those words since just before I left old London, but when the time had come to write them I could hardly see for tears. One Muse I have and always will, who's now a silver crescent in the sky; the other is not with me.

Oh, Liz, this is so hard.

Thursday, 20th September 1803

Last night, I could not write for thinking; neither could I sleep. I do not know if what I've done is right; some part of me it says it is, another that it's not. I tossed and turned for several hours while my two selves played cudgels in my brain. I suppose I must have dozed at last, for my remembered dreams were much the same as usual: great marble palaces glinting 'neath the scattered stars, and lovely large-eyed ladies; then on the sudden I woke up and found that it was daylight. I wondered where I was. I knew it was not home; the seconds raced before I could remember.

This morning, let me gather up my thoughts; for I had promised Lizzie and myself that I would keep a journal. And I would break a thousand oaths before a promise to my sister.

I miss my dear Elizabeth (so sweet to write her name in full, I hardly like to shorten it); a whole day's passed since last I held her in my arms and kissed her fond farewell. I wish I'd never done it. I miss the family home as well, so close to Oxford Street, and all its dear-loved memories: the attic playroom with its wooden steed (to me the Trojan Horse, to her the Princess Liz's much-loved pony); the staircase where I fell, and how she kissed my bruises better; the little garden where, in years gone by, we played at catch-me-if-you-can. It's strange that, now I'm gone, my thoughts run back to innocent childhood days. The apple tree she was too short to reach, and how I teased her for it; how big-eyed she was when at the last I let her eat the fruit. Or how an apple and a twig became the orb and sceptre, the garden seat a throne; and she was Gloriana, I the Earl of Leicester. Or Ralegh on another time, or Essex; but she was always Virgin Queen. Elizabeth, who made me knight with but a stick, and such a charming giggle; and me so earnest in acceptance, nine years old and all my honour and my heart enchained to her forever. And so my thoughts grow maudlin once again.

Yet here I am in Kent. It's true that back in London, I was quite reclusive; I simply had no cause or wish for mingling with others. Here I am surrounded all about with unfamiliar faces; and so I realise I never did quite learn the art of charming strangers, too busy was I with my books. How I wish that Liz was with me; for if she has no greater social graces, at least I know she loves me. What other people think of me, I simply cannot tell.

I know I could not stay in London; yet leaving, it seems such a great mistake.

I left; it was so painful. And yet I did not leave her all alone. Old Mistress Jones will see to all her comforts, her virtue and her safety; and there are all the other maids and servants too. I know if I'd remained behind, I'd never write a word; and I just want to write for her, to show her all my dreams made real. She wants to see me famous; all her admiration of me is so sweet. And yet I know her eyes will never see my faults; and any words I write, I know she'll love them. If others, all unknown, can love my words the way she loves my person; why then I'll know I've written something well, and worthy of my Liz. I hope the Moon will help me do it.

And there's another reason too, to flee. Sometimes I fear we act out ancient myths; and one or two of them perhaps may be quite central to our lives entire, while other times we take on lesser roles. And if with that celestial Muse I like to think I might aspire (with all the Gods a-willing) to be her own Endymion, with her below... I hardly dare to write it here... I would I were not Caunus, but rather fear I am; for oft I think of her as Byblis. And so as Caunus fled, then so did I; and neither he nor I, I know, would wish to.

But see? My Liz she has me in her thrall, though nine miles or more they intervene. She laughed aloud when first I told her she had witchcraft, thought I jested; joked of warty noses, bended backs and chins that reached down to her knees. I told her olden witches had no power; young sweet sorceresses never could be quite escaped. She laughed again and said I was so silly. I told her in return that she was lovely; and so we lapsed then into silence. I remember how she looked that night, all dressed in white and laced with gold beneath a beaming gibbous Moon. I thought she looked a Goddess or a Star-nymph; told her that as well. I swore she was an ideal form, dropped down from Plato's higher worlds; and that I'd never have a sweetheart less the fair than she. She blushed so sweet, right down below the shoulders; she was too pretty not to kiss. Oh, the heaven I descended from, when once I thought to leave.

Yet yesterday at 12 o'clock I kissed her, hugged her, wiped away my tears. Her chestnut tresses tumbling down; the silk-sewn jasmine flowers, so white and richly scented, tucked above her little ears; her pale throat slightly trembling. I told her that I loved her, promised I would write; it was so melancholy sweet to hear her say the same. And after that my arms would hardly let her go.

My trunk already loaded, I climbed into the coach and cursed it roundly 'neath my breath; prayed for sickly horses or for broken wheels. Alas, the Gods would give me neither. Although my arm would hardly move, I thumped my cane against the roof, and then we were away. I looked back out the window, waved a weakened hand; my Liz she raised an arm and started forward uncontrolled, and next I thought she wiped away a tear. We rattled round a corner then; and how I cursed that wall for cutting off my sight. I felt that she might never yet be seen again. Five minutes passed before I could look round me; till then my eyes were simply shut upon the horrors of the world.

An ancient bald-pate parson, face all full of pox-pits, and a florid snoring man obese enough to terrify a child or horse, they were my only companions; I have to think the both of them quite drunk because they slept throughout the journey's long entirety. And so they did not see me weep.

Crossing over London Bridge, I thought of Shakespeare, Marlowe and *The Globe*; of cock-fights, bear-bait pits and raucous pleasure-grounds; and tawdry old Elizabethan stews purveying painful clap and pox to both the highest and the low. All gone now, of course (except perhaps disease), though whether Southwark of the present age is any way the better, I doubt me very much. Then out onto the New Cross Turnpike which, I'm told, improves so greatly on the ancient road, one never would believe it; I have to say I didn't. Or rather, if I did, the former road was quite beyond my comprehension. Past Marlowe's Deptford then; another day I would have paused to pay him my respects, for an olden family tradition told me by my ancient uncle has it that we Morleys share collateral descent with long-gone Kentish Marlowes. I like to think we did (for after all, to have the author of *The Tragical History of Dr Faustus* in the family-line would be felicity beyond compare). Then up the hill at hardly more than walking pace to blood-soaked old Blackheath, the scene, some centuries gone, of battles I forget (and yet, ere that, I know, no lesser person than the Emperor of the Byzantines pitched his tents all hereabouts, for talks with English kings; so high our sovereigns then to draw such embassies, so far indeed from glorious Constantinople of the massy walls and Golden Horn, ere it fell unto the cursed turbaned Turk).

With change of horse at The Old Green Man, our driver Philips cocked his pistols and then applied the whip. The thievish wander even here, though less oft by the day; although I knew the hill ahead more dangerous yet by far. My companions snored; I hated the both of them quite equally: the one who loved a god I long abhorred, the other's god was nothing but his belly (I will not give the Christian god the honour of a capital, though gladly would I enlarge on Goddess; the latter is the All to me, the former I despise). We passed a hundred minor tomb-mounds on the heath; I thought the happy long-dead blessed that they had never lived to see the wretched 19th century. My sister and myself I would preserve; the rest can rot alive in hell. There must be other worlds than this, and finer too by far; and if we cannot find our way to them, perhaps we can create them in our dreams.

A way across the heath we turned onto the Roman road; I knew it straight away, for now the coach no longer lurched on curves. We rattled on through rolling fields of dark green furze and made good time, despite the road's quite execrable state; the recent rains, they told me when I was arrived, had washed out pot-holes everywhere, and some of them quite deep. The bouncing and the jouncing were hardly to be borne.

And so, approaching Shooters Hill, I knew that hereabouts three centuries since plain Anne of Cleves encamped, in hope forlorn of Henry's love. But most of all, I felt the Legions march beside me; felt them stamp and saw them red and silver; heard their raucous songs of buggered Caesar and lewd Bithynian kings. And loved them for their loud and pagan laughter. Though how a Latin laugh might sound, I merely could conjecture.

They nowise would have laughed at how their road was now decayed. I could not ever say what a great relief it was to dismount at the foot of the hill when at the last we were arrived; the road being both so steep and now so muddy that a fully laden coach would have had the greatest difficulty to ascend.

Shooters Hill, it seems, is all of inns: The Fox Under the Hill (though picturesquely named, a hovelish beer-shop and little more than that) at its western foot; The Red Lion halfway up; The Golden Lion down a lane from there; The Bull upon its crest, replacing now The Catherine Wheel; and round its base, on other sides, I gather many more.

The inns were quite apparent; the highwaymen that give the hill its ill-repute were fortunately out of view. I found myself rather disquieted, however, to discover that in recent months these many inns have instituted a system of hiring out armed guards for the journeys made between them, coaches being most vulnerable upon the intervening slopes. I fear to say I have a rather strong impression that these same armed guards, a scarred and surly bunch and quite unwashed, if not hired for the purpose, might well turn out to be the very same depredatious villains that they would otherwise be 'protecting us' from. But such is the way of the world, and as I would be staying hereabouts, I paid my contribution willingly enough, and with a gratuity besides. I laughed to see the priestly and the grossly fat awoken too for similar exactions. The latter paid the more besides, in order not to walk. For all I know, the climb it would have killed him.

The hill is steep, the walk was hard; yet at the last I was arrived, in daylight and with time to spare for supper (a most excellent oyster and kidney pudding). A vast palatial place, The Bull, almost too big to comprehend on first inspection. The sinking sun was flashing on the thick glass panes and so, a moment, then, I thought the building all of silver-golden mirrors. My trunk got down (none too gently) from the coach, I stood a moment looking up toward the tower rising high above the entrance door, its lantern-windows designed quite plainly for the sight-seeing; and knew I wanted that room entirely for myself. All else: the dance hall (or 'Assembly Room' as I later discovered it actually so called), the tap-house, the stables and coach-houses and I know not what, they seem to sprawl in all directions, one, two and three storeys tall, all hardly more than 50 years old, though as I gather The Bull may not have been the first building on the site, some parts might yet be older. Perhaps a greater age would add somewhat to the atmosphere, but I confess the modern amenities are more than welcome. There's much here that I've still to explore; an entire pleasure ground stands, I gather, out behind the inn; there was no daylight left to see it.

I had, of course, written beforehand to reserve a room, though as it seems there are no other long-term guests (or right now even short-term ones, as far as I can see) this was perhaps a little less than necessary. I somehow think the new century treats The Bull unkind; that perhaps its glory-days already lie behind it, and now there's naught ahead but slow decline, from florid, gay *jeunesse* to stiffened, grey *morbidité* (I must remember not to speak French in public while I'm here, the situation being as it is). My suspicion falls upon the current landlord, recently arrived it seems: if ever there was a man suited to kill the goose that laid the golden eggs, he seems the one to me. I hardly like to mention him here at all; but then again, it gives me opportunity to relieve myself of all my spleen and vituperation.

And so...

My host Jude Brown's a balding, surly wretch who dresses most in colours like his name, and that, I do suspect, because they do not show the dirt; I thought him old before his time and, frankly, wish him in his grave. 'Morley the *writer*,' he sneered when I announced my arrival, with all that bristling resentment that only the ignorant can show. I have not cared to enquire how he takes his pleasure; I can only imagine that it somehow involves the torture of small and helpless squealing animals. I thought him oafish and, showing my contempt, I paid him for my room and board a full month in advance, and gave him guineas when he asked for pounds. He became servile. Upon the instant then I knew: I hate him. It pleases me to think ahead and hope I'll hear him screaming as he roasts in hell eternal.

More than this, when I enquired of the tower-room, he bluntly did refuse me. I offered him a guinea more than all I'd paid already. He refused me still, but oh, the torments of cupidity that racked his base and miserable soul; I think I've never felt such deep contempt. He is a worm, as spineless as he's avaricious; and yet, I think, he's poison.

Yet Mistress Brown, his wife, is quite another matter. If dearest Liz was half as old again, they would not look too different: brown eyes so bright, her auburn hair so long, an easy smile, and full of charm. The latest fashions, too, she wears: a long and thin white high-waist dress that almost falls from off her shoulders, and all that fairest flesh exposed above her bosom offset by a chain of garnets. I thought so much of Lizzie then, who wears a dress so like it back at home; but Mistress Brown she fills it rather better than my slim young sister. She showed me to my room and whispered in my ear (charming this, I thought, there being no one near to hear) how Jude Brown charged a penny for admission to the tower room, to those who wished to take the view. I asked her if she thought, late autumn as it was, 250 people would ascend the tower in the month or so I'd stay there; she gave me such a lopside look I almost slipped her the guinea anyway. I cannot think (no, more than that, I refuse to think) of she and he abed; she is too fair, he is too foul; I think she could not bear it either, and thus they have no children. But why a woman so vivacious should marry such a boor, I simply cannot fathom.

Before supper, I slapped a penny in Brown's grasping hand and had him show me up the tower (in truth, it must be said, it was not furnished up for occupation as I'd hoped), so I could look back, sad, to London. I wished that there were telescopes so powerful that I could see my Liz; instead I saw that monstrous heap of Wren's St Paul's. It squats there on the landscape like an awful giant candle-snuff, a crushing weight of that foul Christian church that damns all men to hell with sin.

In Roman times, there was a temple of Diana there.

The views, it must be said, they truly are magnificent, and I could not help but think mayhap that Julius Caesar himself had come this way and, near a century later, Claudius besides, Vespasian, perhaps, commander in his army; indeed, that all of them might once have stood (perhaps a little lower) upon the very same spot as I and looked, whether at barely-founded London, or Troya Nova, or whatever existed then or didn't, across the same broad landscape as I myself did in the fading light, all stretched out there as far as distant Harrow-on-the-Hill (though barely seen for choked and rising smoke of myriad household chimneys in between). And if New Troy was but a fantasy of olden Welshman Geoffrey, how much the more appealing than the sprawl we have today.

Perhaps to me, though, far more important than the sight of London that I have from here is that I *am not in it*, cannot hear its noise, or smell its stinks, nor feel the claustrophobic oppression of its thronging masses. For all I love my sister and the family home, I do not have that robust nature necessary for London; I know that if I had stayed much longer there, I would have gone quite mad. Here, where the hill rises high above that press, and babble and smoke, and all the war-talk and the cursing of the French; and worse, the unclean streets and crush of carriages; then here at last, I might be able to think. And thinking, then, be able to write my thoughts all down. My chief regret, of course, is that my dearest Liz is not here with me now; but I know that if she was, I would not think of writing down a word.

And if I can but think and write, and dream, what marvel phantom palaces might be built, up here on Shooters Hill...

And yet, perhaps, The Bull itself somehow partakes of all that makes me marvel; or someone living in it.

After supper, Mistress Brown invited me to share a drink with her; I thought this was quite sweet of her to try to make me welcome. And yet I could not. I was too tired, the world was all too strange; I missed my Liz. I asked her to excuse me; when I saw the corners of her lovely mouth a-suddenly so drooped, I promised I would drink with her tonight. I almost promised more than this: that if she would but smile again then I would ever be her slave. A moment then she looked at me all quizzical, as if I was some beast incomprehensible.

'Young man,' she said (I almost died for shame to hear her call me so), 'a thousand hulking brutes would lay down flat upon the ground for merest chance to drink with me. I do not know if you are wise, or you are stupid; and yet, I think I like you. So go to bed and rest your head; tomorrow night, we'll drink so much, that surely you will lose it.'

I did not know if she was kind or she was not; and yet, the moment passed, we smiled, and laughed, and so at last I took me to my room. To my great delight, I've obtained a corner room upon the upper floor with windows facing both to east and south: to east I look out over little villages called Welling and East Wickham, and across the wide and rolling Kentish country; to south the trees are far enough away across the road for my eyes to wander up and down a vast and starry sky. More to the point, I can look toward the rising Moon and, with this elevated viewpoint, see the first appearance of her lovely radiant head above the far horizon, then gaze for hours upon my beaming Muse as up she sails serenely to the zenith of the dark-night sky (the sunrise, of course, I intend each day to miss). This causes me far more than merest pleasure. I feel myself thus welcomed to my temporary home, and to the beginning of my work, by the world's oldest and most beautiful Goddess. My pleasure it was somewhat marred by hearing, down below, some drunken wretch upon the road who would sing patriotic songs and, worse, 'god save the king.' So, all frustrate, I asked the Moon above, with all her gracious pleasure, to deliver him forthwith into the brutal hands of the nearest ugly press-gang. My evening, it had gone astray.

I looked upon that sweet and silver crescent; I was so sad to be here on the Earth and wished that I was up there in the Moon. The Moon it is a world of ladies; I hate the world of men.

I woke to neighing horses, clattering hooves, slamming doors and squeals of poorly oiled wheels. And, as I said, I did not know quite where I was, except it was too noisy. I realised at last that even at The Bull, the 19th century was too close; I fear I never will escape it.

I slept again a short while then, and know I dreamt of dearest Liz; I think she wept and missed me, worried for my safety too. I woke and missed her just as much; the more because there was so little I could remember of my dream.

I rose, but kept within my room; the day outside had turned to rain. And so the morning's passed with writing in my journal; I'll now to dinner, and then this afternoon, begin my work. I decided on awaking here to call the story *Somnium*. It speaks so sweetly of the Moon, and Goddesses, and unattainable longed-for love. And hardly formed as it may be so far, I know it's full of joy and pain, and how they coalesce.

Its hero's named Endimion Lee; his darling is Diana.

Friday, 21st September 1803

So, yester-afternoon I scribbled many notes, and arrived at a bare schematic of my story; but far too much, I do confess, I thought of dearest Liz. At last I knew the best for me was but to combine the two. I'd made two promises to my sweet young sister: that I would not return until my story it was written, and more, besides, that before Christmas I would again be home (I think foul scorn upon the wretched festival as far as its religion; and yet I do confess to thinking well enough of roasted turkey, brandy-flamed plum-pudding, and dancing with my Liz). And so I'll write this tale for Liz, and surely be home in time to offer it as a gift.

And more, besides: my story's set in that golden-glowed

Elizabethan era, so close to both our hearts. So when I write each single word about that puissant Queen, it cannot help but bring another Liz to mind.

I went for supper. I think it was stewed duck; I hardly noticed. For Mistress Brown sat down there with me at my table in the hotel dining room. Before my supper it was even served, she had two glasses there upon the table; an open bottle of claret and a smile I thought was rather wicked.

If I'd offended her the previous night, she had the strangest way to show it. I told myself that, as the only rooming guest, she simply wished to make a fuss of me; but, honestly, I do not know the thoughts that put that sparkle in her eye. Young though I may be, I hardly think myself as handsome; and beyond that, she knew no single thing about me. And yet I simply knew that last night there'd be no possible escape: I'd drink with her or all my life here in The Bull, it would be hell. And so I let her fill my glass; for if she wished to make me welcome, I could hardly say her nay. I saw her husband glare at me, while passing to the cellar. I wanted then to tell him that I would quite happily be upstairs; I could not.

And yet, for all my earliest misgivings, I would not have missed that evening for the world. The first bottle of claret we drank there while I dined; she plied me with so many eager questions that I told her, if she had been a papist and a man, then she could easily have found extended work with all those villains of the Inquisition. I asked her if she preferred the rack, the pilliwinks or boot. She laughed and threatened me with further claret, pale sack and, if I would not submit at all, she'd have to resort at last, then, to the kiss. For that, I said, a stronger man than me would tell her anything she wished. She laughed the more, and all I ever thought to see of sauciness was there and dancing in her eyes. Of sin, however, I hardly could convict her. For after all, her dress was white, like Liz's, or a Vestal Virgin's, or rather more than this, I thought, the chaste and lovely Goddess of the Moon.

And so, I think, before too long had passed, I told her all she wished to know; I simply could not help it. I told her how the seizure it had carried off my father, so long ago I hardly could remember; more recently of fever's grip that took my much-loved mother. Of how I'd learned my Latin and my Greek at old St Olave's and St Saviour's Grammar School in Bermondsey, where they had taught the same since the Virgin Queen was sat upon the throne; but having neither cause nor great desire, I'd then foregone a place at Oxford. I fear I may have said too much of breweries inherited in the Midlands, that meant I had no need of work, but gave me time to write. I told her how the family now was nothing more than Liz and I, but what I told her else I simply cannot think. I hope I did not make her think me rich, or suggest to overhearing ears there might be aught of value in my trunk. But whatever I said was said, and cannot be recalled.

And she, in turn, she told me tales of The Bull that made me laugh, or made me gape in disbelief. Of fortunes and of mansions lost and won there in the card-rooms; of teeth knocked out with billiard balls; of highwaymen escaping from the law while dressed up in their mistress' clothes; of fornications on the very dance-floor, and how they said that certain present ministers of the crown were conceived there as a result. With such relish did she tell me, I hardly cared at all to think of truth or silly falsehood.

Yet sometimes, when she paused, I thought to see another, stranger light that glinted in her eye. I could not think quite what it was, but somehow (oh, it sounds impossible) I had the impression that someone else was looking out through her large and lovely eyes, and more, from a great distance too. And whoever that someone was, and wherever she was, the both were somehow more supremely *real* than anything to be found on Earth. And to that cool glance, all the stories dripping from her lips were merely passing entertainments, The Bull a flimsy stage-set, and all this world and all its passing show, but fictions. I confess I do not know if claret made me think this; I am quite certain, though, that with further claret I forgot it.

The bottle that succeeded to the first, we drank it in her private parlour, a room of rather sybaritic comfort (or so it seemed to me) that stands behind the hotel bar-room; the *chaise longue* that she insisted we should share was padded, soft and covered overall with velvet, turquoise-blue and curlicued in gold. She sat quite close and offered up a toast: she to me, and so I offered her another in return. A blazing fire was in the room, and so she cast away the shawl from round her shoulders; and then that fairest skin revealed, betwixt her neck and (oh, let me write it here in private) her breasts, quite took my breath away. A third bottle of claret then succeeded to the second. By the fourth I thought her rather sweet, although I knew a decade separated her from me. No, I tell a lie. By the second I thought her rather sweet; by the fourth I could not tell quite who she was, but thought her mother, sister, sweetest friend and then I know not what. She confused me more by playing soft upon the harpsichord, and so reminded me of Liz, who entertains me thus at home. Or someone played, I'm sure they did. And someone helped me off to bed; I cannot quite say who.

I dreamed once more of silver towers, but now they were confused, somehow, with this vast Bull tavern where I sleep, as if from solid brick rose dream-stuff, sparkling and soaring, to flaunt its gemmeous splendours to a Moon-illumined sky. And one palatial door stood open and inviting; yet all beyond was darkness and I know not what. I was still hesitating on the threshold when at last the dream was ended.

I did not wake before dinner-time, and when I did my head was all a-throb. And going down the stairs I almost fell. I could not quite believe how Mistress Brown was sparkle-eyed and laughing. I told her then that all I wished was milk and more, perhaps, a cool wet cloth to wipe across my brow. She looked at me so sweet and so concerned. I thought she was quite lovely.

She said that she was bad, and helped me back upstairs. She laid me down and placed a wet cold kerchief on my forehead, closed the shutters and told me I should sleep till supper. More, she made me promise that nothing further would I attempt, and when I did so, then she kissed me on the cheek. I knew it was an impulse; she blushed so sweetly pink. I wanted then to call her back and kiss her ten times more; but she was out the door before I could. I thought my head was near to kill me, I could not quite believe it. I lay there thinking:

'Mistress Brown, I do not know quite who you are, or what you've done to me. Last night I thought you angel down from heaven; today I think you dearest demon, and yet I do not know quite what to say. But for that kiss, I think, I will forgive you anything, even though my aching skull should crack and all my palpitating brain escape to freedom.'

I lay there till the daylight went and then, at last, began to feel a little better. Mistress Brown she brought my supper on a tray and served me in my room; I thought that rather kind. She brought a bottle of claret and a jug of cold boiled water from the well; made me promise, if I drank at all, I'd mix the two by halves. I told her that I would, and then I smiled at her weakly; she looked at me so gently. I do not know quite what it is that seems to make dear ladies wish to mother me. I'd think it was because I'd lost my own, but Liz has lost hers too; and when I'm in the grip of illness, then she is more sweet than mother ever was to me.

So after eating supper I felt rather more recovered, and since that time I've lain here on the bed and written all these pages of my journal. The Moon is up, the clouds have cleared; the time has come to work. I'm tempted just to drink the claret, but I have made a promise, and they tell me that the water here is good.

And so, I think, with a half a drink, and a full toast to the Moon, I'll begin to write my story, to bring this world of dreams that's formed within my head to life upon the page.

SOMNIUM
by Christopher Morley
(First draft, commenced September 1803. For Liz.)

When Tiberius Claudius Nero Germanicus Caesar deigned first to set his imperial foot upon the ancient soil of fair Britannia's isle (four entire legions sent before him armed, to teach the warlike locals peace) he progressed triumphant from the Kentish coast toward what would, in latter days, be known as old Londinium, road-building as he came with marvellous speed. Primary road in all the land of Albion, ever the same though many-named... Vitellius' Street, Watling Street, the Dover Road... those of us who stride its straightness now-days might remember, on occasion, that it was builded by an emperor with a dragging limp, unable to place one foot direct before the other.

Eight miles from London Bridge, old Watling Street runs up, and over, and down high Shooters Hill, which ever had but a single name, and no one living knows precisely what it means.

But no, like ancient Claudius too, your author stutters in his speech. In the reign of that most glorious Queen Elizabeth Tudor, the Miracle of Time and Wonder of her Age, robber-haunted Shooters Hill bore an alias besides: the Hill of Blood.

And it is when this tall and wooded eminence bore so sanguinary a title, that our story begs its gentle reader's leave... to begin...

'Why how now, good my lord?' asked Bartholomew Greene, an otherwise amicable young page, excepting only his addiction to the plays, to the cant phrase, and all too loose iambics. Sir Endimion Lee, reining in his horse, just looked at him askance, and wondered at the crinkled autumn leaf that whirled a-sudden round his head.

'Why stop you here, my lord?' continued Greene. 'This hill has all too ill a name.'

'And you, my Bart, have far too loose a tongue,' Master Lee replied in kind. 'I pause because the breeze blows strange, and stars shine far too early. We're benighted when we should be dusked, and the world, methinks, is somewhat out of joint.'

'Oh, let it not be robbers, lord!' moaned Greene, a-tremble in his saddle. But which of his lords he called upon, not even he could say.

Lee stood up in his stirrups then, and cast his eye around. A mile or so behind them, ancient Eltham Palace stood, three centuries old, or more. To their right rose deeply-wooded Shooters Hill, a dark and brooding threat beneath the nighted sky. Before them, the Well Hall Road (a muddy track) ran on to cross the wide hill-vaulting Dover Road that, running to their left, would take them on toward the lovely Palace of Placentia, sprawled along the riverbank at Greenwich. Placentia,

where her Imperial Majesty Elizabeth no doubt awaited Lee's arrival with
her usual fickle temper and the irritated finger-drumming of her hot
impatient soul. A soul that flamed the colour of her hair, worn loose in
virgin style; yet in its cooler moments, storming temper calmed by an
oiled and flattering word, would deign to dance with lesser men and
courtiers, a goddess reaching down to take the hand of mortals. And Lee,
all dressed up in his finest Spanish doublet, embroidered neat with silver,
had clad himself to please her; or so at least he hoped.

All seemed quiet and familiar, and nothing different to the many
times they'd ridden by before. And yet...

It was too dark, too early.

'Ride onward, Bart,' said Lee just then, applying a gentle spur. 'I know
not what's afoot, but let's away from here. The crossroads is not far ahead.'

'The crossroads?' gasped poor Greene upon the instant, eyes
a-bulge to show their whites, iambics all forgot. 'The crossroads are
foul Hecat's realm, and in this dark, her hellhound pack... oh master,
let's across the fields and avoid her howling hunt...'

'And break our horses' legs in unseen ditches? You're a blockhead,
Bart, and those hell-damned playmakers have addled all your brains.
'Od's teeth, but I'm glad you cannot read; otherwise who knows what
twaddle you might spout. Now let's be on, and not another word.'

By all-unspoke agreement then, they put their horses to the trot,
mounting the none-too-steep incline and arriving, in the end, at the
expected crossroads. Far behind them now was Royal Eltham; to ride
on straight would take them down to Woolwich Dockyards, haunt
of raucous porter-swilling seadogs like Master Drake and all his salt-
encrusted ilk. An ilk unliked enough by Master Lee that he'd be glad
enough to make his leftwards turn.

And yet, the darkness thickened.

Crossing himself like a recusant Catholic and muttering soft of
Hecat's dogs that hunt down young men's souls, Bartholomew Greene
pulled hard on leftward rein, and kicked his heels for Greenwich. Only,
a moment later, though, to pull back on the bridle, for Master Lee no
longer rode there by his side.

Greene looked back behind him then, but held his ground. For the sight before his eyes, he knew, was haggard Hecat's work, and could be of no other.

Standing on the crossroads' further side, toward grim Shooters Hill, a curious carriage stood. Greene recognised it straight as one of the new-called 'coaches' (though some did call them 'chariots'), introduced of late from Europe, lighter and faster and more to the passengers' comfort far than olden plodding wagons. But this...

This was all of silver sheen and glinting crystal, its seats upholstered with cloth-of-gold and smoothest satin, with peacock-feathered crests upon the brows of two fine milk-white mares that neighed and struck the stone-paved road with sparking metal shoes. Not from Europe, this, but quite another world. And suddenly the Moon was up, and though he knew it came from hell, the coach was all aglitter.

Neither driver nor passenger was anywhere in sight. But Sir Endimion Lee, that far-too-foolish master to whose service he was sworn, alas, was dismounting from his horse, and had his hazel eyes on coach alone. Bart Greene looked once upon the long brown mane and short small beard, the lined and world-weary face, the night-dark doublet that his master wore; and wondered if he'd ever see the like again. With a discontented sigh and all the urgent speed of a pave-besliming snail, Greene then turned back to join him.

'No sign of robbers, vagabonds, or any ill,' remarked Sir Lee as Greene drew rein, a dozen paces off, his blue eyes paling grey with utmost trepidation. 'But such is hereabouts' repute...'

A long and narrow sword then slithered free, with rasping sound, from out its leathered scabbard. And glinted by that self-same Moon which silvered all the carriage.

'Get you gone to Greenwich, Bartho' Greene,' commanded Lee, a-gesture with his rapier, 'and give your master's compliments to Dudley, Earl of Leicester. Say I offer deep apologies to him, the first, and then, if he'll be kind to pass them on, to our beloved Sovereign Lady, the high and royal Queen. When I've probed this mystery here, I'll follow on; but as the both will understand, I fear some lady may be deep in need of any aid that I might offer. And now begone, and as you ride, remember this: the faster you apply the spur, the slower the devil to catch you up!'

No second bidding needed, Greene wheeled his mount about and kicked it to the gallop. And for all a mile along that old straight road, he never once looked back; and so saw naught of that which fell out next.

Endimion Lee walked once about the richly-holstered carriage, seeing nothing of suspicion. No mud-pressed foot or hoof prints, no sign of swift attack nor trace of unwilled kidnap. At last, shaking his head as he sheathed his sword, he opened up the coach's door and climbed within, sat slowly down on soft seat-cushion and, looking round, once again saw naught amiss.

Now quite perplexed, he let his eyelids close, and on the instant felt the carriage lurch. Hammered iron horseshoes clacked upon the road-pave, banded wheels began to turn. As if a-drowsed with sleep, he struggled hard to open up his eyes again, only now to find that all around seemed bathed in golden light. And yet, although by then his thoughts were dancing brawls and seventeens, he found he could not move.

The silvered carriage, moonbeam-lit, turned itself around unguided, and started up the hill. And, willy-nilly, Sir Endimion Lee perforce went with it.

The utmost peak of wooded Shooters Hill he knew quite well, crowded all about with oak and ash and hornbeam. At least, he knew it well in other days, but on a night like this all former knowledge failed him. At the hill's tall crest the coach turned left and north, along a drive that plainly was not there.

It was not there and never had been and, indeed, he somehow knew, it never would be either.

Nor was the gateway that he passed through next, which opened in a marbled wall; nor the garden spread beyond, with lapping ponds and burbling streams, and marvellous statues all marmoreal, paled and whitened by the rising Moon.

The palace that he reached at last, where the silver carriage halted, was, quite simply, never even seen before in delirium or dream.

Nor Greenwich, no, nor Eltham; nor Hampton Court, nor Richmond; not even glorious Nonsuch, that could not be believed... comparison here made all of these mere hovels. For before him rose up miracle and splendour, and wonder past all telling, enamelled, silvered and bejewelled. All arabesqued it was, in gleaming argent lit by moonbeams, and cupolas interspersed with turrets first, but more with spires next, both rising to the sky. It seemed mosaiced quite in tesserae of crystal, its galleries all filigreed with gleaming gem-flecked bronze; and from within, through oriels so large, came light, and light, and light. And more, about its gateway, there was sweet Diana, imaged up in tiny stones, of opals and of turquoise, and set about with silver, with electrum, and with gold.

And Endimion Lee, who though he'd seen so many things, and thought of more besides, could only sit, and look, and weep. Weep for shame that never human hand had built the like, and weep for joy that he had seen what only dear immortal gods had otherwise beheld.

He sat there, tear-stained still, when the carriage door was opened by a lovely nymph, whose sparkling eyes could only make him think of sweethearts, daughters, sisters, and all those fairest of their sex who are the most beloved. She took his hand in hers, so small, and helped him from the coach.

All dressed in moonbeam white she was, and yet in gossamer light enough to hardly be at all. She gently laughed, now holding both his hands in hers, and tripping backwards nimbly led him on toward a much-begilded door. And Lee, with eyes for nothing but her smile (as surely was intended), thought not to linger with his gaze beguiled by silver towers a-shimmer, by star-aspiring turquoised turrets, or crystal spires that probed the deepest heavens.

The beauty of his charming guide quite silenced all the questions in his mind before they reached his lips. An eyeful of heaven, he thought her, and let her lead him (so it seemed) down deep and mazy corridors lit by Moonish gems (he'd think them all carbuncles, yet they were too lunar), until they came at last to gold-leaved doors, that opened with a mere soft sigh.

Once through those doors, that sweet sprite left him then, although he hardly knew. For now he had his senses back, and she he saw ahead commanded, wordless and by look alone: *O man of Earth, bow down.*

Saturday, 22nd September 1803

I know it quite immodest to say as much, and yet I have to confess that I am rather pleased; the pages of *Somnium* that I wrote last night, I simply do not know quite where they came from. Perhaps they came down from the Moon; and if they did, I love the Moon for sending them. I cannot know what others might quite think of them, and yet I know I never wrote the finer. Endimion Lee, it seems to me, already walks these pages like a real man and comrade; I cannot think at all that I have 'made him up'. Of course, it wrote itself so well I am not sure of each historic detail; but these I can correct when I am home once more, surrounded by my books; besides, of course, it is a work of fiction. And though I did not notice at the time, I find I've used no 'thou' or 'thee', and this seems all the better; a flavour of the time is what I want, and not perfected archaism. I wrote and wrote until the nearly-dawn, and slept the most part of the morning through. I dreamed, and loved in dream, and made my love in some peculiar dream-place; but *who* I loved in dream I really cannot say.

I woke up all fog-brained and did not call for breakfast. My senses once recaptured, I wrote a letter to my darling Liz, to tell her how I missed her; told her she was sweet, a spring-flower blooming still among the golden autumn leaves; told her she was Queen of Hearts and fairer than her royal namesake; told her nothing, I confess, of bright-eyed Mistress Brown, but sent her all my love and kisses. Told her that it hurts me not to see her smiling in the morning; and when I do not hear her laugh, there is no music in the world. I told her, too, how carefully she must guard her health, though all the horrors of my thoughts I could not bring myself to tell her. I could not bear to see her sweet young face all pitted with the smallpox, or to watch her slowly wasting with consumption. O Gods and Goddesses dear, above, if such there be amongst our fates, then let it fall on me. And so I wrote to her, I thought of her, and writing, thinking, thought that I would cry. The further away she is, the dearer she becomes.

I confess I become bemused with Mistress Brown. After dinner (I did not know quite what it was; some dish of chopped-up meat in gravy, served with hot potato pie) I enquired of that wretch, her husband, as to where I could put a letter in the post. He looked at me all surly; before he could reply, and all I think to spite him, she took my arm and led me off outside, proclaiming loudly that it would be a pleasure to walk out with a *gentleman* and show him. The emphasis she placed on 'gentleman' it rather made me wince, for all its implication. And once out on the road, she could not help her laughing. Her motives then, I did not even ask. Her husband and herself are so mismatched, it leaves me quite bewildered.

She walked me halfway down the hill toward old London town, pointing out two large establishments as we did progress. To the south side of the road, quite near the crest, stands Hazelwood House, built a quarter century gone where once there stood the former hilltop inn, The Catherine Wheel (or sometimes, so it seems, The Catherine Wheel and Star; I think I like that better, for so it minds me of the sky, and not the swarming Earth). To the north, a little further down, Broomhall, the mansion of the Lidgbirds, to whom belong the ground rents of The Bull and all its large establishments. Some strange and occult sympathy seemed to draw me to Broomhall. I thought that I would like to see inside; but Mistress Brown informed me that its inhabitants played the eremite, and so were hardly seen at all, except to drive off trespassers.

Some halfway down the hill, we came to that rather inferior hostelry (or so it did appear to me, a lady of the other inn a-clinging on my arm), the Red Lion, where, it seems, the post's collected and delivered daily. She introduced me to the landlord, one Eustatius Wellbeloved, smirked and told him that he'd see me often; for like him, I was quite well-beloved besides. I looked at her askance. And when we started up the hill again, she smiling whispered then: 'Elizabeth.'

I should have been offended. I should have told her this was no one's business but my own. And yet I could not. She is too lovely. Her eyes are too much like my Lizzie's. And more, she seems the younger every time I see her.

I think, the night before last, that when I was too drunk, I talked to her too freely: she knew too much of Liz, and more she seemed to understand how much I love my sister. And so I worry all the more of what I may have said regarding our inheritance. If she were quite alone, I would not care; I'd trust her with my very soul; and yet her husband seems to me a knavish wretch.

Returning to The Bull, I do confess to being loth to lose the pleasure of her company; and so I asked her if she'd show me something of the inn. It is a building quite to match the tales she told me of the place when we were both bedrunk. And so we wandered through the supper rooms, their plastered ceilings painted up rococo-style (not well, but well enough) with naked nymphs and satyrs, the billiard room, the card-rooms and the bar; and so into the assembly room, so huge and high-ceilinged and, empty as it was, acousticked like a church. I stood there for a moment then, just imagining Handel's *Firework Music* played therein, and the majesty it would have had, its woodwinds and its brass high-echoed to the rafters.

Stables for more than 30 horses, she showed me next, with coach-houses, a smithy, granaries, a dairy and an ice-house; a yard, the pleasure grounds all full of walks quite charmingly serpentine; the kitchen gardens, the orchard and the land, all cultivate or grazed by sheep. It is a palace self-contained; no, more than this, it is a self-contained estate, a palace at its centre, and so within itself a state entire: the state of Shooters Hilltop, raised up high above mere London Town, or Kent the orchard county. It speaks to me of palaces silvered up with Moonlight; and so, in turn, I am reminded much of Somnium here on Earth.

The last, she took me to the tap-house, a little public tavern on the Kentish side, where all the passing trade it drinks, and dines, and goes its way. I thought it rather quaint, though verging on plebeian. She told me down below there was a cellar, walled up quite, that legend said contained a table; and on that table lay a horse-pistol, chased with silver. But what the story was that lay behind it, none thereabouts had ever yet discovered.

So arm in arm and full of little laughs, we made our way back to the inn; and how her husband glared to see us.

Frankly now, I am confused. Jude Brown, I'm sure, returns my hatred, and so I fled back to my room as soon as we returned. And even with my cane in hand, I would not care to face him. The tavern's other staff mean little more to me; I know that they are many, though few enough I've met. The serving maids (the two I know, there may be more) look trullish: I think their names are Daphne Squires and Jacqueline Smythe (I wonder if her name is really Smith), and it pains me to say I suspect them both of whoring on the sly. Old Marguerite the cook is all of warts and shares a room with ancient Bates the cellar-man, although they are not married. Young Tom Watkins serves as groom and general runaround; I like his ready smile, but would not leave my trunk unlocked at all when he's about. And there are surly unwashed men who watch Brown's sheep out in the fields behind the inn, sun-browned gardeners and farmhands; those I neither know nor wish to. The staff, I think, are new arrived with gross Jude Brown, and serve the hotel ill; not long ago the clientele were earls and dukes, and all their pretty ladies, the cook a match for any else in Europe... and now? Yet after all, I came to Shooters Hill to write, and hardly for the company. Some part of me it thinks the tavern could be so much better; another part it thinks of Mistress Brown, and suddenly it is. And so I came back to my room confused.

And yet, I know, the world that really is means little now to me; the world that I shall dream, and writing, draw that dream from night to daylight plain... that is the world for me.

I'll to it once again tonight, but since we did return, I've nothing done except to write this journal.

Sunday, 23rd September 1803

Last evening, before supper, I went outside to smoke a pipe or two and look again toward London, and ugly Paul's, knowing that not too far beyond that massive pile of misdirected worship my sweet Liz would, perhaps, be playing the old family harpsichord and thinking sad-sweet thoughts of me. And, simply, to see just where she was, and to feel myself beside her; and how I wished I was.

I thought, then, of how the stinking city it had spread, far out beyond its ancient Roman walls, and somehow (call it vision, or a dream, or clear sight of the future) I had the impression that one day the city of 'London' would have grown (and groaned) and sprawled, and engulfed each single thing, both large and small, between the here and there, washing flotsam as a neap tide does upon the shores of ancient Shooters Hill; which, although my stay here has but lasted days, I've come to think of rather fondly. More than that, I seemed to see the whole hillside quite engulfed in strangely-shapen houses; and I knew the hubbub, and the dirt, the flabby-bellied men who vomited in the street and all their empty-headed squalor, had extended even here. How sad I was to see it.

And yet, somehow, I knew that I was seeing this entire scene through quite another's eyes; of a man of that time, rather than my own, and yet I thought him some way quite like me; and thinking how I'd face such things myself, then somehow all my heart ached at the horrors of his foul existence, while at the same time I found myself upon the sudden proud of his ability to live and move and breathe and swim against the tides and terrors of his time. The best that I could think (or hope) was that he did not make things worse. I know that some may think this sounded lunatic and incomprehensible: but somehow, I felt that he, like me, was a practitioner of the writer's craft, with all the heaven and the hell that that entails; though what 'writing' then might mean escapes me. But somehow, we had that part of us to share. And if he will exist, I wonder what he'll write? For if he is like me, I know, he'll not write of his present time, but rather of the past; or of some ideal world so far removed from all the horrors of the real. And more I know (and how it joys my heart) he'll write all loving of the Moon. And mayhap all of this was fancy; and hap again it may have not been.

With much to think upon I returned within, but decided (wrongly, as I swift found out) to take a little ale in the tap-house. This I merely did for the sake of experience and exploration; only to find myself then trapped in conversation with some local ancient in a *tricorne* hat and, still, a powdered wig, who (when not crying out aloud 'By George!') wished to know my thoughts upon the war; and worse he wanted me to join him in his execrations of the French, the Turks and, I know not why at all, the heathen far Chinee. I told him that I had no thoughts at all and, more, that English, French and any others oversea were all the same to me, alike in stupidity and hypocrisy, and politicians' talk was simply excremental. And more, that income tax for fighting foreign wars was quite immoral, and William Pitt he should be hanged. The greybeard then began to splutter: demanded patriotism, talked of Nelson (pah!), king and country, empire and I know not what. I told him, most politely so it seemed to me, that while I might be forced to live in the evil 19th century, that didn't mean I had to take part in it, that too the more there was of it the less I liked it, and that all his old fool's words were unthought prejudice and downright knavery. I would have told him more besides, of how great my hatred had grown for his madly inbred 'royal' family, and how I spat upon his god as well, but Mistress Brown was passing by, and so she intervened. She took my arm and led me to her parlour, closed the door behind us; and then she could not help herself but burst out laughing.

She told me that the pious ancient I'd provoked was more than four times quite my age; a local miser who, at each New Year, would offer all the barmaids each a golden sovereign if they would but let him thrash them, for the music of their screams. I did not think to ask if he had ever spent his money. She told me he would go before nightfall, for as he often said, 'good Christian men are not out after dark.' And so for her sake I retreated up the back stairs, and took my supper in my room.

Last night the inn was crowded, both with locals and with officers of the Artillery, up from Woolwich, all come to crowd the assembly hall and hear the hired musicians playing jigs and reels, to spend their pay on dance and drink and frolics and, I fear, to pass the time in lewd and riotous behaviour. I thought to stay withdrawn inside my room, although the noise of songs and shouts was all throughout the tavern; but Mistress Brown she simply would not let me. She insisted that I leave my writing, go downstairs and join her in the dance. More, I fear to say, she insisted that I dance with her alone; I simply cannot conjecture why. She plied me then with so much claret ('on the house', as the expression has it) and, dancing, clung so close, that I grew quite alarmed; not with the warm, sweet softness of her in my arms, but rather when glancing at her husband and his all-too thunderous brow.

But stranger still, all through the evening, brash young

lieutenants or dashing captains of the Artillery Regiment would present themselves to her with all their gentlest compliments, requesting then no fairer thing than the honour of her company in the dance; and always she would absolute refuse them. The first or two she deigned to talk to, told them tales: how I was her long lost brother, how the evening was my birthday; after that, she simply did something with her strange and lovely eyes, and would not talk at all. I gaped amazed: first that she would rather dance with me, second that these muscled heroes of the nation would simply wilt and creep away before a single word was spoken. I asked her what she did; and yet she merely smiled.

We danced and danced; a moment when we paused she insisted that, thenceforth, when we were quite alone, then I should call her 'Cynthia' instead of 'Mistress Brown' (though I should always call her by the latter in company, and especially in that of her husband, whose nature, I know full well, it tends toward the jealous). And, although I sought it not, when we were both too drunk for further dancing and I asked her to release me to my room, she kissed me a most fond goodnight. And I confess I did not stop her; neither the first time, nor the second. I looked back as I climbed the stairs and thought that, with the slightest invitation, she would have followed on; I had not thought that I would ever see a woman looking at me quite so sweet and tender as I took myself to bed. And such a gentle smile. Indeed, although I know that I was rather more the drunk than she, I found it hard, I must confess, to turn my back on her. Perhaps the fact that she, too, has such large and bright brown eyes, reminded me of my dearest Liz, and somehow saved me from my baser instincts. Though having written that, I cannot think of why it should.

I dreamt of lovely women in a hall made quite of moonlight, dancing young and naked in my arms, and laughing oh-so-sweet. And all their kisses, each and every one, were nectar and ambrosia.

This morning, being Sunday, I was suddenly awoken by the foul Jude Brown (I think with viciousness and malevolent perversity) at ten of the clock; it greatly did annoy me. One of the reasons that I chose this inn, rather than one in a village further on from London, was because there is no church to be found upon the hill. And so I was disgusted, then, to be informed by the unspeakable Brown that the assembly room (scene last night of such debauch) doubles as a chapel on Sunday mornings, and that a quite insufferable travelling preacher called Kinnock (I will not call him 'Reverend', because from me he deserves no reverence at all) holds weekly service there for staff and guests, hectoring them as to their supposed sins and moralising tediously in a way that hardly would convince a puling child. Being my first weekend upon the premises, I felt obliged to attend for the sake of appearance; though I noticed that foul Brown's fairest wife did not, and so I wondered why I did besides. I need hardly add that I spent the entire hour of Kinnock's ridiculous sermonising praying fervently to Diana, Jove and any of the other elder Gods who might be listening, that the damnable wretch might be accosted by highwaymen, or hauled off to the Clink for debt, or struck down with the French pox, or *somehow* otherwise detained before he gets the opportunity to return here and torment me with his inanities next Sunday.

And when at last I had escaped, dear Mistress Brown she looked at me and shook her head, and on her face was such a puzzled smile. I wanted then to rush to her and make some explanation; but then we both saw 'Judas' Brown nearby, a smirking sneer upon his face, and I know she understood just how I had been tricked.

I came back up to my room to find my copy of Mr Taylor's recent translation of *The Hymns of Orpheus*; and when I had I chanted out aloud the 'Hymn to the Moon' until I felt the air was clean. I think, each night from now, I'll chant it over again at dusk, by way of invocation. This is the only book I have with me; I rather wish I'd brought my *Vathek*.

The incident did depress me. I'd thought that leaving depraved and sinful London I'd leave behind besides the vile patriotism, tricks and lies, the thievish ways, hypocrisy, cant and Christian church (for all of these to me are sin and foul corruption); and yet they're even here. I almost thought to catch the coach, and suffer back at home, where at least there is my Lizzie. Yet here there is dear Cynthia, and if I can but wish away the rest…

Yet if I had but one wish, I know, it would be this: to restore somehow the pagan world, its religion and its art; and more than this, its freedoms. Mr Taylor, I know, he feels the same; yet even if he only speaks of Plato, still the poor man is abused. I feel the loss of all the Christians have destroyed; and more I feel the loss of all that could have been besides. What epics and romances might have echoed down the years, what hymns to sweetest Goddess, what poems of the Moon divine. Who knows, in *Somnium*, or other things I'll write, it may be mine to write a pagan literature of the present day (or not too distant past). I wish I'd been at Placentia or Nonsuch, to write the Virgin Queen in Diana's fairest form, like Lyly, Ralegh and the rest. Yet born too late, I have to write the Moon as she appears to me; and always ere the last few days, she has been Lizzie... and now I do not know...

Dinner done, I took a nap. I know now why I call my story *Somnium*; because I am quite sure this is a hill of dreams. I hardly stop, from candle-out to sun-up, and now I find they continue in the afternoon. I dream of Liz. I dream of Cynthia Brown. I dream of dear Diana, the sweetest Goddess of the Moon (though always in my dreams, somehow, she insists upon the Greek original of her name: Selene). They kiss me in my sleep. They come to me all naked. I wake and wonder where they are; and hate myself for waking. And now I have to find a way to write all this. Ideas I had to write before I came here, all seem nothing now. But dream and wine, they turn my mind quite upside down.

And more, I drink and then I dream, and lovely women quite apart, my dreams are full of palaces. Great spires and towers, and grandiosities the like I never thought; so 'Somnium' is now a palace of the Moon, all builded up of dream-stuff, that sprawls on ancient Shooters Hill. And I know somehow The Bull's a small part of that much-beloved and all-too-awesome structure, a gatehouse to the world of lunar dream. And Cynthia, or Liz, or Diana, I cannot tell them quite apart, especially when they're naked; they wait for me and beckon, sadly smiling, calling me home from all this weary world of dust. They are so sweetly tender; if only I knew how I could accompany them, then home with them I'd go.

But what's to do except to make this so by writing? So supper done tonight, and claret to support me, I'll dip the pen and start again. With someone rather lovely.

Whether she was merely Queen of all the World, or in everything below the Starry Sphere the Goddess, he could not tell, but thought her both and more besides. He looked the once upon her exquisite grace, and saw a vision like to break his heart. If ever there was loveliness under heaven, then it was she, and never was there other.

She sat, enthroned, upon a marble dais, and all around were sylphs the equal of that lovely one who'd led him in. And as those nymphs looked down, from high above, on all the mortal women of the world, so she who ruled here yet surpassed them still, and many times the more besides. She was, in short, the perfection of all the beauty that ever ravished up man's soul, quite since the star-bespangled universe began.

He looked, he loved. What more to say?

Down on a knee he went, and bowed his head; and knew, without her licence, he'd never rise again. And hardly a breath was heard to break the silence of that silvered palace room.

'Good sir,' she said at last, and with her voice the Music of the Spheres matched absolute harmonious. 'This gallant gesture of respect does you the greatest credit, but now you must decide. If terror has unmanned you quite, then merely nod your head, and within the hour you'll awake, and think this naught but dream. If, though... and I believe it so... you have the mettle, then pray look up, for I would rather see your eyes than look down on your pate.'

'As my lady wishes,' he began, the slightest smile upon his lips, and would have more continued. But once his eyes were to their work again, his tongue was frozen stiff.

She sat among those white-clad nymphs, alone a blaze of colour. Gold sandals clasped her small and dainty feet, and wound their gilded thongs about her graceful ankles. Belted tight around her narrow waist, a brocade skirt of cobalt blue, threaded through with beaded gold, cascaded down in broad and tumbling flounces. Above, the neckline of a clinging bodice, welkin-bright and trimmed in gilt, plunged navelwards and left exposed more fairest flesh than ever he had thought to see. About her shoulders, a wide-spaced pectoral mesh of shining gold was studded all with moonstones huge, with gleamy mottled turquoise, with crystals bright a-sparkle; while necklaces of massy pearls hung down in ropes between her lovely naked breasts, so round, so soft, so sweet.

Yet marvelled as he was by all of this, it was forgot when at the last his eyes were cast up to the heaven of her face. Framed all about with tumbling chestnut tresses that spilled down to her hips, they were the dearest features he had ever seen. A fringe swept uncontrolled across her brow, despite the gleaming golden band about her forehead, surmounted with a shining lunar crescent. Above her soft pink lips a tilt-tip nose and, then, the glories of that visage most symmetrical, two enormous deep-brown eyes, with black, dilated pupils, all a-glint with Moonsparks.

And little white-jade teeth, that peeped out when she smiled.

'Ah, now will you stay then nine full days?' her lilting question came. 'For we have wonders here to show, and as you know... no wonder lasts for less.'

'A true wonder lasts forever, dear lady,' he remarked, 'for if it lasts not, it is not true. And may you also live forever, lady mine, for you are wonder too.'

'Oh, I shall,' she soft and slowly said, a sweet and secret smile upon her lips. 'Sir Endimion Lee, I bid you very welcome, and now come near, and kiss my hand.'

'Right gladly, highness... but will you tell me first precisely where I am, and whose the hand I'll press close to my lips?'

'It amuses me to name this palace *Somnium*,' she told him then. 'And if it amuses you, then think of me as Diana Regina, though I have many names, and use them as I will.'

'Then by your grace I'd hope to learn them all, delightful queen,' said he, advancing to the dais. 'But is there time in all the world for such a task as this?'

'No,' she told him simply.

Before her throne he knelt again, and gazed upon the pale smooth softness of her skin; breathed in the perfume of her hair, of jasmine and of eglantine; then pressed her fingers to his lip, and tasted of the Moon.

'Divine Diana,' he hardly more than whispered, 'for I know you more than queen, with this kiss I offer up allegiance, devotion and submission, and all I am is yours, my body, heart and soul...'

'And will you give me mind, as well?' all eagerly she asked, 'and love and hope and dream?'

'I will,' he assured her.

'And your sword? Is that mine too?'

'Even this.'

'And your honour?'

'No, dear lady,' he looked up, and met her earnest eyes. 'My honour is my own alone, and I would no more give it up than I would have you give up yours.'

The radiant smile that lit her face up then was full of warmth and dazzle.

'Sweet knight,' she said, and raised him up. 'Keep your honour, and your mind and soul and hope. And I will give you dreams.'

'And love?'

'Yours I know I have,' she told him then, an eyebrow arched in thought, 'but mine is strange, and far more strangely given. Some desire it, but have it not at all. Some there are who bring it on themselves, but know it not. And there are others yet besides, to whom my love is but a riddle. One or two, perhaps, since this fair and Moon-becircled world began, had it both and knew it... but whether it profited them at all, well, who can say?'

'If a lover finds his love returned, then surely this is profit,' he responded.

'My good and gallant knight,' she smiled, 'this is wondrous sweet and innocent. And for love of men and maids, enough. But do I give my love to men whose love is otherwise for maids? Or to men whose love soars upwards to the Moon? And who, in loving of the Moon, love only maids unconsummate. For those who love the Moon, you know, are lunatic, and special friends of mine.

'But enough of this for now!' she laughed, a sound that ravished up his soul. 'By your furrowed brow I see I've caused you more confusion than intended. These nymphs of mine are special friends as well, so let them lead you to your rooms. When you're bathed and freshly clad, we'll dine and talk more privy in my chamber.

'And so, my dear Endimion Lee, most welcome guest, find ease awhile in Somnium. And within the hour we'll drink each other's health.'

Monday, 24th September 1803

Is there some strange convergence here? For like Endimion Lee, I think that I could also spend my time just drinking with a lovely lady, in a palatial building here on Shooters Hill. Oh, there is temptation in those eyes of Mistress Cynthia Brown's. Last night I saw her looking at me after supper; I had to smile at her and quickly look away, for otherwise I knew my evening would be lost. And writing *Somnium* is so deliciously seductive. Temptation or seduction, who's to choose? Last night I chose to write.

I drank and wrote, and all of it came flooding out again. The strange part is that while I know, and fully did intend, that Endimion Lee should be my surrogate to journey through this world of fiction, he will not do quite what I want him to; he is too independent. And more, Diana Regina is not Liz, nor Cynthia besides. I simply do not understand. I write, but when I do, I am not sure quite who I am; and all my characters, written, they are not quite the ones I thought they were. I wonder if, perchance, I do not write at all, but that my words are written for me by that man two centuries hence. And then I read my lines again and think they're from some ancient book, discovered in a tomb. But most of all, I like to think, they whisper sweetly from the Moon.

At two this morning, when the Moon declined unto the west, I looked out my front window, rather fogged with wine, and thought to see Cynthia sat upon the mounting block before the inn and gazing at the sky. She wore a cloak against the night-time cold, but quite what she did out there, I really cannot think. A shooting star sparked overhead, seemed plunging from the Moon, and then she looked up to my window. The look upon her face was completely enigmatic; and if she wished upon a falling star, I cannot quite think what. And then she stood, and came back into the inn. And so I went back to my writing, and fell asleep at four.

I know it sounds incomprehensible, but I swear I walked the corridors of Somnium before the daylight dawned. It might be said that this was nothing more than any might expect: a writer dreaming of his own creation. But all this was too lucid and too lucent to match the vagaries of dream-stuff, and somehow I trod marble veined with Moonlight, heard the faintest tintinnabulation of some fair lady's distant gem-and-silver earring, scented jasmine on the warm and censered air. I briefly walked a corridor inlaid with sapphires, then stood before a niche where sat a silver statuette, of fair Selene, long hair flowing in the winds of time itself, as on she drove her swift and eager steeds, the Moon-chariot all a-race through skies of deepest night. I paused and leant closer to examine the exquisite argent Goddess, and as I did so she, in turn, raised up her lovely head and gave me *such* a glance, it jolted me awake.

I lay in bed no little time, just thinking of my 'dream'; but in the end I knew not what to make of the experience. Perhaps my head was still a little piece a-swirl with this, when down I went for breakfast; for my strange awakening was swiftly followed by a rude one.

A certain Doctor Gould, of Charlton Village, who drank and danced here on the Saturday night, was robbed of one whole guinea as he walked off home, and some smaller coin besides. I spoke of this to bald Jude Brown this morning, my most innocent and conciliatory smile quite firmly plastered on my poor misguided face, in hope that sharing conversation might somehow reassure him that I had no designs upon his sweet and charming wife. He snarled at me so foully I was quite took aback; then turned away and swore uncouthly, like a common drayman. I will not try to humour him again. I'd wish him nothing but the clap or pox, except I fear he'd give them to dear Cynthia; though as I cannot imagine her ever sleeping with so foul a brute, mayhap he'd never get the chance. Instead I wish him roast in hell, a spit right through his bowels. No longer will I compromise with oafs, or modern fools, or knaves with nothing twixt their ears;

and if my spitting it could reach to Woolwich town, the army there
would have my foul contempt as well. I do not like this world at all. I'd
save my Liz and Cynthia Brown; I'm sure there must be other lovely
women quite as sweet; but men (apart from me, I must confess) I'd
damn them all to hell. Consumption, pox and black-spot plague on
all of them; especially Jude Brown. If he were dead, then who knows
what? I fear I don't. And perhaps it's better that I do not think it.

I find that with each passing day I rise the later in the morning.
Cynthia teases that I am too late for breakfast; I told her from
tomorrow I'll begin the day with dinner. She laughed and ruffled up
my hair as if I was child; I confess I looked around me then, to make
quite sure her wretched husband was not watching.

The afternoons I begin to explore old Shooters Hill; and though
I know that all who live here think it commonplace enough, it is all
strange to me. The stag beetles in the woods are absolute profuse: I
look upon their 'antlers', think of deer, and think in turn of fleet-foot
Diana huntress. All about are springs and wells of cool delightful
water, and in the field behind the tavern, a dewpond; I cannot help but
think how, to the ancient Greeks, the dew was daughter to the lovely
Moon. And pools, in turn, remind me of Diana bathing, and Actæon
turned into a stag, and so we come full circle to the beetles, which feed
on fallen silver birches, the colour of the Moon.

I would be quite content, I must admit, to wander alone
along the lanes about the hill, looking at the views and probing,
dilettantish I confess, into its few but choice antiquities. However, to
my vast amusement, dear Cynthia Brown insists that always on these
expeditions I'm accompanied by that waggish youth Tom Watkins
who, when we step outside, she ensures is always armed with a brace
of pistols quite obviously too heavy for him to properly raise and aim.
'Against the highwaymen,' she assures me, though if any of these
gentlemen rogues were on the sudden to appear, I can only think of
poor young Watkins fainting on the ground. And he, quite bluntly,
told me that he would rather run for life and love and luck than fire
a shot and risk one in return. I carry a light purse on these occasions,
sufficiently satisfying to preserve my life if such should be demanded,

but far from all my funds. I suspect Tom Watkins will have the more from me than any passing highwayman, for I'm gratuitous enough to make his eyes light up with every exploration.

Cynthia, when I asked this afternoon, was prompt enough to provide me with a further bottle of ink, from out the hotel's stores; and told me if I wished for any other thing she'd have it brought from Woolwich. She asked me of my writing; I blushed and told her I had barely started, had no pages yet to show to anyone at all. She looked so disappointed I almost said I had.

And there's a thing. If I was writing sat at home, I'd show my work to Liz, the queen of heart and household; I never thought to have an audience here. But having someone here to 'write for', close at hand; it could be good, to make me work the harder.

But this is all of dreams and fancies. She'd hardly have the time; and surely I've misread her interest.

But *Somnium* itself is all of dreams and fancies. So let's pretend my audience has doubled: my Liz at home and Cynthia here. And now to write, for both these darling ladies, my most embroidered prose...

Maroon the hose Lee wore when next he came to Somnium's Queen, with deep blue velvet doublet, sewn with rows of seed-pearls and slashed to show a scarlet lining. Soft calfskin boots were on his feet, and lace the simple collar round his neck. Rings were on his fingers, all of silver, and he thought that, even in the court of mighty, fair Elizabeth herself, he never had been dressed the better.

'And are the rooms to your liking, dearest sir?' she asked, when he was brought to her again. His answer waited on his eyes, for she had changed as well, and first they needed look their look. Now Queen Diana, still with crescent-brow, was dressed in merest film alone, as evanescent as a dream. He thought of Botticelli or, nearer to his time, of Titian... but there never was a painter here on Earth who could capture any of her loveliness divine.

'I like them much, beloved Queen, and find them quite surprising. I never thought to see a bath like that: a hot pond in the floor, and big enough for seven.'

'For nine,' she smiled. 'Hereabouts, we always think by nines. And ...?'

'And I had not thought your maids would stay with me, and try their hands at my undressing...'

'And let me guess, my sweetest knight... you sent them all away...'

'My dearest Queen, I did. And would a gentleman do any other?'

'And if, instead of them, it had been I... what then?'

'Sweet Queen,' he smiled, and looked her in the eye. 'A lady should not ask.'

She chuckled then, and bade him take a seat at table.

'And the clothes we had prepared?' she enquired next. 'To your taste? A good fit?'

'As good a fit as ever I was measured for, and finer far than any that I wore before. But not, perhaps, as surprising as yours, my Queen, either earlier in the day or now.'

'Ah,' she grinned, 'the first I wore in honour of your English sovereign lady, although she never wears the like. Such was the dress of Europe's first-most queens, in Candian Knossos, Achaean Mycenae, and ancient holy Troy. Such did wondrous Helen wear, to capture Paris' eye. So she was dressed when Trojan Brutus saw his city burn, and set his sails a-westwards. And so I myself appeared in dream to Brutus too, when he slept upon a doeskin in my temple, on Leogetia in the Mediterranean Sea. He promised, when I told him then of distant Albion's isle, to worship me all down the ages, but died before I tired of his adoration. His descendants grew forgetful, until your Tudor queen, who comes yet of his blood. And you, I think, if you return to court, may yet remind her still, that the Moon looks down on Albion and, if only for a while, would make a lunar dream of all her world.'

'Then if you honoured my dread and sovereign queen, I thank you for it,' he replied, a lopside smile upon his lip, 'though the nature of the honour, I fear, she may have found a little hard to understand.

'And these wisps in which you dress yourself to dine?'

'A little for my comfort,' she softly laughed, 'but more to make you welcome, and give pleasure to your eye.'

'Then never was a guest more welcomed or more pleased,' he told her. 'And if Helen launched a thousand ships, then a thousand

Helens you'd laugh to shame.'

'You're gallant, my knight, but rather too much merry; for none should laugh at Helen. For Helen, by her beauty and her fate, became much more than human; became a legend, and a dream, and little short of Goddess. Indeed, sometimes I envy her, for being born here in the world of matter, she transformed herself into an idea that now will last for ever; while I was always of the Moon, and of those spheres above… and though I live as long as her, I have not had her triumph.'

'My lady is too modest,' he assured her, then paused at the entry of her nymphs, bearing cuts of venison, vegetable pies, and strange assorted dainties, as well as fresh baked steaming bread; accompanied all by choice of sack, canary or of Rhenish wine. And while they served, with smiling grace and beauty, Endimion Lee took pause to look around.

The chamber in which he was entertained was hung about with tapestries, all wove with lovely Diana, deer-hunting in the woods or bathing naked with her nymphs. An oriel window opened on a vista, across a fountain-court all lit up by the Moon, of cupolas of selenite and obelisks of jacinth, pylons tall of chrysoprase and domes of gleaming onyx. And everything else his eyes lit on was all of silver or of gleaming gold.

'Dearest lady,' he said at last, 'pray answer me two questions. The first is, how should I address your grace? For I hardly know if you are Queen, or Goddess, or something more than these by far.'

'My knight,' she smiled, and glanced down at herself. 'I hardly bothered to collect a dress, so correct address means little more besides. I told you some small while ago that I have many names; I tell you now that I have many titles too. So call me what you will; I doubt not that I'll like it.'

'And if I called you sweetest heart, or treasure of the world?'

'Why then I'd smile like this, and ask you straight to tell me next about your other question.'

'Then, lady of the lovely eyes, pray tell me… what place is this? And how comes it here on vacant Shooters Hill? And why? And how did I come here? Why have you favoured me with such wondrous sights that take away my breath? And are you really of the Moon? And what purpose, then, in all of this?'

'Sir knight, I think you play the scallywag!' she laughed. 'For now you've asked me seven questions, at the least, or mayhap eight, or more!'

'Nine,' he grinned, and nodded her a bow. 'For, as you see, I treasure up my lady's words, and try to speak her language when I can.'

Her laughter tinkling then like tiny golden bells, she raised a glass of clear canary, a-toasting of his wit.

'You and I,' she told him then, 'I think will be the dearest friends. For the Moon ever loved the mercurial.'

'And did Mercury ever love the Moon?'

'Perhaps,' she said, 'but even Goddesses have their secrets. Yet long ago your ancient namesake loved her; and she came kissing sweetly in the night.'

'Then for the sake of ancient name and long-gone love, I'd hope for nightly kisses sweet.' And there was yearning in his face, which could not quite be masked.

'For your gallantry,' she told him then, and slipped a moonstone ring from off her middle finger, brushed it past her lovely lips and proffered it with a smile. He took both ring and hand in his, and lingering kissed them both.

'My lady's favour, worn with pride,' he told her then, and slid it home along his little finger. 'And now I am your champion knight, my lovely queen of all the fairies in the Moon, my lance all ready at your service... my other questions?'

'Your lance? Ah, you're bold and have a forward wit, Endimion Lee, but now is not the time for tilting at the Moon. Instead ...

'Perhaps you've read, in histories true and false, of those who've journeyed to the Moon. Antoninus Diogenes, and Lucian of Samosata, most honest liars of their times, and many more besides. They've come and gone, have they, and haven't too, and I have loved them with the same pretended love that they pretended me. Dear Lucian I always thought the better of than most, because he thought the worst of me; and because I always dress to please, he always saw me naked.

'But then you dwellers here below, all strange and too perverse, invented up the church, an institution of the mad, that kept your souls in thrall. And never then was loving eye upon the Moon, no compliments paid to lunar beauty, no passion spent for me, except they called it sin.

And all the poetry departed from the world.

'These centuries of the Great Endarkenment passed by, and I grew dull, unloved and unfulfilled. And so, I thought, if merry-minded Lucian, unafraid, could cross the gulf of broad sub-lunar space, then so could I. And so I did, with all my lunar nymphs around me, and if you ask me how we came, then all I'll say is that I dreamed it so, and so, of course, it was.

'And so I dreamed of Somnium, a palace of the Moon upon the Earth and embassy of yet more spheres above, all made of dream-stuff quite ethereal. And dreamed this just for you, and with you too, for without some Earthly dreamer too, then none of this could be. And this is what you see before you, and me, myself, besides, and if I'm not the total sum of all you've ever dreamed, then I shall call you truest liar that ever was, since Lucian walked the Earth.'

'You are indeed the dream of all men's dreams,' he told her, gently sighing, as she poured him more canary.

'Oh come now, sweet Endimion Lee, eat supper, drink your wine, and gaze not so distracted quite at all my tempting flesh, your ears blocked by your eyes, for otherwise I'll tell you naught. Ah, you colour, and you smirk, and I have found you out. But let this pass. Your priests would damn your eyes for sin, but I care not at all. Look all you wish, but listen too, for I'll say nothing twice.

'Why here? I chose your wooded Shooters Hill because, when looked on from the lofty Moon, it has a crescent shape. And more than this, it is all made of selenite; and more yet still besides, the jasmine grows white-flowered here, and never was more lunar scent than this.

'Yet more, it's near enough at hand to your sovereign lady queen, at Eltham or at Greenwich, or anywhere round London. And where your queen is, there are poets, playwrights, makers of masques and plotters of fictions, pamphleteers… and, in a word, *writers*, simultaneous the scum of all the earth, and its very salt besides. For they are mine, and I keep them mused… and in their musings, I am theirs, and they keep me.

'And now, my lusty knight whose lance is mine, I'm sure you'll tell me next why I chose *you* to dine with me, and not just any other.'

'I think I can, although your wondrous beauty distracts me all too greatly,' he shrugged then. 'And, besides, you know already. Our lady Queen has eyes for no one but Lord Leicester and so neglects those, like myself, who've sworn to her the same regard. And yet, upon her next most royal progress, my sovereign honours me by feasting overnight at my decaying manse near Ashford. And so I had a tragical entertainment quite in mind, for my sovereign's pleasure... where, of old, the Grecian youth Endymion, exiled from court and royal favour, and dying more for love, sleeps the years away in darkling Latmian cave, and dreams the fair reviving kiss of visiting queen Selene. It's but a little jest, but heartfelt.'

'And so you wrote of Selene, who is Diana, who is me. And thinking, as you did, of me, so you made me think of you. And so we mingled all our dreams, and so I dreamed a coach for you, and so you dreamed yourself inside, and so, of course, the both of us together, we dreamed you here with me, and me with you. And was there anything ever simpler, in all the world below the Moon?'

'I think, perhaps, there was,' he grinned. 'But are you really of the Moon?'

'Good knight, *I am the Moon.*'

'Then to the Moon I raise my glass, more beautiful than any woman in the world... for all the mortal women of the Earth stand far beneath the Moon. And if ever mortal men loved mortal women, then as you are more beautiful than they, then so much more my love for you.'

'You, my sweet Endimion Lee,' she laughed, 'are near as silver-tongued as any I have entertained since Samosatan Lucian. The difference, I think, is that all your words are truly meant and come straight from your heart; while roaring Lucian lied his tongue to rot, in hope he could seduce me. Which I prefer, I cannot say, for Lucian made me laugh, but you just make me sigh. I sigh, of course, with the sweetness of all this, and yet, at the same time I have to say, you have not yet imagined all my clothes off.'

'Perhaps I never could,' he said, 'or perhaps I never would. For old, bold Lucian, I suspect, for all he saw you naked, probably then gained nothing more. And if he did...'

'He didn't.'

'But if he had, would he have any more than held you down in bed and triumphed in your body? And is that stud-beast mating, then, the all that there could be, even with she who's Goddess quite supreme? I think there's more than this. Your body is too sweet to contemplate, but to love your heart and soul and mind...'

'Yes?'

'It may not make you laugh, my love... but wouldn't you rather sigh?'

'Ah, now there's a mystery you might never solve,' she softly said. 'To laugh, to sigh. Lost in laughter we forget even our own selves, with all our parts, the miseries *and* the joys...'

'While melancholy,' he responded, 'is the most seductive emotion of them all. And if we could combine the two, and seduce ourselves into forgetting all the world but simplest heart-consuming love ...'

'Why, if you remembered naught but love, then I would be forgot!' she laughed. 'And what kind of love is that to offer to the Moon?'

'An impossible love,' he told her, a little flush-faced but raising up his glass unto her honour. 'For once seen, you never could be forgotten.'

'And yet,' (a sudden mock leer upon his lips, suggesting she was overdressed) 'you laughed...'

'At your innocence, my knight,' she told him gently, 'rather than your wit.'

'And have the innocent, then, no hope at all?'

'The innocent...' she inclined her head, '... the innocent have the *most* to hope for, because they have so little else.'

'Then perhaps the innocent should not be mocked,' he smiled, 'for a life that lacks all hope is hardly life at all.'

'It seems to me, Endimion Lee... and now perhaps I say it with a sigh... that the more you drink, the subtler you become. And now you show me wit in innocence, and how the melancholy laugh... and how a mortal man who seems to speak quite straight can even 'wilder up the ever-changing Goddess of the Moon.'

'Dear divine Diana,' he soft remarked, 'far rather would I amuse you than amaze you, although I know them both the same. But perhaps our conversation's grown too deep for pleasant entertainment.'

'Perhaps it has,' she grinned. 'And now we've supped in full, will you take my hand, and walk me to the balcony without?'

'Gladly,' he told her, rising from his seat and offering her a bow. Then hand in hand, they passed through doors of crystal pane and found themselves outside, uncovered to the glowing Moon. And there awaited sweet Diana's nymphs, with virginals and viols, with tabors, hautboys and with fifes.

'And do you dance the galliard, good knight?' she asked, with sudden, radiant smile.

'I do indeed,' he chuckled in reply, 'though hereabouts we think it, like its name, a little too much "French".'

'Admit it, though,' she smirked, 'the "French" is rather to your taste, I think.'

'Perhaps it is,' he then confessed, rising on his toes as the nymphs struck up. 'And never would a man have lovelier partner, more softer or more sweet. And yet… did ever poet think that sweet Diana danced like this?'

'I doubt it,' then she laughed, and so she led him onward, enormous-eyed and lovely. 'Yet up there in the Moon, why, dearest sir, we dance no other step…'

'Then let us dance, sweet Goddess, 'til we can dance no more. And then, with fondest glance, retire…'

Tuesday, 25th September 1803

And so last night, as usual, when the sun set and the Moon appeared, full of claret, pipe a-fume, I began my nightly ritual, withdrawn here in my room. I invoke Diana-Selene-Hecate, I offer her my love and ask her for her help. And then I write in Bacchic frenzy 'neath the beaming Moon, barely sane, pen a-dancing, words appearing, sentence after sentence, in my fervid brain, and scribbled, scribbled scrawlish all across the page, with spattered ink and crossing nib, as fast as e'er I can, to get them down before they're lost. Because they come from Dreamland, and Diana, and from that very Somnium of which I write. And words are in my ears and in my hands, and all my mind is full of sweetest Liz and all her honeyed kisses; who is not here and who I have not got, and only can I summon her with words and metaphors Dianic, and drunkenness, and memories of sparkling eyes (so large and bright), and longing.

And longing.

I wonder if I could ever make her understand, but fear I never could, the strangeness of it all: to write. Not to create from nothing, but to open the mind and let the images flood in: from somewhere; from Moonland; from madness; from that same ideal world I see whene'er I look upon my sister's eyes, so brown, so dark, so large, the perfection of all women's eyes that ever I have seen; her hair so long, her smile so sweet, her skin so smooth, her flesh so soft. A world, not as it is, nor as it should be, but as it is *desired* to be.

Ah, too much claret, too much fondness.

Too much Liz, too far away.

I should not drink before supper; the day's events are all forgot.

I often fall to misquotation (perhaps from old Menander?) that: 'Whom the Gods would write, they first make mad.' Too true, and so I fear I am. But now the way I work can better be summed up: 'Whom the Gods would write, they first make drunk.'

And so indeed I am, and so I should begin to work, invoking lunar vision.

Deep and dreamful was that sleep of dizzied Endimion Lee, when at the last he took him to his bed. He thought, although he knew himself asleep, no sooner had he closed his eyes than Queen Diana came to him in all her godhead's glory and, without so much as magic pass, drew up his soul from out his body. Taking then his immaterial hand in hers, she led him on through walls and down through floors, and quite outside the palace. Across the garden next they made their way, with pools a-glint by moonlight and those pallid statues all regarding them with cool and stony gaze, until at last they passed a silvered gate. Beyond, they paused besides a massive marble slab, all carved up with the bathing of the lovely maiden Moon.

Nearby an ancient Grecian chariot stood, two-wheeled and silver-bodied, covered all in jewels. A pair of harnessed snow-white mares stood there before it snorting, impatient to be off the ground and onward. And sweet Diana Regina, in a short white shift that hardly would have made a half a nightgown down at Richmond or at Greenwich, and which was, besides, all cut away to reveal one full and lovely breast quite naked to his gaze, reached out to take his hand. Together then they mounted swift the chariot's shining car, and so with practised ease she took the silken reins in both her hands, requiring him with jaunty smiles to find him something certain to hold fast to. So trusting all to love and dream, he wrapped an arm around her waist and matched her smile insouciant.

With softest laugh she flicked the reins and urged the horses on, and on and upwards from the Earth, a-gallop for the stars. And Endimion Lee, no longer trusting just to dream, clamped his teeth upon a scream, and hung on to his dear for life.

West they went and ever higher, Thames aglitter far beneath, Marlboro Downs and Mendips giving way to Bristol Channel and beyond, at last, to silver-sparkled broad Atlantic Sea. Over Ocean, higher still, went the Chariot of the Moon, Diana laughing, long hair streaming in the wind; and awe-exhilarated now, Lee looked down on all the passing world below. The Northern Americas now in turn gave way to vast Pacific Sea, and then to old baroque Cathay, of which the Venetian wrote such lies. Wars he saw, and burning towns, locust-swarms and yellow deserts; and yet towers and minarets he saw as well, palaces and glories built in bold defiance still of all the passing tides of time. And he wept for both, the horror to the one hand, and the wonder to the other. Over Tartary and Muscovy they soared nocturnal, Polack-land and German States, United Provinces soaked in blood, and then at last, relieved, back to sweetest England's Isle. And never was a lovelier land, he thought, than that from which they'd left, and to which they now returned. And when the chariot descended from the sky, and landed once again on dear and homely Shooters Hill, he thanked her with the utmost grace for showing him how all the wide and spacious Earth looked from the circling silver Moon, in its glory, and its madness, its birthing and its blood. And when he would have knelt, she raised him up, and looked at him with large and melting eyes, and sighed, and kissed him on the lips.

He woke, to feel the softest, girlish lips, quite warm and moist and brushing swift across his own. Diana's name was on his tongue, but hardly out his mouth, before he heard a giggling peal of delightful feminine laughter, sprung from many sweet young mouths. Opening up his eyes, he saw Diana's nymphs *en masse* and gathered all around, and in their midst that charming maid, all flushed and pink, who'd greeted his arrival. Before her, at the wide bed's side, there lay a breakfast tray, with bread and cheese and golden apples, and the more, a choice of cordial or of wine.

'This looks like mischief,' remarked a voice he knew and loved, although it struck the tittering nymphs to silence most profound.

'Melissa,' continued dearest Queen Diana, all a-sigh as she surveyed the baby-blushing sprite. 'I should have known…'

The Sovereign Lady of the Moon stood framed there in the doorway, a painter's vision of a perfect Roman Empress, filigreed in golden jewellery and swathed in long white silks. Her hair, all curls and ringlets now, was gathered up behind her head, exposing lovely neck and dainty ears a-drip with finest-water pearls and gold-set gleaming gems; and then those loose remaining tresses, wove with little golden stars, spilled far in sweet cascade all down her shapely back. The softness of her swelling breasts above the rounded low-cut neckline made two cushions of display for all the chains of diamonds strung across her lovely flesh, which sparked so bright each time she inward breathed. And on her brow, as ever, the crescent of the gilded Moon; and on her lips, the smile of sweet despair.

'Oh Melissa,' she almost whispered, barely heard. 'Some other mistress, she would ask, all pained: "now what are we to do with you?" But you and I, we both already know.'

'Oh, mistress, please!' Melissa moaned, wide-eyed and almost tearful. And yet, by then, the other nymphs had closed in all around.

'Ah, look not so concerned, my puissant knight,' Diana said, a lovely silken shimmer as she sat upon the bed. 'And rear up not so chivalrous. This is the *merest mischief,* of minor-most degree. And yet, did ever mistress anywhere leave even "merest" mischief unamended? I think not. And up there in the Moon above, this is how we correct, with love...'

A throaty gasp, and then the gathered nymphs, all like a curtain, parted to show unto his wondered eyes Melissa, all blushing pink and held up off the ground. And then a half a hundred elfin fingers, dainty, small and unremitting, began to tickle soft and quaking maiden-flesh: sides and armpits, soles of feet, shapely breasts and squirming stomach, calves and thighs and anywhere that could be reached.

A childish giggle, a breathless squeak. And then the squealing started, growing loud.

'But what has the poor child *done?*' asked soft-heart knight Endimion Lee, eyes all wide and fixed upon her wriggles.

'Usurped the royal prerogative,' his lady said, her perfect teeth a perfect circle biting in an apple. 'For who but *I* should wake a sleeping hero with a kiss?

'And now,' she offered him the golden fruit, a little bit, 'if it pleases you, then it would please me more besides to make you my accomplice in the eating of my brother's golden apples, all stolen from his many west-benighted Hesperides by my nimble-fingered nymphs, while I held bright-gleamed Helius all-bedimmed with soft and too-seductive moonbeams of my smiles.'

'Dear mistress, pray forgive,' he pleaded then all urgent. 'Forgive me please, forgive her too; for if you will forgive not one, then the other is forgiven not besides. And if you'd have my love, remember this, and answer me this question. For which is the greater love of two: is passion, or compassion? And if you say the first, and prefer it to the latter, then neither will you have of me, nor any love besides.'

'Endimion Lee,' a pretty laugh in sudden silence when, at just the slightest nod, those small, tormenting fingers ceased their work, 'I swear you have the rightest questions ever asked, and more you have the rightest answers too. So for your innocent soul's gentility, I forgive; and hope, although I doubt it much, no further such occasions will arise.'

With that she sent her nymphs away and offered up the apple

once again. Some deep down pang disturbed his mind with thoughts of ancient snakes and paradisal gardens, and yet he took it gladly, bit, and ate, his eyes all fixed upon her loving smile. And so he fell not into sin, but rose above it; merest thought of old Adamic error quite washed away and with it that vast edifice of guilt that's built upon it. Sacramental then the bread and cheese and apples, sacred too the wine, and holy all the world around, below the Moon and far above: for realising that there was no sin to pay for with redemption, he found the world redeemed.

He ate, and laughed for joy, and worshipped with his eyes. And if Beauty is Truth, and Truth is Good, and Good is Holy too, then he knew now that before him sat the Holiest Goddess quite, best and truest and more lovely still than all the worlds she ruled. And so his happiness overspilled, until he could hardly see her for the teardrops in his eyes.

His breakfast all consumed at last, he asked for her command.

'Why, every man who'd do me service always starts his day...' she paused, and played him like a kitten with a ball, '... all naked in the bath.'

And then she sat there, saucy-eyed, to see what he would do.

'Oh, come now, bold Endimion Lee!' she laughed, and licked her lips. 'This may be well enough for due-dubbed knights of England's ancient realm... to sit and hug the bedclothes to your breast like maidens all a-quaking... but Somnium's queen demands the more than this!

'Besides,' and now her sweet voice dipped down low, a soft conspiracy of chuckles, 'you and I both know that since I raised the question yester-eve, you've thought much on the answer. "What if it had been I who aided your undressing, and assisted at the bath?" And so your fancies bring you opportunity, and warning.

'The opportunity? To discover for yourself, in truth, exactly how you'd act... and, mayhap yet more apposite, how indeed would I? And would you then enjoy it?

'The warning? Be careful what you imagine, fanciful knight! For dreams dreamed here in Somnium quite often do come true.'

Their eyes they locked then, moment-swift, like fencers quite engaged and looking for advantage. Then all-undaunted, up he stood, bedclothes cast away, and faced her in his nightshirt. Sparkle-eyed, she raised a brow: a query, a temptation and, with merest nod of head, a challenge.

Lee flourished her a bow, and made a leg, a grin upon his lips; and then, as devil-may-care as ever he had been, he turned and marched into the adjoining room. No door to shut behind him, he stood there face-away and stripped himself quite naked, then sank down in the bath.

A moment later, though he knew not how, she was sitting there upon a chair and facing him, appreciative glances (or did they mock?) upon her lovely face. And despite his best intentions, his body started then to betray his admiration. She laughed, a lovely sound, and laughing found him guiltless.

And then his mind reminded him, as minds so often do, that she'd called this a bath for nine, and baths that size were surely big enough for two. And on the instant there she was, a naiad splashing in the water, fully-dressed but clothes all soaked, and giggling like his sweetheart. No sooner had his eyes engulfed her in the bath, than there she wasn't, and back upon the chair she sat. For moments then he struggled in his head, to sort the imagined from the real, and deciding on the former, looked again.

And there she sat, all soaked, with breasts thrust out, a preening vision in wet and clinging silk. And when she stood, and marched off to the door, wet footprints followed her, across the marble floor.

She turned then, wistful smile upon her lips, as if for five-year-olds or charming little boys.

'You see then now, Endimion Lee, imagination's power. And yet, you also see, how all untrained, it lasts not for an hour.

'But be this as it may, and bathe you as you will. And when you're ready for the day, my maids await you still.'

Wednesday, 26th September 1803

I hardly know what to think of *Somnium*. I think it far the better than anything I have ever written before, but how I write it, I simply do not know. I know that some would laugh and say I do not know because I am too drunk. And yet I think the truth is nearer to what I wrote last night: that all this comes from Moonland, and sweet Diana whispers all her story in my ear. And if what I am is but amanuensis to a Goddess, was there ever sweeter task for humble man to bear?

But then again, what if all this were not fiction, and somehow I just wrote down what had happened, two centuries now behind? This is a conceit that pleases me enormous.

Or yet again, what if all of this was happening now in Dreamland, and Somnium was indeed that very place? After all, I see those Somniac towers so frequent in my dreams, I no longer have to think now how to describe them. And if Endimion Lee's adventures are watched by me in dreamtime, then somehow forgotten and buried in the basement of my memory, only released again by claret and by writing ... then writing somehow makes all this quite real.

And so I write the whole night through, and sleep the morning off till dinner; and Cynthia laughs and asks me if I am awake enough to eat or whether she should feed me with a spoon as if I was a little boy. I confess she tempts me to the latter, just to see if quite she would; and if she'd let me fall asleep, my head upon her breast. And something, that I know's against all wisdom, it tells me that she would. I think, while foul Jude Brown's about, it's better that I should not try.

Late morning when I first arose and took me to the dining room for dinner, there was a letter here from Liz; Cynthia presented it to me with such a smile, I almost thought she'd read it, and yet the seal was quite secure. I read it so agog I hardly tasted anything at all. So sweet, so sad, it was so hard to bear; especially the *post scriptum* note explaining how her tears had dripped and caused the ink to run. How the dear girl misses me; and how I miss her in return. She writes so sweet of garden flowers and neighbours' cats, I almost cried myself to read it; of how her comfort was to look upon the Moon whilst knowing that I did the same (that touched me to the quick); of how she missed our goodnight hugs and kisses; and how she sleeps still with the candle lit for, though she knows old Mistress Jones quite close at hand, she is not used to being in the house at night without me. And that, I think, was hardest-most to bear: for if she had not closed her letter with a sweet, imperious command to stay here where I am and write of silver Moon and golden Love, then that single, candle-lit line of hers would have had me on the homeward coach forthwith, to take her in my arms once more and never let her go. She ended saying that she loved me; if she but knew the way I love her in return.

This afternoon, young Watkins and I made further explorations. Some four or five hundred yards along the lane, going northwards from the inn, are half a dozen tumuli; a cemetery, no doubt of ancient, ante-Romanum kings (or perhaps, I like to think, of pre-imperial and uproarious queens). Who's buried there, or when, there's no-one hereabouts who knows. The moster part of them are flattened and eroded by the heavy hand of time, and cropped close by the many sheep that bald Jude Brown grazes here atop the hill; and if young Tom were not there to point them out to me, I never would have seen them. He wonders if they're full of treasure; wants to know if I will dig them soon. I told him these are holy dead to me, more sacred yet than those all buried in a churchyard, because they never heard of Christ. I think he did not understand.

There's one mound, though, all green and grassy, standing by the lane itself, that's well enough preserved and surrounded by a ring of trees. Standing on its rounded crest, I had a notion come to me: that whether king or queen or other they were buried here, their spirit had somehow become the *genius loci* of old Shooters Hill; its God or Goddess, habited here throughout the millennia, watching as its woad-smeared people gave way in turn to Romans, and Saxons, and Danes and Normans, and wondrous Tudors descended from old Trojan Brute, and idiot Stuarts, and crophead Parliamentarians, and maddened Hanoverian line. And *me*, most insignificant of all, but the only one, perhaps, to stand there, thinking, and acknowledging, and saying: 'Oh Guardian of this place, here from long-gone past and still remaining, perduring to the long-becoming future, look kindly on me standing here, a merest eyeblink in eternity, and let me write, not the story of this place as it appears, a cowfield on a Roman road, but as it *should* be, as it *is* in dreams of glory, enamelled with the palaces of the Moon, bejewelled with temples quite Ephesian, the silvered throne of that most puissant Goddess/Queen, who is Diana of the lunar crescent, Titania of the fairies, Elizabeth who's of England both and sister too, and queen of all my heart (and, perhaps, I think, as now

I write, who's Cynthia Brown as well), and *all* of these, insoluble in one mere name, the oldest of them all... Selene.'

(I think it was a prayer made after its own fulfilment; I think this most because, last night, my pen would hardly stop and all my words seemed wrought in gold. So perhaps in praying I merely offered thanks.)

Yet more thoughts then occurred to me besides: that this rounded, Moon-shaped mound, that swells upon the hill like sweet Diana's breast, is perhaps the latest of them all; that the others, now all worn away, mayhap were tombs of former Guardians, or that same Guardian born and born again, and cycling on and on through time. I wondered then if I had addressed the last-most of his line, and how long his position had been held, and if there was another still to come. I like to think there is, and always will be, until the hill itself is ground away to dust.

And more, I thought that this mound it would survive, as all the other five would not. I felt the loss that comes with passing tides of time; and more, the loss, far greater than destruction, when things are quite forgotten. I would I were the Memory of the World, to treasure up the all that ever was; and all that ever wasn't too, besides, for dreams and myths and magic spells are every bit as important as idiot-kings and stupid wars, and an apple-blossomed branch is far more lovely than a mace or sceptre.

But be that as it may, I thought this mound would still be here two centuries hence when, if my late vision held some truth, this hill would all be smothered up with strangely-builded houses and too-unthinking men. Unthinking perhaps, I thought, except for that single future-man who, like me, will walk this hill and write because there is no other thing to do.

At last I walked away from all that sacred earth, though not without the proper farewell words, said soft beneath my breath; and so returning to the inn I ate my supper, took my claret, locked my bedroom door. And now, I hope, no interruption intervening, to write fair words, just like my singular unborn friend, of twenty decades time.

And so his fair Diana left Lee then, to thoughts and solitude. He found himself with little time for either.

Sweet Melissa, all-too-lately punished, peeped around the doorway, blushed, and pattered forward, then down upon her knees she threw herself, at bathside's edge. And hardly knowing whether best to smile, or just to cry, she looked him in the eye.

'Good master, many thanks,' she said at last. 'For but for you, I'd scream away an hour of the day, in agonies of bliss.

'But will you let me tell you something to your good? My mistress is a wonder and a beauty quite supreme, and in her heart is nothing ill.

'*But love her not*, good knight! For never loved she living man, and though she would, she *can't*. At least not in the way you wish, although I know she loves you well enough, at least, as best she can. But blissful passion's fruit you'll never taste with her while living in your body. And never will you hold her in your arms at night, uniting love and sweet delight, unless it be in dream alone.

'And worse, I tell you now, that if you love her and your heart is lost, then *you will never love another*, and all the women on the Earth will seem to you as nothing.'

Dumbfounded by her earnest plea, he could but sit and soak and stare.

'Oh, don't you see?' she continued, all a-rush. 'When you are dead, all things are possible, for spirit freed from matter knows no bounds. And then mayhap you'll find her love, in ways unsought or haply even thought. But if my lady sends you back to lands of daylight sun, and your heart remains behind, then ever after will your senses long for Somnium, and in every woman that you meet, you'll seek for Somnium's queen... her beauty, her smile, her flashing eye; the sound of voice and laughter; the softness of her flesh, the smoothness of her skin; the breath of perfume all around her; the sweetness of her kiss... and you *will not find them*, evermore. And though you think you joy in love, your portion will be all too sad, and tragic.'

'Sweet child,' he said at last. 'Whether what you say is true or not, in truth I've no idea. But I think you mean me well, and for that I give you thanks. If your words had warned me earlier, then even so I fear I would ignore them. And as it is, they come too late. I love your lady, always will, and never will no other. And so it seems, alas, that all is lost; and yet, in losing, giving up, resigning hope besides, mayhap we find a way to win ... although perchance the prize is something other yet than first we thought to gain. I cannot tell, but time it has the answer.

'Oh, look not sad, for sadness sits so ill upon a face as charmed as yours. All men they have their destined fate, and mine has brought me here, and was there ever stranger? And if old fate is but a deck of cards, or perhaps a pair of dice, then I've been dealt a flush of Queens and rolled the Venus Throw, and so I take the hand of Lady Luck and say, "what comes, will come", and play things to the full. For if I did the less, then just so much, the less I'd be a man.

'Ah, weep not, dearest girl, but look upon my smile. For nothing in the world is worse than death, and now you give me hope of bliss beyond, with she I love the best. And such a hope of heaven all-deferred, makes even longest life of hell seem frolic.

'So smile, and get you gone, and let me take my bath, and leave my heart to me. And if you'd please me still, and lessen all my cares, then never more be lady in distress, and free me of your burden.'

He grinned at her; she smiled so weakly back, then turned away and left him to his thoughts. And what those thoughts were, even he, in latter days, would never one declare.

Thursday, 27th September 1803

I dreamt of him last night, that writer who I fore-remember two whole centuries hence. He smirked at me as if he knew that I was looking, knew what I was thinking even, and all his mouth was twisted wry and quite lopside. He's old enough to be my father, hair all greying, lenses to correct his sight, living quite alone yet somehow not (I do not understand it quite: he seems to live with someone only nearly there; perhaps she is a spirit, but how can spirits live with men?). He survives, though little more, upon his works; but what he writes, I know not. And in his time, this very Bull Inn where I write is all pulled down; perhaps rebuilt, but smaller, and so its glory lost. His house is near to where I write, although I'm not sure where; perhaps where Broomhall stands today, though how such a rich-appointed mansion could be ever quite destroyed escapes me. At least, I realised eventually that what I saw was just his house: when first I dreamt, I thought it was a library. But then I realised, instead, it was a house quite full of books, by the hundred, by the thousand. Yet it was not the number alone that removed my breath; rather it was that a single man, apparently of no great means, might own so many. Could they be so wealthy in the future?

I say I dreamt of him last night; of course I meant this morning, for once again I wrote the whole night through. I do not know quite where this story goes, except each night it takes me somewhere lovely. I read over all that I have writ when once I wake up at midday, and do not quite believe it; the most part because I was so drunk I cannot remember any word I've written. At times I wonder if I've written in my sleep, or if some pagan angel moved my hand while I was unaware. I think I begin to fall in love with fair Diana Regina, although she is a fiction; and though I fear she is too sweet for such a one as me. Who would have thought: the more delightful that I make her, the more she breaks my heart.

I went to dinner; Cynthia Brown she pouted at me, whispered that I did neglect her. I told her that I had to write; she looked at me all strange and said that I should write of her. All debonair and too unthinking, I said perhaps I did. No sooner were the words quite out my mouth than she demanded that I read to her the whole that I had written. She was so imperious, I hardly know how I managed to put her off until tomorrow. She looked at me unkindly until I explained: I had to write to Liz. And then she smiled, so sweet and strange, I did not know quite what to think.

And so this afternoon I wrote to dearest Liz indeed, and told her how I loved her. Again some part of me, I know not why, it told me that I should not speak too much of Cynthia, except to say that she was kind. I did not tell my Liz that Cynthia's eyes are much the same as hers; or, indeed, that Lizzie aged, she'd look like Cynthia, or

Cynthia young would look like Liz. And perhaps the difference in their age is but illusion; a decade's nothing when beauty is eternal.

But Liz, I told her to tell me everything of her, of what she does each minute of the day, of what she thinks of in the night. I told her of my writing, but not so much of drinking; I told her of my dreams, though not quite all of what she did in them. But most of all I told her that I missed her, quite as much as she did me. I said she was the sweetest girl; I thought it better not to say that if she had been any other than my sister, then I would have had her for my bride. I know not what she'd think of that; and yet I think she knows it nonetheless. And if she knows it, then she'll know another reason why, for now, it's better we should be apart.

I slipped out with my letter late this afternoon, unseen by Cynthia, Watkins, Brown, or anyone at all. I confess I felt released to be alone, and swaggered down to the Red Lion, swinging my cane quite lustily. I bade Master Wellbeloved a fair good afternoon, asked him for a glass of porter, and presented him my letter. It will not make its way to dear Elizabeth until tomorrow; I hope it finds her well. More's the point, I hope it makes her happy.

Returning up the hill, I lingered by the wall and gate of fairly-built Broomhall. I could not gain admittance; indeed I hardly wished to. Instead I tried to see it not quite there at all; all hammered down and then replaced with strange-built houses of the future. I thought of him who was not born; wondered if he thought of me long dead. Some part of us, we spoke together, though it was not ever quite with words. I confess it made my hair stand up. I thought that we were counterpoint upon a single harpsichord, though who the right hand, who the left, I could not quite decide.

I walked back through The Bull's front door and Cynthia, she looked at me so strange. Demanded all abrupt to know just where I'd been, and why I'd walked out all alone. I started to expostulate, and then I stopped. I realised upon the sudden that she cared about me. I do not know why this should be; she does not make a similar fuss about the others of her clientele. I told her I had been to post my letter; told her more she should not worry so. And on an impulse then,

I kissed her on the forehead. Her blush was oh-so absolutely pretty. And while she stood there all confused, I sped back to my room.

She pouted at me once again, when down I went for supper; I gave her such a grin. I knew her pout it called me 'bad boy'; my grin said 'yes I am'. I ate my supper with great relish; I am not quite certain why.

Friday, 28th September 1803

My writing was quite poor last night. The Moon it was too bright, the sky was full of stars. The night outside was full of silence; within the inn was nothing but a harpsichord. I knew that it was Cynthia, playing galliards, and more she used the lute-stop. I found I had to pause and listen: she played with so much passion I could not help but think she played for me. Yet let me make that clear: I do not think she played to please me; rather I think it was merely to distract me. I knew somehow this was revenge for all my independence of the afternoon. It made me laugh, and so I poured out too much claret.

She played and played and, at the last, as if she knew I'd emptied out by far too many bottles, she played me gentle lullabies. I sprawled down on the bed, still dressed, and let her play me off to sleep, to dream and, at the last, to heaven.

And so I had my strangest dream so far: I dreamt of woman, queen and Goddess, I know not what except she seemed to be all of these, and more than them besides. For she was Diana Regina, the Goddess, queen and heroine who rules my fictional Somnium; and Selene the Grecian Moon-Goddess, that epitome of loveliness who stands there at the start of time; and Elizabeth Tudor with the heart and stomach of a king, on whom the Armada foundered and of whom the poets wondered; and she was sweetest sister Liz all dressed in nothing but her curls; and Cynthia Brown-eyes too. All of these she was, one and all and separate, every single one containing all the others, lovely and large-eyed; and in the end she kissed me. I moaned, it was so heavenly. There may have been more than this to follow, but I awoke, and cursed myself for waking, and wished the world were always dream. Or perhaps it is. Perhaps to wake, and to be parted from that lovely fairy Goddess, nine times more perfect than the very world itself; perhaps that parting is a dream, or nightmare, or a horrid fit. But, the loss. The *loss*.

Saturday, 29th September 1803

So yesterday, when I had finished writing the above, I took me down to dinner, and Cynthia Brown-eyes she was waiting there for me. Sat herself down at my table, wanted to know where all the pages were that I was going to read to her, made it plain that there would be absolutely no escape. I had to chuckle; told her that I could not possibly read upon an empty stomach; and neither without a glass or two of sack to lubricate the throat. She looked at me, pretending ire. I ate and made her wait.

At last, when I thought that she was quite prepared to chase me to my room, rather than let me out of her sight, I confessed I had the pages in my pocket. She pouted so preposterously, my impulse was to thrash her; and after that she glanced around, then took my hand, and led me out the inn's back door.

Although she'd shown me the pleasure garden stretched out far behind the inn, with gazebos, trees and pools, and gravelled walks all serpentine, I had not realised there was a little private garden there just nigh the building, all fenced around and full of eglantine. A little bower on the north, it caught the afternoon sun, and there within, a wooden bench-seat, barely big enough for two. She sat me down, sat herself beside me, looked at me imperious, and all her look was one that did command: said nothing more than 'read to me'. And so I did.

I read until the opening section's end, and then I paused. She put her hand upon my knee and told me it was lovely; I almost gasped for pleasure. Several deep breaths I had to take before I could continue. Even so, she left her hand upon my leg.

So the time passed, and the sun it rode the sky, and then I'd finished all I had. She looked at me so very sweet, said 'thank you' very soft, and kissed me on the cheek. I asked her if she liked it; she told me that she did.

And then she quoted one whole sentence, word for word, from the first page I had wrote, and pointed out where it could be improved with but one extra syllable, to make the rhythm flow. I looked at her astonished. Three other sentences entire she followed this with, and for each a minor correction.

I stared at her, my mouth agape. I was no way offended, for well I knew that she was right. And neither was it that she had a better ear for rhythm than me. It was that on one single hearing she had committed those entire sentences to memory, even when the error occurred quite near the end. I simply had no idea at all just how she did it.

She told me then some things I thought were rather sweet; of how she liked to have a poet in the inn, and a gentleman (so young) of such romantic instincts. She told me I should write the more, and read her each night's work upon the following day, because she'd love to hear it. I was quite touched. And then she laughed and told me that her small improvements did not come without a price.

I knew just what she meant upon the instant, for Saturn's day has come around once more. And so, tonight, it seems, again I have to dance.

Sunday, 30th September 1803

And dance I did, and it was sweet. Her husband gone upon some jaunt of which I cared not to inquire, she had me to herself. And so the dance hall we abandoned; the music could be heard quite plainly in her parlour, so there we drank and danced. We drank too much, we danced too much; eventually we had to sit, and when we did she rested lovely head upon my shoulder, closed her eyes and sighed.

And so much then I wanted just to kiss her. No, I confess, that is not quite the half of it. For all I love my dearest Liz, with Cynthia Brown-eyes in my arms I knew, I wanted to take her straightway off to bed. She looked up then and, oh, her lovely eyes they were so huge, I guessed she knew just what I thought. And then she laughed; her little tongue poked out, all saucy; then up she got, my hand in hers, and demanded further dances. And so the moment passed.

By midnight the musicians left, the inn was closed; and I could barely stand. Cynthia then sat down before the harpsichord and played me nothing more than old almaynes and galliards, and voltas and pavanes. And when she paused, I asked her why she played Elizabethan airs; she told me straight it was the music played in Somnium. Of course I'd read to her of Moon-maids playing so; but now somehow I knew that she was *right*, yet how I knew I am in no way sure. My mind it conjured up an image then, in which Diana Regina and I we danced a slow pavane; it was so sweet. I wished that I could act my fancy out with Cynthia Brown-eyes then, but while she played she could not dance.

I think that woman reads my mind. She stood up then and took my hand; I knew upon the instant what she wanted. And so in deepest night-time silence, we danced so stately a pavane around my lady's parlour; and all the music of the Moon was in my head, and the light of all the stars was in her eyes.

I think back now and find myself surprised we did not collapse into each other's arms all lost in drunken laughter. And yet we did not.

We danced in perfect time and step; we concluded note for note. I bowed. She curtseyed. I kissed her hand and thanked her for a lovely evening, thought I ought to go upstairs and so back to my room.

Instead she helped me up another stair (my feet, but moments gone all full of dances, were somehow on the sudden full of trips and stumbles), and so up to the lantern tower, where we could view the Moon. All silver was that semi-orb, and sweeter to my sight for viewing with a companion near as lovely. A sofa seat she sat upon; invited me to lay my head upon her lap and look up at the Moon while little fingers stroked my hair and fondest smiles were all about her rosy lips. My eyes were all at war: the right it looked up to the Moon, the left at dearest Cynthia; and each demanded of the other that it should share its view. Somehow (perhaps the fumes of wine they misted up my gaze), I thought that Cynthia's face was there upon the Moon, while all the light above the world was shining in my hostess' eyes. I could have laid there thus forever.

She would not let it be, for at the last she lifted up my head and sat me upright, more or less. By then I was resistless; she helped me to my room and lay me down a-bed. Somehow, when she was gone (I hope) I managed to undress.

I dreamt that I was dead and buried in the ground.

I woke and yet I found myself no way distressed at all; for dead I may have been, yet somehow I survived. I cannot say quite how; it was not Christian resurrection, heaven, purgatory, or any of those things. It was as if I'd died to sunshine days, but still lived on in Moonlight. In other times I would have been quite terrified; now, somehow, I found it rather reassuring.

I slept till noon; it was only when I woke I realised today was Sunday. My prayers to all the ancient Gods and Goddesses have been answered quite! The unspeakable Kinnock was unable to deliver his abominations this weekend, being sorely stricken with the gout. And how dear Cynthia smirked to tell me; I swear that woman has a pagan heart to match quite with my own. I thought the man a drunkard from the first I saw his florid face. When I drink, I think of Bacchus, offer him salutes, and all is well; for barbarous Christians, drink is but a sin, and so it strikes him down. On his own head be it, then; or rather on his foot.

And yet, I have to think: if prayers like this can so succeed, what else could be achieved? And more than this: I should not offer any prayer that's ill-considered.

The other news I heard at dinner was rather more the serious. Last night, it seems, armed robbers had burst into an army officer's house in Woolwich, down below the hill. The foolish man had tried to fight, and for his pains had got a pistol ball that shattered all his knee. An army surgeon took his leg off; they say it took but fifteen seconds, and yet I do not like to think of how he screamed. This is too much a world of pain.

Returning to my room this afternoon, I heard the harpsichord again. I thought of Liz to start, and then I thought of Cynthia. I left my room and went downstairs, and followed all those sweetest notes, and found myself once more in Cynthia's parlour. She smiled at me: I knew she'd used those lovely sounds to draw me there deliberate. And so I spent the time till supper all alone with Cynthia Brown-eyes (for having begun to nickname her so, I find now that I cannot think of her in any other way). I wrote a fair copy then of all I had of

Somnium, to send it to my Liz when next I post a letter; she played me
sweet pavanes. I had to smile, and all my thoughts, they ran back to
last night. Some tunes I knew, and some I'd never heard before. Some
were by John Bull; it struck me strangely then to hear them played in
a tavern also called The Bull. And some, I thought, could only have
been written in the Moon. I had to admire the beauty of her playing
(if truth be told, she made my Lizzie sound a charming child; and yet,
at the same time, I thought my Lizzie's playing all the sweeter for its
childish charm); I cried her 'bravo' with each passing piece. The smiles
she gave me in return were, quite simply, lovely.

More strange than this: when I had written all my pages, then
she asked me once again to read them out aloud. I did so gladly,
remembering yesterday afternoon: and as I did, then sweet and soft,
she began to play continuo accompaniment, so beautiful I could hardly
fit my stumbling words around her lovely, liquid notes. She smiled; I
read my text with tears all streaming; I had not ever thought that such
a combination could be quite so oddly pleasing.

And when we finished, she told me that my words were lovelier
than any she had ever heard; more lovely still than they had been the
previous afternoon. I told her that they were not mine; that someone,
somehow seemed to write them through me; and more they only came
to life accompanied by her music. I could not think of any other way to
express my thanks for all she'd added to my work and so, I do confess,
I kissed her (more, I kissed her on the lips). And when I had, I sat back
quite in horror, and blushed for shame; these things they may be well
in dark of night when we are drunk, but in the afternoon? A moment
then, I wished I was in Asia, out there in the wind-blown Gobi desert,
where none could see me redden; and then she smiled and kissed me
in return. And after that we thought it best to make our way to supper.

Oh Cynthia Brown-eyes, how you do confuse me. When first I
wrote of *Somnium's* Diana, so I thought of Liz, and told myself it was
a way to love my darling sister in the abstract, for the world will not
allow me to love her as I would. Now I find I think of Cynthia, just
as unattainable to me, because she has a husband. And yet she tempts
me just as much as Liz, and both of them they know they do it. And

so I wonder if there's something here that tells me more of dear divine Diana: a virgin and a temptress too, for all our artists paint her naked. And so I think of Cynthia naked too, and then decide I'd better not.

And if I'd better not, then perhaps I'd better think of something else. And so, perhaps the best for me is, once again, to write.

At last, new-dressed and freshly-shaved, Lee let the softly-whispering maidens of the Moon a-smiling take his hand. They led him on and outside to a courtyard far-removed from Somnium's entry gate, where Queen Diana, huntress-clad, awaited his arrival.

All dressed in fur and softest leather now she was, with fine morocco boots extending foot to thigh, a tiny skirt of panther-skin, and tiger-hide her tunic. A tiger's head her pretty hat, all jaunty perched upon her lovely hair, its savage teeth in sabre-curves across her charming brow. Centred in her forehead, a cat's-eye sapphire gleamed in gold; around her lovely neck, a chain of garnets hung, all interspersed with topaz, and withal a dripping emerald pendant. Right shoulder burdened with a quiver, her left hand held a Moon-curved bow of ancient close-grained yew, and horn. The leopard-gleam was glinting in her eye, and on her ruby lips a smile.

And yet, for all he thought her ravishing to view, a sight more curious still first captured his attention.

'I'd swear by all my life and she I love, who stands now here before me, that I had slept the whole night through,' he said. 'And yet I see no sign of daylight...'

'And so you will not, gentle sir,' she told him then, a little chuckle in her voice. 'For here in Somnium I allow no sun. All is stars and Moonlight here, and velvet night, aurorae, comets all ablaze and meteors all a-sparkle. For in the day, all men forget their dreams; while here, in nighted Somnium, all remember me.'

'Dear lady,' he responded, 'if ever there was one, below the starry night, of whom it could be said, "once seen and ne'er forgot", then it was you, my bright-eyed queen... for your image is all embranded in my soul.'

'Oh, gallant knight, go to!' she laughed. 'The night is not yet old enough to press your fond desires. Rather, tell me this...

'If given long, curvaceous bow, and quiver-full of goose-quilled shafts... then can you shoot and hit a target, small and far away?'

'Madam,' he told her, smiles awry, 'I have my fingers and my thumbs, and more, I am an Englishman. The froggish knights of Agincourt, or rather still, of Crecy... they would not ask me this.'

'So prove your English skill,' she demanded with a grin, handing over bow and quiver, then pointing to a deer-shaped plaque of wood. 'The target, as you see, is yonder distant hart...'

'Another heart I'd have in mind, if this was Cupid's bow,' he said, and nocked a shaft. 'And will you wager on my skill?'

'Five hits in five to win a kiss,' she told him, saucy-eyed and smiling pertly. 'If you think you can...'

'And if I can't, then bell my cap and give me bladder on a stick, and let me be my lady's fool!'

He grinned, and drew, and shot, and almost missed the mark, it being rather further than at first he had surmised. With greater concentration then, he shut an eye and shot again, his second hit more centred than the first. And so the third, the fourth, the fifth, all hissed and sang and thudded home, a cluster of desire.

Expectant then, he turned and let a sweeping bow demand reward.

'Well shot, my proud and noble knight!' she said, a little minxish in her tone. 'But now before I give you wager's due, pray let me shoot as well...'

She took the bow, and barely looking, shot and split his first shaft end to end. And then in order, one by one, the second to the fifth, she split them just the same. An eyebrow raised, she turned and smiled; and whelmed with chastened wonder, he could do naught but stare.

Exuberant pride now quite forgot, he waited while she downed the bow, then took her gently in his arms. Lost a moment in her exquisite face, at last he pressed a reverent kiss upon her soft and sweet-moist lips, as if the chastest maiden ever living 'neath the whole of wide blue heaven was wrapped in his embrace.

And then her tiny little tongue-tip wiggled in between his teeth;

and with the lingering of the kiss, so he found celestial bliss.

Time-distorted, he knew not whether eternity had been compressed into an instant, or an instant sempiternal stretched; only that her berapturing kiss still ended long before he wished. And yet, at last, his lovely lynx-eyed Moon-cat queen slipped supplely from his grasp, placed a dainty finger-tip quite full upon his nose, and pushed him back a pace. And laughed a little laugh.

'Wooden harts are well enough for practise shafts,' she told him then, 'but moving targets prove one's skill. So will you hunt the deer with me, around about this woody hill?'

'Oh gladly, fairest lady,' Endimion Lee said then. 'Yet this old hill's a robber-haunt, and I'd not have you risk your beauty in the hands of such as they…'

She laughed, and with a little hand she tilted up her tiger-hat, then swept back swift her luscious locks.

'I think we'll be alright,' she softly said, 'for no longer now is this the Shooters Hill you know, but rather is it mine. A Moon-hill here upon the Earth, with Somnium its crown, its oak-woods now a private park, its wells and springs all gushing wine. And here the white hart roams, that killed the once revives the twice, and so provides us sport for evermore.'

'Then, loveliest maid that ever was, I'll sport with you in any way you wish, and if it only lasts for ever, then even this will be too short.'

At that she took his hand and led him from the courtyard, through an arch all painted darkest blue and specked with golden stars. At farther side they found themselves in Somnium's massy stables and the low-roof brick-built kennels of the baying lunar hounds.

'My page, he warned of Hecat's hunting-dogs,' laughed bold Endimion Lee, 'and yet I think that yours could track the comets 'cross the stars and even turn men's dreams at bay, while hers are only fit to course the depths and 'venge on gore and shattered souls…'

'Oh, mine are quite the same as hers,' she grinned, 'for she's the same as me. And if I light the sky above, then she's the darkness of the earth below.

'But these are puzzles for another time. So let's to horse, and on our way. A mare for you, I think, a stallion for me; for we should always ride the other sex, if only for the sake of piquancy.'

A sable stallion and a milky mare were brought forth then, already saddled, by a pair of lunar nymphs. With half a laugh Diana placed a booted foot within the silver stirrup, then sprang and threw a long and shapely leg across the horse's back and sat the leather saddle mannish-style. Endimion Lee was swift in emulation, then leant to take another bow and quiver, handed up to him by widely grinning Moon-maid.

'Dear knight,' his lady smirked awry, 'your face is wonder-baffled, for never have you seen a dame, a queen, or Goddess even yet, who rode the same as I. So if I send you back to court, then tell your lady-friends that riding half a saddle only gives them half the thrill, and never will they gallop, leap or curvet fast as me.

'And neither, I think, will you!'

'Dear Queen,' he laughed, and looked direct into her lovely eye, 'one thing I learned when I was very young was "always let a lady win". And now I've told you this, then you will never know if triumphs that ensue are all of yours or part of mine, and so I think we should agree that sharing honours of our sport is far the best for both, for even kisses won or lost are none so sweet as kisses held in common.'

'No time for kissing now, my friend!' She kicked her horse into a trot, and raised a curving horn that dangled ready at her saddle, brought it to her full and pursing lips, and sounded it sublime. And at its mellow tone there opened up a gate, releasing then a pack of red-eared hounds, all furry-white and baying 'neath a gold-sparked Moon, that swift passed by the skittered horses, muzzles downward pointing to the vaguely fragrant ground.

And then, behind the pack, there came Diana's nymphs, each hardly clad at all, their lovely legs all wrapped around the waists of gargant mastiff-hounds that slavered as they ran. With bows and quivers all were armed, and gleeful laughter sped them on their way. And sped a thought once more to Lee's remembrance then, of young Bart Greene and all he'd said of Hecat's hounds and the terrored fury of her hunt; and thought, instead of down to hell, this pack would take him straight to heaven. So laughing too, he joined them then, and spurred to catch their mistress.

They rode on side by side and out the postern gate, then turned to canter straight along by glorious Somnium's marbled walls. And though old Amphion may have played the louder, to raise up mighty holds and Theban towers, he knew a sweeter music underlay these smooth curvaceous breastworks. No defensive ramparts these, for never army of the world had come up hereabouts, as long as world there was. Inviolate like its queen stood matchless Somnium, and almost quite as fair.

On opposite hand, the hilltop stretched away, both strange and quite familiar. Its woods were oak and ash and beech, and yet they stretched more wide than any he remembered, and so the hilltop too was larger, rounder and more full, somehow, of all that made a tree-decked height appealing to the sense. By moonlight it was gloried, and yet, when round he looked at tiger-clad Diana, all else was quite forgot, except her smile, her streaming hair, her eyes.

The nymphs hallooed ahead and off she galloped, faster yet than moonbeams or the lightning flashing bright across the clearest night-time sky. And as he spurred to join her all he heard was fairy chuckles, gently mocking, and then her lilting laughter calling 'catch me if you can'. But that he doubted any could, unless the lady let them.

They rode on then and swift left Somnium's soaring towers behind. And then they came to Roman Watling Street, and found it quite transfigured.

He knew it, for it ran the same east-west across the hill; and yet he knew it not. For now its surface sparked with marble plates that glittered 'neath the stars, all mortared close with gold-dust. And either side was statue-strewn with all the emperors of the world and, on pedestals raised higher yet, of all the women that they loved. And all those women, in their looks, their eyes, their smiles, reflected something greater; something of Diana, the Lovely of the Moon.

Across they went and down an ancient stony lane, hounds a-howl and mastiffs baying, horns all winding on the moonlit air. On past gushing fountains, spurting springs, and hill-arisen brooks the which he knew, in any world that really was at all, would burble on and rivers soon become, and flush themselves in mighty tidal Thames, the world's imperial stream.

Halloos and horns, and then the hart they saw, snow-white its fur and silver-antlered, silvered too its hooves. It sprang and dashed and brake through bushes, bounded on from rock to boulder, turned a tree and plunged down hill. Arrows whistled (not Diana's), missed, and then away it went, and leaped, and disappeared from view.

All excited now, a tongue-tip to her lip and soft breasts heaving, thighs clamped tight about her stallion's saddle, sweet Diana cried away and swiftly then was gone. And so they rode, sometime together, sometime not, about the hill for most the day. Strange slopes they crossed, that seemed to slide, from top to bottom, into places still unformed; crags next rose up quite unbidden, and from their peaks revealed vistas where the stars skimmed by beneath the Earth; and tree-lined avenues led to shadowed places quite unmapped. All matter then seemed mutable and turmoiled 'neath the Moon; the pole-star of the world Diana's eyes alone. And yet he knew this was enough, for worlds and all their riches count for nothing, next to love.

At last, when they had rode enough for their enjoyment and, it seemed, explored too many permutations of the strange and dizzied world, the white hart turned at bay. It stood, regarding Somnium's queen, and in its eye was all the self-same love Endimion Lee would claim was but his own. And so Diana Regina, arrow nocked and smile forgot, nodded then and drew and shot; and all the spheres above the Earth conspired then to guide her shaft to its appointed mark. A silent sigh and then the white hart knelt and lay its length upon the ground; and all that were around, Goddess, man and nymph and hound, were still-tongued in its honour.

Young Melissa swift dismounted next, took brocade robe and covered up entire the carcase of the prey; and all then joined their queen to turn their backs and offer silent prayer. And when they looked again, the hart was gone; and only seen as distant flash of white amongst the trees.

A fond farewell they bade it then, and thanked it for the sport. And so they next returned, their horses at a stately walk, to jewelled and towered Somnium; which in his heart, if not quite yet his mind, seemed sweet and longed-for home to Moon-besmitten Lee. For there dwelt dear Diana, queen and Goddess both of all he was or wished for.

They supped. They drank. They talked. They kissed. They bid each other sweetest dreams, and parted then, Endimion Lee to bed alone, his lady to he knew not what. And knowing nothing, left her free; and freeing her, he freed himself. And slept.

Monday, 1st October 1803

No sleep for me last night. I wrote until the sky was grey with dawn, though found myself at times distracted. At midnight I heard horses leave; at nearly three they did return. And then for half an hour after that I heard the sound of booted feet about the inn below that, though they tried for silence, still they scuffed; and then there was the sound of something dropped, and afterwards a muffled oath. I stayed within my room and checked the key was in the lock; what Jude Brown does is Jude Brown's business and none of mine, especially at that time of night. I simply hoped that Cynthia was safe abed and sweetly dreaming in her room (I confess that in the evening when I sat to write, awhile I placed my chair quite near the open doorway, so I could glance along the corridor without; and so I watched, and saw, and now I do believe that Cynthia and her wretched husband sleep in separate rooms. Such prying, of course, is no gentlemanly thing to do; and yet I had to know).

And when at last I did retire, I dreamt of Lizzie bathing, sweet and naked, eyes half-closed and mouth half-opened. And, oh, those soft white breasts of hers, with warm and soapy water lapping all around them. So sweet, so lovely. And then she realised that I was watching, and simply smiled, and closed her eyes, and let me look. A crescent then was on her brow, and so I knew her, on the sudden, Elizabeth and Diana both. And when I woke, the dream combining with the hunting scene I wrote last night, gave me thought of yet another dream to write up next in *Somnium*. For if *Somnium* is a world and book of dreams, it seems so right to me that dreams themselves should write it.

Tomorrow I shall have to ask dear Cynthia to send to Woolwich for more paper, and while she does, perhaps for further ink; I had not thought to write so much so quickly (or quite so much here in this journal). Yet everything I write seems well enough, and nothing is to waste. I think my Goddess whispers in my ear and tells me what to write; and every word she whispers pleases me. The *Somnium* we've made is far from anything I expected; and if Diana tells me what to write, then every word it seems to mean: 'Sweet Goddess, how I love you.' And if in truth that's what she wants to hear, I'm more than glad to say it. I'd say it louder, longer, but she knows it's true already.

While eating dinner, I could not help but notice Cynthia and her husband exchanging heated whispers, neither of them seeming pleased in any way about the other. And shortly afterward Cynthia proposed an expedition for the afternoon. I willingly accepted, although I must confess I thought that Brown himself was behind all this, and wanted me away from The Bull for some short time; whether this had anything to do with late nocturnal noises, I'd rather not conjecture.

A half an hour after dinner, I met her by the squat stone mounting-block outside the inn, and both of us were dressed for walking. It seemed we were away into the woods. I looked around for young Tom Watkins, asked if he'd be joining us. When she said he wouldn't, I mentioned highwaymen and pistols; pointed out my walking cane would hardly cry defiance to a child. She merely laughed and told me everyone about the hill knew Jude Brown's wife and how to leave her well enough alone. I told her, with my best, most-boyish smirk, that I was not from round the hill; she pouted at me, eyebrow raised, and said that we should be on our way. And as we went I thought that I would never like to suffer any sort of vengeance handed out by Judas Brown; but somehow I'm not really sure that that is what she meant. Besides, from what I'd seen a while ago, he'd know full well that I was with her.

We started down the road toward London, then turned aside to leftwards and so into the woods; and once we were beyond sight of the inn, she took my hand. She said it was to guide me on the path; I knew quite well it wasn't.

Her smile it was so full of mischief; I wondered what it could portend.

A few minutes walking further on, she simply laughed at my amazement: a castle-tower rose up high before us then, all new and gleaming brick. I simply had not known that anything like this was here on Shooters Hill. She ruffled up my hair again to chide me for my gawping; this seems to much amuse her. I had to tell her of my shock; for when at first I'd seen its crenellations up there in the trees, a moment I had thought before me stood an outpost-turret of dear fantastic Somnium, a night's-dream all a-sudden real by day. She had to lead me on until I touched it; and only when my fingers chafed the brick could I accept its earthly form.

Three storeys tall and all three-sided; three syllables its quite unlikely name as well: *Severndroog*. A single tower and yet it rejoices somehow to think itself a 'castle', though it is hardly ancient, erected as recently as 1784. At first I thought it nothing but a folly, but it seems it is a little more than that: a memorial to one Sir William James. I confessed to Cynthia that I'd never heard of him, knight or not; she laughed and told me to imagine how much the less his name would mean, then, a double-century hence. I looked at her, and wondered why she'd said that; why she'd choose that time.

For the sake of my journal, let me record that William James cleared the Malabar Coast of pirates (led by a certain Conagee Angria, whoever this unheard-of unworthy might have been) in the year 1755, and captured Severndroog Fort, bombarding it from the sea. I imagine it one of those minor skirmishes we seem to like to magnify, for the glorification of the 'British Empire', and all the baggage that entails of 'enlightening poor savages' far across the seas. Nonetheless, the conquering hero left a widow and she, in turn, left us 'Severndroog Castle' in his honour (I had to think of the Mausoleum, and Artemisia finishing off the tomb of her brother-spouse; and so, of course, I thought of Liz). A gallery within has paintings of the battle (our sailors so 'heroic', their foes but utmost cravens; I thought the image quite beneath contempt), and in the vestibule, a collection of the defeated Indians' arms and armour. But mayhap yet: if we still wore armour, and had the less of guns, the world might then be far a better place.

I thought little enough of all of this; it seemed to me of no account. I suppose the British Empire's well enough, though better ruled by queens. I could not help but wonder why dear Cynthia had brought me here. And then she gave the crone who keeps the door a groat, and so we were allowed to make our way up spiral stairs that wind up through the north-east turret. The first floor boasts a fine domed ceiling, rather more an ovoid than a sphere, with gilded plasterwork and lions' heads, with smaller rooms in those two turrets not containing stairs; the second floor is similar but lacks a ceiling, merely showing heavy naked beams below the roof. I rather thought I'd like to live there, reclusive in a forest-tower and high up on a hilltop, far removed from all the mud-bespattered world; to cherish there a single lovely-eyed companion while all the laws and evils of the time pass by. Dear Elizabeth, or perhaps…

At last we reached the rooftop turrets. The view was quite astounding: we stood there level with the tree-tops, and a half a dozen counties stretched out all around. All of London sprawled before us; the Thames ran on for miles. I do not think I've ever seen quite so much of all the world at once.

I stared, and Cynthia ruffled up my hair again. I told her if she did that one more time, I'd kiss her. She did, her wide eyes full of challenge and head all tilted to the side, and so of course I kept my word. How many further repetitions followed, I cannot quite remember; at last she could not help but laugh, and fell into my arms. I laughed in turn and ruffled up her lovely hair as well; she kissed me.

She was so soft all wrapped up in my arms, I did not want to let her go; and yet at last, I had to. We left, though not before dear Cynthia had paused a moment for a private word with the old beldame. From there we came up stony Sandars Lane, and so passed by Hazelwood House, the new villa built where once there stood The Catherine Wheel, not long ago the hilltop inn, now superseded by The Bull. I looked about and some antiquarian part of me began to wish I'd had the chance to drink there; but Cynthia told me it had been but little more than just a house of ill-repute. I've no idea quite how she knew this.

I must confess, dear Cynthia Brown-eyes, she puzzles me enormous. Flirtatious, yes, and how she loves to play the temptress; and yet it seems she plays for no-one else but me. I think (indeed, I *have* to think) that these are no more than pretty games. And yet I cannot help but think of what I wrote last night: that Diana was a temptress too. And Diana is my Goddess quite supreme. But what this means, I simply do not know. For then again, there are some occasions when I see that same strange 'distance' that I found upon our first night's drinking; as if temptation and flirtation were but games to please me, behind which stood a figure far more serious, with plans I do not understand.

Returning to my room, I found suspicious scratch-marks about the lock that guards my trunk. A swift inspection revealed nothing missing, and if my money still remained within I had to believe the trunk had not been opened. I know who I suspect, of course; it was too obvious that Jude Brown wanted me away from the inn. At the time we left, I'd thought this more to do with the noises that I'd heard in the night, and so, I have to think, did Cynthia. My heart it will not let me hold her any way complicit.

That said, I know a wiser man than me would leave The Bull forthwith. But temptress or enchantress, I think dear Cynthia has me now too much enmeshed within her spells, escape her if I would.

The evening, after supper, she wanted me to read to her all I'd written in the night, while sipping claret first, and later port, and sitting in her parlour. I saw Jude Brown, in passing by the open door, his face all full of sneers. I thought it best, when she had heard the whole of what I had to offer, to hasten to my room.

And yet, when I had, tonight I wrote and wrote, and could not write enough. The reason was too clear: the more I wrote, the more I'd have to read to her tomorrow, the more excuse we'd have to be together. Somehow I feel I betray my lovely Liz; and yet I know I cannot have my sister. But then I cannot have Cynthia Brown-eyes either. I would I could have both; and more I wish that they were both here with me now.

Perhaps all this desire's provoked by what I wrote tonight...

And on the heels of sleep, a dream then swift ensued. Back in the woods he found himself alone, with strangely silent hounds, and wandering soft afoot. And yet, somehow, he knew that he was other than himself, but seemed himself besides. Short kilt and sandals now were all he wore, and at his belt a dagger. The Moon shone quite as bright and clear as day.

A-sudden then, his hounds were off upon a scent, and yet he followed not; for somewhere close at hand he heard a peal of lightsome lady-laughter. The woods were thick around him now and grown so strange, it chanced, with flowery vines strung all about and orchids blazing quite too brilliant; and Moonlit moths of giant size drank up florescent nectar through their long and coiling tongues. A faint and eerie fluting drifted by upon the perfumed breeze; lush grass was underfoot; and high above, the diamond-brightened stars were all a-glitter. And all the night-time now was sweet and warm and still, and in the soft pellucid light a Moon-nymph's simple sigh filled all the world with magic.

Still quite uncertain who he was, he stole across a glade; though whether then he followed on to flute, or laugh, or sigh, he never could tell after. Beyond an ancient fragrant clump of purple-flowered lavender, he heard the introspect and liquid chatter of a small loquacious brook, a-babble as it tumbled to a clear and bubbled pool.

And so at last, a little further still, beneath a shading lilac tree that drooped all overburdened with a scented mass of pale and pinkish blossom, he paused, and parted leaves, and looked.

Then wonder flew in through his eyes, seduced his mind and raptured quite his heart.

A wide and sparkle-surfaced lakelet stretched before his gaze, its crystal waters freshened by the onward-flowing stream that entered all-a-gurgle close at hand, then poured itself away so many yards beyond, where silver fishes leaped in frolic play about a coral step-stoned weir. And on the pool-side bank, all flushed and pink and warm with chasing fleet-foot deer… Diana and her nymphs.

A little dress of purest white she wore, that clung all close about her tiny waist and cupped up tight her lovely breasts. From dainty sandals rose up snowy stockings, knit like lace, of softest silk and clasped about her milky thighs with claret garters all of velvet, tied up tight with little golden bows. Around her charming neck a russet choker, sleek and narrow, made of satin, massy pearls a-dangle 'neath her chin; and on her brow, where ever it should be, the curving gilded crescent gleamed with Moonfire. And in her spilling chestnut tresses, two gilt brocaded ribbons and a creamy, scented rose.

She sat, so white and pink and sweet, upon vermilion plush, spread smooth across a grassy knoll; about her lolled her lovely nymphs, exhausted and expectant, their eyes upon their charming mistress.

A little sigh, an arching back, her hands stretched high above her, fingers interlaced, she thrust out then a long and shapely leg, a toe-point to a chosen nymph, a summons in her eye. The virgin-maid approached her queen, her head bowed down and both her knees upon the ground, and then, with tiny fingers dainty as a child's, unclasped the royal sandal. The first removed, the other swiftly followed; a regal nod of thanks and after that the nymph retired to join her sweet companions.

Diana next drew up her knees and, with fingers daintier still, pulled slowly at the little bow upon her velvet garter; then swift untied the ends. The strap fell down upon the plush; she stretched out now her fresh-ungartered leg and looked along its stockinged length with gamine admiration.

The other limb was next released from out its claret band, and unbent then were both her white-hosed legs, knees and ankles both together, both feet pointed straight. And next, a sweet and girlish laugh upon her lips, she wiggled tiny toes.

Her pleasure all too obvious, next Diana flexed a leg, leaned forward and, with delicate twiddling of her thumbs and fingers, so slowly and so sensuously began to downward roll her lacy silken stocking. And inch by inch as stocking rolled, so inch by inch her smooth-as-satin skin was just as much revealed, a sweet and delicate milky pink, from perfect curving thigh (so soft and warm and tender) to rounded knee and so beyond, to lengthy shin and rounded calf, to graceful ankle, dainty foot and then at last, so small a-tip her lovely naked limb, her charming little toes.

He looked wide-eyed and open-mouthed along the bare and beauteous leg exposed before his gaze, a fever-sweat upon his brow. And next, with thunder-pounding heart and panting breath, he watched a second web of lacy silk rolled down and tossed aside, with just the slowness and the same delight with which she'd peeled away the other.

And then the Queen of all his Heart, and Golden Moon besides, stood up, forever young and pertly sweet, and reached behind her neck to gather up her nut-brown hair in both her little hands; then tied it up atop her head (at least the moster part) in brocade ribbon-bows. Next down she reached, her forearms crossed and hand to either hip, and took her tiny dress's hem between her fingertips.

She looked around. His heart rose to his mouth just then, her glance upon his hiding place for long-belingered seconds, before it passed along its way; returning then, her searching gaze was paused again at where he stood there statue-struck and all a-drip with sweat.

And then, with slow inevitability, she did what he expected; what he'd always dreamed of, but never dared to hope.

A tiny wiggle of her buttocks, and then she brought the dress-hem upwards, bit by bit and little by little; and the higher up it went the less he thought to breathe. The bony project of her hip above her lovely thigh: the Moonbeams caught these both... the shadowed dark beneath her smooth-curved belly yet retained its secrets. Her flank (so sleek), her stomach next (so soft), and then her ribs (just seen, so dainty in the Moonlight); all these his eyes did overrun, and then he bit his tongue upon a sob.

The dress drew up above her wondrous breasts, as pale as snow, as smooth as silk and downy-soft, as round as ever full moons were. And though he'd rather stay quite still, he had to wipe away the tears. For fresh-released, her young teats wobbled, bounced and settled on her chest, standing pink and proud. Transformed upon the instant to a little boy who wanted suck, he could but stand and stare.

His transfixion quite complete, the seconds passed, and by the time he had his soul again the dress was high above Diana's head, and then she cast it down upon the plush and stood there, charming, naked. In instants swift ensuing, her little hands ran down from shoulders, over breasts and lovely stomach to her thighs, as if she'd assay the impossible and smooth the perfect satin of her lovely nymphlet skin.

Her maids, as charmed it seemed as he who, peeping, watched her, began to chatter 'mongst themselves about some secret, sweet and much-desired privilege; then rose and stripped themselves as well.

And Endimion Lee, who still remained unsure quite who he was besides, looked upon them not at all, ignored their words, and simply gazed on naked Goddess, lovely in her glory, shining in the Moonlight, old as time and schoolgirl-sweet, baby-nude and perfect woman. And loved her, body, heart and soul; and wanted her with all his being.

A little laugh upon her lovely lips, sweet Diana stepped into the lake, paced until the water lapped her calves, turned and crooked a finger, summoning then a pair of nymphs. And turning all about, let the watcher in the lilac see those things he wished to see: her charming buttocks, sweet and round, that swivelled as she walked; between her thighs, the curl-haired portal of her maidenhood, unbreached for now and evermore, and yet for all of that, desired more than bliss and heaven; and perfect paps more treasured than the world entire.

A moment then she paused, remembering that her lovely neck was still encircled by the choker; reached up both hands behind her neck (and how her sweet breasts rose pursuivant), then swift unclasped the russet satin band and handed it a-nymphwards. With greatest care the maiden carried it ashore, returning with a carven phial of whitest alabaster; by then her naked queen had stepped away to thigh-depth in the middling lake.

Upon the shore, the other nymphs struck up a tune of Phrygian modulation, played soft on flutes and lyres, accompany to a wordless lilt. And Queen Diana, adding then a music laugh, sank down into the water till it lapped about her neck.

She rose up on a sudden, all a-splash, the watery streamlets pouring down her back to trickle off her buttocks; and lovely droplets from her nipples dripped, her breasts all pinked from chilling in the waters.

And in the lensing drops that yet remained to cling upon her skin, the Moonlight sparkled rainbows bright, and dear Diana stood there wetly naked, yet still quite clothed from swinging teat to sparkling thigh in rich prismatic jewels.

Such beauty then he gazed upon, that he could hardly breathe.

She turned and waded back a little way to shore, to stand there knee-deep in the pool; the pair of nymphs, as naked as herself but quite outmatched for beauty, stepped up with smiles to meet her. A little giggle and a nod, then sweet Diana stood there pertly, hands on hips and all arch-backed, her chest out-thrust and buttocks too besides.

The phial upended to the maidens' palms released a flow of creamy unguent; a rub of hands and then it foamed all white and bubbly. And Endimion Lee, nigh fainting with desire, could hardly watch as first a maid spread all that oily froth a-down her lovely back to buttock-cheeks and let it ooze the full length of her legs. And more unbalancing yet to all his equilibrium, in fuller sight the second maid rubbed slippery lather all on slick and softly-bouncing Goddess-teats, and gently squeezed them as they squirmed, left them all a-wobble on release. Then further down those lathering hands they drifted on, across her ripe and lissom stomach, at last to rub and bubble soft and sweet about her thighs, till dear beloved Diana dripped and wriggled, wide-eyed as a child.

All breathless then she laughed and squirmed away from tickle-probing fingers that had so slippery-slipped where never she commanded but mayhap she desired. A pink and panting sweetheart, all a-drip with slick white bubble-foam as if quite covered (no surprise) from head to foot with all that old Uranic spume that, spread upon the sea, gave birth to golden Aphrodite, she tottered out to deeper water, tremble-legged and barely able any more to stand aright... then sank down in the cooling waters with a soft and lovely sigh.

A little longer yet she sat there in the bathing pool, while dreaming Lee looked on, more roused up in his heart and cods than he had ever, ever been. And then her little hand rose up and summoned help; her nymphs advanced and took her wrists and raised her to her feet. And then, a trio mutual self-supported, they made their way back to the beckoning nearby shore.

More pinkish yet she then became, as all her dearest nymphs competed with the towels. She laughed, she squealed, she wriggle-giggled, and yet they would not stop their tickles, command them as she would; a sweet revenge for misdemeanours of their own. Her skin all dry, her eyes as big as dinner-plates, she could but squeak as next they put their long and lickerish tongues to work, and sucking lips that drank up sweetness from the darling tender gooseflesh of her trembling childish form.

Those squeaks of hers brought forth a moan from him, although no sooner was it sounded than he wished it back twice o'er.

The sudden silence that ensued quite filled him up with horror.

She sat up, casting nymphs aside, and looked in his direction. Expecting fury, spite and imprecations, he found then something worse instead. For in her eyes and on her face he only saw then pity, tenderness and vast compassion.

And in that glance he felt his soul was damned, for secret looks had stolen something which, he knew, upon the mere request, she would have given freely. And so he turned and fled; and all the time he knew it was not his beloved that he fled, but rather he and all his secret self.

And yet besides he knew, it was not he, but rather yet the other one with whom he shared the dream, from whom he fled and execrated in his flight. Not part of him, or of his soul (or so he hoped and prayed), and yet the whole temptation of them both; an evil twin called Actæon, whose love had turned, mistook, to lust.

Bounding through the thickets then, he wondered at his four-foot gait; wildered more at silvered antlers on his head, and whimpered in his mind to see the short white fur that covered all of him. His cloven hooves clicked sharply on the ground, he sprang and leaped, and far behind, he heard his own hounds howling, now quite fast upon a scent he knew was all his own.

And so he ran about the hill he loved so much, and knew before the hour was out that sweet Diana's arrow-head would strike, and striking then, absolve him of his sins. And all his heart was full of bliss, to think of death and resurrection, knowing that with each rebirth he'd nearer draw to fair Diana of the Moon and all the blessings of her sweet celestial love.

And thus he barely heard and quite ignored the faint and saddened voice that called him back, and then lamented softly in the moonlight, of lessons that remained unlearned.

Wednesday, 3rd October 1803

Yesterday morn I woke so late (my sleep a-boil with dreams of spired turrets erupting silver-glinted all about the hill-top, like talons reaching for an overripely golden Moon) that Cynthia banged upon my door; told me I would miss my dinner; asked if I was quite alright. I thought it rather sweet of her to ask; got out of bed and opened up the door a crack, while still dressed in my nightshirt. She laughed and said I was a naughty man, to address her while I was so under-dressed. I said that she provoked me.

I ate my dinner, swift and eager, ready to spend the afternoon just reading to dear Cynthia. In this I was completely disappointed. I sought her out and found her putting on her hat; she told me then she had to go to Charlton village for a while to see a jewel-smith. I offered to escort her; made the excuse I'd like to see the Jacobean mansion standing close at hand. She told me it was *completely* out of the question. And then, I was not quite certain why, she told me I should be within my room before the sun set, and smiled, so mysterious. And then she left the inn, and left me desolate behind.

Refusing young Tom Watkins' eager guardianship (though still he got a sixpence), I made my way along the lane to the burial mound that had so much caught my fancy some days since. The autumn afternoon was glorious, low-sunned and lacking any sign of clouds at all. I gathered sweet chestnuts as I walked, split and peeled them with my pocket-knife; sat upon the mound and threw the cases in the air, trying to hit them with my cane. I knew it was a childish game; yet I've no desire yet to be old beyond my years. It reminded me of perhaps the one true thing I remember my father telling me. It was the same year that he died. Embarrassed by some childish prank (quite blotted from my memory) I had remarked that I would grow up one day soon. He told me not to hurry. Strangely, I cannot remember a single other thing he told me.

Nuts all gone, I lay there in the sunshine, thought of many things: of who was buried in the mound; of Endimion Lee and how, at least in fiction, he wrote upon the Moon-Goddess, some two hundred years gone by; of myself, who wrote about her now; and of that other author, two hundred years to come, and wondered then if (perhaps in just my fancy) he might write of that sweetest deity as well. No, I knew it; did not wonder.

A triumvirate of authors then I thought us; though who was

Caesar, who was Pompey, who was Crassus, I could but hardly tell. I think that all of us would have liked to be as rich as Marcus Licinius Crassus; though none of us would have liked his death. Nor Pompey's, nor Caesar's, it must be said. The ancient world, for all it does delight me, had its horrors, I confess. But Crassus was a man who could rule a third the world, and still weep the passing of a favourite fish. More human then than both the others; until one thinks of Spartacus' revolt: six thousand rebel slaves all crucified along the Appian Way. Humans are too complicated; by comparison, a divine simplicity shines upon the brows of Gods. And is simplicity then a sign of Godhead? And are we humans in the world of matter, human just because we are so shattered? One part here and one part there, one above and one below; and myriads more that we simply do not know? I thought perhaps there was a hint of some religion here: that if we could but strip away, or meld together, all our most conflicted parts, we should be Gods. Or, at least, the fewer parts we had, the nearer we would be to the divine.

I tried to think of Diana in her simplest form; or rather more of Greek Selene, for when she's mingled with Diana then already she takes on complicated other parts. I thought of Selene and Endymion, how she kissed him in his never-ending sleep; I could not think that there was anything more essential there than one quite simple thing: *her kiss.* That simple kiss, it seemed to me, contained her essence: the love the Moon has always had for Earthly things below; while at the same time reflecting the reversing path: the yearning love of matter for the divine; of all-too-material human for the Goddess; of humble man, for sweet soft woman, who is the nearest to a Goddess that he is ever like to find.

And after that I thought of Liz, my dear young sister; of that fair queen for whom she's named; of Cynthia Brown-eyes who captures up my heart a little more each passing day; of Diana Regina, the perfect sweetheart of my imagination. And thinking then of essences and simplification, I thought to put them all together as lovely-limbed Selene of the sparkling eyes, the naked Goddess of the dreaming Moon. And if there was a path to find her, then I knew that it was *love*. Not the love that demands the subjugation of the marriage and the legitimated copulation; but the love that is expressed quite simply in the kiss. The kiss that says: 'I love you'; the kiss that cannot quite exist unless it is a sharing; the kiss that, offered, asks for nothing in return. I know somewhere there must be wiser heads than mine; and yet upon a sun-declining afternoon, cool breezes rustling fallen golden leaves, sat upon an ancient mound and resting on the long-dead bones of someone now so utterly forgot their existence was no more than merest imagination, I thought, and all my thoughts, I thought they were religious. I offered up a fervent prayer to dear Selene then: I thought her young, and sweet, and loving, a charming girl of wide brown flashing eyes; and at the same time a Goddess too divine to look upon, an essence of the world of heaven. And if I could not know her as herself, I asked, perhaps she might at least allow me to know her in these lesser forms, both real and but imagined, who I would try to merge together in her likeness.

I thought the more of love, then, of both its forms, unconsummate and consummate. At twenty years of age, I know that many men far younger than myself have long begun to consort themselves with ladies of the night; but the syphilis and its mad incurable death, it frightens me so much. The clap I'd much avoid as well. And so I am a virgin man; Elizabeth, at just eighteen, I sincerely do believe a virgin too. Too many thoughts they then occurred to me: that I hated to think of darling Liz in any other arms than mine, but worse to think of her with lover or with husband who'd give her a disease (to think on this is absolute unbearable). But that if she were mine, and we were virgin both upon our wedding night, all this could be avoided (our parents, they were cousins, after all; and if the church does not approve of brother wedding sister, then neither Liz nor I approve the church). Yet, the law, I know, would keep us both apart as well, and if I'd keep my sister free of scandal and the courts, then kisses chaste are all I have to offer. And Cynthia Brown as well, she has a husband, though I think upon the instant that this could be annulled, for sure as hell it is not cold, she *could* not sleep with him. And yet, in law, she could not sleep with me besides. And so I see myself a virgin evermore with thus two 'virgin loves', and realise just why my Goddess is Diana. She looks through Liz's eyes, and out of Cynthia's too; she says 'how sweet it is to want me; but sweeter yet it may well be, that you can never have me, unless it is in dreams.' In dreams, and fantastiques, and sweet imagination… but not, it seems, in base, material flesh. Only in the sweet Selenic kiss. The kiss of lovely virgins.

And mayhap there as well I have a way to think of what I wrote last night of Actæon; for all it overheated and aroused me, it tells me this besides: I should not wish for what I cannot have, but just accept what I am offered. I'd wondered if the passage might be too erotic; but looked on in this light, I think I'll let it stand.

And then I remembered how before I'd thought this mound the breast of dear Diana. I rolled me over then and, in the spirit of my new religion, kissed it. And then, the sun a-westering, I walked back to The Bull.

Returning to my room at last, I found that Cynthia Brown-eyes had arranged to have two bottles of claret, a cold venison pasty, and a mushroom-and-potato tart, delivered to await me. A little note (I thought the hand quite lovely) said: 'Eat and drink and watch the east horizon. And if you love the Moon enough, then who knows what will happen.' I raised that note up to my lips and kissed it; and as I did I knew that I kissed Cynthia, Diana, Selene and my Liz.

I almost had forgot, but last night was the fullest autumn Moon; and when the Moon is full, of course, it rises simultaneous with the sunset. I realised then that Cynthia Brown-eyes knew this well enough; knew besides how much that this would mean to me. I kissed her note again to show my appreciation.

The sky began to darken. I ate my supper; knew that somehow I could taste dear Cynthia's hand in every bite I ate. Then the first bottle I uncorked. A little glass I poured, then poured it out the window: a libation to Selene who now, to me, was most essential of the Goddesses. Another glass I poured, and raised it up; offered a toast, quite madly, to the sky; told Selene that I loved her, and blew her nine whole kisses. And then I sat me down to wait.

The sky was *perfect*.

As if she thought that punctuality was a virtue, the lovely

Goddess of the Moon began to raise her golden gleaming head above the Kent horizon. I looked and at the first I thought her but a jewel of night; and then I realised she was my love. Another libation, another toast; and then I settled down to drink and watch her rise. I thought I understood a little of old Actæon then; for if the horizon that I looked upon was not quite flat as water, at least my dearest Goddess rose up gleaming naked.

And, oh, she was so lovely.

The 'Man in the Moon' was long forgot, for now I knew her woman. Her eyes then broke the horizon; I thought they winked at me, so saucy. Kisses then just poured out from my lips, arising from my very soul.

And then she leapt up free, from Earth to sky; so round, so golden-pink, so huge. I thought her big and bright as ever I saw Lizzie's eyes. And more, my vision blurred (I know it was not drink; I'd barely had a glass); and suddenly the 'Woman in the Moon' *was* my darling sister Liz, all sweet-eyed, and all-smiling, all-lovely as the nymphs of stream and tree and mountain. She smiled and then her lips were full of kisses; she was the very vision of my most complete desire. I wept to see my lovely sister in the Moon. I wished that she was with me then, to see herself a-smiling through my window. And more, I wished I had a huge and golden net, to throw up into the dark-blue sky; to capture her and draw her down, and take her off to bed.

I poured another glass and looked again. Now Cynthia Brown-eyes, she was all the orange Moon. She looked at me so knowingly, I think my every thought was writ upon my face in letters of desire. Her eyebrows lifted up; she gave a lopside pout. I raised my glass to toast her fragrance and her beauty. I whispered things to Cynthia-as-the-Moon I'd never dare to say to Cynthia-the-woman. I thought I heard her chuckle; I looked around to see if she was in the room behind me. Most certain she was not; that laughter came down from the Moon.

I looked again and lost my breath; for now up in the sky was dearest Diana Regina. All reddishness was gone, and now she was but pure gold; yet stars were all around her now, and they were jewels all set about in heaven, to make her far more beautiful than any man could think. And there was blue so deep, and gold so bright, and there was music in the Moon: lute-notes, so bright and sweet and full of light and, I know not any other word, so *liquid* in the charmful smile of a sweetheart-girl or lovely Goddess, who did no other thing but love me.

I looked upon the Queen of Night and Dreams. I wept. I moaned. I sobbed. I cried out loud: 'I love you!' And '*I love you!*'

And then she was *Selene*. And I simply have no words with which to speak of dear Selene. Selene is too perfect. She is more beautiful than *beauty* ever quite described. And more, I love her so much that *love*'s a word that's simply quite inadequate.

At last, all silver-white, she rose up slow, and all-too-sweetly-stately, and vaulted upwards into the dark-night sky. I looked and wept, and loved her all-amazed.

And then I looked the more, and simply fell into a trance. I could not move; I could but sit and stare. Selene silvered all the world around me, and all of alchemy was sparkling in her light. She shone into my eyes, and quite transmuted all my brain. My blood it then was quicksilver, my limbs were carved of crystal.

I could not move an inch.

Four hours or more I sat there gazing; though for me all time had stopped except the motion of the Moon as up she climbed and soared toward the zenith. No other thing was in my world except that slow and stately progression, a pavane of grace and charm in which the Moon was partnered by the Night, as up she danced across my window-panes. And every second passing by, it made me more her lover.

The ancient Gods were static statues, worshipped by their living, moving adorers; now I was just the statue, and how my Goddess moved; and moving, how she lived.

At last, she rose up beyond the window-frame and vanished from my sight. And only then could I begin to stir. The clock it said eleven'd come and gone. I'd hardly drunk at all. I poured myself a largish glass and tried to pull myself together. The inn was closed and quiet then; I began to wonder how I'd spent the evening.

There was no time for that, for Cynthia knocked upon my door.

She wore a cloak of darkest black, and on her lips a mystery-smile; in her hand she held a lantern.

I gaped. She ruffled up my hair. I was too stunned to kiss her. And when she put a finger to my lips, I knew I could not say a word. She whispered then to take a coat and put on boots, to gather up the pages I would have read to her that afternoon; and when I had she took my hand and led me down the stairs. We went outside and crossed the road.

I protested then, for though she might be safe enough by day, I thought by night that this was madness. She laughed and kissed me oh-so-hotly; all her eyes were full of sweet excitement. She asked me if the Moon was bright; I told her that she knew it was, for I could see it flashing in her eye. The next she asked me, how I liked adventuring, and whether I thought the night exciting, and if I thought her beautiful enough to be the queen of all my dreams. I told her that I liked it very much, and yes I did, and so she was; and before she could say any else I hugged and kissed her till she could not breathe. She laughed and called me naughty, told me to behave; and yet her eyes were so enormous. I almost could not bear it.

She took my hand and kissed my palm (her little warm and rasping tongue, it made me tremble so), then wrapped my arm around her waist; and so we set off through the woods and came again to Severndroog. She had the key; she told me that she'd paid a silver crown to have it for the night.

We entered: found the crone had left us goblets, too much claret, half a pound of cheese, two fresh loaves and a candle. The door securely locked behind us, the candle lit, we made our way up to the roof. At last she drew me up the little wooden stair that led from the roof to one of the minor turrets. We stood there for an instant, looking up at cloudless sky, at sparkling stars and, most of all, at gleaming silver Moon. I hardly can describe what happened then; my hand it shakes to think upon it.

She turned to me, all brilliant-eyed and smiling-lipped, demanded my firm acquiescence to all her simplest conditions: that I should treat her in the way I would if she herself were Diana Regina,

Queen and Goddess quite inviolate, and that nothing more I'd offer her than kisses and embraces. I told her yes to everything, for even this seemed more than I deserved. And the Moon, by then, it had deranged my brain so much I wanted nothing more than just to hold a warm sweet woman in my arms. And hold her till the dawn.

She laughed (her laughter is like sweet white wine and just as heady too) and then she said that as this was a Full Moon night, and marvellous for its beauty and its silver transmutation, so we should allow ourselves to think of Severndroog transformed, quite as I'd thought it yester-afternoon, and, until the glow of rosy dawn defaced the eastern sky, make it serve for Somnium. And more, for these few hours, that I should be Endimion Lee. I told her yes, if she should be Diana; she chuckled then, and said she was already. And then she loosed her cloak, and showed me what she meant.

For underneath, she only wore a nightdress, of sheerest clinging silk and all of purest white, its neckline lowly cut to display a mass of golden necklaces that sparkled, full of diamonds, in the Moonlight.

I looked at her and fell down on my knees.

She laughed again, then looked at me so fondly, all shiny-eyed and head just tilted to the side. 'Sweet boy,' she said, and all her expression said the same, and then she bent forward from the waist (I could not help but look at what she had to show me; they were so lovely and so round), kissed my forehead and ran her fingers through my hair.

'And would Endimion Lee just kneel there all a-goggle?' she asked me next, sweet voice a-lilt with laughter, slipping gold-Moon earrings through her lobes, then placing (I knew not where she got it; though now I think of Charlton and of jewellers) a small tiara mounted with a crescent on her lovely head. 'Or would he help a lady with her boots?'

She spread the cloak across the turret-floor at that, to make a carpet for our comfort, then sat her down and pulled her nightdress almost up as far as lovely knees. I could not quite believe the things that she was showing me by Moonlight.

I unlaced her boots and took them off, and then I kissed her naked feet; it was such bliss I knew I'd always be her slave. If she had asked me then to lay myself full length and let her walk upon me head to toe, I know I would have done so. Instead, she urged me next to open up the wine.

I filled the goblets, offered to her one, and on the sudden thought to ask her if she did not feel the cold; she was so underdressed, the silk it was so thin it almost was transparent. She laughed and said she thought she'd be alright for, after all, she had a handsome man with her to hold her in his arms and hug away the cold; and if that was too little, then surely his hot kisses would more than quite suffice. I confess I stared again. For even when she was not being so surprising, she was so lovely to look at, I simply could not stop.

'Sweet Kit,' she said at that, so gentle and so soft and, ultimately, so kind. 'I think you do not know a lot of women.'

Upon the instant then I thought to bluster; yet no words would come out at all. She put her goblet down, then took my hand in hers (so small) and pulled me close; hugged me quite like Lizzie does whenever I feel sad. It was too much; she was too beautiful to be so sweet. I wept and sobbed. I hated myself for doing it, yet at the same time welcomed the release; and loved the feel of dainty fingers stroking through my hair.

'Dear Kit,' she said, 'I listened to you read last night, and thought you had a soul I'd never met the like. If there are poets of the Moon, you must be of their number. And more, I'll tell you this besides: no better offering could you make to Goddess than the words you offered me, all dreamy-soft and semi-drunken. Oh, be not like to other men, for other men would not sit here all distraught and weeping sweetly on my breast. Be Kit, be blessed, and know you are beloved.

'And now enough!' she laughed and ruffled up my hair. 'I did not think to sit here bathed in tears!'

With that she took my hand and touched it where I'd wept. At first I was surprised by dampness; then by softness; then I realised my fingers they were all a-curl about her lovely breast. I jerked my hand away.

'Oh, Kit!' she laughed and put my hand back, kissed me oh-so-hot and oh-so-long and all the time I felt her laughing in my mouth.

And more, her little tongue was there as well. It tasted quite like honey. Just then, I thought, I would do anything she asked, in any way, for ever more; and more besides, I think she knew it.

So when, at last, we parted lips and sat there all too breathless, then we raised up both our goblets, offered up a toast unto the Moon; after that she made another to Endymion, I then to Diana and, before another word she could intrude, to Cynthia besides. And more, I told her that if for tonight alone, she would not let me love her more than any other on the Earth, and kiss her till the morn, then I'd be over turret-wall and none would ever have my kisses. She put a finger to my lips to stop a further word, so gently but so firmly, told me I could kiss her quite as much as any man could want, and anywhere I wished besides. But most of all she wanted just to cuddle close and drink the wine and look upon the Moon, and listen to me then declaim of Somnium and dear Diana, out there in the lovely night. And if I spoke of Endimion Lee, and how he clipped and kissed his dearest queen, then all I spoke of should be acted out, for now tonight we were in Somnium, where dreams are nothing but the truth. And more, she wanted to be kissed so hot and sweet below the Moon by a dear young man who loved her, and to play my Goddess and let my fond caresses wander where they would.

In all my life, I have not known such bliss. She was so soft, so warm, so sweet. I kissed her and I kissed her; I gazed into her lovely eyes and kissed her all the more. The Moon that had so struck me in the eye when she was upward-rising, now seemed both up there in the sky and down here in my arms. She shone her smile upon me; I kissed her till she glowed. We ate our bread and cheese and thought we feasted on ambrosia; drank our claret-wine straight from each other's nectared lips.

And then she snuggled close and demanded that I read to her from *Somnium*, while the lovely Moon was white-bright in the sky. She held the pages for me, leaning back against my shoulder so I could read and whisper in her ear, and all the while my hands, they wandered where they would. And at the end of every page she turned and let me kiss her; and oh, how I adored her, crescent-browed and sparkled-eyed.

I read to her of Actæon all a-spy; and how she chuckled, eyes all wide with minxish understanding. And when I'd finished next she said, with just a little slyest teasing, that I for certain should have written more; I told her I was glad I hadn't, for nothing now remained for me, but to kiss her till the dawn. A moment, then, she did appal me by refusing; but then she said she'd play Selene to my Latmian Endymion, and I should lay back in her arms and let her kiss me in her turn. And like the sweetest Goddess in the world, she did.

The Moon moved in the sky; the night was all too short. When dawn at last a-lightened, all the wine was gone and so was all the food. The Moon was almost gone besides, and so she told me then that we should be as well; but first (I think—I'm sure—I know it was not merely drink) she pulled her nightdress down for just an instant, let me kiss her lovely naked breasts. The bliss, it almost killed me. Oh Moon and stars and heavens all above, the beauty of her breasts, all rosy-tinted by the dawn; or perhaps I merely wished and dreamed it all, and sweet imagination painted Titian breasts to linger in my memory ...

And then she told me that if I did not help her with her boots, she could not walk, and I would have to carry her; I was tempted, I confess, merely to have her in my arms a little longer; but knew my strength would fail. My head was spinning; all the world seemed dream.

All dressed at last and cloaked, alas, I took dear Cynthia in my arms and kissed her as if it was the last time quite before the world did end. She clung so tight, the tears were in my eyes. And then we left our Somnium-for-the-night, locked up the door on dreams, and hugged our way back through the woods. At Watling Street she suddenly was imperious: swore me quite to silence, told me that what happened 'neath the Full Moon only happened once, and with the coming dawn that all would be forgot and then she would be nothing more than Cynthia Brown as usual. I told her yes to everything, but told her more besides that in my secret heart then she would always be Cynthia Brown-eyes the darling of the Moonlight, and *never* be as usual. And if what happened beneath the Full Moon really only happened once, then she should know that, if for only once and just that little time, I loved her. And last, I would not let her go at all unless she ruffled up my hair; and when she did, I kissed her.

We slipped into The Bull and parting was such pain, the more so for its silence. I made my way upstairs and to my room, and tried to sleep. I could not. I thought of Cynthia Brown-eyes and her loveliness, and all that she had showed me. Her bare breasts first of all, of course, but more than this besides: her love, her kindness and her sweetest understanding. I confess, though, that I mostly thought about her breasts. I do not think there is a man on earth who would have differed from me in this; they were, quite simply, lovely.

I may have dozed a little in the end, for on the sudden I found myself surprised to hear a knock upon my door. Dear Cynthia calling me for dinner; and telling me I had a letter too.

Having laid down fully dressed, I opened on the instant; surprised her quite, still standing there. I told her I must have a private word, took her hand and pulled her into my room, then thanked her, so emotionally, for a lovely night. She looked at me all wide-eyed and all-puzzled, told me she had no idea of what I spoke. More, she told me that I must have dreamed whatever adventure I thought to thank her for, for she knew nothing of it. I must have looked at her so utterly downcast, it made her smile. She ruffled up my hair, and on the instant then (I could not stop myself) I kissed her. She laughed and kissed me back, all saucy-eyed and sweet (at least in that there's nothing changed at all) then told me that my dinner and my Liz's letter waited, and neither of them should be served up cold. I said that I would follow soon. I needed time to think.

I sat there on the bed a moment, my head sunk in my hands. A part of me said Cynthia stood by all that we had said on parting, and held me to my oath of silence; and that her strong denial it was all too-well deserved, for I had sworn her not to mention one mere single thing. Another part, though, wondered if she had been speaking literal truth, and that I had quite dreamed of Cynthia-playing-Diana and Somnium-on-the-turret-top and sweet bare breasts all lovely in the dawn-light. I knew the Moon was full last night and wondered if, by sleeping in its rays, I had become a Moon-struck lunatic, as old Hippocrates says is oft the case. And if it was a madman's dream, then oh it was so lovely, and how I wished that I could sleep it all again. *Seleniazmos* he called it, Hippocrates who was so wise; not 'epilepsy' as the later quacks have made him say, but just to be struck down by the Moon, to have its light shine in one's brain, to feel its tender mercies on one's lips. But I could not tell, or truth or dream, and worse, I knew that now I could not ask, for Cynthia had denied me. So how to tell then, what was real and what was not?

I did not know, but thought it best I should decide; and so to make a decision that pleased me most of all. And that was that the last night's sweet adventure was quite real, and that Cynthia's rejection of my thanks was nothing more than chiding for my broken oath of silence. With that I found myself content, and made my way then down into the dining room.

There, Cynthia herself, she served me with a capon, presented me with Liz's letter, and offered to share a glass or two of sack. All this I welcomed well enough, but must confess, the most that interested me was sweetest Liz's letter. And somehow then, it seemed to me, it was the most of interest to dear Cynthia besides.

I read. I was agog. I lost all sense of time and space. And when I finished I looked up to see dear Cynthia all a-smile, and all my capon carved and cut by her fair hand. Another second and, I thought, she would have put it in my mouth.

The trouble was, I read my Liz's letter, and could not help but wonder quite if yet I did still dream. The first thing that she said was that she wished she was my bride, and did not care for all the world that we were brother-sister. She said she loved me; never had no other. And yet I *knew*, for all I'd wanted to say such things when last I wrote, I had not had the courage. I could not tell if this was merely dream, or all my dreams come true. I hardly dared read more, and yet, of course, I had to.

She told me that she thought of me all day, but missed me most at night. She told me how, one night last week, as she made ready for her bed, she stood all naked there before her glass; thought to see me then all mirrored, looking over her bare young shoulder, staring at her back in life and all her front reflected (I know that glass and many times I've wished I had its eyes to look on Lizzie all undressed). She turned all eager to embrace me; found I was not there. Went to bed all disappointed, dreamt I crept in twixt the sheets and hugged her naked, lay with her and loved her through the night; and how she woke up wishing that I had.

Told me that when I was at home it was so sweet she'd hardly thought at all; but now that I was gone she missed me so, and realised just how much time we'd missed for love. Hoped I'd finish writing soon, come home then and make her happy. Most bewildering of all, said we'd run away to some far town and change our names, live in bliss as man and wife, make love all through the night and have so many children.

And Cynthia had cut up all my meat, and smiled at me, big-eyed yet somehow oh-so-far-away.

And Liz had told me things I could not quite believe.

I felt my thoughts betrayed them both.

I knew I had to eat, or Cynthia would be offended; though all my appetite was buried in confusion. I drank with her as well, and thought she was so kind; a glass or two and then my head began to spin; the world was all too strange. I had to ask her to excuse me; told her that I did not feel well in any way at all. She helped me up the stairs and took me to my room, laid me down and tucked me up in bed. And kissed me then before she left, and stroked my aching head with such a tender hand.

It was only then I realised I'd left my Liz's letter on the table. I know that Cynthia read it; and somehow I was so glad she did. Some part of me it wanted to show myself to her all naked; and if it was not body, then certainly it was my soul.

It's not that I am ill (I think), but I am so confused. A little while I tried to sleep, but all my thoughts were full of Liz undressing. Her chestnut locks a-tumbling down her back, her little tongue-tip gliding round her lips, her lovely breasts and soft sweet thighs. And then a sleepy yawn, a stretching of that supple back, hands held high above her head; and such a beauty's rump, my lovely sister has. And yet, for all she is so sweet and young, the more I thought the more with Cynthia I confused her.

At last, though still abed, I took up pen and ink and wrote and wrote this journal. I'd thought, in setting out the night's and day's events, that somehow they might make some sense to me. Alas, they do not. The world is all a-mix, and who knows what is real? I've sent for, now, another bottle; hope that Cynthia will bring it up herself. And more, I know I hope that she will stay and drink it with me. For if I do not have a lovely ear to talk to, I fear I must go mad.

And yet, perhaps, already that I am.

Thursday, 4th October 1803

Cynthia sent up my claret yester-afternoon, and did not come herself. Perhaps it was as well, for in my state of mind I don't know what I might have said. I was too drunk for eating supper, so I took another bottle to my room instead.

I took back Liz's letter too, and now it seemed so strange. It *almost* said the things I thought it had. It said she *sometimes* wished that she could be my bride, *if we were not* brother-sister; said she *almost wished* we could run away and live in bliss as man and wife, rather than we *would*. I do not know quite what this means; my memory was so clear. And if my memory here's at fault, then what of other things? Was Severndroog, as well, a dream?

I wished so much for all the world to wind back like a watch, and make that letter read the way it did at dinner; for if it did I knew I'd take a coach forthwith and never leave my sister's side. And yet the words defied me.

I thought of many things to say to Lizzie in reply, but was too drunk to write a letter. Perhaps that also was as well; I probably would not have said them if I was completely sober. I fell asleep in middle-evening, woke at midnight to the sound of vile Jude Brown a-pounding on a key-locked door and cursing. I knew that it was Cynthia's door he hammered; thought I ought to rise and go to her defence; but was too drunk to move. At last I heard him stumble off again, imprecations muttered all to Christ. I laughed and thought my Gods were stronger; thanked them for preserving Cynthia in her sweetness, for well I knew her for a co-religionist of mine. And then I slept through to the middle-morning.

I dreamt that I was standing in a Moonlit garden, either back at home or here on Shooters Hill, the earth beneath my feet somehow alive and squirming, as if the roots of some long-buried and colossal tree were about to burst forth into strange luxuriant growth. In dreamtime, then, I suddenly looked forward into the future, saw the tree sprung up renewed and fruited then with heavy golden Moon-globes. Stepping closer, I saw each Moon-fruit now contained a lunar palace; saw my Somnium in the nearest; knew the remainder must be dreams of other sky-kissed sleepers; wondered who they were. Woke up thinking all were somehow me.

I think I must be suffering from exhaustion. Too much work, too much claret, too many late nights and, these last few days, too many strange excitements. Dear Goddess of the Moon I pray: let it be nothing more than that.

And yet I find myself thinking: I write of my ideal world, I see it in my dreams; and these two blur together, for my ideal world *is* a lovely world of dreams. While here and now, so far removed from home, from Liz and all that was familiar, my 'real' world has turned so strange, so dreamlike in itself. Then how to tell the three apart... real, ideal and dream? And can one be turned into another? Or do they merge and all become the same? I know which one I'd transform if I could; but how, right now, eludes me.

I ate my dinner, smiled at Cynthia far too weakly, then came back up to my room, and stumbled on the stairs. I wrote to Liz, and sent her all the *Somnium* pages I had copied; but wrote as carefully as I could. Told her that as soon as I had finished writing, I'd be on the coach; and when I was returned I'd make up to her for all the time she'd missed me; for every kiss she thought I owed her, I would give her nine; and as for hugs, they simply would not stop at all. I told her, joking, of my envy for her mirror and offered then to stand there in its stead and tell her how she looked, in any state of dress she wished (but always would I praise her beauty). I told her many other things besides, though all of love and quite how sweet she is; but of myself I did not say a word. I thought it better not to, lest she think I have a brain-fever. I signed it with ten thousand kisses, told her to imagine them all placed exactly where she liked; then paid Tom Watkins far too much to walk my letter down the hill halfway, and leave it at the Red Lion. And then I slept again till supper; whitebait carted up here from the Thames. I knew that Cynthia had cooked my portion with her own sweet hand; somehow it seems, I taste her touch. I do not know quite how.

When I had done dear Cynthia brought me water with a dash of claret, told me she had boiled the water so it was quite safe; said I should not drink of stronger stuff tonight. She is so kind to me, and makes me feel that I am all her family, not a paying guest.

As if she knew that I was far too tired for any work at all, she later asked if she could entertain me; took me to her parlour, offered sweetmeats, and then an hour or more she sat there at the harpsichord. Played me nothing then but soft pavanes by Orlando Gibbons and John Bull; and when her finale was old William Byrd's 'Jhon come kisse me now', I thought it was so sweet. She saw me to my room; I took my hint from her last tune, kissed her very gently and bid her fond goodnight.

A little writing in this journal; now I am to sleep again.

Saturday, 6th October 1803

I slept on Thursday night and dreamt of Somnium; stood there face to face with dear Diana Regina. My memory it will not tell me how she dressed. She smiled at me all sympathetic, made me think of Cynthia; told me I was soon to die. I woke up with a whimper.

I woke again mid-morning; smoked a pipe or two and finally decided I was feeling better. The way that Cynthia smiled at me when I went down to dinner told me that I looked it too. She sat and watched me eat; told me that it was to make quite certain I had had enough. And when she said those words, and looked that look, I thought to recognise my mother. 'Enough for *what?*' I did not think of at the time.

The afternoon, she walked me down toward old Well Hall, although we never left the woods. She told me thereabouts was where the archers had their butts in centuries gone by; I could not see a sign of anything the like, and why she thought this was the

place was absolute beyond me. Yet here, she said, all hanging on my
arm so friendly, did Henry Eight and Catherine the Spaniard come
for Mayday, find themselves with 'Robin Hood' and all his bowmen,
dining then on venison that was quite plain the king's his own and
yet the robber-band's besides. I told her fie on Robin Hood, there
never was a better archer than Diana; no sooner had I said it than
she kissed me, and such a big kiss too. I did not understand, but if she
kissed me then, I thought to kiss her back, and so I did. She laughed
and pointed to a squirrel, tufty-eared and red as robin; when I looked
around to see it then she kissed me once again and ran away before
I could offer anything in return. I told her she was Lilith and if she
did such things again, I'd make her pregnant quite with demons;
she laughed and looked at me defiant. I chased her then all through
the woods, but no wise could I catch her; she simply lifted up her
skirts about her knees and fled me, laughing, like a deer. Or more,
I think, like Diana herself, the huntress of the forests. I chased her
and I chased her, but oh she was so swift, and so at last I had to cry a
loud 'Enough!' I sat me down beneath an oak that showered me with
autumn acorns, caught my breath, and waited for her slow return.
And though my chasing had been fruitless, I think it was done well
enough to gain her approbation.

She kissed me once, so hot, so sweet, then put a finger to my
lips and said that, for the nonce, we'd kiss no more. I told her I
was disappointed; she said there would be other times for kisses.
I told her I relied upon it; more than that, I would insist. She
laughed and said, for that, I'd never get another kiss unless it was
beneath the Moon. I told her every kiss she'd given me so far had
been beneath the Moon, for always did the Moon look down on
kisses. And if she had any other riddles to propose like this, I'd
think that just a kiss was far too small a prize for me. She looked
at me so strange as if, upon the sudden, then, she thought I had
grown up.

All sudden then, she came into my arms, hugged me close, and
then she led me up the hill. Her little hand was clasped in mine; her
lips were firmly shut. And so we came back 'home' (for so The Bull

has come to seem to me; I know it's 'cause she lives here) without another word.

She is a puzzle, but a lovely one; flirtatious as she is, I rather think she loves me nonetheless; and yet I see no cause to hope for any more than kisses. I think that if I ever understood her, then the world would end, and there would nothing left be but the Moon.

Yet at the same time, too, since Severndroog I have to think that all the sweetest things we've shared, like kisses in the woods... they may be, too, the things I've most imagined.

And yet again, I do recall my thoughts upon the burial-mound: that all Selene's love is found within her kisses; and all there is of kisses is Selene's.

And if all those kisses should be both imaginary *and* Selene, then do these kisses make a syllogistic common-term, which means Selene *is* the imagination? And writing my imaginings of her, then, do I simply write down what she tells me? Now there's an idea to please me.

And more besides, if I interact with Selene-who-is-imagination through her kisses, does that make *me* Endymion? And if *I'm* Endymion, who's Endimion Lee?

There are too many thoughts that run about my brain. So let me merely concentrate upon my journal.

Last night I managed to escape from further distraction; disappeared to my room with three full bottles of claret; and wrote. And when the wine had eased my mind, the words began to flow. I still ponder as to whether I write those words, or they write themselves, or someone writes them for me. However it may be, I had not expected them to turn out so erotic. If it's me that writes (I know this sounds absurd; some part of me says it is of course), I think I understand: the thought that Cynthia will hear all this, it has a frisson; and just as much, that Liz will read it also. And more than this, I verge unto the risqué in the hope that they will feel this frisson too. I thought that Liz would have the pages that I sent her by last night; I thought the more of her abed, and mayhap even naked, reading what I'd written. And that was most distracting too.

I fell asleep, and dreamt the strangest dream. I walked straight up a rainbow; Endimion Lee was on my right, the unnamed of the future on my left; and so we came to a crystal palace of the Moon which was and wasn't Somnium. Four ladies there awaited us: my Liz, and Cynthia Brown-eyes, and Diana Regina, and one who was too Moonlight-bright for me to see; I know I could not look her in the face because she was so beautiful. We danced, each man of us with all of them in turn; I thought it sweet to share my ladies with these friends of mine and could not quite distinguish which of them was real and which of them was fiction. The lady all of lights I danced with last of all; and as I did so I looked round and saw we were alone. I knew the others had not left us, but somehow we two now were all of them combined. And then I knew I slept; and more, I knew she kissed me as I slept. I woke and could not help but cry: '*Selene!*' It was a sob torn from my very soul. The Moon was shining through my window. My watering eyes had made her difficult to see; and so I know with whom I'd danced, and who had pressed her lips to mine.

At noon I woke and went for dinner; I rather wished I hadn't. Jude Brown was drunk and shouting at his darling wife with oaths and curses quite horrendous. She simply looked him in the eye with a disdain as lofty as the Moon; and so he stopped and stumbled off outside. I was just too amazed.

She came and sat down at my table; smiled at me as if no word had ever passed between them. She said that if I had an hour to spare this afternoon, she'd like to hear me read again. I think the expression on my face must have betrayed my fears; she laughed and told me Judas Brown knew better than to burst into her parlour. And from the way she'd seen him off just then, I thought perhaps that she was right.

So after dinner I took my pages and my pipe, and joined her in her parlour (it was too rainy for the little garden in the rear). She offered me canary; said it was good enough for old Ben Jonson, but she preferred the words that claret put into my mouth (or rather, in my hand). I confess that I was flattered beyond all measure, although I told her the comparison was quite absurd.

The thing I did not quite understand was that when I began to read, she asked me to go back and start where I had left off Sunday last when we were in the garden. I began to tell her that I had read her several more pages in Severndroog, but such a blank expression was on her face, I stopped. And so I read her what she wished, and as before she played the softest lute-stop harpsichord accompaniment that almost seemed the music of a dream.

I came back to my room a-wondering, and sat again to write. I'd thought her denial of our Full Moon night on Severndroog explicable, resulting from my oath. But if she will deny all memory, besides, of simple pages that I read her, then now I have to wonder: did I read them out at all? Or was it just a dream? Oh, Selene, dearest Goddess, what is dream and what is real? And how to tell the difference?

Endimion Lee, he woke, although his head was still all full of dream, and wondered at its meaning; and still was pondering sin and guilt, the latter's load and former's expiation, when up he looked to see Diana.

She sat there on his bedside, quite alone, with early-morning wine and breakfast ready on a tray. Her dress was simple, slightly pleated, all of silk that shimmered palely blue and white. Below a cobalt velvet zone that tightened at her waist, the skirt fell down about her ankles, and yet was slashed on either side the whole way to her hip; so when she placed one knee upon the other, all one leg was quite exposed, naked, smooth and lovely. Above, a loose and low-cut bodice slipped its sheening-silk half downwards, almost baring rounded breasts; and short sleeves, only palm-width long, slid lower ends toward her elbows. About her lovely neck, and all her other jewellery 'cept the crescent, were aquamarines and sapphires, lapis lazuli and Himalayan turquoise.

'Good morrow, fair and noble sir!' she gaily said, and laughing asked: 'And did we dream of me?'

He blushed and bit his tongue.

'I rather think then, that we did!' she chuckled next, and all the lights that lit her gleaming eyes partook of the divine. And all embarrassed as he was, his longing fought it down.

'Oh, dear Endimion Lee,' she said at last, with sudden tenderness. 'No more teasing for the nonce. Eat and drink, and bathe and dress, and when you're ready, step outside. A nymph of mine, she'll be there waiting; and let her take you by the hand, and then she'll lead you on, to join me in the library.

'But first, sweet knight, will you just do a little thing for me? And kiss me gently on the lips? And tell me that you love me? Because for far too long, I've kept me in the Moon… and mortal men, that live and love and die… o heaven and the stars above… I *miss* them.'

'Diana, queen and Goddess, mistress of my heart, come here' he said, extending out his arms. 'I love you now, I know somehow I always have, and know for sure I always will.

'And if you send me far away, I'll love you still. And if you tell me "nevermore", then any woman that I see will always be the less than you.

'So now, as if there never was another chance, beloved, let me kiss you.'

And so she came into his arms, and as she did her dress slipped down below her breasts. And neither of them noticed.

All cuddled close, he kissed her then, with love the like of which was never seen beneath the sparkling stars. No tongue, no teeth, but merely lip to lip, and mingled breath, and two hearts quite as one. And more than this, two souls all merged in lovely love, one human, one divine; and so in each they found the other half, and all the wholeness of the worlds, celestial, material, they merged in something more.

At last, although they wished it not, they found the kiss quite parted. And yet, embraced, they lingered on, and gently wept a little, hugged in other's arms.

And then he knew, though naught was said, their fate was soon to part. How long before he had to leave, how long he'd live thereafter… these he would not ask. Instead, all tender-fingered, up he raised her dress about her shoulders once again, and covered both the sweetest breasts in all the cosmic worlds. With fingers just as delicate next he gently pushed aside her fringe, and brushed his lips across her brow.

'And now, Diana, divine as light and sweet-eyed as a child, I'll ask a thing of you, as well. And what I wish is simply given, for all I ask's a

smile. And though it's only small for now, then mayhap it will grow…
and let's away with sadness.'

'Endimion Lee…' she soft began, then faltered all too soon. His
finger, never tired to touch her skin, it raised up then her little chin, and
so his eyes caressed her own. And what it cost them both to smile, they
never ever knew; yet thought to see their smiles returned repay them at
a profit.

'And so,' he sighed, 'unless you wish to feed me, bathe me, dress
me like a mother… and though I know you would, I think you'd better
not… I'll see you in the library.'

[I am not sure about this passage here, about Lee's mayhap-too-fond
awakening. I read it out to Cynthia, and she queried if perhaps I'd
portrayed Diana too much by far a human woman, too little far a
Goddess. For my part, I wonder if the piece reflects too much my own
yearning to take someone lovely in my arms and feel my love returned.
I do not know. Perhaps I should revise it and somehow make it more
'divine'. And yet I cannot imagine anything more divine than simple
love between man and deity. And so for now I leave it as it is.]

Too long by far the time that passed before he joined her there, although
he hurried all he could. She waited for him, quite recovered, sweet
with smiles and touched with mischief, a coy and charming maiden all
impatient as she stood before a gem-encrusted door. The guiding nymph
then turned about and left them quite alone.

'Sir knight!' she laughed, a naughty temptress look upon her face,
a giant silver key a-glitter in her hand. 'Will you thrust this in my lock,
and open up my secrets?'

'I will indeed, fair maid!' he chuckled, bowing, gallant. 'Though if
you ask such things again, I have a better lock-pick…'

'I know you have,' she laughed all soft, although she blushed. 'But
lock-picks are for thieves… and English knights, due-dubbed by red-
haired queens… for sure they would not steal a maiden's treasure!'

'Oh dearest love! Go to, for now you jest and tease! Or have you not been on the Earth for sometime since, and so forgot that men have cods and think of little else? Or more precise, they have no gods but stones and cods, and maidenheads are all they sacrifice.

'So now, my sweet girl, that's enough. Let's open up your doors and see what we shall see…'

'And would you speak to fair Eliza so?' she asked amused, and handed him the key.

'The Queen of England loves herself, and flattery, and mayhap Dudley too; but not Endimion Lee. And so I hardly speak to her at all, save "by your leave" and "if you please".'

'But how you will,' she told him then, all serious on the sudden. 'And when you tell her what I teach, you'll gain her love as well… though never near as much as mine, and never more, I think, than fourth… besides herself, and flattery, and Dudley too.'

'If that's my lot upon the Earth, so be it,' he replied, inserting then the key into the lock, and turning tumblers sweetly with a click. 'For having gazed once upon the lovely Moon, the Earth means nothing more.'

With that, he opened up the doors, and stood there all amazed.

Before him, long and wide and tall, there stretched away the library hall, and shelf on shelf of books, the thin, the thick, the large and small. Above, around the soaring walls, there ran along a railed gallery; and further up beyond, more shelves again besides. Ten thousand tomes within his sight, ten thousand more above; perhaps as many more again, beyond his estimation.

'Sweet Diana, are there now as many books as these on all the Earth?' he asked, a-wondered in his brain. 'Johannes Dee his library I have seen, the largest in the land, and barely would it fill a corner here. How came you by so many books? And what do they import?'

'Oh, let's be in and take a look,' she laughed, her little hand a-sudden in his own. 'I think you'll be amused.'

She led him to a library shelf, and just for once her lovely looks found competition fore his eyes; for all around were words and books, his lifelong love and always first, before he met Diana. Endless shelves of endless tomes; in corners, racks of ancient scrolls, and cabinet-drawers of single sheets, and tablets, clayed and waxen both. Bound manuscripts of smoothest vellum and printed paper books, leather-bound or pressed in slats of wood, they drew his soul up through his eyes, and made demands: read me, learn me, treasure all I say, for every written book's unique, a mind-child of the brain.

Dear Diana kissed his hand and let him have it back, then pointed all along a shelf. 'Now here, in Grecian, Latin and the English too, we have dear Lucian's *Dialogues of the Goddesses, Icaromenippus, The Fly, Alexander the False Prophet* and *True Story*... all those works, surviving down the age, in which he speaks of me, quite often sweet, but on occasion slander too. For both I love him well enough; and even naughty, still he makes me laugh. But here's one that you'll never find in any library on the Earth, for only here a single Latin copy yet survives: wry Lucian's *Diana Fornatrix*, its circulation barely public, the manuscripts all burned by Christians. And here's another of his own, he never even wrote, but thought of; and so by dream it comes to be, a book existing here alone in Somnium, but never down below: *Selene's Private Sleeping Chamber in the Moon (and how I slept there with her).'*

'There's books here lost, or still unwrit?' he asked her, mind a-whirl. 'But how?'

'Oh all too easy, dearest knight,' she laughed, and briefly kissed his wildered lips. 'For Somnium's a palace all of dreams, and so its dreaming library too is full of dream-books... and more, of fantasies unreal, and lunatic songs that drift away on moonlight. And after all, a thought of a book is a real thought... and so a book that's thought of too is too a real book. For "real" and "dream" mean nothing here, and mix them as they will.

'Now here's old Ptolemy's long and detailed *Selenographia*, a marvelled description of the Moon, all written from his trip there, so many said he'd never made. They called him liar, burned his book; and yet he held a smile, because he had seen mine. Herodotus, too, he travelled to the Moon, for lunar entertainment. I told him all the history of the Moon, of all my life and loves and ventures; he wrote them down. Your learned men, they spat; they tore his pages, drove him out along the roads. I gave him comfort as I could, in dreams, until he died; and quite the greatest comfort that he knew was this, that though down in sub-lunar worlds his work would be destroyed, I'd save it for him here. And read it, for him, by him, to him, love him for it too, until the end of time.

'And so you see, my library here is all of me, by many, many names... Diana, Selene, Cynthia, Mene, Artemis and Luna too... dark Hecate and Phoebe and the golden Moon besides. Whatever's writ, whatever's printed, here a copy comes; whatever's lost is here preserved; and even books, or essays, verses too, conjectured once and thought of me, if no one wrote them down, or have not writ them yet, then they are here besides. And here's a shelf for you, my love, although it still remains unfilled; but as the years pass so it will, I know. And, oh, the sweetness that you'll write, for me; I hardly dare to think on...'

'Then if you think it sweet, dear queen, I'll happy die and nevermore write any else. But can it be, that *every* written thing, or printed, sketched or thought, about the Lovely Moon who Lights up all the Skies, it ends up here, or writ or not, for dear Diana's delectation?'

'It can indeed,' she laughed. 'And some of it is wondrous strange! So many things men think of me. They see me virgin or they see me not; they make me Goddess, then down to Earth they bring me, make me wife or mistress, harlot, mother, daughter, little sister... write me hymns, all full of sacred words... hold me down in pornophilic lust and rip my maidenhead, suck my teats and fill me up with seed. Have children by me, rape me, whip me, bind me tight with ropes and sodomise me till I shriek. I care not where their madness leads, nor ill-think of their strange perverting lusts; because they write, and think of me, and even in their awful, weird and bestial desires, they offer up what little bliss they can achieve, perverse and strange and all their own, to me... and somewhere in that offering, smothered up with all their selves... they love me.

'Now here's a favourite, from three centuries gone, and still another city of the Moon, not far besides from London. 1279, and strange, perverse and bell-capped Perkyn of old Hampton, he wrote me this, and set it all to music then besides. A sweet thing with an odd and rhyming title:

Howe Priapys mightey wande
Tooke Dianas swete behonde;
Howe she shreked, and howe he spent,
When she was all overbent.

'I read it then, and how I laughed. I take it off the shelf sometimes, and laugh and love it still. He was so sweet, and yet for all he thought of transgressed violation, of yards all swollen huge and virgin Goddess-buttock, he thought, in all of this, to give me pleasure. And thinking so, he did. A sacrifice of quite fantastic dreams; of things so large and male, and things so small and other-sexed, that drained him of his bliss in volumes by the kegful.

'And many more I've stored up here besides. Blind Homer's lost *Seleniad*, Artemidorus' book, the whole of which was dreams of me, he called *Oneiroselenicon*, and Sappho's lunar longings. Of Latins, dull old Virgil wrote me little, though bold Petronius did, and outraged all his peers, for Rome would never have me any else but virgin; and so his *Scandal of the Lunar Vestal* was instantly suppressed. Seneca's *Diana's Fury*, that's gone too, except for here. Yet since Rome fell, too little. Of late we have the minstrels' lays, of Luna and her loves, and dear Diana's dreams. And then more recent still, *The Romance of Lady Luna of the Silver Castle* by Morion of Lyons; Ariosto's long and long-lost *Merlin of the Moon*; and Chretien de Troyes' *La Somniacque*... and more there are, to tax your patience quite.'

'I think not so, my love,' he told her then. 'In all the world I think there is no bliss, unless it comes from you. Your form it ravishes up the eyes, your voice the ears, your skin the touch, and so the other senses; and greater yet than all of these, the sweetness of your company. And if deprived of any these, I'd think of nothing dearer, than to gaze upon your image, to read of you or, better yet, to write you into being, to love you and invent your love, to take your kisses second-hand, and send you on adventure.'

'Oh dear Endimion Lee,' she sighed. 'You have an author's heart. Such sweet romances will you write, and love me in the very ink they're wrote in. And last night's dream... I know it well, and blush not when I tell you... I think therein you'll find your inspiration. At least for your beginning script, and as for after… oh, the dreams we'll dream… and dear my knight, how beautiful you'll make me.'

'No more than you already are,' he gallantly responded. 'And yet, I think there is more here, than quite I understand. For I'm a man, of single form, perhaps who'll write of you, but only one of many. And you, there never was the like of you, and even 'mongst a thousand Gods and Goddesses besides, there would not be another. And yet, though quite unique, you have a myriad faces, and show to each a single one, to every man who loves you.'

'Oh no, I show them all the same, but all their eyes are different. They make me what they will: a Goddess, whore, or both, and oftener yet besides, they make me like their long lost loves, and through me love their loss. I would not stop them, if I could; for if a little piece of me, however I appear, could help them through the horrors of their lives, then let it be. And if my image then they take, and all frustrate, pervert it to their lust, it harms me not at all; for all the men who'd think me wicked things, a hundred more there are like you, who'd wish me love and think me all bejewelled. I know the proverb often on your lips, that "many men have many minds", and so it is with me; for many men have many Dianas. Or so they think. But I am one, and always was, though loved in many forms. And so, my dear Endimion Lee, you look upon me as I am, though others see me different.'

'Then sweet Diana, all I look upon is love, and beauty, and longed-for, hoped-for bliss. For if ever I saw my sweet beloved, I tell you now, it's you.

'And yet… these vast productions… all inspired by you…'

'More complex yet than this, sir knight!' she oh-so-gently laughed. 'For yes, I truly am the Moon-Muse of a myriad starry nights, a maiden darting to and fro in dreams; the darling of the poets, the model of the artists, the sweetheart of romancers. But if they need me, know the truth… I need them just as much.

'For Goddess never did exist without men's minds to dream her; and men who dream of God are nothing but perverse. And I, as changeable as the Moon, yet each and every night aglow up in the sky, am simply Goddess quite supreme.

'And yet, without men's minds, the Moon is but a rock. And for me to be at all, I need my Lucians, my Homers, my sweet Endimion Lee... and many more besides, all forgot or yet to come. They bring me to the world, and shape me with their love; and no man ever made me ugly.

'And so you'll understand, the nature of the Goddess, is ageless, deathless, beauteous ever more... as long as ever there are men to dream me, and as long as ever there is love. For love lights up the stars, and glows all in the Moon, and if ever love should disappear, then so would men, and dream. Then no more Diana, no more Selene, no more big-eyed Goddesses of the warm delightful night. And all of this would all be gone, and with it me besides.

'And yet I promise this, my most beloved man: nor death, nor universe's end, will ever take you quite from me. For even non-existing, still the echo would remain: that once there was Diana, and once there were sweet dreams; and once in Somnium's crystal spires, I loved Endimion Lee, and he in turn loved me. And so that love will never die; and so we'll always be.'

'My love,' he said. 'My Goddess, too... I doubt that ever words of mine will ever do you justice. Indeed, I doubt that words were ever writ, that even ugly women fitted. And you... why, even Homer's words would fail him. I tell you, love of mine, the only way I could describe your beauty... is to call it past description.

'And more, I'll tell you this. If words are the offerings you demand, I doubt I'd better these: "I love you". A hundred thousand books surround us here, and all of *you*. And yet, believe me: they're *nothing*. In words, as men, we speak of you, because we have no other way. But words are not enough. And so, while in the here and now (and who knows of the future?), my eyes drink up your sweetness... then let me tell you this. In all your names, in all your forms... *I love you.*'

She looked him in the eye awhile, then came into his arms. A loving kiss, and then her head she rested on his shoulder.

'Endimion Lee,' she next began, 'there are Three Fates controlling all the world. Nor I, nor any, even Jove, can countermand their say; and what they say's "not yet", for first on Earth you've tasks. But know this now, and keep it close your heart: I love you too, my sweetest man, and

if the Fates allowed, I'd instant make your dreams all true. But first you
have a life to live, so live it just for me.'

'For you alone, and never any other,' he told her then, and hugged
her close once more. 'But if the Fates so cruelly do incline, then let's defy
them to their faces, however long we have; and smile and laugh, and sing
and dance, embrace and kiss and love each other. And show them, all
their doom is nothing to our love.'

'Brave heart,' she sighed, amidst of all her kisses. 'The times mere
mortal men and women show the Gods how best they should behave! No
wonder Jove destroyed the race of heroes, when lesser beings yet can still
surpass him. Oh, dear my knight, you are too fine…'

'Not fine enough for you, my love,' he forced a smile, and wiped
her eye of slightest dew. 'And now…

'Pray tell me, sweet, how best I can delight you? Whatever length
of time the Fates will give us here together, I know it far too short; so let
me please you best I can and try to make you happy.'

'Then darling man, I'll tell you what I'd like, if only for an hour
or two,' she told him next, unclasping both his arms. 'Firstly, always
hold my hand, or other part of me, and break you not that contact.
And second, kiss me when you please; and when I please as well. And
thirdly… come this way…'

And so she led him past the shelves, to where the library wall bayed
out into an oriel window. Through the glass, the moonlight shone upon
a broad divan, holstered all in cloth-of-silver, bolstered up with velvet
pillows. Close by stood wine and goblets.

'And now, my love,' she grinned, 'my third request's simplicity
itself. Select a book, or two or three, lay down and let me snuggle at your
shoulder, then read to me aloud.'

'No more than this?' he asked, a-wondered.

'No more,' she sighed, all soft. 'As if we were just man and wife,
not knight and queen, or Goddess and her hero. For if we cannot love as
man and wife, at least we'll pass the time as they do. We could play cards,
or dance or sing… but now I want to hear your voice, devoted to my
pleasure, and rest my head upon your chest, to hear the words a-throb
within your breast, all rolling and all rounded.'

'Dear darling girl,' he said, and smothered all her face and neck with kisses, 'for now I think you'll let me call you this, and probably prefer it. I never thought to hear as sweet as this request, unless you asked to fall asleep, all wrapped up in my arms…'

'Perhaps tonight, or soon…' she hinted, blushing, 'if you'll give the Fates your word.'

'A harder word I never gave,' he laughed. 'But for you, my love, then even this…

'But now, if I pick two of all these books, and you another two besides… and then we'll pour ourselves a toast, I'll kiss your sweet and soft young lips… and read to you in bed.'

So hand in hand, they wandered round the shelves. Two books he picked at random, knowing them not at all; while dear Diana, sweetly smiling, selected both her best-beloved. A toast they drank to love, and to each other's eyes; and more than this, to both their hearts, that each the other owned. Then down Endimion Lee he laid himself, right-handed with a book, left arm stretched out to pillow dear Diana's head. She cuddled close, her head quite to his chest, then took his left hand, kissed his palm, and slipped it down her dress.

And so, a sighing Goddess in his arm, Endimion Lee began to read.

Or tried to read aloud, for all his breath was took away, the further that he read. For what he read was nothing but a journal, though how his mind did reel to read its dating, which began 'September 1803'. He wondered how he could be reading a journal written two centuries up ahead; but Diana merely kissed him and told him to read on. And as he did, he found one 'Morley' writing a narrative that, it seemed, was nothing more nor less than that same story that he lived through, which spoke so plainly of Endimion Lee, long dead by then, and of his dear Diana.

And this, to him, made little sense at all. And yet, he was a-wondered.

Sunday, 7th October 1803

I do not know quite how the idea occurred to me to make Endimion Lee find and read this journal, there in Somnium's library.

It seems too pretty a conceit to have merely come from out the claret bottle, so perhaps Selene sent it. Perhaps, in the end, it may be an idea that does not work, and so will have to be removed when the time comes for revision. For the moment though, I'll leave it as it is; it amuses me, and more it makes me think.

Somnium is, after all, a fiction, and though our present novelists always write as if they told the plain historic truth, there's no one who would think that *Somnium* was ever else than fancy. And what if fictional characters *did* make contact with their authors? What if heroes knew that cowards wrote them? Or parsons' daughters knew their author was a drunkard who, one glass the more than usual, could write them into whores? Now there's a game for winter nights...

But more than this... suppose the story and the characters were true, and the author was a fiction? Suppose there really was a *Somnium* and Endimion Lee was really there, and reading in this journal. And if this journal's written there, and has been centuries gone, then who's the one who wrote it, and put Kit Morley's name upon it?

I've thought much of such things, and thought them merely fun at first. But after Severndroog the border's blurred, between the real and the not. And remembering that, I've tried to put the rest far from my mind.

I did not write last night; sweet Cynthia Brown-eyes wanted once again to dance. We started in the dance hall; once again she brooked no opposition, and all the army simply then surrendered. The Moon came up at ten, and when it did we danced outside. At eleven the musicians stopped; and so I simply hugged her for an hour, and kissed her in the Moonlight. When we returned inside, she cooked me Welsh rarebit in the kitchen; insisted that she feed me with her own sweet hand. It was too hot; she blew on it to cool it. I ate her breath, and thought to partake of the divine. I began to blurt; she kissed me then again, and sent me off to bed.

I dreamed that Mister Beckford had come up from Wiltshire, leaving behind for the present the building of his Abbey at Fonthill, in order to advise me upon the construction of Somnium, here on Shooters Hill. He told me, with great precision, that the project would require 81,000 dreams, each to be compressed, not into a brick, but into a book, from which dream-books the palace would itself be built. And if I built in dream alone, he solemnly assured me, all I architectured thus would far outlast such mere concretions of stone and mortar as he himself was currently erecting. I thanked him for his kind advice, and wished his tower-building well.

The wretched Brown (I could hear a gloating malevolence in his voice) banged upon my door this morning, told me I should be 'in church'. Secure behind my well-locked door, I told him that I did not care, and thought that sleep to me was more important far than the absolution of my soul. He told me I would roast in hell; I laughed and told him *he* would. Elysium was the place for me, or better yet the Moon. And more I told him that, if he and foulest Kinnock wanted both to go to heaven, they should crucify each other on the instant. And if they did, I'd help them hammer in the nails.

I confess I was quite pleased when, at mid-day, I went down for my dinner, that Brown was not in sight. I thought my pleasure spoke of cowardice; on the other hand I was so pleased to have told him what I thought.

And Cynthia, she knew I had. I could tell it from her smile.

This afternoon, she walked me in the woods again.

I love her.

I dare not tell her, though I know she knows. No woman of her age (she must be almost thirty) would marry such a youth as I. Besides, to love her is to betray my darling Liz, and that I do not know I ever quite could do. Oh Selene, dearest Goddess, I know you here on Earth in both my loves, but who's the best, and how can I decide? If I was but a swarthy Arab, or a distant East-Chinese, more than one wife could I have (though even then my sister, she would be forbidden). I want my Liz; I want my Cynthia; I want them both at once. I know I can have neither; and so I think of Selene dear, the darling of my dreams. If Goddesses would let me love them, my life would be so simple.

We sat beneath an ancient oak all wrapped up in each other's arms. She asked me how I liked the 19th century. I told her not at all. I said I wished we were in Greece or Rome, or anywhere before the awful Christians came. For a moment I thought to see illimitable sadness cloud her lovely eyes, but then she laughed and said those times had passed by long ago. I told her we could recreate them, furthermore that they partook of heaven; and so, I told her, did her kisses. If she should kiss me, then the pagan world would be restored.

She did, and so it was.

The treasure of the world is in her lips.

I came back to The Bull, and found myself a-sudden full of strangest inspirations. Perhaps that kiss was full of potencies I did not comprehend...

Endimion Lee, he read awhile in this strange and futuristic journal, but found it for the most part past his comprehension. There were so many future-things he did not understand; he knew there was no tavern there atop of Shooters Hill and St Paul's, to him, looked nothing like a candle-snuff. Yet Morley did, so plainly, love the Moon, and if he was a little moonstruck, then where's the harm in that?

The sticking point, it seemed to him, was Morley's claim to writing *Somnium*, and inventing all the palace he resided in, himself besides and dear Diana too. This seemed to him, the first, impossible; and more than this, a heresy. He had no thoughts upon himself, but the idea, perchance, Diana Regina might in some way not be real... that was too much for mortal man to bear.

So, some few pages gone, he put the book aside, and tried to think about it not at all. Diana then, she handed him *The Romance of Lady Luna of the Silver Castle* and told him, how Morion of Lyons being two centuries dead, and not two centuries yet a-born, he might perchance prefer it.

So Lee, with more than slight relief, began again to read.

THE ROMANCE OF LADY LUNA OF THE SILVER CASTLE

by Morion of Lyons

I. HOW THE LAND OF PARALOGRES GLITTERED MUCH BY MOONLIGHT, YET DULLED MUCH BY THE DAY.

Of all those fallacies to which mankind at large is prey, the most widespread and pernicious is the belief that unity is in some way more upright, or desirable, or perfect than diversity. Thus the races of mankind have laboured, sometimes mired for aeons, under such delusions as that there is but one Right, though many Wrongs; that there is but one God, while multiplicitous Gods are therefore false; or that there is but one Real World, and never was there Other. Other worlds there are, and always were, we do avow; and only God the One is false, when any fool can see the others; of Right and Wrongs we do not care to judge at all. One world, indeed, may have one God; but other worlds have other Gods, and these are where our fancy roams.

When Arthur ruled in hallowed Albion's isle, and Guinevere was quite the Helen of her times, nine dozen other worlds lay close at hand besides. And far off in the Land of Dreams was lovely Paralogres.

In Paralogres never was there Christian God, though all the olden Gods of Greece and Rome, and more than these besides, resided there and breathed the smoke of incense and of sacrifice. But most of all, and far above the rest, in Paralogres reigned Selene, the beautiful, the luminous and the charming; who, the more that she was loved, the more she beamed her lovelight in return. And so in Paralogres, ladies and their lovers rose at sunset, and lived their lives the night-long through, and danced by silver Moonlight, and went to bed at dawn; and only thieves and villains went abroad by day, all tanned and damned by sunlight on their skin.

In Paralogres all was silver, never gold; and jewels so large and fine and sweetly cut to mirror all the Moon; and flowers opened up by night, so coloured and so scented, that called to moths so large, with patterns so fantastical, and tongues so long to drink up all of nature's nectar. And never was there woman there the slightest less than lovely;

and more than these by far were beauties; and some there were with eyes so large, so liquid and so luminous, they seemed no less than Goddesses. And if they thought themselves competing with Selene, she smiled so fondly at their high pretensions, because she knew they never would, nor could.

Except for one, perhaps, more charming than the flowers and the stars, too sweet for even moths to seek, and near as lovely as the silvery Moon herself.

II. OF LADY LUNA

Within a forest thick and vast, and known to all about quite simply as The Deep Green Sea of Leaves, there rose an opalescent hill all shot with caves that tempted lovers, poets and divines. And on this hill, that some called Latmos-flown-from-Asia, there stood the Silver Castle, turrets soaring to the sky. No quaint poetic fiction this, for all its walls were of that very metal, and how it gleamed and sparkled in the Moonlight. Within there dwelled the castle chatelaine, the darling Lady Luna, her charming friend, the lovely Lady Sweetheart, and oh-so-many dearest girls and ladies, whose looks, unclad, could charm down stars and planets from the deep nocturnal sky. Yet none of them competed quite with Luna; and if so many others compared her with Selene, herself she never thought to do so. For Luna looked upon the lovely Moon, and sighed, and wished and wished for beauty quite like hers; and Selene, if her words were only heard, would tell her straight how nearly then she had it.

For Luna was so sweet and slim and youthful, and wide-eyed as a child; and all her chestnut tresses spilled in lovely hyacinthine curls right from her head down to her tiny toes, and just a little further too. And when she smiled, the world smiled too; and when she laughed, the merest sight of rosy lips and jade-white teeth and shapely little tongue-tip, could only make one wish to kiss her. And when she danced, her dainty little feet would make the music follow suit, for all the musicians in the world would watch her steps and play her sweet accompaniment. And many were the handsome knights who thought it fair to win her love; yet none so far had done so.

So Lady Luna, orphan though she was for some years since, did reign and rule the lands about the Silver Castle. And though she knew that other lords in wondrous Paralogres had laid a heavy hand on all their suffering subjects, she preferred, herself, the soft caress; and so, of course, she was beloved.

III. HOW LADY LUNA BEGAN HER NIGHTS

At sunset, measured quite precisely, by sight or by the court astronomer if the sun was wrapped in cloud, a pretty page, but eight years old, would enter Luna's chamber, taper lit and held up high above his little head. And then he'd light the triple candelabra, nine in all, about the room and draw back all the curtains, so all the chamber then was filled with starlight, and with moonlight, and with candlelight besides.

That done, and all a-tiptoe, hardly drawing breath, the page then next approached the bed where Luna slept all folded up in Lady Sweetheart's arms. And parting then the curtains, he crept so silent to the pillows, and oh so gently kissed the lovely girls awake, precisely as instructed, and only on the lips. And when they sighed and yawned and opened up their big brown eyes, he swiftly scrambled backwards, and left the bed, and bowed so low it almost seemed he'd kiss the floor; and Luna always smiled to see his charming rump raised high up in the air. And when he asked her, hardly daring, why she wished it so, she told him never was there more a charming prince to wake a sleeping beauty with a kiss; and then she kissed him once or twice, or more, until he blushed and looked so boyish and becoming, he had to run away.

The bath was next, and big enough for two, of course; for Sweetheart, Lady of the Bedchamber, was Lady of the Bathchamber too. And then those lovely girls, one dark, one fair, would take themselves, all naked, up a turret; for there the Lady Luna had her private chapel, which was observatory too. Next followed evening prayers to sweet Selene, offered up with love; and as they wished the most part to the Goddess her own happiness, she of course gave to them precisely what they wished for her in turn. And sometimes there were Moon-Fairies seen, a-flight about the sky, on errands strangely lunar, who smiled down so sweetly as they passed; and sometimes there were shooting stars, that sparkled in the dark.

Prayers all done, descended from the tower, they'd break their fast with honey-cakes and nectarines, while hid behind a screen, a valet played a slow and languid flute. And then, all braced up with a goblet each of sweetened spicy wine, they'd deck themselves in turquoise and in moonstones, in garnets and alamandines, all set about with silver; and if the weather or decorum so demanded, perhaps a silken dress.

So Lady Luna of the Silver Castle, in the lovely land of Paralogres, prepared herself for all the business and the pleasures of the night.

IV. OF A CERTAIN ILL-BODING COMET

There came a time when, for half a month entire, the skies were curtained quite with boiling, sulphurous clouds, and neither Moon nor stars were anywhere to view; and all was heat and stillness, curdled fog and dank miasma. Yet finally, with the waning of the Moon, a wind sprang up at last; and when another night was past, the skies began to clear.

And so when Luna went to say her evening prayers, she looked upon a starry night (the Moon not yet arisen), and half across the sky was flung a blazing comet. A banderole of doom, it seemed, all ghostly pale and pregnant of the plague, of deadly war and unmitigate disaster. And Lady Sweetheart whimpered at the sight, while Luna pondered deeply what it might portend. And nowhere were the Moon-Fairies in the starred nocturnal air; and all that once was fine seemed now decayed to evil and to death.

So Luna summoned then, forthwith, her astronomers and astrologers, her diviners and all the priesthood of Selene. And all of them she asked exactly what it was the comet did portend; and knowing this, precisely what to do. And all of them they said they'd have to look then in their books, and consult their fellow sages, and that they needed time to ponder.

And Lady Luna frowned, and how the court assembled thought it ill to see it.

V. CONCERNING THE KNIGHT ARCADIUS

Originating in the snowy north of wondrous Paralogres, where all is thickened forests full of ice-demons and mountains roamed by white-coat wolves, the knight Arcadius had already ridden many weeks toward the summerlands when first the comet did appear. His armour, lance and weaponry (his sword alone excepted) was loaded on a pack-mule drawn along behind him; tunic, breeches, boots and a wide-brimmed hat seemed more than sufficient to him, who'd trekked for miles through mountains decked with glaciers and windblown snow. Besides, such light attire spared the snorting, strutting jet-black stallion that he rode, and never yet had he come across a problem more potent than the sword that hung about his waist.

Of comets, though, for all he knew they boded ill, no single idea could he conceive of how they might be fought, placated, or sent upon their way.

Some twenty years had passed since first Arcadius saw the lights of night, and always had he doted on the Moon. A handsome, fine-boned face with deep brown eyes looked out from underneath a mass of bushy curls, each one as black or blacker still than the inky steed between his legs; and all those curls spilled disarranged across a pale, smooth brow. Long and narrow fingers grasped the reins. Lightly-built and supple-waisted, you'd think him more a dancer than a warrior; and yet he seemed too languid to be either.

A poet then: with sword in hand and Moonlight in his eye.

And so Arcadius idled through the woods, a minstrel lay upon his lips, of Selene and her loves, and how he wished he might be numbered with them; and high above the Goddess smiled to hear his fond conceits.

And yet she sighed to know the reason that he sang so sweet of her, was that he had been disappointed by all the ladies that he'd found so far, who lived their lives so vainly 'neath the Moon.

VI. HOW ARCADIUS CAME UNTO THE HERMIT

The day was almost breaking, the golden Moon was almost sunk, when Arcadius looked around and found himself still deeply in the forest. And so he began to look for shelter from the day.

The ruby sun was just begun to rise when Arcadius came at last upon an ancient oak, quite leafless now and gnarled with passing centuries. So vast a trunk, and lightning-scarred besides, had long been hollowed out, by nature first and later by assisting hand of man; a doorway cut and windows too, and up above a roof of beams and thatch. Within an ancient hermit dwelt, who looked all night upon the Moon, and all the time upon his lips Selene's name was spoken, in hymns and prayers and simply for its lovely sound. His beard was white and, left alone, would drag upon the floor; yet on his leftward hip he tied it in a knot with hair that fell behind him quite as long, so neither forward nor behind he trod upon his head's excrescence.

He'd loved the Moon from first he had been born, and loved her still past ninety; and if the Goddess so desired, he'd love her past a century.

Lilæus was his name.

Arcadius came, and saw, and knocked upon the hermit's door. And Lilæus, closing up the holy book entitled *Selene, Who is All, Her Litanies and Liturgies, with a Compendium of Daily Praises*, made way, so slow, one foot before the other, across the tree-trunk room, and opened to the world at large.

He was not disappointed with the man he saw before him.

It was not that he saw himself, made young once more; but rather that he saw the better. And more than this, he thought him worthy of the love of Goddesses. And so, of course, he bade him enter.

Arcadius thanked him, took a while to look toward his horse and mule, then gladly entered in a tree so holy. And Lilæus gave him wine, and rough-baked bread, and apples that he'd knocked down with a stick, himself. Arcadius thanked him for his kindness, then spoke no other word until he'd eaten up his fill.

Lilæus, meanwhile, took him once again to his devotions, and opened up a triptych of the lovely Moon, at centre all unclad, and either side the clad and half-clad views, and all of them so lovely. And, lost in contemplation, once again he mumbled out Selene's name.

Arcadius, washing down the food with wine, first heard, then looked, and all his mind was full of Goddess. With hurried step he paced across the room to where Lilæus sat before his treasured icon, looked again more closely now, and fell down on his knees.

'Get up, boy!' Lilæus snapped. 'She has no time for grovellers!

What Goddess ever loved a man with dirty knees?'

Arcadius, all a-blush, got up and tried his hardest to explain. Of how the icon was so lovely he thought it, for an instant, 'The Perfect Image' that he'd dreamed of finding since his early youth. Of how he'd thought his quest was quite completed even though he barely had begun. And even if it wasn't, still this was an image of the Goddess that he loved above all else. And tailing off, he then began to stutter, of how the triptych seemed so holy, and how he'd never seen a better, and how Selene was his life and mistress of his soul.

And then Lilæus saw himself made young once more indeed. And like an old man with an infant, took Arcadius' hand in his, and patted it so gentle; invited then the younger man to draw a stool up close and sit him down to listen.

'This triptych of the lovely Moon I painted long ago, when I was young and sprightly as yourself; and every man who loves the Goddess would do well to paint the like, precisely for himself. For Selene has so many forms, and likes, I know to please us. So paint her as she seems to you, and how you'd like to have her, loved and held close in your arms. And so she will appear to you, in dreams within the world we do inhabit; and in the otherworld, in truth, she'll be as you have dreamed.'

'Old saint,' the knight said then (and really did he mean it), 'I fell down on my knees because the painting you had made was quite the same as that dear Goddess of the Moon who smiles so sweetly in my dreams. And more, who, with a charcoal stick, I long ago essayed to daub. And so I think, for all you say Selene has so many forms, in fact she has but one... and all we mortals in the lower world we see the same, although we think we see the image made precisely for ourselves. For she is ever-lovely, and more than this, she ever is herself. And if your image is the same as mine, then more than this I think it is, besides, too near enough The Perfect Image I have dreamed of since a child, and which I've ridden from the north, with all its snows and longer nights than here, in hope to gaze upon, but once before I die.'

'Young man,' the hermit said, 'if your quest is for The Perfect Image, then you are more than doubly welcome here. Three times in ninety years I've thought to see it, and even then I've only seen it but in dream, in frenzy, or in sickness close to death. But how it ravished up my soul, and nourished more my body, so I hardly ate for weeks. And all of these were blessings, select and irreproducible, of Selene, that only when I had attained a state of grace, I saw. I have no further hopes to see The Image in the world below; but when I'm dead (not long, if Goddess sweet is kind), I hope to gaze upon it ever more… or rather more than this, upon its sweetly-smiling subject.'

'I'm sure you will, old friend,' Arcadius said upon the instant, 'for looking on your face I know, I never saw a man the more beloved of the lovely Moon.'

'Perhaps,' the old man said, and if he was too pleased to hear the compliment, then just as much he thought it well to act as if he wasn't. 'But young and handsome men have far more chance than ever such as I of gazing on that Image, face to lovely face. And if you seek for this, which is, we know, felicity quite beyond compare, then know as well you have my prayers for your success.

'You know, of course, the story of The Image?'

'I have been told,' Arcadius said, 'but that was long ago, and she who told me was my mother, when she was still so young, and sweet, and more than this, alive. I'd think it more than fortune now, to hear the tale again; and more so if it fell from holy lips quite like your own.'

Lilæus then closed up the triptych, sighed and wished he had the more of teeth for assisting pronunciation, and so began his tale.

VII. OF THE PERFECT IMAGE, AND HOW IT CAME TO BE

You know, of course (he started then), how some would say that fair Selene first came down to Earth upon an Orient mountain far away, called Latmos in the land of Asia; but some would say that 'Asia' was another world entire. There, they say, she gave her love and visions to the Sleeping Priest Endymion. And he, who woke a bare month 'fore he died and went to heaven in the Moon, passed on the teachings and the visions to that holy college of lunar priests who built the city-temple-state, Selenium, upon the slopes of Latmos.

And just before he died, it's said, Endymion, unable quite to make the others understand precisely what he'd seen, he fell into a frenzy.

Asked for brushes and a palette full of paint; and then he let his dear
Selene guide his hand, and paint herself through him. And so she did,
and so The Perfect Image came to be. And Endymion, at last come to
himself, looked waking on the face and form of his beloved, of she he'd
kissed in dreams. Endymion then looked upon the work, and thought
that it was good; but when he showed it to his fellow-priests, disaster
then occurred. For they were nowhere near as much so sanctified as he
in all the mysteries of the lovely lunar light.

The different tellers tell a different tale. Some say that nine went
blind, to look upon The Image; and some say ninety-nine; and others
yet, they say nine hundred and ninety-nine in all.

However many it may be (I think it one, at most, and even then
that seems too many) we know that sweet Selene would not willingly,
in any way at all, be the cause of suffering here in the world below the
Moon; and the suffering of blindness is, perchance, the worst, for then
we cannot see the Moon, the symbol of Selene. And so she took The
Perfect Image back, along with loved Endymion, to that fair heaven of
the silver light that circles round the Earth below.

Selenium, we know, it grew and throve, and all its learning was
enormous; so its library too, and mostly written in its precincts. Some
centuries, then, the praises in its temples rose up to the Moon. And yet,
at last, the populace about fell into barbarous ways; and so the Selenites
they upped and forthwith took to ships, with scriptures, icons, statues
and themselves, and sailing for the Land of Dreams, they somehow left
their ruined world behind, and came to Paralogres. And here the true
religion has been practiced since, for if we stand beneath the Moon,
then surely we'll adore her.

Since then, they say, The Perfect Image has been seen, here in the
world below, on more than one occasion (how many times, I do not
know; to count would be inane); but only by the pure of heart, when
perfect of devotion, for others would go blind. The Moon-Fairies, so
they say, they fly about the Earth and show it to the chosen. And I, who
have but seen it in my dreams, I think myself so blessed, and hardly
dare to hope for more. But to see it with the waking eye... oh, fair
young man, I hope you do, for if you do, I'd think myself thrice-blessed

indeed, to have offered some small hospitality to one more loved of loved Selene than myself.

VIII. OF SELENE, SPEAKING SOFT IN DREAMS

And so Lilæus spoke, and so, at last, Lilæus ended. Arcadius, fallen into a meditative trance the while, at last aroused himself and thanked the hermit for his story.

'From what you say,' the young knight next continued, 'it seems mayhap that riding out on quest to find The Image may be fruitless. For if the beauteous Moon-Fairies fly the world around and take it to the blessed, then hardly is it in a place to find. So what's to do?'

'Why, first, young man,' Lilæus said, 'the thing's not to despair. Rededicate your heart and soul and mind to dear Selene on the instant, and vow you'll never cease your search, although it may take longer than your life. For even if you never should attain your goal, a life spent in the service of Selene, dearest Goddess of the Moon, and lived all in the lovely light she sheds, so silver from the sky, is reward quite in itself, and more it earns the love of she we both adore.'

'I'll gladly take that vow again,' Arcadius said, 'although it's vowed before. And more willingly yet I'll swear if, in return, I'll take away a blessing from so holy a hermit as I see before me, to speed me on my quest.'

'You have it, though you'll have it once again before you leave. As for what's to do and where to go from here... well, some would say to take yourself far west, to the Mountain of the Satellites, where centuries past the priests of old Selenium established themselves in lovely Paralogres. A life of study in the libraries, of prayer and contemplation in the temples, or sat upon the snowy peaks among the pines by Moonlight, chanting lunar psalms; well, there's the path to heaven; and hap before your life ends, you'll see what you have sought. But for a handsome and a dashing knight... no, I don't think that's the way at all.

'A more romantic fate for you, I think, my boy, and Selene always did smile sweetly on the handsome, for would they not remind her of her dear Endymion? For you, the quest, the bold adventure, the careless smile with all to risk. But where you go and what you do, from here, I simply do not know. And so I'll ask the Goddess.'

'You'll ask Selene?' Arcadius did exclaim, wide-eyed.

'She comes to me in dream whene'er I sleep,' Lilæus said. 'And so I have her knowledge and her conversation. And, indeed, we should sleep now for, well I know, the sun is much arisen in the sky.'

Then offering up a prayer, or more, Lilæus took him to his pallet; a blanket on an inch of straw. There being nowhere else to sleep, Arcadius then accepted the old man's invitation, and gladly shared so sanctified a bed. And so they bade each other fond good-day, and put themselves to sleep.

About mid-day Arcadius woke, to find Lilæus muttering Selene's name and sighing; and more he moaned, and then he gasped and panted; and after that, he lapsed once more to silent sleep. Three times in all, throughout the day, Arcadius heard the same.

And so, at dusk, they rose, and broke their fast with nuts and cheese. And when he thought enough time had passed by to make polite enquiry, Arcadius began the conversation.

'You dreamt and spoke with fair Selene, old saint?' he asked. 'For when I did awake, I heard you speak her name, and... and...'

'And heard us making love, asleep there in the dream world. Oh, yes, you did; and do not think it impolite to say so. Each day, the Moon no longer shining in the sky, Selene comes, or mayhap sends a dream-emanation of herself, to love me in my sleep, as long ago she loved her own Endymion. It is a special dispensation and a blessing given, although I hardly feel it is deserved, for my withdrawal quite from the world. Most days she comes but once, and more is most auspicious. Three times, it seems to me, must be, at least, an omen.'

'How blessed you are!' exclaimed Arcadius then, but added, just a touch uncertain: 'If ever such a thing should happen to befall me, unworthy as I am, I fear I'd think it was a succubus...'

Lilæus, how he smiled, to hear the question so implied, and how politely was it phrased.

'Young man,' he said, a saucy sparkle in his eye. 'I am, as far as I recall, the more than ninety-one years old, and dear Selene has held me in her arms and loved me each single time I've slept, for fully seventy-five of them. If this is *not* Selene but a succubus, I think I'd have to say she's rather less than harmful, and if anyone's gained anything at all from this, I think it must be me. When I was but sixteen she came to me, and sixteen then she seemed herself; and sixteen still she seems to me, though I have aged and aged. I think this rather sweet of her, to stay always the same.

'Besides all this, she tells me things I need to know.'

'Forgive me that I ever doubted!' Arcadius cried then, and had to be restrained from throwing himself upon the floor in penance. 'But has she told you aught of me, or aught I need to know to carry on my quest?'

'She has indeed, and what she said is this. Some way to south of here, a night or so by horse, there rises up the Silver Castle; and there dwells lovely Lady Luna, beloved of the Moon, and near, some say, as beautiful. So there's your first-most destination. Ride there, and pass whatever test is set; then afterwards… Selene did not say…'

Arcadius then asked Lilæus if he might see his holy triptych once again, that they might offer thankful prayers together, an hour or so, and so they did, and pleased Selene with their fair devotions. Then Arcadius asked the blessing of Selene and Lilæus both, kissed the old man's hand for kindness and for guidance, and bade him fond farewell.

Some minutes later, stallion, mule and knight Arcadius were once again upon their way, beneath a starred but comet-riven sky.

IX. HOW ARCADIUS CAME TO THE SILVER CASTLE

That night he rode, all through The Deep Green Sea of Leaves, and slept the day away beneath a spreading oak to one side of a shady glade, where roe deer passed upon their way to water at a sun-besparkled stream. With dusk he rose and rode; another moonlit midnight passing by he came at last upon that quite same Latmian hill where soared the bannered Silver Castle, and how his heart rejoiced to see it.

He paused a little then, to dress himself in fine; a purple velvet tabard sewn with tiny opalescent moonstones and pointed up in silver thread (embroidered by his mother; rest her in the Moon); a cap of softest leather dyed the same, and sporting such a pheasant-feather; a massy turquoise ring upon his finger; and in his hands a treasured lute, all set about with nacre, its notes so liquid-sweet that when he played the Moonlight could be heard.

Remounting then, he rode unto the castle gate, all the music of the world there at his fingertips, a song self-writ upon his lips, that spoke of lovely maidens, high adventure, and of that wine of ecstasy that young men drink, by Moonlight, and by starlight, and by the light that only shines in much-loved ladies' eyes.

And when he was arrived, he asked forthright an interview with lovely Lady Luna. And such a boyish smile was on his face, and how he looked so handsome, the curls all flopping on his brow.

The men-at-arms that stood there at the gate, they greeted him most courteous, and asked him to dismount and take his ease; and yet they would not let him in forthwith. For no one, then they said, had ever yet been admitted straight unto their lovely mistress; and first they had to send for Lady Sweetheart. And ladies being as they are, they could not say when she'd arrive; and so they begged him, pray relax, and take a little wine. And Arcadius thanked them, said he would, but asked besides for water; and so they looked with wonder at a man so moderate.

Arcadius, though, he had his reasons; for sent upon his way by such a holy hermit, already he'd decided quite to treat the Silver Castle as a temple, and lovely Lady Luna as a Goddess; and hardly could he speak to her, all lost in fumes of wine.

X. OF WHAT THE WISE MEN TOLD THEIR FAIR YOUNG MISTRESS

Within the castle hall, Lady Luna, dressed now in a sheath of silver clinging close about her shapely form, a crystal crescent on her brow and ropes of pearls about her swan-pale neck, sat upon a throne all carved with scenes of Selene and Endymion. Her little hand was held by Lady Sweetheart, standing at her side; before her eyes were gathered all those priests and sages who, before, she'd asked so sweetly to advise her of the comet. The books were closed, the pondering was past, the disputation over; and now they'd come to tell her what she sought.

'Sweet Mistress,' old Theophilus began (and how he was so worthy of his name, for how he loved his Goddess), 'we have consulted much, and searched so much within *The Prognostics of the Lunar Night*, and so at last we have arrived at near-unanimous conclusions.

'It is agreed by one and all this comet is unholy, boding ill for all. It portends evil, retreat of Gods, and all those horrors that Selenium's priests fled long ago, the whence they came to Paralogres.

'The more we do agree upon the proof against this ill. A quest, successful made, to find The Perfect Image; to hold it, then, up to the sky, and let its radiance cleanse the foulness of the comet-polluted night.

'But where we come to blows, dear Mistress, is upon the question, who's to find it. For some of us say man, and some of us say woman; and I alone, abused by all the rest, say both.'

And Lady Luna smiled so wryly then, but before a word was past her lips, a page appeared, informing Lady Sweetheart and herself a minstrel-knight was now presenting compliments at the Gate of Pearl, and asking straight for Lady Luna.

So Lady Sweetheart, though she'd rather stay to hear how Luna did respond, accompanied the page to see what sort of man had wished himself upon them.

XI. THE TESTING OF ARCADIUS

She found him fair indeed, and fairly spoke besides, and all her heart cried out to please him; and rather wished he'd asked for her and not the castle's mistress. And yet her heart was sweet in truth, and so she did her duty.

She bade the swains to stable both his mounts and porter his belongings; herself she took his hand (the other held his lute; he would not let it go) and led him to the Tower of Moonlight Longing, where guests were always chambered. She saw him fed (a message passed that said 'no single thing that's less than best') and well-supplied with wine; and every thing pertaining to his comfort she ensured, for after all, he was so handsome. And then she left him, returning only with the nearly dawn.

And more, she brought with her a sweet young maiden, who, slightly prompted, introduced herself: 'Sir, my given name it is Liselle, but twelve years old, no more. And so it please you, lord, I am a virgin; sworn to love Selene, never man.'

Arcadius looked on fair Liselle, and thought she was so charming. He thought no more except to kiss her hand and send her on her way.

'Not so, Sir Knight!' said Lady Sweetheart then, a-reading of his thoughts. 'This is your test, and sir, I somehow think you knew already that you'd have to face it. And, sir, you have to pass it, if you would see Lady Luna.

'So sleep all day with fair Liselle, quite wrapped up in your arms. And, sir, before the night-time's come again, then you must breach her maidenhead, and leave her blood all spread across the sheets. But more than this, she must remain a virgin, for she is Selene's. I leave you with this small conundrum; and if you've solved it by the morrow's night, I'll take you then to Luna.'

Then Lady Sweetheart did depart. Arcadius took Liselle into his arms, and kissed her oh-so-sweetly.

And though she trembled like a fawn, he took her off to bed.

XII. HOW THE NIGHT-TIME CAME AGAIN, AND WHAT THE DARKNESS DID REVEAL

The bed it lacked for curtains, and so Arcadius thought he would be watched; and so indeed he was, although he hardly could conjecture who might be a-spy. It would, besides have made no difference.

So Lady Luna, informed of all by Lady Sweetheart (and that the stranger was so handsome), saw Arcadius first turn away his sight while Liselle attired herself for bed; and when she was, he stripped down to his undershirt and joined her.

What happened then, a little later, right there within the fullest light of day, gave Lady Luna such a smile; and so she took herself to bed as well, enormously contented.

She did not say what she had seen to Lady Sweetheart, and so she let that darling girl herself find out if Arcadius had passed the test. And so he had, for when she went to fetch him at the fall of dusk, she found

Arcadius ready dressed, though still Liselle she slept all innocent.

For when she was no more awake, a little nick he'd made there in her scalp, above the hairline where no mark would ever show; and when the knife had done it's work, before he stopped the bleeding with a gentle hand, he'd drawn a fingerful and written on the bed '*intacta*'.

And so he'd breached her maiden head, and spread her blood across the sheets, and left her yet a virgin.

And Lady Sweetheart smiled and kissed his hand, and full of joy she led him from the room.

XIII. HOW ARCADIUS AND LADY LUNA DID SURPRISE EACH OTHER

A little walk about the Silver Castle (all of shining metal strung about with gleaming gems), and then she brought Arcadius to a private small reception room, where Lady Luna waited, old Theophilus at her side, and half a dozen courtiers.

And Lady Luna, all in silver thread and pearls and crystal, and both her sparkle-eyes so wide and brown, she looked so much like fair Selene; and more, to Arcadius she looked besides just like The Perfect Image come to life. And so he dropped down on one knee, all gallant and all reverent, and hardly could he look.

'My Lady,' Sweetheart then began, as formal as the occasion did demand. 'I present the knight Arcadius... [here she smiled]... your latest suitor...'

'Oh, no!' the words escaped Arcadius' lips before he thought to stop them. 'Fair Lady... and you are the fairest lady ever I did see, that walked beneath the Moon... forgive me, please, for now I have to tell you that I did not come to woo.

'Yet seeing you, I know that if I could, I would; for never could a man aspire to any such felicity more delighting than to have you as his wife, unless Selene herself should condescend. But I am vowed to other things.

'From farthest north, I've ridden south, with but one thing in view, to which my life is dedicate. For I am sworn to find The Perfect Image...'

And here he paused, to hear so many indrawn breaths; he could not understand quite why.

'And so, dear Lady,' he continued, 'forgive and understand. Two nights a-gone I came to the holy hermit, old Lilæus, who, I think, you surely know [and here Theophilus nodded sagely]. Consulting with the sage, of how I might continue with my quest, he slept, and dreamed, and loving spoke with sweet Selene. And what she said, through him to me, was I should ride straight here, to your most wondrous Silver Castle, and pass your test perplexing. And after that, alas, she did not say.

'I think Selene, if I dare read her intentions, would have me ask my lady's favour... a scarf, a glove, some talisman... that I may carry with me on my quest. I do not seek your love itself, although I'd joy to have it; but some small token, given with your fairest wishes, I know would speed me on my way. And so I seek for nothing more than but a tiny kindness.'

'Sir Knight,' said Lady Luna then. 'Pray take a seat, and take a little wine and cheese and bread, and let us talk as friends. And if you do not seek my love, then more's the cause for me to say, you have it.

'You must have seen the comet, long and foul, polluting all the sky. My sages and my counsellors both tell me it is evil quite unspeakable, and only will we mitigate its ill, if we can find The Perfect Image, and show it to the sky.

'And so I take it as a happy omen, that you are here on such a quest. I do not know if you'll succeed, although of course I hope you do. Some here say man will find it, some say woman; and one alone says both.

'My friend, for so I'm sure you'll be. I will not give you glove, or scarf, or talisman.

'Arcadius, be Selene's sweetest knight, and so be mine as well. For if you seek The Perfect Image, you need much more than favours. You need a hand to hold in yours; and if we do succeed, why then, Sir Knight, you'll win it.

'And yes, my friend, I mean exactly what you think, and should these grave advisors then be scandalised, it matters not at all.

'My handsome knight, wherever, in the end your quest should lead, then please do understand.

'Your Lady Luna's coming with you.'

And so Lee read, and thought this was more charming, and more sane; and having read enough, they ate. And having ate, they drank. And having drank, they danced so many voltas, sweetly 'neath the silver Moon.

And having danced, they kissed.

And having kissed a fond goodnight, they took them to their chambers; and if their eyes were sad at parting, then none will be surprised...

Monday, 8th October 1803

I do not know quite where *Lady Luna* came from; it all spilled out in one enormous rush. Like Endimion Lee, who reads it in my story, I find it rather charming; and yet it is unlike whatever else I write. I almost feel as if I had no hand in this at all, and that the spirit of Morion of Lyons (who, I am quite sure, he never did exist) had written the whole through me, ghostly hand all clutching mine; as if he wanted his story to exist here on the Earth, as well as in the library of Somnium. Oh, fancy I know all this to be, and yet... yet it is the sort of pagan romance that could, perchance, have been written, if the Christians never triumphed. A vision of a pagan world, then, and of its literature, that never was... and never having been, the sweeter then it is, to have it.

A pagan world restored, indeed. And never more will I discount the power of ladies' kisses.

Lady Luna's story would, no doubt, be long enough to make a book quite in itself. And yet, I think, what's there is quite enough (besides, no more was given me). It speaks of fair Selene, very sweetly, and more, it does foreshadow what's to come. So, leave it as it is, and let's be on...

Last night I decided that it might be wiser to retire to my room immediately after supper, for after what I'd said to Jude Brown in the morning, I thought better than to speak with him at night. I feared the worst as I retreated then and met him on the stairs. He sneered at me, as so he always does, but nothing more. I did not stay to ask him why.

I *know* I said those awful things to him, of crucifixion nails. And yet I *knew* that I had spent last Monday night in Severndroog Castle, with Cynthia of the Moon.

I confess that this begins to make me fretful.

What worries me besides is that so much of *Somnium* that I write it merges dream and fancy and desire with what's of everyday and what's of Goddesses of the Moon. In fiction I am all the more deliberate in this; in the waking world I'm not.

And yet it seems to me that while I build up Somnium in my writing, somehow it builds here in The Bull as well, with Cynthia as its queen; and neither has the room for Christ or church. So if I wished them all away, and with them Reverend Kinnock, and nothing then ensued... then what to make of this?

It is too strange a thought. I cannot think it through.

Last night, indeed, I lost myself in claret, dreams and lovely words; and all the world was magic, for I wrote it so myself. And what was written out of claret was there to see in dreams; and what was seen in dreams was written out with claret.

I woke for dinner; wandered down the stairs; found Cynthia waiting for me, mischief in her eye. She sat and watched me eat, and all her smiles said: 'hurry up and finish.'

It seemed her husband was departed for the afternoon, driving his wagon down to Woolwich, with its docks and shops and warehouses, to arrange for new deliveries: casks of sack, and hogsheads of ale, bales of pipe-tobacco and (most pleasing news to me) more bottles of the finest claret. When I had eaten, dear Cynthia Brown-eyes left the hotel in the charge of barmaid Daphne Squires (the bawdy strumpet looks at me quite oft, and all her looks are invitation; blue-eyed, though, as she is, she's thus, to me, repellent), then took my hand and insisted I accompany her into the tavern cellar. I did not know quite what she was intending; sometimes she's so surprising, I no longer am surprised.

As everywhere in coaching inns, the cellar of The Bull is vast, for storage of its liquor; yet this seemed bigger yet than most and, at its western end, there was an empty space. There, by lantern-light, she asked me to look down and tell her what I saw. And there (as she knew full-well I would) I found the remnants of an ancient wall, protruding upward through the rammed-earth floor. From its construction, and its depth below the current level of the ground, I guessed it Roman. I did not know quite what to make of this, and sweet Cynthia did not help my concentration, seeming far more interested in pressing herself too close against my side, 'the better to illuminate the old remains.' Perhaps, I suggested, this had been some Roman beacon-post; a similar one, they say, had been built here in Armada times, and now the Admiralty Telegraph rises up in ugly splendour, a little more to Londonwards on the far side of the road, its shutters a monument to misplaced modern invention. It seems each technical advance we make must then be paid for with a loss of beauty.

There was little else to see. In fact, as rather I'd expected the case would be, dear Cynthia was, by then, becoming becomingly importunate for kisses in the shaded cellar underground. Yet somehow I thought this was, to her, a game; and kisses were a merest part of some far greater plan. Yet be that as it may, I have to say, I did not tell her no. We were disturbed by footsteps on the stairs; the annoying Daphne Squires had sent Tom Watkins down for further bottles. In all honesty, I do not think she really needed them, but rather used young Tom to gratify her curiosity second-hand. He made too much noise, though, to take us unawares.

Our minds now concentrated once again on olden things, dear Cynthia showed me then an ancient door, set in the north wall of the cellar. I know not where it leads, though obviously not back up to the inn above. They say there used to be a tunnel leading south-west from the Catherine Wheel to Eltham Palace, but this is simply in the wrong direction for aught to do with that. The hinges rusted and the door-panels eaten up with woodworm, I judged that door to be above two centuries old; though the inn itself is said to be more recent. An ancient and enormous lock, of dark-patina'd bronze, prevented further explorations; yet Cynthia, grown big-eyed and, so it seemed to me, just a little tipsy (we had, while down among the casks, been sampling of the tavern's wares) assured me that her husband had the key, and all it needed was but to wait until he slept, to silently make away with it. I told her then (forearmed as I was by all my previous spying) I simply did not believe she shared a room with Judas Brown; she laughed, and kissed my nose, and simply would not answer; and, oh, she looked so saucy. She told me then that beyond that door, though she had explored it little, were tunnels, and caverns, and further old remains of the most startling antiquity and quite bewildering artistry. I know that, given the opportunity, I will be unable to resist her offers of further exploration. And if we end up in a cave below the ground, and all she wants to do is kiss me in the dark, then I'll say yes to anything she asks. I know not what will happen next; I confess I am intrigued.

I really know not quite what she intends. I'm sure she leads me on, but why, and toward what, I just have no idea. I know, if only from Cynthia's warnings about the inhabitants of Shooters Hill themselves, that there are evil people in the world; my brain says there must be evil women too, but my heart will not believe it. Most of all, I cannot think one single ill of Cynthia herself, or that she could ever take advantage of my innocence. And if she has a plan, untold to me, I'm sure it's for my good. Perhaps I am a fool, upon the edge of a precipice. Who knows? I put my trust quite simply in the Moon, wherever she may lead, to heaven or to hell.

And yet I cannot help but wonder, what lies down there in the cellar, what underworld below the hill..?

But let's again to write.

With night came bed, with bed came sleep, with sleep at last came dream. He stood there on a tower-top, all crenellate with jewels, with Somnium spread palatiate below; while high above there rode the narrow crescent of a waning silvery Moon.

And by his side Diana stood, now dressed in black, a strange enticing sparkle in her eye. A robe of sable velvet, sewn about with silver stardust, swathed her lovely body from the neck unto the foot; and when his mind it conjured up the pulchritude all hidden there beneath, he wished away the robe, but even dreaming found he couldn't. Her eyes a-twinkle told him: 'more work needed yet.'

With finger-rings and ear-rings pendant, and necklace too besides, all made of gleaming jet surrounded up with silver, the only gold about her person now was mounted on her brow: the crescent that she always wore. The long dark feather of a raven's wing sprang jaunty from above her ear, and all her long loose hair seemed swirling in the breeze.

Himself, he wore the darkest garb as well, but dreaming never quite discovered what; besides, the vision by his side... the fairest beauty wrapped in midnight black and smiling red-lipped with delight... quite drew his eyes away from any other sight.

Her little hand was clasped in his, the gentle inclination of her head it promised reassurance, said: 'trust in me, and trust to love'.

Then hand in hand and foot by foot, they stepped quite off the tower.

His stomach rose, his mind turned over, and then he felt the pressure of her hand. From looking down, a hundred feet above the ground, he turned, sick-faced and pale, and lost all fear with one quick glance at laughing eyes and smiling lips, and in his ears the Moon, she chuckled soft. Then dear Diana forward-leaned, her body all-aslant, and so inclining, so inclined him too.

And then away they drifted, soaring on the winds.

They looped the air round Somnium's towers and Lee stared all amazed at star-besparkled turret-jewels and windows crystal-paned, at rearing marble walls and minarets of moonstone. Looked down on from above, the palace made a matchless gem, that glittered on the maiden brow of Moon-shaped Shooters Hill; and though he'd ridden up and down the hill on occasions all too often, and thought it nothing more than barrier to travel, he saw its magic now. And knew a magic all the same would shimmer anywhere upon the Earth, in any spot how humble, had we the eyes to see it.

Her hair all streaming out behind, she flew him on, then drifted down a-circle to the hillside that faced out northward to that old and Moon-beglimmered Thames. They landed on a grassy slope; she kissed him once for bravery, then kissed him once again, for love. Then up the hill unto a crag she pointed, and at its foot a cave.

Like lovers laughing in their bliss, they made their way uphill. At cave-mouth, two large torches then she found, and lit them with a look.

She glanced back next to see him staring at the stars, at old Polaris never wet, at Deneb, Vega, musical Capella and pulsing-strange Algol, the frightener of all the far-off Arab lands. A little sigh she gave out then, to see such innocent wonder, delighting in the lovely sparks of night.

Her hands quite full of torches, she put her tongue into his ear, and gained all his attention. And then to tunnel's-mouth she brought him, and led him under-hill.

Along the shaft she led the way, his hands clasped round her waist; and though she thought it just a way to keep him on the path, the both, they knew, they liked it. She liked his hands, he liked her waist, and in the dark was everything forgiven.

An underground lake they passed by then, all swum about with fishes luminous, gleaming in the dark. Above them, all the weight of Shooters Hill; on top of that was Somnium besides. And narrow was the tunnel, black as ink, with spiders, rats and crawling things; and every horror that there was proclaimed Diana's beauty by its fearsome opposition.

She took him through a maze of tunnels that, he knew, without her aid he'd never quite escape. All turnabouts and forks and crossings, quite unmarked, and oh-so-deep beneath the hill, and oh-so-deep the dark. And so at last she opened up the massive brazen door to dear Diana's underworld; an underground apartment quite the like he'd never seen.

She led him in and placed her torches up in sconces high upon the wall; then both together started lighting candles first, and lamps. Old books bound up in dark and crackled skin, lay yellow-paged and open on their lecterns in the corners of the room. The walls were covered round about in arras black, with silver-thread designs of all the Mansions of the Moon; inlaid upon the floor of jetty granite, pale Etrurian marble traced a magic circle, strung about the rim with names of lunar Goddesses. And at the circle's edge, in a smoky-dark obsidian mirror, gold frame carved with naked Goddesses all-embraced, he saw, although he knew not how, the decrease-crescent of the silver-sickle Moon.

A censer next Diana lit, and filled the room with jasmine incense, mingled all with musk. Two goblets then she filled with rainbow-glistened nectar that he knew was nothing less than dew dripped down directly from the dark eclipsèd Moon; she laughed, and told him *aphroselenos* it was, the like of which was never gathered since those old Thessalian dames expired with the pagan days of Rome. But not yet would she let him drink it.

She asked him next his date of birth (as if she didn't know it), and drew up then his astrologic chart; drew another for that very night; and laughed a little laugh.

And next she bade him draw a couch into her magic circle, gave him then a book all writ with menstrual blood, and hung about his neck a garland wove of moonwort. Then passed him both the goblets, and told him to be still.

He watched, all wide-eyed then, as she unstrung the velvet robe, and let it sink about her ankles. And seeing what he saw, he sat down on the couch.

A snug black stitchet, all of leather, banded up with clasping silver, laced up far too tight about her tiny waist: he wondered how she breathed. Black silk stockings, knit like darkling spider's-webs, lizard-skin garters silver-buckled pinching close to bulge the soft flesh of her thighs. And sandals, sable-leathered, heels both tipped with diamond points and rising up far higher than her toes, while thongs wound tight about her shapely calves.

Her lovely breasts, all full-Moon round and full-Moon pale, they bulged and thrust above the leather banding close her ribs, their whiteness shining through a film of sable lace.

And nothing else she wore, save jewel of jet and raven feather.

She let him look, as much he liked; because she knew, as much he liked to look, so much she liked to show him. A charming smile, and then she pouted, mouthed a little kiss; told him then to open up the book and, when she started circling, to chant a certain chant.

She picked up next a giant key, the like to open Hades' door; a glint-edged silver dagger, sharp as death itself; a whip, nine-thonged upon a hazel shaft and fit to drive the dead. The key, the dagger and the whip she buckled next her waist, then took up once again her hell-belighting torch, its use to light the way down to the underworld, and waved it swiftly till it smoked. And then, completing her ensemble with a shed-skin symbol of eternal resurrection, a nine-foot python next she wrapped about her hips, its long, forked tongue all flickering out as if to lick the lace from off her satin breasts.

Around the circle's rim she moved, strange cantrips spilling softly from her lovely ruby lips, and let the serpent coil about her where it would: between her legs, betwixt her breasts, beneath her scented armpits, its quick tongue licking where she liked. All breathless then she soon became, and circled all the faster; while he, in turn, gave voice to words so strange he feared to understand.

Blue mist trailed out behind the torch, and walled up all the circle in a strange translucent vapour. And as it thicker grew, her path it spiralled inward, until she dowsed the torch and joined him on the couch. The serpent struck out then behind his back, pulled him close and wrapped around them both, squeezed him tightly to her pulsing breasts. She kissed him like a hungry beast, all open-mouth and nipping teeth, her tongue all long and hot breath gasping in his throat.

The next, she put his hands about her waist, leaned back and, calling out those barbarous names that first were given to the Moon when men no more they were than apes, began to raise the dead.

And Endimion Lee, for all he dreamed, he knew young Greene was right: for here he was, below the Earth where Hecate reigned supreme. And knew her for Diana too; and loved her just the same.

The mirror, all volcanic glass, it misted then and cleared. Surrounded by her prancing beasts the lovely Circe next appeared, half-Goddess descended of the Sun, half-naked, wholly wanton. All winks and smiles she blew a kiss, it seemed in Lee's direction, a saucy minx with magic eyes and ocelots about her ankles. And then she turned about, and with a wand, she pointed out a pig; the next an ox; and lastly-most a wolf. And then, an eyebrow raised, an eye all wide beneath, she seemed to say: *Be careful what you wish, for anything you wish you could turn out to be.*

And next Medea, daughter of Æëtes, she appeared, a haughty beauty, proud of breast and long of leg. She looked the first to Hecate-Diana, and made obeisance, though Lee he thought it grudging. All ruthlessness was in her face, but vast he knew her power. *With magic you can rule the world, her message all too plain. Give up your soul and cease to love, then take and take and take. Take riches, women, lives and all, and crush the lesser under foot. And I'll be there to laugh and ravage with you.*

Diana at his side, rejection was too simple; and yet Medea made him think. He told himself that, never had he seen the Moon, he'd say her nay quite natural; at least he hoped he would.

Semiramis next, the gorgeous Queen of Babylon, and naked as its Biblic Whore. By turns she rode her horse, and let it ride her too; dressed herself in soldier's weeds, executed husbands, slept with guards and conquered half the world. Said: *Believe and nothing there is you cannot do, even disadvantaged as a woman. For Babylon I built, that was the city of the world, and never was there like it. Its fame is older far than any other, and more, its fame, it will survive far longer than the others too. And this is mine, and while its memory lives, so I live on immortal too.*

At last, fair Helen she appeared, the bane of Ilion and, he knew, the darling of the world. A golden girl and lovely past compare, she had no message but her beauty. Diana it was who spake on her behalf. Said: *The apex of all beauty can be yours; the aspiration all men sought and failed to find within their wives and sweethearts; the longed-for-one that patterned all men's dreams for twenty-five whole centuries, and will another twenty-five besides. All your life, in any land you choose, you'll spend in bliss, with Helen. With Helen of Troy, the World's Desire, and like there never was. And as for me, you cannot have me while you live, and all you have's my word that anything might follow. And I tell you now, we Gods, we are capricious. So, dear Endimion Lee, I ask you now to choose.*

'There is no choice,' he told her then, 'and needless did you ask. My dear Diana, Queen and Goddess, and call you what you will, I love you. No other will I ever choose. And if, beyond these merest days, I love you unrequited, then sweet Diana mine, I love you just the same. And if I die, and find there's nothing more, I'll tell you this, my sweet: the little love we've shared, though others think it unrequite and far from consummate, to me at least, *it will have been enough.*'

Diana then she was again, and Hecate no more. She clasped him close, and wept, and kissed him, sprinkled him with tears and pressed his head unto her lovely breast; then raised him up, her eyes so wide, and kissed him all again.

At last, she banished all the mirror-images, put aside the snake, the key and all the other aspects of the Carian Goddess; made away with Hades-stuff, laid him on the couch and beamed Selenic on her love. A deep, snug cave within the English Latmos now they occupied, her own Endimion with his own and much-beloved Diana.

A goblet next, with Moondew brimming, she placed into his hand; raised the other in her own. The toast was Love Eternal, tender, sweet and all-consuming; the foaming draft a nectar to the tongue. Almost, lost in lovely depths of wide brown eyes, in drinking he forgot to swallow; but did, and knew he'd never drunk the like. If ever the essence of a young and tender Moon-girl had a taste, then surely it was this.

He drained the goblet quite entire: *aphroselenos*, it warmed and bubbled in his stomach, spread its lightsome glow down to his groin and perineum, rushed up then along his spine and burst out effervescent in his brain; and wheeled on down again to tingle all his cods and stones. Such bliss he never felt before, not even spending in his first-beloved. Entire body ravished up from toe to crown, he sank upon the couch and trembled, gasped and moaned and shuddered as the waves of fearsome pleasure pulsed all through him, all unbearable, raptured more than he could ever think, his mind quite gone to heaven. Transported with beatitude, enchanted up to paradise, his pleasure *would not stop*.

And second after second, stronger then it grew, and hours they seemed to pass away, and still there was no cease. And sweeter than was all of this, he heard Diana sigh besides, and knew she felt the same.

And so eternity passed in bliss, until he knew no more.

Tuesday, 9th October 1803

As I wrote last night, and smoked, and drank, I thought much of the cellar, and all its underworld connotations. The inn is new, the cellar old, that door is older yet. And beyond it? Æonic darkness? Ancient tragedies? Antique hideousness?

Or is Diana Regina's Hecatean cave down there, obsidian mirror of the waning moon and all?

None of these, I expect. But I must go back and find out soon. It preys upon my mind. As does the fact that I have not had a letter from my darling Liz. I wish that she would write.

I did not dream of cellars last night, and yet my dreams were strange. On other nights my dreams are quite full up with Lady-Goddesses, from Lizzie and Cynthia to Diana Regina and Selene, a cluster of lovelies in my mind who seem, somehow, to all be aspects of a single wondrous Moon-girl; last night I dreamt again of that strange future-author living close at hand in space and far away in time. I wonder sometimes whether he will ever exist in daylight (or Moonlight) reality, or is simply manufactured of my fevered dreams. I know not. But what I do know (and yet I don't know *how* I know) is that *he dreams of that self-same Moon-woman*, who is Selene guised as Liz and Cynthia, and all the rest. Occasionally, I feel I should be jealous; at other times I rejoice to share a treasured love with another of the same mind. For I know that he is Moonstruck too, though whether in quite the same way as me I cannot tell; indeed, so much of his life and times, and how he thinks, are utterly incomprehensible to me. It seems to me he lives and works alone, to a pace of his own choosing, and that far slower than the common population of his time; and yet he achieves more in one day than I would in a week. Or, perhaps more to the point, than I would *want* to. Strangest of all is the way that, dreaming, I see him write. He does not use a pen, but rather plays at something like a harpsichord; yet when he hits the keys, not musical notes but words come out. I simply do not understand it.

I confess I'm thankful that I do not live in the high-speed hell of future-time. Perhaps, if ever I finish my Annals of the Palace of Somnium, I might write a romance of the distant future, where time is, simply, *fast*. Where journeying to the Americas takes but a single day; where food is cooked in minutes; where love is made in seconds. And all the world is full of mad, unending chatter. Sometimes, my thoughts are frankly *horrible*.

And yet, if I did write so, and made that writer of my future-dreams a character, would I then, or *could I then*, write him into full existence? And if I could, then of whom would he write? Of *me*? And would he then make *me* exist?

I think perhaps it's time I thought of something else.

And yet: if I made *him* exist, and he made *me* exist; then what of Endimion Lee? I *know* I made him up; he never could be real.

And yet...

And yet my mind keeps straying away from this to other things. I cannot any way forget the cellar, and all the underworld of dreams it represents...

I think I've not been awake for long enough to get my thoughts in order. So let's away to dinner.

Wednesday, 10th October 1803

I hardly can begin to say what happened yesterday afternoon. I tried to write a letter to my darling Liz describing it, but gave up after a page or two, because I knew it sounded drunk or mad. I don't think that I am either, so let me try to write things down within this journal, and see if writing makes them sense. Such wonders I have seen. So many marvels, buried beneath the ground, has dearest Cynthia revealed unto my awestruck eyes. I wish I had the draughtsman's skills of Signor Piranesi, to show them to the world.

And more than this. The night before I wrote a Somniac underworld; but yesterday I found myself within one.

I woke refreshed, and enjoyed a dinner of boiled bacon and leeks (though the fat I left beside my plate; I know that others eat it, but it merely makes me retch and choke). I heard the rattle of the midday coach, just leaving as I ate; then Cynthia was sitting there beside me all-a-smile. It seemed Jude Brown was on the coach, a-posting off to London, intending there to stay on business quite unknown to me, and not returning until tomorrow late. She asked me if I had things to do that afternoon; when I said no, she told me I should dress me for adventure. I was not sure quite what she did intend.

Returning to my room, I barely had my boots pulled on when she was at my door. The key to that ancient cellar door was in one hand and, I have to say, I cannot think to ever have seen the larger; in her other hand, a ball of thread; I did not know quite why. She looked so saucy, with her eyes so full of mischief, I hardly knew what best to do: to laugh or just to kiss her.

The plan proposed was simplicity itself: that leaving the running of the inn to young Watkins and the harlots Squires and Smythe, she and I should once more descend into the cellar (alone, and quite deliberately in the absence of her husband, and with the upper cellar door locked behind us this time to shut out further intrusions; all of which things were most emphatic in her description of the scheme) where, fortified with claret and illuminated with a flickering pair of lanterns (only two, so that she might hold my hand and lead me on), she would open the forbidden door, and show me mysteries, and darkness, and I knew not what. Some part of me thought this a scallywag's invitation; that perhaps she wished to seduce me and play the strumpet down there in the dark, her husband gone and none to know her loose ways in the cellar. Another part remembered Severndroog, and what she did and did not permit there; and yet a third part thought that Severndroog had never ever happened. All this was quite forgot when, at the last, beyond that cellar door, I saw just what I saw. Oh, Liz who is my sweet, and Selene who is my Goddess, the things I saw beyond that door. The wonders and surprises. The things that should not be.

But I get ahead of myself once more. Descending to the cellar with our lanterns lit, we then found a bottle of claret and poured ourselves two large glasses, and she proposed a toast: to Diana and the Moon, to Somnium, to me, and all I loved here in the world; I told her, of the last, she should include herself. For that, she smiled and kissed me softly on the cheek. The second glass, the toast was mine: I do confess, all couraged up somehow, that in the blithest fashion then I consigned her 'loving' husband (who, I know not how, I thought was on some business most nefarious) straight away to hell; not only that, but added imprecations too. And when the words were out my mouth, I wondered what I'd said. And yet, she looked at me all wondered and delighted, and then she gave me such a grin. Thereafter (and only minutes later than it had been opened) we emptied out the bottle.

She led me next toward the ancient door and paused a moment then, her lantern in one hand. In the other she held up the brazen key, tapped it once or twice against her chin, looked at me big-eyed and licked her lips with the sauciest of smiles. I knew, before she spoke a word, that little tongue would soon be licking mine; and yet I could not help but think her gesture so familiar and Dianic, I almost expected that, beyond the ancient door, Somnium's longed-for library would be found. I put my lantern on a nearby cask, held out my hands, and so she flung herself into my arms.

She clung so soft and kissed me then so long I asked if anything might be wrong. She shook her head and hugged me all the tighter. I thought this rather strange. Nonetheless, when at the last the embrace was broken (by whom, I cannot quite remember; I doubt that it was me, she was so warm and such a comfort in my arms), she took the key and inserted it in the lock. It turned so easily I was surprised; it seems that someone has been keeping it well-oiled; unlike the hinges. I had to put my shoulder against the door to move it, it was so stiff.

Beyond was, simply, blackness.

She took my free hand then in hers and, raising up her lantern with the other (as I did mine as well), she led me through that ancient doorway; paused and demanded that I push it almost closed behind us. I half expected further kisses then; instead she paused and tied one end of her thread around the door-handle. I realised then she played at Ariadne, and this would be our clew of thread in labyrinthine darkness; I hoped we'd not meet the Minotaur. I hardly had the time to mention this before she took my hand once more and started for the darkness.

To begin with, I thought that on the other side of the door was simply another cellar the same as that we just had left. A couple of old chests and boxes stood there to my left but, squeezing my palm warmly, sweet Cynthia led me past these swiftly. And what I'd thought to be a simple cellar turned out to be, instead, a broad corridor, some ten feet across and thirty long. At its end, a flight of nine stone stairs led downward into deeper darkness yet.

At the foot of the stairs she paused, lantern held up high, and turned toward me. Her hand slipped out of mine and slid around my waist and, as she pressed herself so close, she confessed (rather sweetly but obviously rather trepidatiously) that twenty feet further on than this was all, before, she'd ever dared to go. I really was quite touched.

Rather than being the adventurous Amazon I'd thought her in the past, she suddenly seemed so soft and trembling, and reminded me, I confess, of dear young Liz. I took her in my arms and kissed her once again, and from that fond embrace she seemed to gather strength. It's only now I write of it that I realise she may have been offering more than I could quite perceive. My Liz has always told me that I do not understand women, and perhaps indeed I don't. There've been times when I've had *her* in my arms like that, and wanted many things, but never known quite what to do. But now the time's gone by, it does not matter anyway.

But more's the point, with further thought, I have to wonder. If she never had been farther, how could she have hinted, Monday afternoon, of all the wonders found beyond there in the darkness? I cannot solve this mystery.

We stepped away from the stairs then, arm in arm, onto an uneven floor of earth and stone, as if we walked across an open field, up above there on the surface. How high the roofing was above us, I've no idea at all; the lantern light failed to penetrate that far, and the ground below our feet continued to slope gently downward. Again, the walls to either side seemed out of reach as well, and as for what might lie ahead, I simply did not know.

The first things that we found (a little beyond the twenty feet dear Cynthia wide-eyes said she had explored) were three or four ancient, fluted column bases carved, with the most exquisite craftsmanship, from pink and sparkling marble. They were shattered no more than a foot above the ground, while close at hand lay a Corinthian capitol of the same stone, its leaves almost (if not pinkly veined) compellingly real. What building once stood here, I could not tell. I knew not if this was Roman, Greek, or what; and even if I had known that, the workmanship seemed far too fine for provincial craftsmen, no matter how near they might have been to old Londinium. My first thought was that I looked upon a temple, but the palatial remains we saw thereafter leave me without any clue at all.

A few feet further on, I was completely staggered to find a giant slab of whitest marble lying horizontal to the ground. And somehow, though I could not tell anyone how I knew, it seemed to me that this was imported stone, brought all the way by ship (and carted somehow up the hill, I can only think by oxen) from the quarries of old Etrurian Luna, the city that the Byzantine Stephanos called *Selenopolis*. More than this (again, I have to explain by intuition, or Goddess-given revelation) I knew that this marble had been brought up here by choice, *because* the stone was *lunar*. And the carving of that marble: Phidias never carved the better, and neither did Praxiteles. The exquisiteness of those reliefs (no, not reliefs, for some of that carving was fully in the round), I simply cannot describe its loveliness. The entire surface of the slab, except the edge, was carved as water, lapping in gentle waves and heaped up by the tides. In its centre, sweet, sweeter and sweetest Diana rose up all lovely from the swirling water (not relief, but fully rounded; and rounded oh-so-gently), bathing her lovely naked body in the world-encircling Ocean stream, her two-horse chariot standing by, her beauteous Moon-nymphs gathered all around, though submerged all breast-deep in the milk-white sea. And smiling, all of them, naked, playful and playing with one another in sweet and sparkle-eyed Sapphic delight; and dear Diana with the crescent on her brow, just as naked, far the more delightful, and looking so much like my Liz, my sister and my love. And yet somehow I was not so utterly surprised, when Cynthia clutched herself quite close, and told me that she thought, in that dearest image of Diana, to recognise *herself*. I confess that when I heard that, I looked the more at bared Diana's form, till Cynthia plucked my sleeve and simpered. We both knew exactly why I stared; but who's the deeper blush that then ensued, I really cannot say.

Some ten feet square that marmoreal slab it glittered in our lantern's light, more marvellous than any sculpture anywhere in all the museums of the world. If Periclean Athens or Imperial Rome they ever saw the like, I doubt it very much. This was, quite simply, divine: the artistry of the dreaming Moon, the sculpture of a supreme Selenic hand.

Yet there was more, though this itself near robbed me of my breath and put my brain to sleep. Another descendant flight of stairs, nine more again, and what had been a corridor before expanded widely out to either side; and I knew that, though so far beneath the surface of the ground, we stood now in a cavern of a size that grew unfathomable. And somehow then, within the glass-panelled lanterns, the candles began to flicker, and it was all that I could do to lead poor trembling Cynthia onwards (if this, too, was not itself an act); and yet, she seemed so tightly wrapped around me, I thought I had to walk for both of us. Only a few feet around us did the lanterns light; beyond was illimitable blackness and the unknown void. How glad I was for that small clew of thread; without it I feared we never would escape.

The low ruins of a broken wall appeared next in the stuttering light, marble again, but flecked this time with gold and bearing the shattered remains of a relief: of chariot wheels and horses' hooves, of maidens' feet and the merest beginning, I thought, of a curious representation of the wide-expanding ocean of the stars. What palatial building this represented once I could not possibly conjecture, but after tracing its course a few feet further on we came to the broken stumps of a pillared gateway. I realised then that this was merely the remains of a surrounding wall, rather than that of a building itself.

Collapsed between the gateway's pillars were the remains, still recognisable though tarnished and betwisted, of a pair of gate-leaves, wrought of silver and decorated, in amongst the arabesques, with combinations of the star and crescent. Yet no Mohametan swarthy hand was e'er involved in this. In that openwork of silver struts and curlicues, there was an elaborate name-plate; and when, at last, by lantern-light I was able to read it, I confess, I fainted. It was too much. I cannot say I grew dizzy, or that the world span before my eyes, or any of those other old clichés. One moment I was there, and looking; the next I simply was not. Not there, not looking, not conscious. Simply *not*.

When awareness returned, I found my head was cradled in warm Cynthia's lap, face across her softest thighs, her fingers stroking, worried, at my hair. I raised my head and tried to speak; before I could, she pressed my face against her lovely breasts and, I confess, I suddenly thought of mother, and was contented then to stay there while I gathered up my thoughts. Finally, she let me look up, to gaze upon the relieved expression lighting up her face. She said she was so glad I was alright; I wanted then to say so many things, but simply could not speak. And then, hugging each other tightly for support, we followed the thread back to the ancient door. No, I confess, she hugged me more than I did her; but it was I who needed the support by far the more than she. Regaining the familiar cellar of The Bull, we locked the door behind us, and then she helped me to my room.

She laid me on the bed, and stroked my hair, and kissed me; and oh, her concern, it was so sweet. She sat and held my hand until I fell asleep, the finest doctor of them all. I needed that. My mind would not accept at all the thing that I had seen. That name-plate simply could not be. And yet it was. I say again: it could not be, and yet it *was*. The word that name-plate spelled, all twisted and all battered, it was that single word that made the world entire a dream:

Somnium

That should have been enough shocks for one day. Alas, it was not.

I awoke again at evening, my dreams all filled with Moons that hid in caverns and lovely palace ladies who, though different, all were one; had my supper sent up. Dear Cynthia brought it up herself, and as I lay there propped up on the pillows, she fed me with a spoon. It was so sweet, and how I loved her for it. She told me I should neither drink nor write, and try to get more sleep. The darling woman blamed herself for all that had befallen me; I told her she must not; and if she would but kiss me once, the world entire would be set to rights. She did; my eyes they must have shown it was not so; and so she kissed me once again before she left me.

I tried then to write my letter to dear Liz, but failing as I said, I lay there on the bed and tried to understand what I had seen. That marble slab, it so surprised me down there in the dark, I had forgot just then that I had written such a thing (so briefly) when Endimion Lee, a-dreaming, takes his chariot-flight about the world; the palace name-plate, I did not know if it was real or just absurd. Yet I had seen it with these very eyes; and more, the sight had been so real it made me faint away. How could it be that, down below the surface of the hill, beyond the ancient cellar door, there yet remained the antique traces of a palace (of a world; of a merest, nebulous fantasy) that *I had invented* and written down within the last three weeks? *That* is why I fainted. My mind it simply could not conceive how anything so strange, so extraordinary, could exist. And yet my own eyes had seen it. At least, so I thought. But who could say? Was it real? Was it a fantasy of my own devising? A dream? Or did I have the brain-fever I had not wished my Liz to think I had? At last, I decided that I simply could not tell. I knew I wanted Lizzie here with me, to tell me what was real and what was false, to hold me in her arms, and kiss me, and tell me all was well about the world; the same then that she always does when I am quite unwell.

Of course, that could not be. My Liz was far away; my only cure to hand was further sleep.

And that was not to be either.

I do not know how late it was, but as I lay there half a-doze, there was a sudden rattling at the door, which, though I'd locked it earlier, suddenly burst open. It seems dear Cynthia possesses duplicate keys, which, with afterthought, says little of the privacy and security promised hereabouts.

As I said, how late it was, I know not, but Cynthia was in that same nightdress I thought I'd seen before on Severndroog tower, all sheer and clinging in the Moonlight; I confess she looked quite charming. She told me then, in great excitement, that she'd just received strange news, by trusted messenger, directly from old London town.

Her husband, she informed me all agog, though hardly with regret, had been taken by the officers of the law, as a highwayman and a controller of highwaymen, a burglar and a common thief, and worse a murderer too, and was, upon the instant, immured in Newgate Prison. She babbled something of information laid against him, but I confess her décolletage distracted me, as it had when last I'd seen her in her night attire, and I remember little else except she said they'd surely hang him. Then she thrust that heavy, ancient key to the cellar door into my hand and begged me, if questioned thereabout, to hide it and deny all knowledge.

I naturally agreed (I think I would do anything she asked, and even risk my soul); and besides, the thought of some profane thief-catcher being let loose in that caverned underworld, unable to understand its glories or, worse yet, shattering those delicious depictions of Diana, was quite too much to bear. She kissed me hotly then, the more than once, and told me breathlessly how I was 'a darling boy' and how, before the month was out, she'd 'make my dreams come true'. I had no idea at all of what she spoke, but when she paused for breath I thought at last to ask her where Jude Brown had been arrested; she told me it was Oxford Street and, it seemed, not far away from my own house; and suddenly she was gone again, leaving me bewildered and alone, and quite unable to sleep.

What this means, I know not. My first thought was that already my dreams were all too true, and little has this to do with my charming and, I suspect, all-too-confusing Cynthia Brown. But second thoughts came rushing in to follow: that Jude Brown, discovering my address and thinking me a rich one, after failing with my trunk had then been on his way to rob my house. A third thought then appalled me: that breaking in and finding sweet young Liz, he could not help but rape her; and leaving behind then none to testify, he surely would have killed her. The thought, it made me sob and groan; for her presumed escape, I thanked the Goddess of the Moon, and whoever it might be who'd laid the information leading to her rescue.

I finally slept again, after I know not how long, and dreamt that Liz had come to me all naked, and thanked me for her rescue, and said that we could love, and even marry, siblings as we are, but not in quite the way that I had thought, if I would only give up something here and take a journey with her; and at the same time she was Cynthia, naked too, who told me that she and I could love and journey just the same, for some obstacle (I naturally have to think her husband was intended) had shortly been removed; and even more than this, she was Diana Regina, Mistress of Somnium and a Goddess who (I have to think) is a literary creation entirely my own, and the journey she wanted me to take it had its destination in that lustrous city of the lunar night wherein she reigns. To convince me of the message's earnest import she, or they (by which I intend the entire trinity) slipped sweetly into bed with me, kissed me, embraced me; and I woke up moaning, to find it then full daylight.

Young Tom Watkins, it seems, absconded in the night, suggesting that he, himself, might have been one of Jude Brown's cut-throat gang; all of which implies to me that the 'protection' he afforded me in previous days depended rather more on his involvement with the blackguards than his weaponry. I'll be glad if he makes his escape. He was a personable lad, and I would not see him swing, or anyone else so young and apt for leading all astray; and swinging, I gather from the officers who arrived from London late this morning, is Brown's predestined fate. The information laid against him, and the evidence found upon his person, apparently, put together, make the case conclusive. I know not where the information came from, though Cynthia, of course, denies responsibility; and, likewise, the greater part of me refuses to believe that any woman would betray her husband so. Another part, however, remembers how she looked when I did curse him in the cellar, and how these things have coincided. And that part too, it warms, I must confess, to think that if anyone knew Jude Brown's plans it must have been herself; and if a choice it then was made, between husband and myself, and that sweet sister who is the half of all my life, then I would love, because I had to, the person who had made that choice, for all it may have cost her. Yet this cost, I think, is something better left unthought of.

But thinking of that curse again, I cannot help but wonder. I wished him dead, although I could not say it quite unto his dear wife's face; the least I wished him instantly removed from all I had to do with. And so it seems he will be. This gives me much to think on.

Well, there's nothing I can do. They tell me Jude Brown's case is thought so serious that a special Sessions will be convened within a day or two; upon his certain conviction, the following day they'll bring him back here to the Londonward foot of Shooters Hill and hang him by the crossroads, just outside The Fox Under the Hill (coincidentally, that's just where I had Endimion Lee first board the silver coach; but whether there's significance in that, I hardly can conclude). Then they'll parade his corpse up past this very inn and take it down the Kentish side, and leave it hanging in a cage to rot on Gibbet Field, as a warning to all the others of his kind. I'll neither attend the hanging nor go to see his body crow-pecked; and nor, agreeably to me, will Cynthia Brown-eyes either.

The officers, of course, were searching for other members of Brown's gang who numbered, on occasion, some seven or more, I'm told, ranging everywhere from here to Blackheath and even as far as Deptford dockyards where, long gone, poor Kit Marlowe, daggered in the eye, expired, and took with him to other worlds all those wondrous words unwritten that might, perhaps, have been (I fancy if he had a Moon-play in him, it might be found at last in Somnium). All that Doctor Gould and the Woolwich army officer suffered too is laid at Jude Brown's door; and far more than this besides. Some of the things I heard the officers talk of simply do not bear repeating. They questioned me, as they did all the inhabitants of The Bull, but Cynthia (corroborated, I gathered, much surprised, by the unattractive Daphne Squires) swore the most atrocious oaths by that god I know we've both abjured, that I had arrived here with the falling leaves, and that I was a strange one (I winced to hear her say it) who rarely left my room, and a writer poetical who was, to my great good fortune, able to produce page after page of manuscript to confirm all this. Lastly, she asked them if they thought I looked a brigand; of course I was relieved when they said no and yet, somehow, I felt myself diminished.

Much more relief to me, of course, was to discover from the officers, by questions indirect, that Brown had been arrested before the perpetration of any London crime; and so my Lizzie, she is safe and well.

The officers' other task was, of course, to search for Brown's ill-gotten gains. Having already satisfied them that I knew nothing of the case, I was allowed to withdraw to my room, as a result of which I had no embarrassing questions to answer about the ancient cellar door; still less about its equally-ancient key. Cynthia told me afterwards that the officers battered at that door but, being made when last a true Queen sat the throne, with all the wondrous workmanship of that bold and mightiest imperium, it withstood all their efforts, impregnable in itself as she was virginal. No key being traceable (I had it hid beneath my mattress) they gave up at the last and, by middle afternoon, departed for the city; and I could tell, simply from their angry bickering as they left, that had they found the loot they sought, no great part of it would have been delivered by them to their masters. Thief-takers, I fear, take almost as much as the thieves they take in turn.

Cynthia brought a bottle of claret to my room when they were gone, and laughed aloud; I could instantly conjecture why. Those chests stored just beyond the cellar door had no part of their origin in the ruins of Somnium that lay beyond.

If Somnium exists. Ruined, whole, or merely dreamed. And if it does, then what place is this? Who is Cynthia? And who am I, and what then have I wrought? I do not know, and am no longer sure: am I here in The Bull Inn, new-built in 1749? Or far more ancient Somnium? Or Bedlam? Or fainted, lost in some bewildering delirium, never quite woke up? Or even written by another, two hundred years ahead? Or but a story in a palace of the Moon?

I asked sweet Cynthia, when the bottle was empty and I thought she might be prone to answer, how her feelings were on what had happened, and who she thought had consigned her husband to his doom. She laughed and put an arm around my shoulder, pulled me close and whispered all conspiratorial; swore me quite to silence, then murmured that Jude Brown had never been her husband and, as for who had laid the information, she simply did not care. Before I could ask her anything else at all, she kissed me swift and left me all alone.

Thursday, 11th October 1803

Last night I thought of many things; but most of all I wondered why I had not heard a word from Liz. I wrote to her again this morning, but hesitated far too much on what to tell her; so many things have happened (or at least, I think they have). In the end, I told her that I loved her, missed her, had so many things to tell her that, upon the instant she received my letter, she should hire a trusted guard and take the next and fastest coach to join me here. I know that many other rooms are standing empty in the inn (though I'd rather Lizzie shared my own); but what Cynthia would think of having Lizzie here, I simply do not know. More important to me, right now, is that I *need* my sister here to hold me in her arms.

And yet, right now, I am no longer certain-sure at all I actually have a much-loved younger sister, Elizabeth Melisandra Morley, brown-eyed, warm and sweet as honey, to whom my letter was addressed. But let me believe, because I have to believe in *something*, that I actually have. I signed my letter 'From your loving Kit' and sealed it with ten thousand passionate kisses, and all my hopes: that somehow she would be *there*, to receive it and to read it. And that she'd come, or at least write back and tell me that I am not mad, and that I have a sister who loves me (oh, I want to hear her say she loves me), and that all of this, and I myself, am really real and not just some fantasy made up by another.

I never should have left my Liz. Never. She is my dearest, darling sister, and now that I am gone I realise how sweet it was to be with her. And more, far worse than the thought that I myself might not exist, is that she might not either. And to think of a world without my Liz; that never had or never will have anyone as sweet as she; that is too much to bear. But if she's *not* and yet I *am*, then I think I'll soon be quite as she is.

But what if she were, and I was *not*? Now there's a thought. Oh, sweet beloved Lizzie, I know nothing of what may happen, to me, or you, or to the world itself. But if you read this, simply know: if ever I was, and had a reason to be, it was to love you. And I do.

Friday, 12th October 1803

Yesterday the inn was closed, which hardly was surprising. Having written my letter, I took it down to the Red Lion myself, there being no-one else to take it. It took me half an hour to extricate myself from Eustatius Wellbeloved and all his silly questions. I tried to tell him that I knew nothing of Jude Brown's notorious past; little less of what had happened in the last two days, and nothing again of what might happen next. His curiosity, though, was quite insatiable. I left him disappointed.

I returned and found The Bull apparently deserted. In my room I found a note from dearest Cynthia, telling me she was gone out ('to put things righter for the future'), and I should help myself to claret and a cold supper from the kitchen; and that she would see me 'in my dreams'. And so last night I wrote and drank and slept, and know that she was right; I remember little of my dreams, but lovely laughing Cynthia certainly was in them, and oh, she seemed so happy. I woke in pre-dawn light and wondered: if she could will to be there in my dreamworld, what other marvels might then follow?

I had some inkling when I woke this morning and found The Bull entirely filled with delightful female laughter. It seems that Cynthia's lengthy expedition was for no other purpose than replacing the inn's entire staff with personable young maidens of the most extraordinary beauty. Everyone hereabouts before, apart from Cynthia herself, is gone: Tom Watkins, Daphne Squires and Jacqueline Smythe, Bates the cellar-man, old Marguerite the ancient cook, and all, replaced with alluring lovelies all of whom, it seems, bear flower names: Rose, Lily, Violet, Iris, Ivy, Daisy and more than I can quite recall, all serving under their charming 'matron', an equally young maid called Flora who, it seems, prefers to dress in boots and britches, a man's shirt and a waistcoat. Shepherdesses are now found out there in the fields, lady-grooms bring out fresh horses, dear damosels set forth upon the cart to visit the warehouse in Woolwich; while housemaids, cooks and serving-wenches are all as eye-delightingly beautiful as the sweetly-scented flowers whose names they bear. All are dressed in purest white but Flora who, besides, has a brace of pistols chased with silver, in case some stranger seeks to trouble her sisters in the slightest. Apart from dearest Liz and Cynthia (who is infused, upon the moment, with a sudden, surprising, enormous and quite charming vivacity), I've never seen a lovelier collection of sweet young virgin maids.

I went downstairs before the inn was open, to discover the source of all this girlish hilarity. Dear Cynthia lined the gigglers up and introduced them one by one; and one by one they curtseyed smiling, hugged me close and kissed me on the cheek. I thought this was so lovely. I asked them if they all were given flower-names upon the day that they were born; it seemed to me unlikely. Every one of them assured me then this was indeed the case; yet every one they tittered as they said it, and so I ended up believing them not at all. Then Cynthia put an arm around my shoulder and told her lovely minions that I was a special guest and all of them should treat me like a brother; she winked so slyly when she said they were my sisters, I hardly knew quite what to think. In spite of this, I told them next I thought that, one and all, they'd charm the stars down from the sky. I started then to tell them other things besides, until I saw dear Cynthia pout. I stopped, of course; the lovely girls they tittered once again.

Cynthia and I we ate our dinner together in her parlour, and how she was so full of smiles. I asked again about her relationship with foul Jude Brown; she laughed and winked and said she was his sister. I said I simply could not believe her. She chuckled then and spooned some soup into my mouth; and after that I knew she would not answer. And when I asked her where she'd found her lovely flowers, she simply told me in the fields about, and plucked them here and there.

So after we had dined, I wrote an ode at her request, on Cynthia and all her lovely maids, to be found now at The Bull; some inspiration made my descriptions of them all partake of the divine. It was so easy, for all of them have beauties quite celestial. As soon as I had finished, dear Flora she appeared and took my words away to have them all transcribed by that delightful sisterhood. I gather now that copies of my words are already to be found in Woolwich, Charlton, Blackheath, Eltham, Welling, Plumstead, and who knows where else. Inspired by all that's happened in the last few days, my ode says Lady Luna and her Lovely Nymphs are now to be found residing in The Bull, where all the Beauty of the Moon is now exalted up in Taurus; I doubt that anyone hereabouts will have the astrology to understand any of this, but simply will they think that young and lovely virgins now will serve them with their wine and ale.

When all of this was done, I asked sweet Cynthia if she thought that she could run the inn without at least a single man to help; she laughed and said that she had me. I said indeed she had me for the while, but time would come when I would take me back to Liz. She smiled a little faintly at me then, mysterious; I did not know quite what to think.

This evening, when I went for supper, she would not let me eat out in the hotel dining-room. Rather now, she told me then, I would be eating only in her parlour, and we would share our meals; and furthermore, although next week I should be due to pay her once more for my room, I would not. She told me then I was no longer guest, but much-loved member of her 'family'. She said again her maidens were my sisters; I asked her then just what *she* was to me. She grinned and answered with a lover's kiss; then told me like a caring mother I should eat my supper now, and save my talk for later.

And when we'd eaten, then she said I should select whatever wine I wished, and take me off upstairs. If I would spend the evening writing, then she said, when the inn was closed she'd come and kiss me sweet goodnight. My part of the bargain's quite fulfilled; and now I wait for her, and hers.

He woke at last, his mind exhausted with his ravishment, his body all a-comfort. And sweeter yet besides, he saw Diana sat upon his bed. All smiles she was and loveliness.

A raven feather in her hair, her lovely breasts all laced about; a stitchet tight laced up and black silk stockings. And still he dreamed, he knew he did; and yet, perchance, he didn't.

He sat up, all bewildered quite, and stared and stared and stared. And while he did, she threw the bedclothes back and eyed him in his night-shirt.

'So one of us is dressed to please, while yet the other isn't!' she said then, and laughed a lovely laugh. 'No time for slug-a-beds, when queens are up and waiting… the bath for you, my boy!'

He blushed all red and could not speak; her kiss was consolation.

'Dear Queen,' he said at last, 'how can it be this morning that I find you dressed, or rather under-dressed, exactly as I dreamed you in the darkest night?'

'Sweet man,' she said, all winsome and all wistful, 'it's time you learned that what you thought was but a dream last night, and what you think the morning light makes true, they are the same. More obvious this should appear, the while you stay in Somnium, and yet I tell you this: *all* the world's a dream. High Olympus, or the starry and the planet spheres, we dream them; and all the Earth you think so real, why that's a dream as well. And if there is a single thing I'd have you learn while you are here with me, I'd like to make it this: the art of dreaming lovely dreams, and dreaming them all real. And now, before you form the question on your lips, the answer it is yes.'

'The answer it is yes?' he echoed then her words. 'But I have not asked a thing!'

'Oh dear Endimion Lee, my innocent and charming love, there is no need, because you have imagined. The thought of dream, and sweet desire, and all I've tried to teach you, they finally came together in your mind, although they did not reach your tongue.

'So yes, my love, I'll join you in the bath, the same as you desired from the first. And as a mark of my affection, I'll let you, too, undress me; but whether you can do this with your mind, or still will need your fingers, that we've yet to see. But first, sir knight, you must remove your night-shirt.'

Wide-eyed and open-mouthed, he looked upon her then; and no words could he utter.

'Oh, dearest man,' she sighed and simpered. 'Just think a thought for me. I like to see you naked, just the same as you do me. We ladies have our fond desires as well.'

At that he laughed, no other could he do; and when he did, he found that she laughed too. And laughter, laughed however, and whatever so the cause, it makes the world all innocent.

Away with bed-clothes then and night-shirt too; and so he faced her naked, and showed her what she liked. Her sandaled foot she next placed in his lap, and smiled all saucy-eyed.

'And now, my love, although I need not tell you: the straps of sandals, and of garters… but, oh, you know the rest…'

He wanted then to kiss each single inch of fairest leg that was revealed unto his sight, and yet she told him no. And when the disappointment shone there in his eyes, she sad and wistful told him: 'The wise man he accepts and takes what he is offered; the fool, he tries to take the more.'

'All lovers tempt to foolishness,' he said, 'for given joy, they seek for more. Take it complimentary then, and know, for you, my eternal adoration.'

'I know,' she said, quite simple. 'Now sit me up and take me in your arms. The rest, I think, you can do with your mind and thought; your fingers can caress me.'

He sat and pondered for a while, his eyes all closed, of how he was to do this. Imagination was the key, he knew; yet when he thought of her quite naked, desire got in the way. At last he gave it up, and thought it far more important just to have her in his arms, and just to have her love and love her. And on a sudden then, he opened up his eyes and looked, no longer dreaming (so he thought), on dear Diana naked. And never was a fairer sight, or sweeter under heaven: her rounded breasts, her incurved waist, her rotund shapely hips, her long curvaceous legs; he loved them to distraction. Yet none of these they matched her eyes, more glorious far than all the Moonlit nights that ever were, and all the stars that twinkled.

He kissed her for her loveliness, then looked at all her beauty quite exposed, and worshipped.

He worshipped all her lovely body, worshipped more her shining eyes; worshipped her entire soul and all her Goddess-head besides. Divine she was, divine she is, divine she always will be: the Moon, all young and old, a mother and a child, a mistress and a sister; all-changing and unchanged besides, the constant sweetheart of the mad and sane.

Raven's feather then she took from out her hair, pressed it to her lips and breast, put it in his hand and whispered: 'keepsake'. He kissed it too and called it: 'treasure', placed it safe aside.

And then, upon the sudden strong and manly, next he picked her up all naked in his arms. She laughed, she sighed, she kissed him, threw her arms around his neck and kissed him twice again. A sweeter armful heaven never made; she was too lovely.

'Sweet heart,' he told her then, 'in London town, the town of all the world, I thought I understood the love of women; thought I knew the love they offered, thought I knew what they required. And now I understand that they were only *women*, and you, my love, are *woman*. And though the difference is too strange for words, I know it in my heart.'

'You know it in your mind as well,' she told him, snuggled close. 'For they are women quite of flesh, and I am all of dream. My kisses, though, and all my love, partake of the supernal. I'd offer more besides, but now the Fates forbid it. The Fates allow me dream my way down from the Moon to here on Earth, and better yet, allow our interaction. But doing so, to share embraces and your eager kisses, I dream myself material; and while I am material, I must remain inviolate. And so, my love, the laws of fate, they make me virgin 'gainst my will. And yet, when you have passed beyond this heavy world of matter, then soul to soul and spirits all entwined, I'll love you all the better.'

He took her then into the bathroom, kissed her oh-so-hungry, clutched her softness with his hands.

'You know what happens next,' she said, her breath all short and eyes all wide.

'I do indeed,' he laughed, and threw her in the bath.

Her squeal was all the Music of the Moon.

The bath was long enough for her, though half enough for him. And then she left him, sweetly naked, to his dressing; left him to his morning meal besides; rejoined him in a long black cloak, the like he'd dreamed her in the night before. And then she took his hand in hers, and led him from the room.

A passage took them, then, to two large doors, which opened of themselves; Endimion Lee discovered then that Somnium had a theatre. *The Orb*, she told him it was called, a laugh about her lips, and told him he might see the joke, about the century's end; he shook his head, bemused.

She sat him down among an audience of fair Selenic nymphs, his seat before the stage. And yet she did not join him.

'My fair and scholar knight,' she said, 'we hope to entertain you. A short and tragical drama, but lately writ, though full of antique charm, it has a speaking cast of five. Three male parts are taken by my fairest nymphs, though painted in disguise; Melissa plays the maid; and I, myself… I play myself…'

She kissed him then and left, just as he guessed the author; but how she might have got the text, that never had been copied, he could not quite decide.

A Moon-maid offered wine, and so he did relax, and laughed, and stretched his legs, and so prepared himself to see…

LADY SELENE & THE PRINCE ENDYMION

ACT ONE

SCENE ONE: *The silver barge of the Moon, coursing through the starry night. SELENE sits beneath a curved stern-post. AURORA, her hand-maiden, nearby amongst TWELVE SILVER ROWERS.*

SELENE:	Eternity, who measures such a thing?
	An insect lives the summer days, and dies;
	Undying Gods pass æons in their dreams
	And bring the millennium when they wake.
	Yet only men (no more than God-spawn'd apes,
	A half-race mix'd in part of life and death,
	Of Heavenly-descent, yet Hades-bound)
	In all beneath the sky, alone they stand
	And count the hours, the days, the months and years.
	With calendars they seek to shackle time,
	With dials and gnomons, mathematic art
	And charted stars, they try, oh, how they try,
	To capture Chronos with a grasping hand
	And bend his aged shoulders 'neath the yoke
	Of measur'd science; proudly thinking this
	A great achievement that is all their own.

Yet in their time, too short alas for most,
How many pause to shake their heads and think
That all their human arts depend on this:
The movement of the Gods across the sky.
My fire-eyed brother, wheeling round the world,
Their days and years describes, both short and long;
And this, this sluggish silver barge of mine,
So slowly circumnavigates the month
And drags the leaden tides from high above
While cutting through the stellar seas of night.
And each and ev'ry night we follow on,
The course the same, the stars, the sky, the Earth.
No other life but this can I enjoy
Once darkness spreads across the world below.
Old Chronos shackled? No, Selene is,
Bound tight by Titan-overthrowing Zeus
And by his slaves, the grey unfeeling Fates.
The purpose of my round? Zeus knows alone.
And Zeus it is who wills 'the barge moves on',
With me as captive captain ever more.
Ah, what a waste is this 'eternal life',
When timeless Godhead empties—Hold! Who comes?

                    [AURORA approaches from among ROWERS]

AURORA: It is Aurora, Lady, by your leave.
               But, Mistress, did I see, a moment since,
               A tear of crystal, sparkling 'neath your eye?
               What sadness drains your so-pale cheek like this
               And draws up those sweet lips of yours so tight?

SELENE: I know not; but that Time's revolving wheel
               Repeats the evil like a jesting fool.
               We journey nightly, trailing brother Sun
               Now close, now far behind, from east to west,
               A darkling voyage upon an endless sea.

Eternal dusk; it is too much for me...

AURORA: But days are spent in bliss celestial
                 With merry feasts among the jesting Gods;
                 And if with twilight dim the barge arrives
                 Then let it carry too your memories!
                 Retain those treasures of the day-lit hours,
                 Fill dreams with them beneath the wand'ring stars...

SELENE: I'll not! Such memories as these bring gall.

AURORA: But why? They satisfy your company...

SELENE: Too fickle the affections of the Gods!
                 Too much are they in cups, too gross their jests!
                 Æonic dicing fritters time away,
                 Compliant Goddesses and nectar sweet...
                 No more will radiant Selene shine
                 At revels such as these! I'd rather spend
                 The sun-lit hours as mortals pass the night,
                 Dim-eyed, close-lipp'd, limbs bound by Hypnos' hand,
                 Than once again attend that rout of fiends
                 That unwise worldly men call 'Most-High Gods'!

AURORA: Oh say not so! Calm yourself, my Mistress!
                 You must remember that this very morn
                 Just past, great Hermes, fair of face, did give
                 You tokens of his fine and deathless love.
                 Accept his grace, and put your heart at ease!

SELENE: That trickster! Within hours I saw that cur
                 His kisses shower on an earthly maid!
                 And worse, she let him do as he desir'd
                 Or said he wish'd to do with me alone!
                 Zeus, Hermes, both alike! Away with them!

My time is better spent alone, it seems!

AURORA: Then they are poorer for it, I would think!

SELENE: So be it! I have palaces myself
              Where western waters deep receive the Moon
              Beyond the distant silver-sanded isles;
              And there I'll spend my hours with maidens pure
              Whene'er the world is by my brother blest!

AURORA: But, Lady, I have heard those lips divine
              Speak oaths like these a hundred times before...

SELENE: And meant them too! And kept my word, you'll mark,
              For many long years, only to relent,
              When humbl'd Gods, diminishing their pride,
              Gave such fine promises and blandishments
              That I believ'd their oaths all true. For shame!
              Their word is broken swifter than old Zeus
              Can wink a drunken eye and crack a smile!

AURORA: My Mistress, dare I say this anger seems
              To me not to the point. Some deeper grief
              Afflicts your heart, but what that wound may be,
              Alas, I cannot grasp. I wish I could...

SELENE: It is a mystery to me as well,
              And yet... speak on, perhaps some pleasant word,
              Some idle banter may discover yet
              The wriggling worm of discontent that gnaws
              At my sick heart, a plague as yet unknown...

AURORA: Ah, Lady, this seems far too great a task
              To impose on a humble serving maid.
              It is Athene who gives counsel wise,

As ever she did since that awesome day,
She sprang full-form'd from her cleft father's skull.
She too disdains the frolicking of Gods;
Perhaps to her you should confide your woe?

SELENE: No more than Artemis who romps with bears!
The one my ear with homely wisdom dulls,
With hunting tales the other offends me!
Words spring out from their supple tongues in hordes,
Each loose-lipp'd as the other! Fie on them!
A housewife and a bloody butcher-maid!
No wonder that the Gods will seek them not!
No time to kiss—their lips are fully used!
But none of these protective faults have I
And so I am pursued, my favours begg'd.
'Tis Aphrodite they should gaze upon.
To her, such glances never go amiss.

AURORA: Sweet Lady, you distress yourself with this.
Think not on it, but rather turn your mind
To pleasures tried and true. May not the stars
Be pluck'd and set into a sparkling crown?
The tails of comets wove into a scarf
That trails all sequinated through the sky?

SELENE: Enough! Such simple pastimes also cloy.

AURORA: Then let these silver rowers catch your eye,
That old Hephaestos did himself well forge
When this fair barge he made. See now the gleam
Of silv'ry muscles, all twelve pulling strong,
Superbly tim'd in silent rhythm swift...

SELENE: What use are such as they? They have no mind,
No voice, no life; they feel as much as stone!

I'd conjure them to stop if I but could!
Our height, however... that I can command.
So tell them now, Aurora, to descend.
We'll skim the mountain peaks and close survey
The world of peaceful sleep and dreaming men.

AURORA: No word of mine is needed here! E'en now
                   We drift down slowly from the starry sky...

SCENE TWO: *A windowed gallery in the Carian villa occupied by Endymion,*
Prince of Elis. Night. Enter ENDYMION, solo.

ENDYMION: My Soothsayer! Does sleep o'erwhelm you? Come!
                   It is your lord commands your presence here!
                                   [Enter PERSES, painter, running]

PERSES: What ails thee, Highness? But a half-hour since
                   You were abed, your eyes quite clos'd, asleep.
                   How comes it now I find you shouting here?

ENDYMION: 'Twas Apollonius I call'd, not you.
                   Confound it, Perses, where's my soothsayer?

PERSES: He comes, my lord Endymion. Be at peace.
                       [Enter APOLLONIUS, the soothsayer. PERSES to him]

PERSES: Our lord is raptur'd once again, I think,
                   As oft he's been since we from Elis sail'd!
                   Speak soft with him, old man, and soothe him well!

APOLLONIUS: If possible at all, I shall so speak.
                   But I can only tell him honestly
                   What heaven's portents do indeed foretell.
                   The soothing you must do, with rhyme and sketch,

As many times before. My art is sooth,
Not soothing; your fair talent is for that!
Fetch charcoal, linen, whate'er you may need
For swift performance of your wondrous art,
And him I'll gentle meanwhile.

[Exit PERSES]

APOLLONIUS *[Aside]*:   Wretched Prince!
How pale your face, how languorous your form!
Your temples hung about with darkling clouds,
Most certain signs of some impending woe.
This stately villa will not echo long
With your sad sighs and moanings dolorous.
It will be winter soon; I doubt it much,
Alas, that spring will find you living still.
But all is with the Gods. I'll speak to you.

[Re-enter PERSES]

APOLLONIUS: My Lord, your servant, bent-back'd already,
Bows deeper still! And also, Perses comes...

ENDYMION: Who sent for Perses? Still, it matters not.
You may stand by and listen to our words.
My sleep is visited with dreams, old man,
And you will tell your Prince their true import.

APOLLONIUS: No other words these lips will speak, my Lord.
But tell me first, why gaze so fixedly
Upon the full-orb'd Moon that nestles still
Among the woody growth of Latmos Hill?

ENDYMION: Because my vision's subject was herself,
O ancient one! Be patient, for you'll hear
Each little detail. All, from start to close.

APOLLONIUS: Do this, my Lord, omitting not one word.

ENDYMION: You know I lay me down to sleep at dusk,
                   O'erwhelm'd by a delicious drowsiness.
                   Yet as I clos'd my eyes the Moon appear'd,
                   More brightly glowing than that vision fair
                   Which hugs the hills e'en now. The shining whelm'd,
                   'Came blinding and, before my eyes, dissolv'd
                   In glinting curtains, sparkling fiery pure,
                   That faded fast away in vacant air.
                   I saw ahead a sea all flashing stars
                   And I like wing-foot Hermes cross'd the swell
                   In flight, it seem'd, toward a silv'ry barge
                   Which rode the gentle waves, oars plashing soft.
                   And there Selene I beheld, most sweet...

APOLLONIUS *[Aside]*: I like this not, good Perses! Not at all!

PERSES *[Aside]*:   Nor I, for she hath wander'd through his dreams
                   Too many times, though always veil'd in mist
                   Or passing half-seen through a ruck of clouds...

ENDYMION: Such dazzling beauty is not often seen
                   By mortal men, I know; and yet I gaz'd
                   And saw the fairest face that ever grac'd
                   The lovely form of womankind...
                                                        [Pause]

APOLLONIUS: Speak on,
                   Good Prince, ere rapture draws you more away...

ENDYMION: I hover'd, calling, but she heard me not.
                   'O fair Selene, Lady of my heart!'
                   And other such endearments pass'd my lips,
                   To no avail. Her lovely ears were clos'd

To every word I spoke. I watch'd her still,
And then a hand-maid suddenly appear'd.
She had a crystal tray on which she bore
A bunch of grapes to quench her lady's thirst.
And when the Goddess rais'd them to her lips...
Those fruits, I swear, I could have picked at home.

APOLLONIUS [Aside]: At home in Elis? No, I like this not...

APOLLONIUS: How many grapes did this bunch then contain?

ENDYMION: Some fifty perhaps, I know not. My eyes
Were fully fix'd upon those redd'ning lips
Instead of that which painted them that hue.
And juicy were those grapes; she suck'd them dry.

APOLLONIUS: How many so?

ENDYMION: Why, all of them!

APOLLONIUS [Aside]:   Alas!

ENDYMION: Then lips full scarlet like a blossom wild,
She stood, and bade the rowers cease their toil.
The barge, becalm'd, then drifted; while the sea,
Already still, grew mirror-like and show'd
A fair reflection of her lovely form.
And sweet Selene, stripping off her dress,
All naked slipp'd into a silv'ry sea.

APOLLONIUS: You saw all this, my Lord?

ENDYMION: I did indeed,
And saw the ripples that her frolics made
All sparkling bright amid the ocean's glow

As like a dolphin pale she cut a wave.
Then close I swoop'd; her beauty nothing hid…
A grace unknown in this sub-lunar world,
For all Earth's maidens fair beneath her stand.
And when her small hand beckon'd, I plung'd steep,
And lost all sense in darkness submarine,
Swift sinking down, and down, and down…

PERSES [*Aside*]:   To drown…

ENDYMION: I woke, and found myself abed, alone,
And utterly despairing. Tell me now,
Good Apollonius, what you make of this.

APOLLONIUS: I trust you will allow a moment, Lord,
As I must contemplate each item here.
                    [*APOLLONIUS & PERSES withdraw to one side*]

APOLLONIUS: I fear this vision, Perses, bodes not well.

PERSES: But why? 'Tis said to dream of Gods brings luck!

APOLLONIUS: Of Gods, perhaps; of Goddesses not so.
To view their naked beauty utter sin!
Lewd Actæon was torn apart for such,
And Cadmeian Teiresias grew blind!
The vine of Elis… this must be our Prince.
The fifty grapes… the store of years he hath.
The juice suck'd out… their fullness drain'd away.
The years his due, like morning dew itself;
And just as dew turns vaporous at dawn
I fear his life by sunrise will be spent.
Alas, the dream's dark ending does confirm…

PERSES: By Zeus, you cannot tell him that, old man!

APOLLONIUS: This life of mine is led by honest stars
                And so I can do naught but speak the truth.
                If these plain words should cut my thread of fate,
                We'll meet again beneath the Earth as shades.

PERSES: Now, wait! Err only thus if you'd not lie:
                A little truth with much forbearance mix,
                Revealing nothing of his coming end.
                And should the present night turn out his last,
                At least he'll pass it all in merriment!

APOLLONIUS: So be it then. But I'll not stay to watch
                Infernal Hades snatch his soul away.
                If you can bear, till overwhelming sleep
                Strikes gently at you both, amuse him well;
                See him to bed, and know a blameless dawn.

ENDYMION: Good Apollonius, speak! What means this dream?

APOLLONIUS: It means your present troubles soon will end,
                My Prince. A true dream, surely, much disguis'd.
                The outcome fated, such is heaven's will.

ENDYMION: Just this? Explain the more, or I'll grow wroth!

APOLLONIUS: I... cannot...

ENDYMION: Fie! You mean you dare not, man!
                Come, out with it! I'll know it, good or bad!

APOLLONIUS: My Prince, pray do not question me on this!

ENDYMION: I will, in truth, have truth from servant's lips!
                You are commanded! Speak!

APOLLONIUS: As you so wish.
                My poor doom'd Prince, I cannot lie to you.
                This dream is evil and your life is short.

ENDYMION: What blasphemy is this? It cannot be
                That visions fair and sweet as this bode ill!
                You jest, old man, but jokes become you not!
                On pain of death make quips no more, old wretch!

APOLLONIUS: My life is yours, my Prince, as is my love;
                And knowing this, you'll know I would not jest!

ENDYMION: This cannot be believ'd! You are mistook!
                What use is wrong divining? Get thee hence!
                Away with you, old fool! I'll listen not
                To dotards' rambling errors! Now, begone!
                And should bright dawn still find you 'neath this roof,
                I'll have you strung!

APOLLONIUS: So be it, Lord. Farewell!
                I lov'd you much, but cannot bear this ire.
                To Athens I'll go; you, I fear, to death…

PERSES [to APOLLONIUS]: A fine night's work is this, my aged friend!
                How swiftly does your ancient brain forget
                Wise counsel. There's no setting this right now!

APOLLONIUS: What matter? This is but unfurling fate
                And nothing can be done. All's lost with him.
                I've spoken true and yet his ear is deaf.
                Alas, divining ever was like this:
                For good words welcome, but for ill words rue!
                So farewell, Perses! Loyal be, and true!
                      [Exit APOLLONIUS. PERSES to ENDYMION]

PERSES: My Lord, I think this harsh dismissal wrong,
                     Although I know I risk much saying this.

ENDYMION: Who's this? Oh, Perses, it is you, my friend.
                     I had forgot that you were still at hand;
                     So brightly does the Moon attract my gaze.
                     I think I almost see her once again,
                     She was so fair…

PERSES [*Aside*]:   Alas, unworldly Prince…

ENDYMION: What brings you here, good Perses? Did I call?

PERSES: You call'd… at random, Lord, and so I came.
                     Yet being here, mayhap I can you serve
                     With my unrhythmic rhymes and sketchings poor.

ENDYMION: A sketch? Why, yes! I'll have that Goddess sweet
                     On whose fair form I raptly gaz'd in dream.
                     Draw beautiful Selene if you can…

PERSES: I hardly dare to, but at your command
                     Will try my best. Describe her as you saw…

ENDYMION: Too coarse are words, alas, for such a task.
                     Image the fairest woman ever seen,
                     Then elevate her to a form divine;
                     Still raise her, till fair Aphrodite seems
                     No more entrancing than a milking maid…

PERSES: More subtle be, my Prince, lest you incur
                     That much-adored lady's vengeful wrath!
                     Choose words precise and simple terms: her hair,
                     Her form, her face, her raiment's cut and cloth…

ENDYMION: Not tall, yet shapely: pale her so-smooth skin.
      Her flowing hair, loose-tumbling, dark about
      Her shoulders, framing her pert smiling face;
      Fair-cheek'd, sweet-lipp'd, soft brown her star-bright eyes.
                  [PERSES draws]
      Her dress was like an Attic girl's, and yet
      Of dazzling cloth with pearly gleaming hue,
      Loose-gather'd with a girdle crystalline
      That star-like flash'd upon her rounded hip;
      About her neck, pale gems and turquoise blue.
      And like the Moon half sea-sunk, barely seen,
      Or rising from enveloping cloud-bank,
      There rose, it seem'd, from beneath that bright dress
      Two lunar orbs, as I have never seen,
      Or ever think I could, on mortal maid.
      The Moon again upon her brow appear'd
      In horns of gold—but now, enough, no more!
      The mere remembrance brings me grief so great
      I wish no more to live. This dust-blown Earth,
      This empty world, this prison vile...

PERSES: My Lord!
              [Shows him the picture]
      Instruct me, Lord, How seems this sketch to you?

ENDYMION: The nose a little smaller make, the eyes
      A little larger... aye, 'tis well enough.
      It is the finest portrait I have seen
      And lacks but little; even so I think
      No picture drawn by human hand would do
      Full justice to my lunar Goddess sweet...

[ENDYMION takes the picture and stares at it silently for some moments]

PERSES: At dawn I'll have it hallow'd by the priest
                   And placed amongst the temple deities...

[ENDYMION hurriedly rolls the picture and thrusts it into his tunic; then
turns away toward window]

ENDYMION: Do not so trouble yourself without cause.
                   My dream has sanctified it well enough.
                   Instead I'll shrine it next my loving heart.
                   How strangely lingering the Moon doth seem
                   Upon the slopes of Latmos, like a lamp;
                   As if reluctant to ascend the sky...

                                                   [Turns back]
                   The stable, Perses! Fetch my horse at once!
                   Perhaps the Goddess waits for me this night!
                   Why, yes, my dream is much disguis'd in truth;
                   Upon an earthly mountain, not the sea...
                   And yet, are not all mountains merely this?
                   Uprising islands in a sea of stars?

PERSES: Be calm, my Lord! Your rapture overwhelms...

ENDYMION: Yes, raptur'd now, with raptures still to come!
                   Why stand there, dullard Perses? Fetch my horse!
                   Methinks I'll gallop 'neath the night-dark sky!

PERSES: My Lord, this is not wise, for who can tell...

ENDYMION: Obey me, Perses! Wretched man! Obey!

PERSES: Restrain yourself, my Prince! Here safety lies,
                   Yet outside who knows what the Fates intend?

ENDYMION: The Fates? They promise bliss for brave men, or,
                   They promise death for fools! What care have I?

I laugh at fate, not fate at me. I'll ride.

PERSES: If so you are resolv'd, I'll to it straight,
                   Though begging you again to stay at home…

ENDYMION: I'll not! The stars will guide my course right well!

PERSES *[Aside]*:   Then ride out, Prince, but I'll be close behind;
                   Where'er your will doth lead, there follow I!

                                                         [Exeunt]

ACT TWO

SCENE ONE: *Night. The slopes of Mount Latmos. A rock, to one side. Enter SELENE and AURORA, opposite, wrapped in black cloaks.*

AURORA: Alas, methinks this night's adventuring,
                   If not ill-suited, is at least unwise.
                   To leave the silv'ry lunar barge invites
                   The wrath of Zeus and risks all cosmic law;
                   To even grace a lonely peak so wild
                   With your supernal beauty tempts the Fates
                   To wretched plots and trickeries connive.
                   Not like to high Olympus is this place…

SELENE: Fie, girl! The lunar barge no steersman needs,
                   Nor need those silver slaves a word's command.
                   Let Zeus upon it unattended come
                   If he can cease his wenching long enough
                   To cast his dull wine-clouded eye about!

AURORA: E'en so, this place is wild and brooding strange,
                   Grotesquely shadow'd with a wind so chill…

SELENE: Is this the speech of an immortal maid?
               Go tend the Moon-barge if you like it not!

AURORA: I think of your good comfort, nothing more.

SELENE: Adventuring's my comfort this strange night;
               It smoulders within like a latent fire.
               And if these chill winds fail to fan it bright,
               Mayhap we'll find our warmth in lovers' arms
               Before my sister wafts the night away!

AURORA: Oh Mistress, now I know you can but jest!
               Now, who upon this lonely peak is there
               To shower your sweet Goddess-charms upon?
               A lonesome shepherd ill-deserves such bliss;
               Or would you take a black-heart bandit foul?

SELENE: Why not? And boast it in the halls of Zeus!
               Or taunt that split-tongu'd Hermes with his pledge,
               A stolen gem-stone dangling round my neck!

AURORA: Oh, Mistress, no!

SELENE: Be not so simple, girl!
               E'en so, I sense the weaving Fates conspire
               To cast a web around this mountain height—
               A web most curious, like Arachne weaves—
               Yet what the warp, and what the weft, who knows?
               Nor what it catches, netted unaware...
                                     [Sound of hoof-beats, off]

AURORA: Now listen, Mistress, someone rides this way.

SELENE: We are invisible; it matters not.
               Besides, the speed he rides he'll pass us by,

And vanish swift in darkness thick and deep,
To slip away like dim forgotten dreams,
And leave us wond'ring why he rides so swift.

[Hoofbeats cease]

AURORA: Perhaps not so! He draws rein, stops, dismounts...
He comes this way, my Lady! Let's be gone!

[AURORA draws SELENE to one side. Enter ENDYMION opposite]

SELENE: No, wait, Aurora, here is much to please;
He's nobly form'd and has a princely air.

AURORA: He looks to me, my Mistress, much the same
As any other mortal I beheld.
Be not deceiv'd by looks! Full handsome too
Is Hermes who you do abhor so much!
And this young rider—why, in face and build,
They strike me much alike!

[ENDYMION sits upon a rock]

SELENE: What nonsense, girl!
I tell you straight, with aid of sight divine,
This cannot be that wretched God disguis'd!
But look how sorrow creases his fair brow!
Observe how desolation o'er him hangs!

AURORA: I'd guess him lovesick, Lady!

SELENE: Hold! He speaks!

ENDYMION: O heaven that looks down on fools, look well!
'Great Prince Endymion', lord of widespread lands
So far across the sea—now all I have—
A little rock, and an unruly heart.

SELENE: A prince, you see? No ill-bath'd shepherd this!
                  I wonder what afflicts his tragic soul?

AURORA: 'Tis love, I swear, and that will equal strike
                  At prince or fool, unmanning both alike.

ENDYMION: It seems this ride was but an idle whim,
                  My loneliness to drown in lonely night—
                  It cannot be! But where then shall I find
                  The solace comforting a splinter'd heart?
                  A crowded palace seems an empty waste,
                  A lonely peak too crowded with ill thoughts.
                                    [Takes out picture, looks at it]
                  Here only, in her image, in her eyes,
                  Is cooling balm that my delirium soothes,
                  Yet also fuels its fires and burns me too!

SELENE: How contradict'ry is this lovesick man!
                  Disguise yourself now like a vagrant wind,
                  Aurora—go to him, and from his hand
                  This image snatch away. In truth, I'd see
                  What doe-ey'd creature plain can smite him so!

AURORA: It seems a cruel jest on this poor wretch…

SELENE: A wretch? A prince should have a sterner heart!
                  What's stolen by the wind can soon return
                  And anguish him for moments only, girl!
                  A single glance will more than satisfy!
                  Now be about it, else this cherish'd sketch
                  Will vanish 'neath his doublet once again!
                                [AURORA crosses, snatches the picture, and returns]

ENDYMION: What, no! It cannot be! Oh, cruel wind
                  That mocks me, snatching off this one small joy!

Oh, jesting Fates, your wit is far too grim!
[ENDYMION gets to his feet and starts searching for the picture]

AURORA: I have it, Mistress, but I like this not!
Observe how agonis'd he now becomes!

SELENE: It seems this girl has power to bewitch
That Aphrodite's envy would arouse!
We'll see—

[Looks at picture]
By Zeus and all his thunderbolts!

AURORA: Is this some monster that offends your eye?
Who is this tyrant queen that rules him so?
[SELENE shows her the picture]

SELENE: It seems it is no other than—*myself*!

AURORA: Yourself? Why surely this is mockery!
I swear no mortal dares aspire so high!
The features are a little part alike,
But beauty as she is, 'twould flatter her
If with your lovely self she was mistook!

SELENE: The mortal hand has but a little slipp'd,
Unus'd to rendering the higher ones.
Myself it is, no other! This I know...

AURORA: I dare to say you have an error made.
This picture is coincident, no more!

SELENE: He speaks again!

ENDYMION: Selene, dearest dream!
Oh, blackest night! Now even your sweet image

Is stolen away by the looting wind!

SELENE: He speaks my name! It is myself! It is!

AURORA: What kind of brute is this, that leaps so high?
               Oh, strike him down, my Lady, with all haste!
               Such pride must swift be punish'd, lest it grow.
                                    [SELENE gives picture to AURORA]

SELENE: Be hush'd! Throw down the picture at his feet.
               I cannot bear to see such great despair
               As settles now about this raptur'd prince!
               Be swift, Aurora! Get about your work!
               [AURORA tosses picture. ENDYMION picks it up, kisses it]

ENDYMION: My Goddess! Now at last you reappear
               As when you burst forth from the banked clouds.
               Perhaps the Fates are smiling once again!

AURORA: See how he kisses it! Disgusting sight!
               That ever man should be so arrogant!

SELENE: Perhaps he is a mite bemus'd, indeed,
               But there's no cause to take offence at that!

AURORA: Yet see! He kisses your fair image so,
               Again and again, and again still more!
               All with such passion and enthusiasm,
               And taking liberties as such he might
               When merely fondling willing palace maids!

SELENE: Well, is he not a prince among his kind?
               And were I one among his serving girls
               I think I'd gladly to his will succumb!
               For there is tender passion in this prince

That all his raptur'd cries can ill disguise.

AURORA: These words, I think, are quite the strangest kind
                  That e'er I heard escaping from your lips!
                  I'd almost think you willing to agree
                  To changing places with a palace slave!

SELENE: Perhaps I would, for kisses such as these!

AURORA: Oh say not so! You cannot think of this!
                  Not bow the knee to mortal will and whim
                  And let his hands caress your form divine!

SELENE: Such high alarm, Aurora, only spurs
                  Me further to adventures strange! Besides,
                  I am a Goddess, not a mortal slave,
                  And he it is who'll bend the knee to me!

AURORA: Oh, Lady, you'll not…

SELENE: Fie, now! Silence, girl!
                  Methinks I'll bandy kisses with this prince!
                                  [SELENE moves toward ENDYMION]

SELENE [Whispers]: Benighted prince, why clutch you so this daub
                   And press your lips against its lifeless cloth?

ENDYMION: Because it is my fair—
                                             [Looks round]
                                  Whose voice is this,
                  Both soft and sweet like notes struck from a lyre,
                  That floats so lightly with the midnight breeze,
                  Yet emanates from nothing, so 'twould seem…

SELENE: Why, prince, did ever nothing speak so fair?

Perhaps your sight is dimm'd by lover's tears.
Fear nothing if you cannot see my form;
I bring no harm and swear it by the name
Of that fair Goddess who you hold most dear.

ENDYMION: I must be craz'd! The darkness seems to speak,
             Its voice most like a mellifluous girl!
             And yet, if real, where came that voice sublime?
             No vile deluding-hag would swear such oaths.
             Then could this be a mountain-sprite, perchance,
             Or vapid nymph, ris' from a sparkling stream?
             Aye, that's it! Nymph, though beautiful you be.
             You are as nothing to the one I love!
             Away, dull nymph! This prince is not for you!

SELENE: Is there no curiosity in you?
             Not e'en to glimpse the one who speaks these words?

ENDYMION: Were even Aphrodite standing here,
             Her magic girdle only 'bout her hips,
             Not even this would tempt my love to change!

SELENE: How now? Who is this woman you adore
             And raise above the Golden One divine?

ENDYMION: No mortal maiden, but a Goddess sweet;
             The fairest quite among great heaven's host,
             Selene, Queen of Night—'tis she I love!

SELENE: O bold and shameless man! How can you dare?
             Repent, lest Zeus should hear, and strike you dead!

ENDYMION: Then let him, I care little. Life or death
             Are much the same if love is not return'd.
             I love Selene—let the lightning strike!

For without her I am already dead.
Away now, nymph! Torment my mind no more!

SELENE: These words are harsh for one who loves you so!

ENDYMION: Forgive this mortal fool, it must be thus.
Selene has this heart of mine in thrall;
My eyes will look no further for a queen...

SELENE: Then lift those eyes and gaze at she you love!
[SELENE opens cloak, revealing shining dress]

ENDYMION: What awesome light is this that dazzles bright
These eyes of mine, long-dimm'd by bitter tears,
Its shining like the silv'ry Moon above?

SELENE: I am none other than the Moon herself,
The Goddess you have worshipp'd from afar!
Your bright Selene stands before you now...
[ENDYMION prostrates himself]

SELENE: Oh, come great prince, has your ambition flown?
Your chance is here to take—no grov'lling now!
I'd think you but ador'd an ankle fair,
Or does my robe's low hem attract your love?
Rise up, Endymion! Clutch me 'gainst your breast!

ENDYMION: O beauteous Goddess—this I cannot dare!

SELENE: For shame! I thought you bold and true of heart!
I tire of being Mistress of the Moon;
A prince's mistress now I wish to be!
Rise up, I say! And kiss these hungry lips!

ENDYMION: How can I dare? Those lips are too divine

To sully with a lowly mortal's kiss!

SELENE: In truth, I hope you'll dare much more than this,
               When love's sweet magic overcomes your awe!
               Be bold and rise, or never more set eyes
               On she you worship, she you idolise!

                                           [ENDYMION stands]

ENDYMION: Such loveliness of face I ne'er have seen,
               Nor form so sweet—I scarce can draw a breath!
               Too profligate is fortune now I fear!
               Such bliss must surely fade and be no more;
               I fear such fortune; fear to use it up!
               I fear the more I have, the less remains!

SELENE: Now hush, Endymion! No talk now of fear!
               All things I permit! Kiss your Goddess straight!

                                              [They kiss]

AURORA *[Aside]*: How strange to see my mistress so entwin'd!
               Observing this the Gods would snigger loud!
               But from such folly no one can be sav'd
               If once their heart is set upon this course.
               And I can only watch the hilly slope
               And see no gross intruder spoils their sport…

                                          [Exit AURORA]

ENDYMION: O nect'rous kiss! These lips ambrosia drip,
               And make my former life mere nothingness
               Compar'd with this one moment's radiant bliss!
               These sweetest lips begin my life anew.
               I'll kiss you once again, my Goddess fair,
               And should I die the instant after this,
               I'd think the time between such kisses sweet
               A life well-spent, and ask for nothing more.

[Kisses her again]

SELENE: But more there is, my now-embolden'd prince!
             Another kiss will double your new life.
                                      [Kisses continue]
             It's trebled now, and I'll not stop until
             You're quite immortal made with fond repeats!

ENDYMION: This smothering of kisses, lovely one,
             Entrances, leaves me little time to think.
             Oh, could those palace-scoffers see their prince,
             His arms about his Goddess, tight-embrac'd,
             They'd tear their eyes in jealous disbelief!
             Indeed, I scarce believe this for myself,
             That such a wond'rous dream should turn out true!

SELENE: A Goddess truly, but a dream I'm not!
             Is not the flesh I have both soft and warm?
             And now it longs for passionate caress,
             So come away to some wind-shelter'd spot
             And give free rein to amorous delight...
                                      [Exeunt kissing, left]

SCENE TWO: *The same spot, some time later. The picture of Selene on the ground. A glow, as of Moonlight, at left. Enter AURORA, right.*

AURORA: But once I've travell'd swift around this peak,
             And yet my mistress' voice already drops
             To private whispers, soft seductive sighs...
             How oft does silence interrupt her words,
             Her lips now gagg'd by mortal kisses hot!
             Those kisses turning giggles swift to moans,
             Those moans each moment far more passion'd grow;
             She gasps and some new liberty allows,
             That liberty now taken brings a sigh...

Well, let them frolic so, this must be fate.
There's naught to do but circuit once again.

                                            [Exit left]
                        [Enter PERSES, right, with bow and quiver]

PERSES: My master following, I have arriv'd
                On Latmos' peak, and found his tether'd horse;
                But of my prince himself, no sign at all.
                Perhaps no longer does he walk this Earth;
                Yet servant's duty calls me, honour too,
                To seek my prince on this wild mountain peak.
                I'd curse the Moon that thus afflicts him so,
                Yet rather give it thanks for shedding light—

                        [Sees picture on the ground, picks it up]

                But hold! What's this I see upon the ground?
                Selene's picture that I drew myself
                So little time ago—now cast aside!
                An ill-foreboding steals upon my heart!

                                    [Crosses toward left]

                And see, this light which first I thought the Moon
                Instead upon the mountain has its source!
                I fear that sprites make mischief here tonight,
                And terror makes me reach for bow and shafts!
                Perhaps an arrow will defend my prince,
                Or better still myself, if need should rise.
                But soft, I hear a voice upon the wind...

                                    [Peers through bushes, left]

ENDYMION [*Off*]:   O eyes, o lips, o flesh! O bliss divine!

PERSES: Is this my prince entangl'd with a wench?
                'Tis strange, but—nay! No earthly girl is this!
                The glow I saw which lights these hills so bright
                Doth shine out from that woman's monstrous form!
                'Tis some foul mountain-sprite disguis'd most fair,

My prince entrancing, sucking out his life!
I see the old diviner's words come true;
She drags him down to dark oblivion sure,
And all too willing goes he, like a fool!
Yet how can such a one as I now help?
Were I a fighting man mayhap I'd charge,
My blood run hot, and swift this demon slay...
But sight of this foul witching, I admit,
My knees doth shake, and chills me through and through.
A shaft must speak on my behalf instead
And may the Gods and Fates make true my aim!

[Draws arrow and nocks it]

Forgive me, prince, for though it seems to you
I steal your joy away, these joys are false,
Are best forgotten and will vanish straight
When this good arrow hits the demon-mark!

[Shoots, toward left. SELENE screams, off]

My shaft is true, I think, all praise the Gods!
Well done is this, deserving good reward!

[Enter AURORA, running, from right]

AURORA: What deed unspeakable is this, you wretch?

PERSES: Another! Coming on me fury-like,
And I've no time to draw a second shaft!

AURORA: I hear my mistress scream and find a cur
With murd'ring weapon tightly clasp'd in hand!
Whate'er's occurr'd, vile man, you'll know this true—
By dawn your soul in Hades will reside!

PERSES: I pray to all the Gods 'tis otherwise!
But prayer goes oft unanswer'd—let these feet
Assist these finest words with swiftest flight!

[Exeunt running]

SCENE THREE: *A cave on Mount Latmos. Enter SELENE (front) and AURORA, carrying ENDYMION between them, an arrow in his back.*

AURORA: My Lady, should it comfort you at all,
                 Then know the wretch who shot this shaft is dead!
                 Pursued by me, he pass'd your grieving self,
                 Saw all too well his deed's result, most foul,
                 Then running swift he came upon a cliff
                 And plung'd all screaming into Hades' maw!

SELENE: It comforts me, Aurora, not at all!
                 O awful night! O vile and cackling Fates!
                 A bronze-tipp'd shaft has stole your life away,
                 Beloved prince, but still the fault is mine...

AURORA: The fault is yours, My Lady? Say not so!
                 How can this be? I saw the one myself
                 With bow in hand and holding still like shaft!

SELENE: The fault is mine, I say, it surely is!
                 If I'd not dallied on this night-dark Earth,
                 Abandoning my barge and proper state,
                 This handsome prince would now be living still!

AURORA: Restrain these tears now; 'tis the shaft, not you...

SELENE: Foul shaft! This wood was once a living tree,
                 These feathers once a flying goose adorn'd;
                 Now dead, they both together have conspir'd
                 To aid that black-heart murd'rer kill my love!
                 Away! I cannot bear this bloody sight!
                                 [Pulls out arrow and throws it aside]

AURORA: His soul has fled away then, Lady mine?

SELENE: It yet remains, but life will not return.
              His noble soul still flutters here within,
              Retain'd by love and powers mine alone;
              Yet nothing can revive this handsome frame!
                        [Cradles his head to her breast and weeps]
              Ah woe! We barely had begun to love,
              Some fifty kisses given and receiv'd,
              When like some vicious parody of Fate—
              Like little Eros' dart—an arrow struck
              And found his heart, the seat of all his love,
              And still'd life's bubbling fountain, lightning-swift!

AURORA: Why not to high Olympus travel now
              And beg almighty Zeus on bended knee
              Restore his life, and love return to you?

SELENE: Ah no, for Father Zeus would merely laugh
              And call me fool to love a mortal so!
              Besides, it cannot be, for should I leave,
              My dear Endymion's soul would slip away
              And darkest Persephone clutch it tight!

AURORA: Then what's to do, my Mistress? All is lost!

SELENE: Aye, lost for me, at least! All lost as soon
              As sweet Endymion's life was snatch'd away,
              My arms embracing him, my lips on his!

AURORA: And yet perhaps this bitter grief will fade
              To naught with passing time and length'ning years.
              Away now, let the silver barge—

SELENE: Be still!
              Unfeeling girl! Have you no wits at all?

How plain that love has never touch'd your heart!
Can you not see? Endymion sleeps for now,
And while I yet remain he'll slumber still;
My touch divine alone retains his soul—
By leaving I consign him straight to hell!

AURORA: Forgive me, Mistress, for I did not think.
And yet this cave is no appealing place,
E'en with your love, to pass away the years...

SELENE: Then should you wish, Aurora, leave and go
To high Olympus, barge, or Earth below.
I give you freedom, but myself will stay
And with this sleeping prince I'll make my home.

AURORA: But, Mistress, think, how long can this endure?

SELENE: How long? Why, through eternity, of course!
Eternity... now, after all, it's short!
Nay, hardly time enough to hold my love
And count out kisses press'd upon his lips!
Perhaps a kiss will stir his soul to dream;
In dream he'll know Selene loves him still.
Yes, now I see it clear: a life of sorts
Can dear Endymion still enjoy in sleep.
Ah, lips still warm, now feed upon my kiss!
Here's one, my prince, and two, and more to come;
And with our arms entwin'd and lips press'd close
We'll share this cave on Latmos ever more.
Eternity. Who measures such a thing?

CURTAIN

Endimion Lee, he watched all lachrymose, to see his own play so performed, and more, the lovely Moon played so sweetly by herself. And when she joined him afterwards, and kissed his tears away, he asked her why she'd done so.

'To encourage you to further efforts,' first she said, 'for as we know that by 'Selene' you hint 'Elizabeth', so in time you'll do again, by other lunar names; and this is what I'll ask of you. But more of this anon.

'And more, to give you confidence in what you wrote, before you offer it to the Queen herself. To give a first performance in the Lands of Moon and Dream; and is that not amusing? To consecrate your work, as well; for if your Goddess was not pleased, she'd hardly deign to act it. And last, to show you that, writ or not, we really do have all your works stored safe here in the library.'

And then she kissed him once again, and asked him how he thought her acting was; and he could only kiss her, oh so sweetly, in reply.

Saturday, 13th October 1803

At one this morning, Cynthia kept her promise; came into my room all night-dressed, kissed me fondly, glanced at what I'd written, said I was by far too much in love with Diana of the Moon, and in these hypocritic days I'd surely cause a scandal. I told her that I hardly cared; two readers were enough for me, and well she knew the other.

She smiled and then expressed surprise at just how much I'd written; as if somehow I'd cheated. I forthwith did confess the *Endymion* play I'd written back at home, not long after I escaped from school, and brought it in my trunk. I'd never thought to place it in my *Somnium*, but something (someone?) told me there it did belong. And because I always trust these 'whispers of the other', so it was included. She nodded then, sighed something of a 'youthful effort', said she understood now just why Selene rode a barge, and not the chariot that I'd given her in *Somnium*; and then she smirked and told me 'Aurora' was a Latin name, ill-fitting with the Grecian others. She looked so saucy as she said it, I greatly wished to spank her.

She told me next The Bull had never had a better Friday night.

She said my ode was all to blame; I told her it was nothing of the sort, but rather of the darling girls it did its best to describe. She laughed and said I probably was quite right; and if all her sweethearts had their maidenheads by evening's end, they probably owed them more to Flora's pistol-butts, wielded all too freely, than any other cause. Then all those lovely girls were at my door, so sweetly blowing kisses, and calling Cynthia away. And so she left, and left me to my writing.

I fell asleep full-clad at four, hardly having written more at all; there was too much to think on. At eleven in came Flora and dear Cynthia (I no longer see a reason now to lock my door), with hot water, soap and a razor frightening-sharp. I had begun to grow a beard, but Cynthia would no longer have it: Endymion, she told me, was ever-young and not maturely bearded. I acquiesced; I do not argue with two beauties, especially when one of them has a razor. So Flora shaved and Cynthia smiled and I just sat. When all was done, 'to test the smoothness', the pair of them they kissed me on the cheeks. A tittering at the doorway told me I had yet a greater audience.

It seems now then that, whenever I step out of my room, I find myself encountering, or surrounded by, the most startling examples of feminine pulchritude. Yet I know my Liz would be nothing discomforted amongst them; indeed, as she belongs in any company of angels, so she belongs with these. Cynthia does not call them angels, though. She laughs and calls them 'Flora's nymphs', or sometimes her 'lovely daughters of the Moonlight' or, most simply and affectionately, 'my girls'. But whence she found such extraordinary creatures, or how so quickly, I cannot quite conjecture, although I think I see her reasons. Perchance when Jude Brown led his masked and thievish crew, she might have been thought guilty by association with their heinous crimes. Surrounded now by soft and laughing-eyed young maidens of surpassing beauty, whatever crimes there may be committed hereabouts, suspicion is hardly likely to fall upon the charming mistress of The Bull.

Indeed, Cynthia seems quite content to leave the running of the inn to Flora, as capable in mind as she is startling in looks. I mentioned this at dinner, and asked dear Cynthia how she now intends to spend her time. '*We*,' she told me, 'will continue our explorations of the cellar's mysteries. And *you*,' she said, 'will write your book, not for your sister, or any other love, but for, and inspired alone by, *me*.' So big-eyed and so earnest, and so lovely, was she as she said this, that for a moment I believed her quite completely. And then, perhaps, my face betrayed another betrayal that I felt, and she laughed, and kissed me on a sudden, and told me that I could write for any that I wished, so long as she was woman, and young and beautiful, and if I thought her of the Moon; and so long as, no sooner had I written, she would be the first to hear it. I thought back then to Severndroog (if ever that lovely night had happened), and how the Moonlight had glinted softly in her eyes as she had spoke to me, and burnished up her chestnut locks; and I said yes, and promised that, if ever the book was published, I'd dedicate it both to lovely Liz, my sweetest sister, and to darling Cynthia who is, quite simply, I know not what. She is too much surprising.

His fairest queen Diana left him then, and when she next appeared she wore a scanty garment made of cloth of gold, all shaped up like a doe-skin; and that was all she thought to wear. Her lovely loins were barely hidden; one sweet breast uncovered, bare; the dress strapped but one shoulder. Naught else but golden necklaces, crescent, bracelets and large rings for both her ears and fingers; not even shoes, and nothing making up her face.

A little elf she was, so small and barefoot, pattering sweet about the room and half-dressed like a big-eyed child. Another look, at all that ivory flesh exposed, and gold; and but for moving all about, chryselephantine statue then he thought her.

So simply dressed to please, he never thought her sweeter, more lovely or divine.

He sat her on his knee, clipped her close and kissed her.

'You've a question in your mind!' she chuckled then, unmindful where his hands were all a-roam and giving kisses one for one.

'If you know that, my darling girl,' he said, and hugged her closer, 'then I don't have to tell you what it is. You can simply answer.'

'To make you feel the more at home!' she told him, lovely-eyed. 'But many things I've done for that, so many questions that could answer. The one you had in mind was, why does Somnium look in part like Nonsuch, Greenwich, or old Eltham?'

'I told you that I dreamed it here, my love, and so I dreamed it in a form that you would recognise. I dreamed it like the palace of your mighty queen, and yet I glorified it all the more, to make it like the palace of a Goddess. Your queen she is quite special now, but I am rather more.'

'You are indeed, my sweet,' he told her twixt his kisses, 'and if I said that in the real world, sedition's price I'd pay! And worth it, well enough!'

'Oh, say not so, my love!' she told him, all a-horrored. 'I know sedition's vicious cost, and would not have you hung. Your legs should only kick to dance, your yard should stand for love, your tongue... oh slip your sweet tongue 'tween my lips... and never more speak such nefandous words!'

He kissed her as she wished, and held her oh-so-close. And so the minutes passed away, before they spoke again.

'Dear heart,' she said at last, 'do nothing to endanger your sweet life. For though it means I'll wait the longer, till we can be one... still each minute of your days and nights, I'll watch them from the Moon. And, love, I could not bear to see you suffer. Live out all your natural span in loving me, and do the task I'll set you. And then, my man, the kisses that I give you now, they'll seem as nothing, though they seem so sweet, compared to what's to follow.'

'My love, my queen,' he told her then, although the words would barely come, 'your word it is my dear command. So, no more jests. I would not have you all upset, my sweetest dear, although to kiss your tears away, such bliss I'd truly think it. And now, my elfin sprite, continue on with what you meant to say.'

'I meant to say, beloved man, that if familiar stones they pleased you not, then on the instant, with a twitch of dream, we'd change them. So, shall I show you things today, that you have never seen? That never were on Earth before, although I ever had them in the Moon? Or else I'll make this Alexandria if you wish, where Alexander strutted proud and Cleopatra worked her wiles, where all the Ptolemies took their sisters off to bed. Or old Baghdad, and all my nymphs, they'll play your houris if you wish. Or Semiramis' Babylon... I've always thought her half of me... or Zenobia's Palmyra. My love, I want to please you.'

'Then please me best by being most yourself,' he told her then. 'And if you wish to show me palace reconstructed, then show it to me most the way you'd wish to have it. Show me where Diana lives, Diana sleeps, Diana loves. And everywhere Diana goes, I beg you let me kiss her.'

'A bargain, then,' she smiling said, and pouted for a kiss. And swift as payment was received, she hopped down from his knee. Her little hand it found his own; her toes they pattered on the floor; and so she led him to the theatre's door.

Sunday, 14th October 1803

Last night the inn was packed out in a way I never thought to see. It was Saturday night, of course, and so the musicians gave a dance; but word of Cynthia's lovelies had obviously spread far and wide besides. And more than this, I thought: with Jude Brown gone, and all his gang, and all the former tavern staff associated with him, it seemed as if The Bull had somehow shrugged off base material form and risen now above its hilltop ground, idealised, partaking of the celestial; while nymphs and angels served up gobletsful of nectar and ambrosia, and all around was Moonlight and cascades of lunar rainbows.

Half the army seemed to have marched up all the way from Woolwich; a half a legion of civilians had come to join them from the local villages. And all of them they seemed intent on dancing all the night with Flora's dearest flower-fairies (at least to dance to start with; I suspect their real intentions went considerably further). The lovely maidens being far too few; the soldiers and the locals eyeing each other with mutual disapprobation; an hour or two of ale and wine a-flowing: I frankly expected a riot at any minute, especially as dear Cynthia, who is so sweet, still refused to dance with anyone else than me.

Yet Flora was magnificent. Her pistols were discharged but twice. Her first ball she put into the wall, to attract the attention of a brawling mob, no less a dozen strong. A drunken corporal, not quite understanding the message of that first shot, received the second. She warned him first precisely what she'd do, and then she shot away his earlobe.

After that, there was no further trouble.

It was gone two before we expelled the last-most reveller; I was quite drunk, and darling Cynthia had danced me to exhaustion. The takings from the tap-house alone were, I gather, quite enormous, the Assembly Room yet better, and the musicians were paid a bonus like they'd never seen before.

I'd thought to stagger to my room, and write a while, then sleep. An innful of the loveliest girls had other ideas for me.

It seemed that every one of lovely Flora's blossoms had watched me dance at some point in the evening, and now I was surrounded by prospective partners, all of whom insisted that I drink with them and dance a step or two. They were so lovely, and they giggled so delightfully, and I knew that Cynthia was laughing near at hand and egging them on; for otherwise, I knew, they would not dare to strip down to their fair white petticoats to dance.

I was not then quite sure what music played or whence it came; but each dance started with a glass of sack, and oh, those darling girls they all were so vivacious. We whirled and twirled and tripped and hugged; I kissed them every one. My dizzy head was full of floral scents, my arms were full of sweet young virgins. I danced with every single one, until I got to Flora, who was so energetic; by then I was so tired and so drunk, I tried to slow her down. I am no longer sure; I think my pawing hands tore even her chemise. I know I saw a pair of lovely breasts, but just as well they may have been my Cynthia's. I know she took the final dance; I almost think she was quite naked. And yet by then I know that I could hardly see at all, and dancing had, for me, become a little more than being held up in a lovely woman's arms; the music, I thought, was nothing more than lovely girlish giggles.

They carried me off to bed; that much I do remember. Nothing more. I woke this morning to find they had undressed me.

Even now, I blush to think of this.

I dressed and took myself downstairs; it was still early, but all my dancing had left me with an appetite, and for a change I wanted to eat breakfast (surprisingly, my head it did not ache at all; yet I know I drank too much). Everywhere I went within the inn, those lovely girls were waiting there to kiss me fond good morning; and oh, those charming smiles. Every single one of them, I realised, has large brown eyes; though Cynthia's and my Liz's are the bigger. If Cynthia's maids were made to please me quite, they could not have been the better.

But Cynthia was in her nightdress once again, when at the last I'd kissed my way into the kitchen. I pulled her close and hugged her. She told me then that what I wanted was an omelette; a part of me agreed.

Before I'd hugged enough, or she could start to cook, a small disturbance at the door distracted us. Dear Flora, she was being Flora once again, but this time even more so; and I never thought to see such a wondrous sight, not even in these modern times. The 'reverend' Kinnock, unfortunately now without his gout, arrived this morning to preach his nonsense to I know not who; and dearest Flora put a pistol-ball straight through his boot-heel and sent him hopping on his way, calling absurdly on his Christ, his God and, I've no doubt, in time upon his doctor. I laughed and laughed, and threw one arm around slim Flora's waist, and round beloved Cynthia's the other, and kissed them both in my delight. I decided then, I would not let them go, the pair of them, until I'd taken them both with me to the tap-house, and called on lovely Rose for claret, to toast in truth the overthrow of God, and of his damnable church; and to call on Goddesses everywhere, and their nymphs, and their priestesses, and the soft beloved sisters of all who worship them, to laugh and dance and kiss and sing for joy, and to say that here and now, upon this strange and Moonish hill, we damn all preachers straight to hell, and all their masculine religion with them, and gods themselves and sons of gods we roast them; and that I (most especially, because I would not ask any other to do what I would not do myself) and *we* (being those lovely young ladies embraced up in my arms, and more than this, that dearest sister Liz who is never, ever quite removed from out of my beating heart) cry out instead that we love Diana (as the Romans call her, one breast bare) and Selene (as the

Greeks, all naked to the waist) and any other lovely Goddess who is of the Moon above, and of its beauty and its charm, and only in her arms is bliss, and that anything besides is nothing, and *nothing*, and that the world is empty without *her*, who is beauty, who is beyond description, who is, to any of the masculine sex, just *everything*.

And Cynthia looked at me so strangely in my exultation, and smiled a smile that was, somehow, quite small about her lips but enormous in her eyes, and told dear Rose to leave the claret where it was. Instead, she led me then behind the taproom counter and showed me there an earthenware jar that lay upon its side; I thought it vaguely like an amphora, but told myself it could not be. She took a jug, then knocked the plug, and asked me if I would tilt up the jar; and when I did, a brownish 'white' wine came thickly pouring out. The jug filled up, the jar replugged, she arranged a dozen glasses on the counter-top, and began to pour. My expression must have been full of questions.

'Falernian,' she said so soft, and then I know my face was full of disbelief, for I knew full well that genuine Falernian was quite undrunk upon these shores (or anywhere else) for a millennium or more; I mean by this the ancient wine, laid down in jars for 20 years or more, and not the weakling imitation coming now from Italy. More staggering yet, I realised that just last night I'd noted out a section where Diana Regina gives Endimion Lee Falernian there in Somnium; on a page *I've neither writ nor yet read out* to Cynthia. All that apart, I simply *knew* this could not be old Falernian.

Such a mischievous smile my dearest Cynthia she had then: spilling out a drop or two of wine as libation on the counter, and then applying to it a taper's flame. The wine (for wine it was, not spirit; I know that from the drinking) it then caught fire.

I know not how, but Cynthia Brown-eyes had Falernian, brewed, it must have been, when gilded, marbled Rome still stood and lorded half the world.

And this, said Cynthia brightly, was the only wine for toasts and libations to Diana, and that if I meant what I had said in my excitement just a moment previous, and would say it now again in duly considered seriousness, then Falernian would be all I drank for ever more. I knew, of course, that drinking Falernian ever after was mere symbol of reward, and the look in her eyes it simply said: 'renounce!' Renounce your old god, your religion, your society, all the life that you've led heretofore. And fair Diana looked at me through Cynthia's bright and sparkling eyes, and I know she said: '*surrender...* come to me and lay your head upon my naked breast and dream eternal in my arms, where anything is possible and everything can be done; and I will comfort you, and live with you, and we will love together and forever in the Moonlight, and by starlight, and the light of eternal bliss, even if the world goes mad and the sun turns black and there is nothing more in the eternal night than *us*.'

I told her yes, and renounced the world, my body and my soul, and *everything except Diana*, who is Selene, who is Cynthia, and darling Liz, and all and any that I have ever loved or considered worthy of my love.

And I drank the Falernian. And damned the rest. The unwashed world can waste in hell. Nineteen Christian centuries are too long; I pray there'll never be a twentieth.

And every single one of 'Flora's nymphs' they entered the taproom then. I know not how they knew what had occurred, but suddenly they came and took their glasses, ready-poured, and laughing first for joy, they toasted my 'conversion', and then they raised a double toast, to Cynthia and myself, and Cynthia embraced me, and we kissed, and drank that ancient nectar from each other's lips.

And after that I simply passed out in sweet Cynthia's arms, waking only at sunset, to find myself undressed (again, I have to assume by ladies) and put to bed in my normal room. Rising, I found the tavern once more its usual self, though just as packed with drinkers as on previous nights, and Violet at the harpsichord while Iris played the violin, and there was dancing, and revels, and laughing that I had not thought to see again in these tempestuous times.

Dear Cynthia brought me claret (although I swear it tasted of Falernian) and asked me how I felt. I told her not to worry of my fainting fits; never had I tasted wine quite like that delicious Falernian and, besides, last night my most loved Cynthia and her darling girls had simply tired me out.

We ate together. An hour later now, I cannot remember what at all, though Cynthia's presence made it taste quite of ambrosia. I asked her then if she'd excuse me; another evening's rumbustious entertainment probably would have been too much, and besides I felt I wanted to write. She smiled at me so sympathetic, said she'd see me later, and sent me back upstairs with such a charming kiss. And another bottle of claret.

And so I've spent an hour or more just writing up this journal.

I confess I'm still perplexed. The ruins down below the cellar simply cannot be, and neither can the Falernian; I do not quite believe dear Flora's nymphlets either. Are all these like that full Moon night on top of Severndroog?

Am I mad?

Not *going* mad, but mad *already*.

The Falernian it may or may not be; the charming girls, I hear their giggles down below. And Somnium's ruins? I simply do not know. With Jude Brown's capture and all that's happened since, we've had no chance to return. Yet I *think* they must be there.

I am bemused. I thought to make a fiction of the Moon-Goddess's palace, high up on its sacred hill; which at the same time was Endymion's cave. Now it seems it's come to be, and I cannot tell what's what. Is the cellar that old Latmian cave, and Somnium in The Bull? And who is Cynthia?

And who am I?

And why, O Goddess of the Moon above, have I not heard from my Liz?

Monday, 15th October 1803

I wrote a small amount of *Somnium* last night, but halfway through the evening lovely Cynthia came to see how I was getting on. We talked and drank, and then I read her what I'd written. She said the Moon was on my tongue; I said its light was shining in her eyes. She left me when the time came for the inn to close; and so I tried to write again.

I write now with my door wide open, for no ugly men are left about the inn still to distract me; and charming girls I'll stop for any time. And so they stop me far too much. All those lovely floral nymphs, they wander through the corridors in night attire, or flimsy robes, or less, a-giggle and adorable, and I can barely think. Especially when dear Cynthia, dressed no more than they, brings me wine and honeyed cakes, and tells me that I should think only of sweet and Moonlit things as I sit and write. And so I always do. But, oh those darling ladies…

Not long after dawn this dismal rainy morning, they hanged Jude Brown between two other thieves, down there at the foot of the hill. I was so glad it was not up here where the Moon reigns on our sacred peak. The Fox, I'm told, was selling ale and beer before the sun was up, and all the crowd were drunk. They jeered the cart as the men arrived and shouted foul abuse as the nooses they were tightened, sang ribald songs that quite drowned out the priest, and cheered and tossed their hats up in the air as the bench was kicked away. They say Jude Brown abused them till the last. I was just glad I was not there to see it; I did not even like to hear about it later.

The other two, I gather, when they had finished kicking, were transported back to London town and handed to the surgeons' apprentices for the cutting. Brown (and I know not whether this is the more merciful or otherwise) now hangs in the Upper Gibbet Field, food for crows. They paraded him past his former home, without a thought at all regarding to his widow, with singing, shouts of exultation and bawdy jokes. We heard them, Cynthia and I, but refused to look; and the dear woman seemed so grim I almost wept for guilt that I had ever thought she might have been the one to betray him. I took her in my arms and sat there hating all the outside world. Indeed, some inhuman members of that rowdy mob that followed Jude Brown's lifeless shell sought to burst into The Bull in search of further drinks to toast his taking off; only to find the handsome Flora standing there in boots and britches before the tavern's locked front door, with pistols in her hands and venom in her eyes. She did not have to shoot them; I rather wish she had.

The inn remained quite closed beyond the hour of dinner. We ate together, all subdued: myself, Cynthia, Flora and all her nymphs; and though none of us could find it in our hearts to say a good word about the late Jude Brown, we all agreed that that barbaric crowd deserved their thirst.

Yet later in the afternoon, Eustatius Wellbeloved sent up his man to present me with a letter. I thought at first it must be from my Liz, yet when I looked upon the envelope, it was so passing strange.

The address was as I might expect (my name, though, perhaps a little informal): *Kit Morley, Esq., The Bull Tavern, Shooters Hill, Kent...* and yet somehow it seemed to be *printed* on the envelope, not written with a pen. And in one corner, overstamped all blurred in black, a tiny coloured engraving of a woman's head seemed glued.

And when I opened it, many sheets of paper were within, and all of them were printed like a book. I simply could not understand it. The first sheet was a letter, and the more I read of this, the more I do confess my head span. I thought it best, then, until I'd tried to understand, to go back to my room; though Cynthia looked at me with questions in her eyes.

The sender's address was given as *The Palace of Dreams, Shooters Hill, London SE18*. I realised at last 'The Palace of Dreams' might perhaps have been a private joke in a letter whose recipient would know the writer's address well enough. But to find that Shooters Hill was now in London, not in Kent, reminded me then of all my future visions. And then I saw the date.

Friday, 7th November 2003.

I read it twice or thrice, and looked away, and looked again. And *still* it said *2003*.

So after that, I *had* to read the letter.

Hello Phoebe! it began. *How's my big-eyed girl?* I was appalled. Such vulgar over-familiarity. I would not even write the same to Liz.

And yet... thinking how I write so much the less of English than Will Shakespeare did, two centuries gone before me, I had to wonder how they'd write two centuries after I was buried in the ground.

But if I was confused by this, I also had to smile. Whoever he was who'd written the letter (and all my intuition told me that I knew exactly who it was), the Phoebe who he'd written to, she had a lunar name. And so, of course, I had to read the more.

How're things down there in Hastings? next the letter asked. *Give yourself a hug and kiss from me, and I'll see you in your dreams.*

I'm still writing, as much as I have the time to, and I thought I'd send you down another little story. Just finished it last night. Of course, you know I can't write anything about the ghastly present day, so it's set in late 19th century France. It's complete in itself, and, naturally, it's a bit of a distraction from my main work on Somnium—

Here, of course, I had to stop. Rose, I noticed passing by then in the corridor, and asked if she'd be so kind to bring me up a brandy; but not to tell dear Cynthia. She looked at me so strange.

By the time she brought the brandy, I'd long forgotten asking for it.

Except for Liz and all the ladies of the inn, I'd told no one my story was called *Somnium*, yet here was this apparent 'future-author' writing a story called the same. Worse, I somehow had the feeling that the title wasn't the only thing coincident… that somehow too (though Gods and Goddesses of the Moon and Stars above, I cannot quite tell how) the *story* too was likely-most the same *as well*. I had to lie down then, at full stretch on the bed, before I could read on till the end.

… distraction from my main work on Somnium, *though some of the ideas obviously overlap. The young man far from home, the silver castle, the library. I don't know what I'll do with this. I wrote it just for fun. But sometimes it occurs to me: I might insert it whole in* Somnium. *Now isn't that a mad idea? Let me know what you think when you've read it, angel.*

As for Somnium *itself, I'm getting near the end. And I've grown so fond of Kit Morley as a character* [fortunately, at this point, dear Rose, she brought the brandy]. *I dreamt of him last night, back there in the old Bull, scratching away by candlelight with his steel-nib pen. When* Somnium's *finished, we'll have a celebratory drink in the* **new** *Bull, okay?*

In fact, he's become so real to me, I sometimes have this really strange notion. What if I were to write a letter to him, addressed to the (old) Bull *tavern… then would I get a reply? And what would it say? I actually had a very suggestive dream about this last night, so let me copy it here, straight from my dream-diary:* 'I was walking past The Bull with Alan, talking about *Somnium*, and I told him I'd decided to include a sequence where he and I were walking past The Bull, talking about *Somnium*, and including a sequence where he and I (etc., *ad infinitum*), and I was also going to include a letter, to Kit, from me in the present.' *In fact, the more I think about it, the more I like it, as one of those artistic pranks— 'author writes to his character; wonders what the universe will send him in return?' In fact, let's do it now, same time as I'm getting your letter ready.*

Anyway, my love, hope you enjoy the story, and I'll look forward to hearing what you think. I'll give you a ring next week [this seemed to me a rather casual way of proposing].

All my love,

S

I read it all again, and still I had no slight idea at all exactly what to think. I had to guess that 'S' had put his letters in the wrong envelopes somehow, and I'd got Phoebe's letter, while she, no doubt, was puzzling over mine. But surely such things only happen in farces on the stage. And no-wise could that possibly explain how a letter could travel back 200 years in time.

And yet, I have to think... it's only two or three days since I'd made the fair Diana Regina say that 'all the world's a dream'. And now it seems that what I said in fiction, might be true in fact.

I could not get to grips with this at all, and so, instead, I started then to read the story...

THIS DULL WORLD, AND THE OTHER

Even though some few short weeks had passed by since his arrival, Théophile Delore still couldn't quite understand why he had been selected for the post of assessing librarian at the shadowy and sequestered Château D'Argent. It was true that on his arrival la belle Comtesse had jokingly told him, with a soft and musical laugh, that she was fond of puns, and that 'Delore' would add a golden aura to the silver-frosted walls about the old château; but that hardly explained why one of such comparatively junior years as he was, fresh from the Sorbonne and with no practical experience whatsoever, should have been awarded such an elevated position without even a personal interview. There were times when he thought he must have been the only applicant; but then again there were times when even he thought such a thought inane and quite ridiculous.

Nonetheless, he had found the post advertised in a small and dusty bookshop that he frequented on occasion in Montmartre, and thought the idea of cataloguing the library of an ancient château just on the near side of the towering Pyrenees precisely what he needed in order to defer such unpleasant decisions as young men have to make (or have to have made for them) regarding careers, or marriages, or military service. Applying forthwith, before he changed his mind, he promptly forgot all about the prospect in favour of those rather sweet distractions offered by the Comédie Française, the Folies and the Moulin, waking up one morning two weeks later, not entirely sure quite where or who he was, to find a letter most graciously addressed to 'Monsieur Delore, Savant', and slightly scented too.

The Comtesse Eugénie de Sylvaire ('Mademoiselle', he noted with a certain astonishment) had written, in a very dainty and sophisticated hand and rather risqué purple ink, to accept his application, and to offer an extremely reasonable remuneration, from which there would be no deduction for his board and lodging (this being, she pointed out, a little less luxurious than he might be used to, as a denizen of la belle Paris). He was, therefore, invited to make his way to the château, by railway (changing at Toulouse) and hired coach from Pau (again, his expenses would all be reimbursed), arriving no later than the fourteenth of October, and to bring with him whatever he thought needful for a six-month tenure, free of interruption. A 'librarian's livery', he read with even more astonishment, would also be provided (and more astounding yet, it fitted to perfection). And so, his head quite full (of Roncesvalles and Roland, of the Moors, and the mysteries of Andorra), his travelling bag the less so (the clothes he owned were few enough, and even a dog-eared volume of Baudelaire, the tenderest of letters from his sister, and a bottle of absinthe 'for emergencies', could not quite pack it tight), he said farewell, without a second thought, to fair, immortal Paris of the marbled boulevards; the pleasures that she offered, though, he wondered if in time he'd miss them.

He arrived at the château, so high up in the foothills, its turrets soaring even higher, on October the twelfth, thinking punctuality a virtue; and found his welcome warm enough. By the fifteenth of November, the winter blizzards blew, and all his shivered dreams were icy hells with lanky, stalking frost demons.

The establishment of the Château D'Argent, first built in 1564, he thought was somewhat strange. Within the main house lived only Mademoiselle la Comtesse, a butler, cook, two chambermaids and himself; a small number of other staff, gardeners, handy-men and veterans of the colonial wars who saw off wolves, both bestial and human, were billeted within the outer walls, quite separate. Without those limestone walls (quite tall and thick, he noticed from the start) were shrunken, twisted pines, large rocks and tumbling screes and, later, snow and ice.

La belle Comtesse (and très belle, too, he thought she was) explained that she had been travelling much abroad, and only in the last few months, inheriting the château from an aged uncle, had she returned to France. She did not say where she had been (he rather thought the Moon, her skin it was so fair), but simply told him that her long-gone forebear Comte Alphonse, some century and a half ere then, had gathered such a library that now it filled up four entire halls, within the western wing. His duties, which she trusted he would carry out in the exemplary fashion of a Parisian savant far older than himself, would be to work each day from nine till half past four (Sundays excepted, if he wished) to conserve and catalogue the Comte's collection; and on Mondays and on Thursdays, in the evening, he would dine with her and report his progress and whatever notable or peculiar discoveries he had chanced to make. The Comte, she warned him, though he died so long ago, had something of a reputation thereabouts, as a devil and a heretic, and so she had every expectation that the library would contain a number of items that would startle and surprise. She looked forward to his full reports;

and Théophile, who thought he'd never seen such large and sparkling deep brown eyes, looked forward to his dinners.

The library of the Comte was strange indeed (if far too dusty and neglected), and more than half of it deserved to be transferred forthwith to the Bibliothèque Nationale. For here were incunabula from old Württemburg and Mainz and London, by Gütenberg and Caxton, and manuscripts from old monastic scriptoria as far apart as Dublin and Byzantium. Here were tomes inscribed 'Johannes Dee, his librarie', lost volumes, rare beyond all price, of Livy and of Claudius (the *Etruscan History*, how it made his jaw drop); the *Cypria*, complete, and all five books of *Dream Oracles* by Hermippus of far Berytus; and next to these were other works which, if not quite the grammaries of darkest demonolatry, were somewhat on the uncouth side, and very odd indeed. The most part, though, it seemed that Comte Alphonse had been obsessed with manifestly cryptical works of ancient Grecian mystery, and, more, of all the iniquities of antiquity, so manifold and so diverse. And on Mondays (when she dressed in white) and Thursdays (when she dressed in gold) he told the Comtesse all he'd found. And when the autumn leaves were turning crisp and brown, she called him Monsieur Delore; and when the first snows drifted down, so many things he had discovered, she called him Théophile. And then one night, to his delight, before a roaring fire she told him that, at dinner, and at brandy afterward, he might call her Eugénie, if so it pleased him to, but not before the staff. And Théophile, a young man as he was, he thought she was a Goddess; though which of them, he could not quite decide. The lovely chestnut locks that tumbled freely round her shoulders, he thought were just delightful; but there was something in the structure of her facial bones, he thought was quite unearthly.

On other nights than Mondays and on Thursdays, she kept herself apart, and what she did he never had a slight idea at all. So absinthe drunk, and Baudelaire all read (again), he kept himself within the library, in search of wonders and new finds, with which he could delight her. And so, one icy midnight, when the righteous and the true are fast asleep in bed, he sat before a blazing fire, and opened up *The Eight Great Wonders of the Ancient World (Now Fallen into Disrepair Save One, of Pyramidal Form*). The strangeness of the title, unexpected, hardly registered with Théophile at all; instead, his thoughts a-wander from his much-beloved sister Délia (of whom he'd dreamt the night before), through the Delian isle, to ancient Artemisia, he turned straight to the chapter on the Mausoleum.

By then, it must be said, the weariness was pricking at his eyes; his lids began to droop. And so he read (in old, barbaric French, it has to be remarked), how swarthy long-haired Mausolus, who loved his sister in a way that Théophile could only envy, had, long before his death, begun to build his tomb, with space enough for two and gold enough for thousands. The Sun he thought himself, his lovely sister was the Moon; and so each month in darkest night they'd come into conjunction; the tomb, he thought, in which they'd sleep forever, enfolded in each other's arms, would be, not just a wonder of the world, but a monument to all the joys they shared, diurnal and nocturnal.

And so, at last, the crinkling pages said, old Asiatic Mausolus, he died; and quoted some lost work of Suetonius the racy to say he did expire loud gasping in his sister's bed. And Théophile, for all he thought of Délia, he thought of Eugénie as well. Distracted as he was, he hardly noticed then the things that he was reading next: how Mausolus' brother Idrieus, already married to his second sister Ada, took Artemisia too into his ménage... and how the three of them then, too busy with each other, neglected to complete the Mausoleum. How Mausolus, robed in cloth-of-gold and crowned irradiate with amber, befitting to the Sun himself, rose up from out his tomb, a-rotting, with fiery eyes and lipless mouth of ivory teeth, and walked the streets of Halicarnassus, and gnawed the passers-by for blood and flesh until he came at last unto the palace; and all the things he did there to his sisters and his brother, too horrible for human tongue or hand to make account. And how he raved and haunted till the city was deserted quite, and only when Alexander, passing by upon his way to glory, gave orders for the tomb to be completed, did Mausolus at last rest peaceful in his storied Mausoleum.

So startled was Théophile by this curious revelation, so widely variant to the history that he thought he knew, that not only did it fright him quite awake and make him drop the book, it filled him also with a sudden, unreasoning panic. The next he knew, he'd left the library and was fleeing, all blundering in the dark, along the corridors and staircases of the old château. With no idea at all just where he was, he clattered into a table, bruised his shin and knee, and fell down, howling, on the floor.

A moment later, a door creaked open and the wide-eyed Comtesse Eugénie appeared, a silver candelabrum in her hand and, in a rather querulous and puzzled voice, asked: 'Théophile?'

And Théophile blushed that she should see him lying there like that, but looking up he blushed the more; for in her haste to see what made such gross disturbance in the silence of the night, she had no more than thrown a silken negligee (though trimmed with ermine, nonetheless) about a nightgown that was wisp of gauze and nothing more. Most graciously she helped him to his feet, and then the memory of what he'd read overwhelmed him once again.

'Oh *God!*' he cried and threw his arms about her, decorum all forgot.

'Théophile!' she exclaimed; then, more sternly and upbraiding: '*Monsieur!*'

And Théophile, who suddenly realised he had his employer in his arms, all décolletée, and warm and soft, at midnight, in the dark, stepped back, and stuttered, and tried to find some way he could apologise.

He must have looked so red-faced, so nervous and so utterly terrified, she smiled and took his hand, and asked him, very softly, what was wrong.

He tried to tell her, but all that would come out, a-sputter, was 'library' and 'book' and 'wrong' and 'Mausoleum'. And so she gently said that he should show her, and led him back along a trail of tumbled furniture and tapestries all disarranged, until they'd come to where he'd started.

The first thing that he noticed, when he found it on the floor, was that the book was now called (he could not quite think how) *The Seven Wonders of the Ancient World (Now Fallen into Disrepair Save One, of Pyramidal Form)*, and when he opened up the page it read as he would quite expect: how Artemisia, much distraught, had finished off the tomb, with love,

and died, and joined her brother in it; and after was succeeded by Idrieus
and by Ada... and never a word of rampaging Mausolus revenant.

He slumped down in his chair and held his head, a moment, in his
hands; she found herself a stool and sat down, sympathetic; and then,
three deep breaths after, he told her next precisely what he'd read. And
more, he told her that he *knew* he'd read it, and even if he had been
awfully tired, he couldn't understand why he should think to read of
anything that was quite so utterly *mad*.

And Eugénie then, standing up, she took his hand and pressed it
very sweetly, commented not at all, and told him he should go to bed.

And so, bewildered more than he had ever been before, he did.

Next morning in the library, he thought that every book it wore
a smirk, and mocked him when he turned his back; and whispered to
its neighbour, of all the saucy secrets it contained, and how he must
be stupid if he thought he knew the things he thought were true. And
the books he catalogued were all of riddles, magic and illusion, and of
making things appear quite other than they were.

And when, the butler having brought his luncheon, of strongly-
reeking Roquefort and of fresh-baked bread (still warm enough to
melt the salty local butter), with one large glass of old Bordeaux, he
paused to glance once more at *The Seven Wonders*, he found that it was
bound in brown morocco; and the previous night, he knew, it had been
bound in *vert*.

The snow was falling very gently, in large flakes, outside;
within the library, old logs were burning with a quiet sigh; and inside
Théophile, the lunch that sat there in his stomach gave a warm and
placid satisfaction. And so, to open up that same notorious book and
read then of 'the five-sided pyramid of Cheops' was, for a moment,
nothing more than natural. A moment later, of course, it was nothing of
the sort. And Théophile then ground his teeth, and jumped up straight
away, and slapped his hands about his sides, and looked again, and found
a pyramid that had four faces, as he'd really known it should. And when
he looked again, four sides it had indeed; and so it had all afternoon.

At four o'clock, the Comtesse de Sylvaire came into the library
and asked him, rather gently, how he did; and when he looked a little

baffled, she took him straight away, and told him they were playing cards (he lost) until the cook had readied up some supper. For even though it was a Wednesday, and she was dressed in neither white nor gold, but green (her jewellery all of bloodstones and dark garnets), she thought it would be better if he did not dine alone. And Jacques the butler played the hautbois, and a bottle each of Burgundy they drank; and then at half past eight she bade him sweet goodnight and told him *not* to read.

But once apart, of course, he went back to the library, his head a little piece awhirl, and opened up old Quintus Curtius. And read how god-like Alexander Magnus, resting there in hot and hoary Babylon, as old as all the world and twice as sinful, too, had passed away of neither drink nor fever; but Ptolemy, it seemed, surprising him asleep, had inserted up his fundament two long and slippery eels, flesh-eating and voracious. And Alexander, waking on the morrow, had suffered inexplicable stomach-pains, and soon thereafter died.

Green, the book was, when he looked; and when he looked again it wasn't. And when he looked a third time, Alexander, drunken, died of fever, just as Arrian always said he did, and Quintus now did quite agree.

So Théophile, he rang for Jacques and asked him, employee though he was, if he might have a little brandy. And Jacques, who had a better soul and broader smile than all the other butlers in the world, then gave him what he asked for. And left the bottle too.

So then he reached for Plutarch's *Lives*, and opened it at *Caesar*. And there he found that handsome Brutus and the lean and hungry Cassius had used no knives at all, but rather with their pointed teeth and tongues had sucked up Caesar's blood, for they were vampires both, and all the plotters too.

And the book was bound in green.

And then, again, it wasn't.

One last attempt he made, with much-loved and familiar Homer's *Odyssey*; and there he found that, just arrived on hemitheic Circe's isle, the *moly* fed by Hermes to Odysseus had made him quite complaisant, and when that lovely sorceress had turned his men to grunting swine, he gladly roast and ate them, and swore Penelope whored each night with every single suitor in their turn, and renounced the world of men and mind for Circe of the raven locks, delirium and spasm, and let her change him to a woman, evermore.

So after that, Théophile, who thought perhaps the brandy might have played a part in all of this, left it behind him in the library, and took himself, with haste, to bed.

Next day he merely cleaned the shelves, and dusted books, and noted down some titles, and looked at falling snow outside, and low dark clouds, and shivered; and never once read anything at all. Yet being Thursday once again, he dined as usual with his dear Comtesse.

All gold she was, and gold her jewellery too, with just a hint of amber; and Théophile remembered what he'd read of Mausolus. Some little wince must then have crossed his face, for when they'd eaten and progressed to coffee and to brandy, she produced some Turkish cigarettes and asked him, very precisely to tell her all the things he'd read since first he had disturbed her in the night. And that mere mention of how he'd presumed to hold her in his arms said: 'tell the truth, or pay the price.' And so, of course, he told her every single thing, and spared her not one awful detail, not even of the eels.

Quite pensive, then, she did become, and asked him if he'd noticed any change about the books themselves; and when he told her that, in their most delirious and obnoxious condition, they were quite as green as absinthe, she neither laughed nor looked at him askance, but nodded most decisive, as if this news was simply as expected.

'Théophile,' she said, and poured him out another brandy. 'I must confess, I have not been entirely open with you and now, perhaps, I'm only going to be a little more so. I knew five years ago my uncle designed to leave me this château, and with it Alphonse's library, to which I had been previously denied. And so I used the time to good effect. I knew the ancient Comte had spent so many years collecting books and, more, the wisdom that accompanied them, in Istanbul and Cairo, Damascus, Calcutta and even Samarkand; and, less exotic, in cold St Petersburg, Berlin and rainy London too. And so I followed in his footsteps, best I could, and added Marrakesh and other places too, attempting to learn the same as he. I will not tell you all the things I did, the bargains that I made, in order to find out what I sought; and never ask me of Bokhara, nor of its evil Khan. Some men would think the less of me for that, though some might think the more. I do not seek your judgement, and as the snows may chance to keep us here, together, for up to three months more, it may perhaps be better not to give it. And yet, it seemed to me, from what I'd learned, that what the Comte Alphonse had finally discovered, and somehow had brought back, was not a little treasure.

'In Cairo, I read certain crumbling papyri in bastard-Greek, all mixed up with Demotic and old Coptic, about the dark and reeking mysteries of ancient humid Memphis, the city of the evil opalescent night; refined young ladies of our current age would normally find them horrid. Two things I learned within those texts: the first of great importance to myself; the second will explain your presence here.

'You perhaps have heard of *The Smaragdine Tablet of Hermes Trismegistus*, that states succinctly 'As above, then so below'. I tell you now, that tiny text is nothing but a fraud; and, oh, the wasted ink that has been spilled about it. The true *Smaragdine Tablet* is an emerald-covered book, thrice-blessed indeed, but writ by Hermes, not by Trismegistus; yes, by Hermes, God of magic, trickery and spite, one eye a-wink through all the tides of time. And Alphonse, though I know not how, although I do suspect the price perhaps was more or less his soul, obtained that book, or brought it, all hidden and somehow just beyond his grasp, here to this very library.'

'A green-bound book…?' then interjected Théophile, a-wonder.

'Yes,' she said, her voice so low. 'But first, let me finish. The second thing I learned in Cairo, forgive me if you do not like. It was that, in the art of scrying, virgin boys or innocent young men were far away the best. In Singapore, a Chinese priestess of the Moon, white-faced and strange and oh so languid-eyed, before whom I laid out all my problems and designs, told me that such a book as this I sought, that was not quite of Earth at all, would best be seen indeed by eyes that, unlike mine and hers, had not been clouded by the dust of all this sinful world.

'And so, my poor dear friend, your blushes tell me that you know what I've to tell you next. Seven applicants I had, to be librarian here, and six of them, in any real sense at all, were far more qualified than you were. But you had youth, and I had agents there in Paris who told me that your sins were little more than drink; and when the drink was a little more than little, a fist-fight or two perhaps, but little more than that. And they told me too, and this may cheer you, that you were fair to look upon, and honest, straight and true. And so I brought you here to help me. And everything they said of you was less than what you are.

'And more than this, you have succeeded, more than I had hoped. For you have seen the book I seek, in all its strange disguises.

'And now we have to find a way to grasp it.'

'Eugénie,' he said, and leaned a little closer, emboldened by the brandy, so he thought. 'I fear you've studied more than I, for here are things I hardly understand. A book which hides in other books...?'

'And rewrites them as it does so, but only for the instant you're aware of it; and awareness only comes upon the fringe of sleep, or curious distraction; and once the realisation wakes you with a start, it slips away and hides elsewhere, as mischievous as its author.'

'And are such strange things possible, in modern days like these?' asked Théophile.

'You forget, my dear young friend, this book was written by a God, and is a thing of Gods itself. Discard the learning that they taught you at the Sorbonne; the logic and the science of the 19th century are little use for this. The library at Alexandria might have contained the key, for there was found so much of magic and of theurgy, of Egyptian rites and of the Indian gymnosophists, Thessalian witchery and drawing down the Moon, and more, much more, besides. Rather more to the point, I half suspect that Hermes' verdant book, if we can but clasp it close, *contains* the library of Alexandria itself, with all those myriad volumes collapsed somehow within. I wish I knew how Alphonse had discovered it or brought it here, but on this his diaries, which I discovered hidden in an oaken chest in uncle's house in Paris, when I was but a teenage girl and long before I acquired the château and the library, are, alas, quite simply silent. All he tells is how he could not clasp the book itself, although it seems to have had a mischievous propensity for tormenting his young son. Again, an innocent boy, you see…'

'Then how on Earth do *we* capture such a thing as that?'

'We, or rather you, have made a good beginning. For you have seen the book; or perhaps more to the point, you've attracted its attention. And that, perhaps because of those same atrocious bargains that I made, was something I could never do. And so, tonight, my Théophile, I do propose, if you have for it the heart and stomach, that you and I should pass away the midnight hours together in the library. Oh, Théophile, do not allow yourself a smile, for nothing more I have in mind to clutch at than that book. So, no more brandy now; but… have another cigarette.'

So Théophile, although he found the Turkish tobacco rather strong, tried his best to refrain from coughing, and asked the Comtesse what she had in mind. Instead of answering, though, she took his hand and raised him to his feet, led him to the library, and said she would explain as they began. And so a few minutes later, sitting in a deeply-padded old armchair beside a roaring fire, in pale and golden candlelight, he took a copy of Plutarch's *Life of Antony* into his hands and let her then explain.

'This trickster book of Hermes,' she commenced, producing a little gold vaned wheel on a stand which, when a candle lit below began to warm the air, span round and round and sparkled like the moonlight on a wind-blown darkling sea, 'appears upon the fringe of sleep. But once it does, you either fall asleep completely, or else the shock of recognition jerks you quite awake. And so we need to keep you in that borderland a long-extended time.

'The Turkish cigarettes we smoked, forgive me that I did not tell you, contained no small amount of fine hashish, the best the Ottomans can produce; and green, besides, just like the book. But that is just the start. I next propose to use upon you the subtle and magnetic arts of Mesmer, or as the moderns call a similar technique, 'hypnosis'. For that you'll look upon this whirl of glinting lights, and listen while I lull you with an old soft song I learned in Isphahan, where choirs quite like the houris sing so sweet of paradise beneath the wind-bowed palms. And when you are a little touch entranced, I'll tell you then to take up ancient Plutarch's book, and so begin to read. And being then both in and out of Hypnos' hands, we'll hope to trap that other book here long enough... just long enough...'

'Long enough for *what?*' he asked, lighting up another of the tainted cigarettes, yet hardly thinking what he did.

'For you to turn back to its opening page, and tell me then the title written there. For as the ancients knew, especially the Egyptians, if we can find the true and secret name of either God or thing, then it will fall at once into our power.

'And Théophile,' she continued after a pause, 'you *will* do this for me, won't you? For once we have the book, then we can do so many strange and lovely things... together...'

'Of course I will, my dearest Eugénie,' he said, already half-entranced, not merely with hashish, but with her beauty too. Her smile, at that, was perhaps a little wry.

And so he looked then at the whirling wheel, its rays and all its sparklings, and listened as she sang a wordless song more sweet than any old Ferdowsi ever wrote, of silver mists and golden autumns, of silks and satins, of aromatic scents and harems of Circassians, and peach and pear trees too, and sherbets chilled with snow, in old and perfumed Persia, where lithe young princes jewelled with sapphires dreamed such wondered dreams. And though his eyes stayed open wide, his mind fell half asleep.

And then a little later, she commanding, he commenced to read, aloud. A small amount of minutes passed, and then he spoke of Cleopatra, how she and Ptolemy were a pair of Siamese twins, joined side by side but full of hatred nonetheless, who slept with Caesar and with Antony, the both of them at once, the whole night through, in varying combination, and wheedled each for power. And then she coaxed him very gently, told him first he must stay calm, and then requested that he turn the pages back until he reached the start.

The book, although it seemed a little green, had slipped away before he found its opening. So Eugénie then softly kissed his forehead as a mother does, and lullabied him to a deeper sleep, this time with songs from ancient Luristan, unknown to all of Europe, and told him then to read once more. He opened up the book at random, found that Caesar was a werewolf on the full moon night alone and Antony, addicted to the lotus, had ate up four young girls alive, and died of satiation. And once again, at her instruction, he slowly, calmly, returned to the beginning.

And on the title page he read, and roundly did pronounce, 'Opusculum Mercurialis', though why Greek Hermes made his book a Latin thing, he could not quite decide, unless it was for humour and confusion. And green it was, and green it stayed, and when he looked again, it still was called the same besides, and green its binding too. And Eugénie smiled, and sighed, and snuffed the candle, stopped the wheel, and woke him with a kiss that, administered while he was still a half asleep, he hardly knew at all. And then she gave him another brandy, and sent him off to bed; and Théophile, still half bemused, did everything she said.

That night he slept and dreamed, and Hermes came to him, caduceus in his hand, winged sandals on his feet, winged helmet on his head, and such a smirk of debonair duplicity upon his face that, even sleeping, Théophile was forced to laugh. Then Hermes brought his darling Eugénie, brown-eyed and naked, to his bed, and charming sister Délia too, without her clothes, and when that wasn't quite enough, that lovely Goddess who, the Queen of all the Night-time Air, and Mistress Leader of the Stars, wheels round and round this cold, unfeeling Earth and never stops except for love of young and handsome shepherd boys, with javelins in their hands. All three of them he clasped to him, so close, and unlike other dreams, he did not wake until he was satisfied entire. And Hermes watched, and laughed, and told him if he kept the verdant book quite to himself alone, then all these bright-eyed lovelies he would have for harlots evermore, and none would ever gainsay him at all. And Théophile then woke up all in terror, for everything he dreamed was sin, and every sin he dreamed was sparkling with allure.

And more than this, before he'd had the time to realise it was indeed the dawn light shining through his window, Eugénie had burst into his room, still wearing that same wisp of nightdress that cried out loud 'dream all your lovely dreams of sin, and I will dream them with you, so sinful till the whole world ends'. But Eugénie had other things in mind, and ordered him at once to rise and join her in the library; and when he did, all dressed up in the proper style, she hadn't changed at all.

And then she told him he should stoke the fire and strip down to the waist, so she could paint Egyptian hieroglyphics foully on his chest that came from ancient Karnak, and several words in Greek, that evil reeked, and certain Hebrew letters too, that seemed to him the worse, for they were angel-script and spoke of naught but demons. And when she had, she stripped herself quite naked, all unblushing, and told him he should paint the same on her; and how he trembled as he brushed those burning words across her soft young breasts. Then standing hand in hand, they called upon the name, *Opusculum Mercurialis*. Or he called it by its name, at least, and she sang noxious incantations hardly heard since golden gloried Rome fell from its might and crumpled like a craven to the conquering Christian horde.

Ten minutes passed and nothing happened, yet they did continue just the same; then Théophile's attention wandered somewhat. For the beauteous Eugénie was swaying nakedly before him as she sang, and once again he saw her young bared breasts, and all the rest of her which, not exactly flaunted, was not exactly covered up. And sin began to heat up Théophile's imagination then; and from the corner of his eye he saw a vagrant greenness first and, almost shyly, that quite improbable book slipped across the gulf of time and space from its strange, uncertain world and nestled snugly in his hand.

And Théophile, who rather feared the holding of it would burn his flesh away in agonies quite transcendent, then remembered all he'd dreamed, and tempting promises of Hermes, and six bright eyes that sparkled 'yes', and all the sin of his desire, and how it did allure... and handed then the book forthwith to eager Eugénie.

She clutched it close and made it fast with certain noxious recitations learned in Smyrna, that orient city scented all with myrrh and unbecoming foulness, and painted symbols on its back and front that would not let it get away, back to its own and other world, no

matter how it sorely wished to. Then, without the merest thought of
covering up her nudity, she took a pace or two toward the fireplace,
opened the little, innocent-looking book and began to read aloud such
evil things he thought he would expire.

How Remus had been sodomised to death by Romulus while
giant birds of prey pecked out his bleeding lungs until he had no breath
to scream. How Helen, cursed by all the Gods at birth because her
beauty was too great, aged never more than up to twelve until her
dying day, and always was a child in bed who did not understand at all
the things that men desired, and did; and ever wished that she could
die, and didn't. How handsome Antinous, because he was too loved,
was cut in tiny pieces by old Hadrian his lover, fried with onions, most
sacred plant of Egypt, and eaten by the emperor, all his blood-sauce
drunk as well, and bones boiled up for soup, till nothing did remain.
And how Pyriphlegethon, the fiery river, rises up from hell each night,
to burn the innocent as they pray to all their innocent Gods, who quite
refuse to save them. And of the sex-life of the dead, decayed, which was
more lewd than all the whores of Paris could imagine, put together.
Of living stones that turned to fiery lions, all-hungry in the all-too
evil night; of gates to other worlds where everything was worms,
and maggots and corruption, stinks and blight. Of oceans turned to
crimson by the blood of sacrifice, and all for nothing but the charm
of coloured death. Of sepulchres that glow on moonless nights and
spiders twice as large as Athens ever was. And hordes of giant rats
that ate the sun itself when it settled on the horizon. So many things
the slim, unwholesome volume seemed then to contain, he knew
they would not all fit in, and somehow it was more than first it did
appear... so many times more over.

And Eugénie, she stood there naked by the fire, and read with
such a lickerish look upon her lovely face, that Théophile cried: 'hold,
enough!' and asked her to explain. What meant this awful book, and
why had she desired to have it?

Then Eugénie glanced up, and saw the look of innocent, tremulous
pain upon his face and, if not for long, the spell the book had wove on
her was, for the moment, broken. She put it on a table (it did not

disappear), invited him to sit down in a chair nearby, sat down herself, and took his hands in hers, so small.

'Dear Théophile,' she said, a phrasing he thought rather pleasing, naked as she was, 'I've always known, in ways that you perhaps have not, the difference between what's *real* and what we *think* is true. For what we *think* is true is mostly what we have been told, and not what we have seen with our own eyes. And what we have been told about the ancient world, is lies, and lies, and lies. The Christians, when they took the world, they made it over as they wished, and so they made it plain and dull and boring, denied all mystery and all sensual entertainment, declared that incest, sodomy and bestiality, necrophilia too, and both the ways of Onan, all those things that make life sweet and full of interest and variety, were foul and horrid sin. And banished Gods and fauns and nymphs, lamiæ and sphinxes, chimeræ and wyverns, Mormo, Baubo, Gorgons, gryphons, gigantic worms that fed on shuddered maidens' flesh till they were done away with quite by heroes armed with adamantine blades of orichalch, though always then there came another, hungrier than before, and larger too... and more, they did away with sorceresses, with their violet eyes and lovely breasts, and red hair swirling round their dainty ankles, who thought it fine to fornicate with fauns and pans beneath a golden gibbous Moon, and make sweet music with their sighs and gasps and cries and moans; and so they did away with spells and wonder too; and tombs that housed the living dead, and parricides that slept then with their mothers and charred their hands and feet besides, and drugs that show a glimpse of heaven and blind us then for ever more, and women with the heads of crows and feet of mice, and ladders quite of diamonds leading to the very stars themselves, that glitter in the night of time, and tell eternal hours of pain in hell. So hardly surprising was it then that men were bored, and prayed unto the Christian God to save them from this dullness. And he, of course, so full of goodness, leaves them as they are. Do you wonder then that men do open up a vein and die, a-weltering in red blood that's all their own? The only surprise to me is that they do not do it sooner and more often.

'No, Théophile, I will not live in such a world and nor, I hope, will you. I want to live in Hermes' world, which, though it is not here with us, was never quite destroyed. It *hid*, and saved itself for those who sought it, such as me, who thought it not a sin to live a sensual life, and think such thoughts... such pagan, *lovely* and, by Christian standards, *evil* thoughts as I do. I know you think me sweet, my dear, but all the line Sylvaire have been voluptuaries since the pagan Franks they first arrived, and took their joys promiscuous. And if I cannot gratify my body and my mind, destroy my foes like angry Mars and love my friends like soft and lovely Venus, all perfumed, and think then all the thoughts that can be thought within the world at large without a moral judgement just the same as Hermes-Mercury, trim the fatheads like young smirking Glycon, naughtier far than man and snake together, storm like triple Hecate when she magic-makes the world as she desires, and sleeps with all her dogs so dark, or copulate like Thracian Bendis of the leather dildo, then what's the point of living, and what's the price of body and of soul?

'And more, I know, for there is one thing, earlier, I did not quite reveal... that Comte Alphonse he never died, at least as far as this world knows at all... there is no grave, there were no masses said on his behalf... he simply disappeared. And if his journals mention nothing of his finding of the book, I suspect that, having found it, before he wrote another word he then departed, simply, for another world. The book, I do believe, is more than just a history; it is a gateway too, and bridge across the worlds. For if it is but hardly here, and so 'unreal', in what *we* call the 'real world', then if we make the *book itself* quite real, then *our* world fades away, and so the book's world too becomes the 'real'. And using certain awful heretic spells I learned, all breathless and all gasping, writhing too, in Syrian Harran where even God was named for Sin, and old Cyclopean Baalbek next, foul incantations triple-wove that speak so sweet of peacock Gods like Melek Taus the evil, but worse by far of oiled, voluptuous Atagartis and her bloodstained doves and squirming fish that wore the golden earrings in their gills, then I shall make it so, and follow handsome, lewd Alphonse, and never once return.

'I'd like to take you with me, if you'll come. For Théophile, a life with you, my handsome friend, so virile and so charming, so ripe for sweet corruption, of sin quite dreadful to our parents, and just as much to those we know today in Paris and in Orléans, would seem quite sweet to me. I do not wish to shock you, and never will I speak to you of love, but Théophile, I *want* you… and more, I do not want you *here*, I want you in that *other* world… where you are father, brother, son and everything forbidden that here I may not have… and I will be your sister, mother, daughter, and we will sin, and sin, and cry our pagan bliss until the starry heavens weep their diamond tears of joy. And Théophile, my darling boy, I tell you this, if you refuse to go with me, then I will go myself, alone, and I will find Alphonse, the never-dead, and he will then be everything to me that once you could have been, and in his arms and bed mayhap then once or twice I'll think of you as centuries pass, but mostly then, I know I won't. And you will never have me, as all too well I know you wish to.

'So will you come, or will you stay? I need to have your answer. Now.'

And Théophile looked once then at her soft, fair flesh, made golden by the flickering, flaming light, the magic letters he himself had painted on her lovely breasts that matched the letters he bore too from her, the stars that winked like Algol in her bright, enormous eyes, and decided there and then he could not let her go. And so he murmured: '*Oui…*'

She grinned a grin of such corruption then, he almost thought to see a snake's forked tongue coming flicking from her ruby lips. But even that, which passed away, could not erase the simple realisation, which, he knew, within his heart, he'd known for many days: he loved her. And if that lovely face were but a mask for sin, he loved her none the less. And if he could not have her here, in a château in the Pyrenees, then he would have her still, in any mad and wicked other-sphere she chose.

The magic inscriptions painted on their skin they left exactly as they were, but dressed and ate and fortified themselves as best they could for the journey to a destination past the edge of this known world. Jacques, and all the other staff, she paid too much and thanked and sent them on their way; they seemed so sad to leave her, kissed her hands and wept such salty tears that spoke of all their love. And then at nightfall, when the Moon rose up above the horizon, round and full and staring down upon the world, an empty-eyed skull, it seemed, the colour quite of ancient bone, they hugged the once and kissed the twice, and took them to the library.

That book (for ever after would he stammer trying to pronounce its name) she held and opened for the final time, and read how when the Christians came the Sun itself, protesting, had expired, and after that the world was never lit but by the Moon. And this she thought a happy omen, standing there by lunar light that shone in silver through the window.

Then Eugénie began to sing those skirling Levantine enchantments of which she'd spoken earlier, that book clutched tightly in her hands, her eyes so full of flames that, looking close, one might have thought to see the fires that Nero set to fiddle to as all about him burned down wondrous Rome. And as her voice rose higher still, the very air began to shudder, and then she screamed so loud for Hermes Argophontes, Hermes Charidotes, Hermes Chrysorrapis and, glancing then at Théophile, for Hermes Epithalamites, but most of all for Hermes Chthonios and Hermes Psychopompos, to guide them on their way. And all the world was full of strange irisian shimmers, tiny lightnings too, and there upon the Moon's face was a smirk, and in the air were scents, both sweet and foul, the like he'd never known.

And Eugénie, she shrieked and shuddered, all unstrung, writhing as she rent the universe in twain, her back all arched, her breasts so proud, her legs collapsing so she fell down on her knees; and then that lurid hell-gate opened wide, and skull-face Charon beckoned then that they should cross the Acheron, no obol needed for his boat, for Hecate and Aidoneus loved them both and wanted just to please them, wanted to initiate them in oh so many lovely worlds of necrophilia and corruption that made the worm their special friend and partner, till they tired of life and death together, and sought for pleasures yet more vile.

And Eugénie cried 'yes' to all the Gods and Devils offered, fire-tongued, without a second thought, and surrendered spirit, body, soul.

And looking back once to Théophile, she cried out: 'Will you come with me? Oh come, oh come, oh come!'

And Théophile surrendered body, thought he knew not what a spirit was, so relinquished that as well, but stumbled when it came to soul. For some old voice of Catholic God, of parents, or of schooldays, said 'do not so, my child, oh do not so', and so he hesitated but an instant.

An instant was too long.

For when he looked again, the lovely Eugénie was gone into another world, quite gone, and gone, and gone, and he was still in this one. And with her went that book of books, and all his dreams, and all his fond desires.

So Théophile, quite simply, fainted.

He woke at some time in the night, beneath a smiling golden Moon that seemed so sweetly sympathetic, looked round then once and realised, he sat there in a ruin. For everything of Eugénie, the things she had and all the things she loved, save Théophile, had accompanied her to hell; the library, the furnishings and half the château too, all were gone and one would think, on looking, had departed quite a century since. Or worse, perhaps, were never there at all.

And Théophile, upon the sudden frozen to the marrow, could only howl for Eugénie, and everything he'd lost, and stumble down the mountain, a beggar dead to all the world, for after all it seemed somehow his soul had gone with her in fact, and nothing but his body had remained. And spirit, well, he knew not what it was, and so he never realised he'd lost it.

They say he wandered ever after that, like Ahasuerus the Jew, with loss so plainly written on his face, and 'Eugénie' forever on his lips; and ragged, drunk and odorous, he oft frequented libraries and bookshops, asking always, with a stutter, for the *O-O-Opusculum Mercurialis*, the like of which no man had ever heard, and so he never found it.

Decades later, they still spoke of the 'mad and mumbling Delore', much as they spoke, on other times, of the well-known Flying Dutchman. And so he passed away from out this world and on into the land of legend.

But whether he went further still, to Eugénie and hell besides, that, no one ever knew.

But those of us who think it sweet to die, if only once we've tasted love, would like to think he did…

I did not know quite what to make of this at all. Some things, of course, I did not understand; but again, I have to think, that Endimion Lee would hardly understand such present things as the wretched Admiralty Telegraph, when beacon fires were all he'd know.

I too could see the similarities mentioned by the story's author: the library, the silver château on the mountain, the writer and the character's love of paganism and rejection of the world in which he lived; but all this treated with a bold and cynic hand, that spoke to me of an older author, even more world-weary than I am. And yet I was so sad poor Théophile had failed and faltered at the end. I thought then of Endimion Lee, and how I think to end his story. More though, I thought of myself, and how I might react if ever I was in a similar situation. I'd like to think I'd go where Théophile did not, my love of all things pagan is so strong. And yet I do not know.

Besides, I know such things they cannot be, and happen only in stories.

But then again, I thought: this 'S' says in his letter that he writes a *Somnium*, in which *I* appear as a character (and when he is not writing that, he writes another story just not quite the same); I write a *Somnium* about Endimion Lee; and Endimion Lee, Diana tells him, *will* write all of her. What, then, if there were *only one story* at the heart of this, and we three simply wrote it out in all our different ways? Or more, what if there was *only one story*, and *all three of us were in it*? (And what of Morion of Lyons? Now surely *he's* a fiction…)

I hardly dare to think of this. At times I think I am too much enmeshed in fictions, and would be better on the coach away from here, to somewhere in the 'real world'.

But stories are the life and soul of all the world to me. And after all that's happened today, with hangings and with letters, I think my best escape is found with pen and paper.

So let's be back to Endimion Lee and his elfin Queen Diana, as next they leave the theatre…

A corridor, the same as he had seen before, he expected then to find. He didn't.

Before him stretched a mighty hall, of crystal walls and columns; its oversoaring ceiling, lapis lazuli it was, decked out with constellations. To start, he thought them diamond twinklers, but then he recognised them: stars. Though whether they were dream or real, he never could quite tell; and hap it didn't matter.

Carnelian and tourmaline mosaiced all the floor; a thousand Moon-nymphs stood upon it naked, singing cosmic harmonies. At hall's end rose a nephrite dais, nine steps leading to an amethystine throne; behind were all the banners of the Moon, its oriflammes and streamers, its pennants and its flags. The mostly blue and gold they were, though variegated white. And long and straight they blew out silky, a-snap and cracking in a wind that was not there.

And perched above the Goddess' throne, the golden Moon-disc glowed, corona'd like a gem.

Endimion Lee looked back across his shoulder, wondering how from theatre he had come to here; and yet no door at all he saw. His sweetheart, though, remained at hand, and whispered in his ear:

'Look forward, don't look back, my love. Who knows? Perhaps tonight, you'll find a sweeter chamber!'

He thought to find a hint of promise sparkling in her eyes; but then she laughed and, tugging at his hand, away she ran amongst her nymphs.

She led him to the dais and up it; far against his expectation, sat him down upon the throne and jumped into his lap. Her arms all flung around his neck, her bare breast in his hand, she kissed him long and deep. A tenth of a myriad Moon-nymphs they looked on, with smiling eyes and laughing lips, then sang their naked song.

'Dear love,' he said, when at the last she gave him pause for breath. 'And is it right to put me on your throne, when all your maids are watching? And then to give me softest breast and kisses sweet, and such a lovely lapful?'

'You asked to see Diana's home!' she laughed. 'And in Diana's home, Diana does those things that please her. Besides, millennia have passed away, Diana kissing nymphs: they are no longer jealous.

'But if you'd rather be alone, my love, one further kiss and then we'll go [he kissed her with his might and main, as if he'd never kiss again]. But I have one condition: until we leave this giant room, my darling man, then you must let me carry you!'

'*You* carry *me!*' his laughter was explosive, as down she skipped onto the floor, all sweet, petite and lovely.

'My man,' she said, both serious and a-laughing, 'I know you see me, dressed like this, all small and soft, your lovely little darling. It's time of this you were reminded: *I am, besides, your Goddess.*'

And so without another word, she picked him up and tossed him 'cross her shoulder. Then running lightly from the throne, she crossed the dais and passed out through another door.

She put him down and while he stood there all amazed, she tip-toed up and kissed him.

'You see?' she tittered sweetly. 'You thought you'd got to know me! All those old thoughts that your mind might hold at home... of "mighty man" and "little woman"... for a moment, they were coming back. That queens would somehow be a-lessened, giving throne and showing love unto a man, and showing all the "weakness of their sex". I know your queen, she suffers much the same: men cannot see that "love" and "virgin" go together. So should she show a smile, or give a kiss, they'll make a woman whore.

'Oh, love, I know at heart you did not think it so, for if you did you'd never be here. But throw aside what others think (not just in this besides); their thoughts pollute your head. Your heart, my dear, should always rule. Your heart is what I want.'

'My heart is yours, sweet girl,' he told her then, although he looked a-wildered. 'And if in heart, or head, or any other way, I've sinned against your love, I beg you now, forgive me.'

'Dear knight,' she sighed, 'you never did, and if you had, I would. But, love, this thought: that women, they deserve far better on the Earth below, I wish you'd take back to your world. For if there is a teaching of the Moon, that is not learned and mayhap never will be, I tell you it is this.

'And now look where we are!'

A giant window, all of glass, he found himself before. He looked out on an empty place, with stony mountains rising in the distance. All sun-dewed gold they soared up high, beneath a dark and starry sky; and climbing upward to the zenith, a globe of blue and brown. Mercator never made the like, although he tried his best. Europe then and Africk too he saw, and when he squinted up his eyes, Eliza's lovely land.

''S'teeth!' he gasped, and grabbed her shoulder, reeling at a world all upside down.

'Sweetheart, are you well?' she asked, a-sudden. 'I meant you no alarm. A small surprise, and nothing more, intended to amuse you!'

'If this is small surprise,' he laughed, a little thin, 'then I'll forego a big one!'

'Come this way,' she led him from the window, and through another door.

A long and lavish gallery stretched out far before him then, all windowed down one side. He could not help himself: he looked, and saw the Moon up in the sky. She hugged him all apologetic, sat him down upon a couch, sat herself upon his knee, and kissed him oh-so-tenderly. She was too sweet to faint beneath, so breathing deep, he upped and played the man.

Opposite the windows, all the wall was covered quite with paintings; spaced along the floor were sculptures. And every one, in oil or stone, they all portrayed Diana, sometime naked, sometime clad; sometime queen or charming child. Here Diana, there Selene; three-form Hecate, magic, stern and mild. Sky-girl, huntress, night-lamp, priestess, all of these she was and more; and all her stories they were there besides. Here was Actæon, bold Orion, sad Niobe too; Endymion sleeping, horn-god Pan with thrusting yard; bed of Zeus and both their daughters, Erse dewy and Pandia all agleam; dark of Moon with Helios and nine months later, all the lovely Seasons.

She led him all along the gallery, showed him every one and told its story; and every time she did, he hugged her with a kiss. So they passed an hour or more, and all the time was sweet.

They wandered on, all hand-in-hand like lovers. Sometimes she led him up the stairs, and so into a basement; or otherwise they downstairs went, and climbed up to a tower. An inner gate, it led out to the gardens; and going out beyond, they found them back inside. A-mazed, he thought him, truly, then.

But all its upward-soaring spires viewed exterior, just the way she liked it, rather than the way she made it just for him… then what a palace Somnium was. No tower tall that rose up more than five whole storeys had he seen before; Somnium overleapt it thrice. And all its walls and turrets, they were coroneted quite with jewels; and more, besides, of crystal they were builded. And tessellated domes, they sparkled opaline beneath the stars; and glorious banderoles, all a-glint with fiery gems, streamed long below the Moon.

A wondrous building, fitted quite for such a lovely Goddess. And when he saw her standing there before it, he thought that beauty's surfeit, it would make him blind.

Within once more, she led him to a temple, built and dedicated just to her. All silver, moonstone, crystal were its walls; its floor, in gold and turquoise, mapped the full-formed features of the Moon; its ceiling was a dome of sapphire strewn with quartzy comets. And circling ever overhead, the phasing, changeful satellite, a disc of purest ivory.

More statues of Diana, nude, were placed all round the walls; he thought, perhaps, they were unclad for him. A swirl of fragrant incense wafted clear across the room, and scented up a vast, imposing throne. And then Diana, tiny feet a-patter, left him, climbed up on the seat and turned to face him, beaming lovely smiles.

A Goddess in her temple, then she was, awaiting his admire.

He dropped down to a knee; she ordered him to stand. In Athenæ and Roma, then she told him, one stood up to adore. The slave religions, they bowed down; but she preferred to look her lovers in the eye.

He offered then extempored praise, and told her how he loved her. He wished herself felicity, and everlasting bliss, and told her how he loved her. He called her blessings on himself, and on his queen and country too, and told her how he loved her. And many other things besides, and when he'd run out quite, he told her how he loved her.

And bliss to hear it from her lips, and in her temple too, she told him that she loved him just the same.

And so the day, it passed away. She showed him treasures of the Moon; she showed him things that never were on Earth. And all the time she kissed him. She showed him things from long ago; she showed him things more recent; but none unto his eyes were lovelier than she. She showed him all the best she had, because she wished to please him; and never was a better way for him to show his pleasure, but to hug her close and kiss her in return.

With evening and the brightening Moon, she led him on to chambers far more dainty. All frills and lace and feminine things he found about him now, and flowers oft en-vased upon the tables. The scents about him, too, far stronger then they grew; and sweetmeats melted on his tongue that seemed to him ambrosia.

A boudoir then she took him to, its carpet-floor all strewn about with cushions. A silent nymph tapped out an ancient earthen amphora, and poured out strong Falernian wine, a whole millennium its vintage; and then she left them quite alone to drink. And drink they did, and loved and laughed, and cuddled up and kissed. She pressed all close and let his hands go wander where they would; and let him kiss her anywhere he liked as well. He thought, since all the world began, two hours had never passed the sweeter.

All soft and charming drunk she was, when up she stood at last and took him by the hand. The boudoir's inner door she opened then; Brazil-wood, red and dark it was, he noticed, and all inlaid with nacre. But once beyond, he paused, and thought himself in heaven.

He knew then, as she looked at him, all wide-eyed and all-lovely, she'd brought him to her bedroom. Nine feet diametered was the bed, a perfect Moonish circle, its sheets of whitest silk. Its mattress all of softest down, he knew, before he even touched it. And pillows shaped like round full Moons, he never saw the sweeter.

The gleaming lamps were crystal globes; the rugs were furs of polar bears. A fireplace of rowan logs, it heated, and it lit. No tapestries here; white lace hung all about the walls; above, a dome of glass, and through it shone the Moon. Beyond, a bathroom, mosaic-walled in gold; within, more wine, and crystal goblets, comfits and confections too.

'Dear heart,' she said, and kissed him oh-so-sweet. 'A while ago, we talked of Fates, and given word, all hard. And now, my love, that test it is at hand. A test of all your love.

'The question's this, my dear: do you love me, quite enough, to hold me in your arms all naked, sleep with me all night, and more, within my very bed, that quite was made for love, to leave me all a-virgin? My sweet, I tell you, if you can, I'll love you ever more; but if you can't, then all is lost, and though I'd never harm you, you will not know me ever more again. There is no choice; the test is here; you cannot now withdraw.

'But if you hug me all night long, with nothing more than kisses, then, oh my love, eternity it beckons.'

He hardly knew what words to say, or what to even think. He took her in his arms and kissed her eyelids, nose and lips, and gathered up his wits. A deep breath then he took, and said:

'My love, a hard word's never given easy, and this is hard as I can bear. To have the thing I most desire, and in the moment it's obtained, to give it up entire; why, that's a trial, too. And yet, they say, we only get the things we want when we have quite renounced them. And more, when we have no desires left, we've no desires unfulfilled.

'Oh, love, Diana, sweetheart mine. My heart says yes. My body does not know. I think, though, that with all my soul I love you. Mayhap I love you quite enough, to even give you up.

'But let's to bed and test me. And even should I prove to fail, I tell you now, my love, the crowning moment of my life so far, will be to hold you naked in my arms in bed, and kiss you sweet goodnight.'

A little tear was in her eye, as up she stood on tip-toe, for to kiss him. All charming then, she helped him to undress; and very sweet she was to let him take her dress off too. Quite naked then, they turned and faced each other, eyes all greedy for the other's form.

His yard was never standing bigger. She took his hand and squeezed it, sympathetic, said: 'Come to bed, my love, and kiss me.'

The bed was far too large for what they had in mind, for all that either wanted was to hold the other close, and closer yet besides. In tight embrace they tried to melt into each other; in constant kiss they tried to breathe the other's breath.

He told her that he loved her quite; she said she loved him too.

No other words were needed then, and so they used their lips to kiss. Sometimes, their smiles spoke little odes; more oft their tears spoke volumes quite enormous. But all the time their lips were used for kissing.

He could not sleep for hours, just waiting for the dawn.

Tuesday, 16th October 1803

At last, then, yesterday evening, after early supper (and much impatience on my part), Cynthia and I handed over the running of the inn to Flora, with strict instructions not to stand for trouble or uproarious celebrations of Jude Brown's too-deserved demise; and if she cracked a skull or two, we'd think her none the less. The smile she returned for that was quite delightful; she is a marvellous wench.

And after that, dear Cynthia and I went back down to the cellar.

I thrust the key into that ancient lock and turned it, and found the door more willing to be opened than it ever was before. And I have to say that this time all my nervousness had disappeared and that, with our lanterns lit, it was I that took fair Cynthia's sweet small hand in mine, and led her on. Not only because I wanted to see the more of what remained down there, but because I wanted to adventure with a lovely woman, hand-in-hand, and to face the great unknown beside her, and to feel that this time, if anyone needed aid and protection, then I should be the one to clutch *her* in my tender arms, and kiss her from her faint. Of course, for all of that, a part of me also knew that if Cynthia played the wilting maiden, all would be an act; for that same part suspected all of this a puppet-show, where Cynthia pulled the strings. Well, be that as it may...

My eagerness, of course, was quite misplaced. We followed once again the thread, left in place from our previous adventure; and as before, the first thing we came to was that sculpture of the whitest marble, portraying dear Diana bathing in the world-surrounding waters of the Ocean; except that this time *she was no longer bathing*.

Instead, she'd stepped out of the lapping foam all dainty, and stood there now on tiptoe poised as all her wondrous nymphs (in whom I thought to recognise young Flora and all her lovely sisters) dressed her in a short and thigh-revealing chiton. And once again Diana was my Lizzie, and sweet Cynthia, and all those to whom, on Sunday morning, I was all too willing to swear away my soul. How these things can be, I know not; and yet I know quite well they are.

This first shock I managed to bear, I admit enwrapped in Cynthia's softest arms, without undue alarm. The second, when we reached that ruined wall, was rather more the difficult. For that same wall had grown up high somehow, I'm sure it had; was taller than it was before. And now, in lunar marble, I saw chariot wheels in full, and maidens carved in stone up to the breast, and gazed upon sufficient to know that here was Diana, taking leave of her lovely and beloved nymphs, as she prepared to drive the silvery Moon-chariot swift across the starry sky. And I know it's not my memory that's at fault; that wall *was* taller than it was before.

We moved along the marble wall to the gateway we had seen before, and there was that name-plate once again, the one that read, but should not read, the quite impossible *Somnium*. I thought to take it back with us, to examine it more carefully in my room, and to have some *proof* of what we'd found; but Cynthia told me no. Better, she said, to find some way of propping it firmly in the stonework by the gate, and so to reinstate it and the palace (or whatever it is that we have found down there) that it names; or, perhaps, to *re-found* it. And so that's what we did, though I confess I'm not entirely sure exactly what she meant.

This time, being better prepared and, in my case, still quite conscious, we decided to move on through the gateway. An avenue led onwards into darkness. A few feet to our left, the remaining wall cornered and then followed along beside the broad paved path. To our right, a little flight of steps led down some three or four feet. Taking these, we found ourselves in what had once, quite obviously, been a sunken garden of some extent, and a water garden besides. No water now remained, or plants either, of course, but wandering the paths we could trace the outlines of the various-patterned ponds and the water-channels connecting them, the shapings of the flower-beds and, more poignant far than any of these, the tumbled or broken statues that lay where they had fallen, appearing suddenly from the darkness as our lantern-light revealed them. Mostly of the whitest marble, all of them distinctly female, they portrayed the most beauteous Goddesses, and winsome nymphs, and lovely priestesses, in various states of dress or less; and when I saw one of dear Diana, crescent-browed and breasts exposed, I could not quite resist. I had to help her to her feet once more (she looked so sad, all tumbled and all overthrown), and then I knelt before her, head bowed down, before rising up to kiss those pure white lips, oh-so-perfect and oh-so-cold, before we moved once more upon our way. But before we did so, Cynthia clutched my arm and turned me round, and showed herself by lantern-light, quite posed as sweet Diana was, and with all her dress pulled down (or disappeared) and beautiful breasts exposed; and I kissed her soft red lips, oh-so-perfect and oh-so-warm. At least, I think I did, for the next that I remember she was dressed quite as before, and looking as if she never had been otherwise, and I was leading her onward through that garden and up the steps at its far side. And thinking back, I simply do not know if it was real, or if I dreamt that moment, inspired by the statue; or if I dreamt the entirety of what happened in the cellars last night. After Sunday morning, having abjured the Christian god and all his works, and any of the world that is not Diana or her own, it seems to matter very little; but last night when we returned from the underworld, it gave me much to think on.

That sunken garden I had not mentioned, I'm quite sure, in my own (far too poor) description of fair palatial Somnium, and thought I must include it; though last night when I read my manuscript again, I found out that I had. How this can be, I really do not know. All things Dianic and Somniac now become as strange and fluid as Moonlight dreams, and 'facts' they merge with 'fiction', and who knows which is which? Perhaps I'm mad, but think I'm not; or perhaps I'm not, but fear I am.

We rejoined the avenue at the garden's farther side and, walking

on a few paces more, we suddenly found ourselves in a world I knew
(or thought) that I myself had written. A gatehouse rose before us,
ruinous, I must confess. And yet *I knew it*, for I had described it exactly
as it was, its outward surface covered entirely in plaster, in which were
set mosaics composed of naught but precious and semi-precious gems,
interspersed with gleaming gold. Two towers rose to either side of the
broad gateway, with lovely and loveable images of divine Diana: one
portrayed her as the earthly huntress, the other as the gold-girl of the
Moon. Her lovely locks were done in agates, her lips with rubies, her
skin with corals and tourmalines, her nipples with upstanding garnets,
her dress, what little was to show, of shining diamonds, and topaz were
her golden jewels. And how those gemstones *sparkled* in the lanterns'
light, and how I wished that I could look upon them in the brilliant
silverings of the radiant full Moon. I trembled to see those mosaics,
and moaned to see those broken turrets, that once forefronted up the
lovely palace of the Dreaming Moon. For though it may be a strange
and wonderful thing to build a palace in the imagination, to see it real
quite takes the breath away; but to see it ruined shatters the soul in a
way that I simply cannot tell of.

I looked upon the ruins of my fondest dreams, sat down upon
the ground, and wept. And wept, and wept, and wept. I know not how
long it lasted; it seemed I wept forever.

But lovely Cynthia who, with every passing thought, becomes
to me yet more in truth the beauteous Diana, embraced me with a
sympathy that told me fully that she understood, and kissed my
tears away.

We then passed far enough through that great and lovely
gateway to see an open space beyond, that our lanterns were far too
weak to penetrate, and I knew that stretching before us was a spacious
quadrangle; knew it most of all because I'd already written it so. I
know this sounds like madness, and it *is*, and it's *real* besides; and any
thought of rational explanation I abjure, and leave it to any who think
the world is simple, and objective, and comprehensible. And I leave it
to them with my most vulgar scorn, because they have no dreams, no
magic in their souls and, perchance, no souls at all besides.

But all that aside, by then the candles in our lanterns were burning down so low, that I began to fear that we might be stranded there in darkness before we'd gained the safety of The Bull's familiar cellar. I have to say that, as we debated our situation, I could not help but think that, Liz apart, there was no one with whom I'd rather be lost in cloying blackness than with Cynthia; Cynthia whose eyes, so enormous-pupilled, were so sweet and sparkling in the lantern's light. And I thought, from the faintest smile upon her lips, that she understood my thought and, for a moment, considered it; and then that same thought broadened her smile into a grin, and we agreed to retrace our steps, returning again on a later occasion with extra candles for the lanterns, and mayhap Falernian wine, and cold venison pies for a subterranean, nocturnal picnic; and I cannot think of anything else than Cynthia smiling at me at that moment, brown-eyed and lovely-locked, and looking at me with a mother's love, as if I was a small boy who needed to be taken home, and put to bed, and lullabied to sleep with a lovely-voiced and lunar song.

And I can only imagine that indeed she performed that kindest service for me, for I remember nothing more until I woke this morning, abed alone, in my room which now, somehow, was full of sweetly-smelling flowers, the door wide open and nothing to be heard throughout the inn but the most musical feminine laughter, and giggles, and occasional sighs. And I knew then that there's nothing more lovely than the sound, to man, of woman, when she's happy and delighting in the world.

Although I must have slept for many hours last night, I found myself so weary when I woke that I could hardly move. Young Violet, passing by my door all frilly and delightful in a pure white petticoat and seeing me awake, blew a kiss and went upon her way; a minute or two later dear Cynthia arrived. She felt my forehead and told me that I had the slightest fever; her touch was feather-soft upon my brow. I asked her if I'd dreamed last night; she grinned and told me only I would know.

The worm of thought that kept on wriggling in my brain was this: that desolate as I had been to see the ruin of my dreams, yet still those ruins had grown taller than they were before; certainly the carven curtain-wall had risen by two or three feet. Yet how, with passing time, do ruins rebuild their former glories? Does time in fact run backwards here, ruins un-ruinating themselves with every passing hour? Or if Somnium is somehow manifesting here (from Dreamland, or the Moon?) must it, for some reason, do so in reverse? I did not mention these ruminations to my nurse-in-chief, lest she think... well, whatever she might think...

She left and came back with a cordial, helped me sit and plumped up all my pillows; I almost called her dear Mama. And then I asked her if I had some letters; she shook her head so sad. Oh Liz, my Liz, what's happened? I can't believe you have not written.

I wanted to get up then and write, but Cynthia would not let me; I confess I was so tired I allowed her to persuade me. Instead she gave me a broad and wooden tray, on which to rest my journal, to place my ink-pot, my paper and my pen. I wrote a page or two of this entry for today, describing most of what had happened in the night, then Cynthia came up with oxtail broth and fresh-baked bread, and fed me with a spoon; I told her I could feed myself, she simply would not hear of it. Flora and Rose were looking in the door all sympathetic; after I had eaten, darling Iris came and played the lute until I took a nap.

Half-waking in the afternoon, I thought the Moon itself had come down from the sky and shone there in my room; a lovely face it then became, said: 'Come on home to me, you are so weary of the world.' I wanted then so much to just shrug off my tired and aching body and soar up to the realms of bliss. The Moon was beaming in my eyes; I wanted but a lunar kiss. And then my vision cleared, and Cynthia sat upon the bed before me, looking down with sweet concern. I reached up then and pulled her close and kissed her; and only then I noticed Flora sitting on the other edge of the bed, a pistol lying in her lap.

I must have looked embarrassed. Dear Flora laughed and said I had a devil in me; thought she ought to shoot it; wondered if it could be done without shooting me as well. I smiled and told her all my devils were quite invulnerable to bullets, but scared to death of kisses. So for a little while (not long enough) two lovely ladies took their turns to kiss me. I said my devil was the most recalcitrant kind, and needed all the ladies of the inn to kiss it quite away; they pouted then and left me. Though soon as they were out the door, I heard their charming giggles.

I love them all. They are so sweet.

So after that I wrote another letter to my Liz, begging, if she could not come, at least to write and let me know that all was well. Flora said she'd see it posted.

Wednesday, 17th October 1803

Quite early in the evening, I once more fell asleep. Indeed, I seem to sleep far longer than I ever did before. Exactly why this is, I really cannot say.

I think I was delirious last night; for if I was not, then I know that Cynthia came to bed with me and held me in her arms all night and smothered me with kisses. And yet I'm sure this cannot be; I woke this morning all alone.

Perhaps I become the more and more Endymion; and was it fair Selene then who kissed me? And is *that* why I sleep so long?

Once again there was no letter from my dear and lovely sister, and so I am bereft. No, more than that, I wept in Cynthia's arms when she brought to me the news. I simply cannot understand how Liz could fail to write to me, knowing how I love her, and how I miss her, and what she means to me (and I know she knows exactly what she means to me, though neither of us would plainly mention it). Oh, and her sweetness, and her loveliness, and all those familiar intimacies we have exchanged.

An evil part of me, that almost is suppressed, though still it has a tiny, jealous voice, says while I am away my sister's found a lover, and so she has betrayed me. And yet I will not any way believe it; she simply could not do that without a word to me. *I know her far too well.*

I must know soon that dear sweet Liz is quite alright, or else I will be torn in two. She is my dearest dear one (Cynthia notwithstanding), and a part of me cries 'back to London and embrace your Liz, and satisfy yourself that she is safe'; but the other part fears that if I leave, then ruined Somnium, sleeping now beneath my feet, will never be restored; will cease to be, and with it all that I have written. And if *that's* lost, then what of me? And what of dear sweet Cynthia? And more, what of Selene?

And writing that, I think the more: and *what of sweet Selene?* For surely she is there in both the others, in Somnium, and everything about the Moon and all below it. To me she is, quite simply, Goddess. And if I lost Selene... oh, *everything* would be lost.

Oh, write to me, my Liz. So much of all I am depends on this.

I love you and I miss you.

Friday, 19th October 1803

Still I've had no letter from my Liz, and fall into despair. I despair of her health, her safety, her happiness, and in doing so I despair of my own as much. If anything's happened to her; if she no longer *was*; then what of me? Oh, worse than this, my lovely Liz, what if you had *never* been? For I can no longer find your letters, or any other of your keepsakes. I *know* they must be here somewhere; oh, I *hope* they are. But, mad though it may be, I begin to wonder if, in abjuring all but Diana-Selene, I've abjured them besides; and worse abjured my Liz as well. (As well as this, it seems that now I cannot find the letter from the future either, or, besides, its story).

Oh, write to me, beloved Liz, and save me swift from awful Bedlam's hell.

And yet I think it's only Liz that ties me to this world of dust, for all my other worlds are full of dream. I stayed abed on Wednesday, and thought perhaps my feverishness was caused by the dark of the Moon; for when there is no Moonlight, the world is full of pain. Dear Cynthia stayed with me throughout the evening, leaving all the tavern's business in bold Flora's hands (and never were there safer). I wrote a little, and Cynthia sat close by upon the bed and sang to me so gently, and so sweetly, as I wrote. So musical a voice, as soft as Moonlight, the words all tumbling and all trilling like the trickling babble of a burbling brook, or the lapping waves a-breaking oh-so-gently on a sparkling gold-sand beach. And the songs she sang: of the Ocean's old eternal longing for the Moon above; of the pale Moon's loving of her brilliant brother Sun; of maladroit and ancient Actæon, and Endymion all asleep, and that mighty star-crowned hunter, Orion of great fame. And there were times when I looked up from my work, and thought to see my Cynthia as Diana herself, or Diana Regina of whom I wrote, or Selene-the-Perfect, of whom all the others are reflections. And sometimes she was dressed, and sometimes night-gowned, or chitoned with a bow in hand and one sweet breast exposed.

And sometimes she was naked.

And when she was all naked I thought to see my Lizzie looking out of her big brown eyes; and whether my Lizzie *is*, or whether she is *not*, I know that I shall never erase that image from my mind, of seeing my lovely sister Liz quite naked, and so young, and so *beautiful*. Oh Liz, my Liz; oh *please* exist for me, for if you do not, then all the world is damned.

And if the world is damned, without a second thought, I'll leave it all behind.

We supped together, Cynthia and I, then supped again at midnight. And then she stroked my hair and kissed me fond goodnight.

I did not wake again till last night's sunset; I probably would not have done so then, but Cynthia woke me with a kiss. The darling sweetheart wished to know that I was quite alright.

The way I wrapped my arms around her, hugged her close and kissed her breath away, it said I was recovered quite. She laughed and pushed me back against the pillow; said Endimion Lee he never would have been quite so forward; I told her Lee, he had to do with queens and Goddesses. She laughed and slapped me soft around the head; asked me what I thought that *she* was. I said I thought she was my darling, and so I'd kissed her; and just to prove my point, I held her close and kissed her once again.

She grinned and said I was a naughty boy. I laughed and told her yes I was, and then I kissed her once again. And last, because I thought she wanted to hear it, called her 'Cynthia of the Moon'.

At that she laughed and took my hand, kissed my palm and

pressed it to her breast; then said she'd send up supper and my claret (it tasted like Falernian once again) and left me then to write.

I think that *Somnium*'s almost done. I'll be so sad to finish with it, yet I think there's little more to say. It is a world I'd love to live in, created all for me; and *Somnium*'s queen is all the ladies that I've ever loved. If I could simply give up all the Earth and soar up winged to heaven, I know I'd find a bliss like that.

And yet I have to think: perhaps I *have* created Somnium. For what's a 'dream', and what's the 'real world', I now no longer know. If Somnium's just a tale I wrote, then what's that down there in the cellar, that's grown since first I saw it? And if those ruins lie halfway between the here and there, half real and half of dream, then which way does the balance swing, twixt Somnium and The Bull? One's real, one's dream, but which, at last, is which? And more, if my *Somnium*'s published as a book, will that be like an *Opusculum Mercurialis*? Not providing a gateway *to* another world, but *for* another world, by which palatial Somnium might be here established. And can a story come to form, if writ so close to one's ideal... that ideal forms emerge from pre-material dreams and shape themselves all solid 'fore our eyes? And if so many authors write a story much the same, does that suggest that *there is something there*, unseen by most but yet eternal still, existing in a way we cannot yet quite understand? Existing in a strange 'outside', perhaps beyond our grasp (or mayhap, with a little more belief, within it?)... then if it grows more as we imagine it all the better, then does it too transform the world we normally think is 'real'? For all I look about me at The Bull, since Jude Brown quite was hanged (and did I wish it so? The question still is with me), the more it seems all Somniac, and Cynthia, Diana.

So when the inn was closed last night, with dear and perfect Cynthia Brown-eyes I descended to the dining room, joining Flora and her lovely and beloved crew for a second much-belated supper (by any other's terms). And they are all my sisters (though not quite so beloved perhaps as Liz), and all of them they treat me as their brother (and oh, oh how they kiss me); and later, when much wine it had been drunk, they all became delectably *décolletée* and lovely to behold. And they laughed aloud so soul-delightingly and sang with such honey-sweetened voices, of love and Moon and stars, and they were all so beautiful to look upon that, on occasion, I could not help but cry.

And later on I read them all my latest pages; they listened so attentive and looked at me large-eyed. And when my narrative saddened, how sweetly then they sighed. Then Ivy said I was a poet, while Daisy whispered I dreamed lovely dreams; and Cynthia pleased me most of all by saying I did both.

At last he slept, or thought he did, but never really knew. For all she'd spoke to him of dreams before, had caused him much confusion. And this he thought the strangest yet, but still the most familiar.

One part of him, he knew, was Knight Endimion Lee, a modern man who lived, by Christian terms, in latter sixteenth century. That part it slept on Shooters Hill, that now was dreamt as Somnium, and slept besides in softest bed, in dear Diana's arms.

The other part, although he was not certain sure that it was part of him, or if it merely lay before his eyes, was legendary Endymion, who lay encaved on Latmos hill before the Christian nightmare quite began. All wrapped up in a sheepskin was that form, and dreaming; and lovely Grecian Moon-Selene (who was Diana too), had come down from the sky and thrown her arms around him. He slept, and dreamt she kissed him; she kissed him as he slept and gave him dreams.

And all was merged together, the dreamer and the dreamed, on Latmos hill and Shooters Hill besides. Endimions both, Diana and Selene, they merged alike in everlasting bliss that merely passed an instant.

And all was given then, that never wanted taking; and all that was received, it never had been asked for.

And when he woke to morning light, and found her there beside him, nothing gained but nothing lost, with nothing he was more than satisfied.

She woke up in his arms, all naked and all-lovely, and kissed him sweet good morning. And all the same, he knew at once, he'd gained her and he'd lost her.

'Oh love, I know how hard it is,' she told him, tears and smiles. 'But yes, we have to part. For matter though I dream myself, I am a spirit quite; and love you as a spirit, yes I could; but love you while you live, I can't.'

'But, sweet, I'll love you from the Moon, and every passing day, a day less it will be, until we are united. And then, my love, the joys I've only hinted at so far, they'll all be ours, forever.'

'And will you tell me quite how long I have to wait for love?' he asked, his fingers in her hair, his lips all tracing round her face.

'My man,' she said, 'and yes, I mean it so, for so you are indeed, succeeding as you did, the first I'll tell you of your task. Your Queen, she plays the virgin just like me, and so provides us opportunity.

'Diana, Selene, call me what you will, I am the Moon. And men, and women too, enslaved quite by the church, they have not looked in my direction, since old and proud-aspiring Rome it fell. But even to the dourest man, I am the Muse, I am Art's spirit, I am Poetry and Beauty. And I am Dream. For dreams are from the Moon, and all the Moon is made of dreams besides. My dearest love, men need me. They need my art, they need my bright creative spark, or all their lives are hell. They need the dreams I give them, they need to dream of me. And more, I need them too. For if men sleep and do not dream, the Moon falls from the sky.

'And so, sweet heart of all my heart, I have to send you back to Earth, and back to London Town. The task I'd ask you undertake for me is this: to make your Queen as much you can like me. In poems, masques and revels, songs and symbols too, draw down the Moon quite from the sky, and deify Eliza in my name. Call her what you will, Diana, Cynthia, Titania and Phoebe too, but sing her all of moonlight, sing her queen of lunar fairyland, and love me in her person. Your tragical entertainment made a start; now write of nothing else but *me* as Gloriana, and make Eliza's court a Moon-land here on Earth.

'For if the Moon does not return, to startle men with dreams, why, long before the years have passed away, then I'll be all forgot. And if I am forgot, then, love, I will not be. And if I'm not, then poetry it disappears, and all those other arts besides. And this, my man, then, is your task, to keep me quite alive. And if you can, then I am yours; and, love, there is no other love like mine.'

'Diana, Queen and Moon,' he told her then, 'for you, I would do anything, and even love you in another woman. But, love, oh heavens, love, how long?'

'Oh, sweet, the universe, it works in curious ways. You will of late, I know, have heard a story out of Wittenberg. A certain Doctor Johan Faustus, he sold his soul to some strange devil called Mephisto. Two dozen years of bliss he then obtained, and even Helen as his leman. And in the end, the devil took his soul and dragged him screaming off to hell. Or so it's said.

'My love, the contract I would make with you, it is reversed. Two dozen years of hell I offer you, with neither love nor leman; worse, with all your thoughts of me, but quite without me too. And all you'll do is work, to make men think of me. And making others think, so then you'll think the more of me, and suffer for it too. But if two dozen years you can pass by... oh, dearest, then you'll die... but come to your reward.

'Dear man, because I love you, so I'll give you one last choice. If you would never ever suffer, then all my plans I will renounce. And if you choose, then back you go, with memories none at all. No joys, no pains, and nothing of Diana. No harm, no love, and all we've had, it never will have been. And who knows, then, perhaps, you'll find a Lady of the Chamber, marry her and breed another Lee, or two, and live a life of fair content.'

'My love, I'd never give you up. How could you think I would?'

'I never did,' she smiled awry. 'I've seen into your heart.'

'It's very hard to part,' he told her then, his arms all round her tight. 'These days and nights I've spent here quite enchanted, a-looking in your lustrous eyes, they've taught me all the worth of love, and oh-how-lovely is the Moon. And honey has a bitter taste, compared with your sweet lips. You are my heart, my soul... oh dearest queen and Goddess, I cannot say the more.

'My love, I'll miss you.'

'I'll miss you too, my darling man,' she told him then, and kissed him. 'But dream of me and all my kisses too, and then the years they'll speed away.

'And when you hear these words, "the Queen is dead", my love, you'll know it's time to die as well. For once Eliza's gone, the joy dies in the world, for many years to come.

'And then I will be waiting.'

Her head she rested then upon his shoulder, hugged him tight, and sighed.

'Dear heart,' she said, 'it's best that presently I send you back to Earth, before goodbyes become too long and fond. And rather would I have your mind recall me at this instant. So kiss me nine times long and deep, and tell me that you love me.'

The tears then streamed down both their cheeks, their lips seemed almost grown together.

'Dear Queen Diana of the Moon,' he said at last, 'I love you.'

'Dear knight, my own Endimion Lee, I love you too.'

She raised a hand up to his face, about to close his eyes; he stopped her for an instant.

'My dear, one question at the last, before I go. And tell me, was it Fate or mother's whim, that named me for your love?'

'It wasn't Fate or whim at all,' she gently said, and smiled. 'I whispered in her ear.'

I almost was in tears, on reading this aloud, but Cynthia softly kissed me, and said she knew that *I* could be as brave as Endimion Lee myself. And so I had to smile; or else I'd let her down.

More wine then followed (oh, how those lovelies *do* insist), before they all proposed a little game of 'Blind Man's Buff', played out there in the dance-hall. Being the only young man present, naturally it was I on whom they tied the blindfold, and then they made me swear by sweet Diana's love I would not cheat at all; and so, of course, I couldn't.

They made me stand there rather longer than I expected, then Cynthia's voice cried out 'now begin' and all around were titters. Hands outstretched, I tottered forward; suddenly clutched a petticoat. Stood there all confused.

There was no darling maiden in it.

I must have looked so baffled; for suddenly all around were peals of lovely laughter.

I looped the petticoat around my neck, so the rascal who had shed it would not have it back. Bare feet they pattered on the floor. My hands stretched out again.

My fingers brushed on softest skin. A moment later I was touching sweet young maiden flesh again; I tried to clutch, but it was gone too quick.

I realised then that Cynthia, Flora, and all those sweet young girls had taken all their clothes off.

And I had sworn by dear Diana's love I would not look. But, oh, what I *imagined*…

I do not know how long they played their game with me; but all the time they giggled. One moment, a soft and bouncing breast was in my hand; the next, one darling girl would grab my wrist and place my hand upon another's ripe young rump; again, I'd hear some darting feet and then two warm moist lips would sudden press against my blushing cheek.

I like to think I played my part, and laughed and chased and let my fingers wander, but never quite did catch a girl; and never did I touch the blindfold. Some part of me, it knew this was a test that meant as much to me as Endimion Lee's did, sleeping with Diana; and if I looked I knew I'd wake up from my dream and find myself in muddy ditch, or Newgate Gaol, or somewhere even worse.

At last the giggles ceased, and footsteps only shuffled. And then a moment's silence, next followed by dear Cynthia's sweet command: 'unmask!'

I did, and looked around, but they were gone, and nothing then remained but petticoats all scattered round the floor.

Sweet Cynthia called again: 'Dear Kit!' I looked around to see her leaning round the door, her face, her arm and naked shoulder, nothing more. She blew to me a saucy kiss and then she dashed away.

I made my way back up to my room; my pocket-watch said four o'clock. I sat upon the bed and wondered if I'd passed.

'Yes, you have,' said dearest Cynthia, appearing at the door. Now nightdress clad, she bore two glasses and a claret-bottle. She sat beside me, kissed me swift, and poured us both some wine.

And so we spent two hours in each other's arms, drinking, kissing and embracing, talking then of many things, I hardly can remember. And then she laid me down upon the bed (no longer could I move), kissed me fondly, wished me sweet good morning, and left me then to sleep.

I woke this afternoon, two hours before the sunset, and found that it had snowed.

Saturday, 20th October 1803

When I had written up my journal, I went down to the dining-room and found a blazing fire. I could not linger long, for Cynthia, Flora and certain other of their dear young girls, all dressed in furs and rosy-cheeked, insisted I should go outside. We played at snowballs for a while, and all the time they laughed and pelted me until I fell down in the snow. A snowman then they proposed to build; I insisted on a snow-Diana. And when I placed two snowballs on its chest, they pouted, mock-offended, and pelted me again. I did not care. Already I was on one knee and praying to the Goddess whose image I had made. I prayed to her for Liz, for Cynthia, for Flora and her maidens; for all of womankind that ever was or is or will be, anywhere throughout the world; and woman's local representatives spattered me now and then again with snow.

I laughed and chased, and Cynthia let me catch her. All furry in my arms, with snowflakes falling all around, I kissed her ruby lips. She was so soft and sweet. And all the other girls, they simply stopped and looked.

I picked up darling Cynthia then (the other maidens, they applauded sweetly) and carried her back into The Bull. I don't know where I got the strength. She was so light I almost thought she was not there at all. I carried her across the threshold too, as if she was my bride. She wriggled then, but I just would not put her down; I laughed instead and kissed her.

Wet clothes demanded that we change, and then I joined her in her parlour; another fire was blazing there, and yet another glowed quite in my heart. Roast venison served in sauce of wine, it was our supper; we cut and fed each other; laughed and clutched each other's hands. I knew I was in love, and never had been more so.

So fed and fortified with claret, the night all thick and dark outside, then lovely Cynthia sparkle-eyes she took my hand, and led me down below, to that underworld which, in equal measure, fills me with unspeakable delight and quite bowel-trembling terror. I knew that it should only be the former, for Cynthia was with me; she told me then that I was more-than-mortal whenever my hand's in hers, and all my mind so full of love, I know I did believe her. But all my frail humanity's not yet quite shrugged off, and there were times… well, there were times when I feared to see the sights before my eyes. Lovely they were, but frightening.

I had suggested, when we first went back down those stairs and through that ancient door, that Flora, at the least, she should accompany us (though I confess I'd rather have, at every moment of the day, the entire bouquet of lovely floral nymphs all ringed about us as a posy), if for nothing else than to provide us with the extra illumination. But Cynthia put a finger to my lips, and simply would not have it. These particular adventures, she told me, were ours alone, at least until we had explored in full, to be shared with no-one else. No other hand would she have placed in mine and, if the fear and trembling should be on me, no other lips would she have warm upon my own. No other moistened female breathing would she have inside my mouth but hers, no other breasts placed soft against my chest, no other arms enwrapping me in tight embrace. And when she spoke so sweetly, how could I say her nay?

We returned then, with a bag of extra candles for the lanterns, claret, goblets, and honeyed dainties to take us through the night. And this time I was no longer shocked (though I confess myself disquieted nonetheless) to find pale marble-sculpted Diana fully-dressed and mounting on her chariot, nor when I found that curtain-wall raised higher still, and dear Diana likewise chariot-carried there. We skirted the water-garden, though I had brought a flaming torch beside the lanterns, for added light to see by; I was tempted then to stop, for it seemed that *all* the statues now stood restored to beautiful and edifying verticality. And when we reached the gatehouse, there was Diana all in gems and nothing ruined, and we went through into the quadrangle beyond.

I raised my torch, while Cynthia held up both our lanterns, and saw, oh, *such* a palace. No Whitehall, or Placentia, or Hampton Court, was ever quite like this; not even wondrous Nonsuch, all plastered up with pale divinities, the loss of which is crime and tragedy, alas, beyond recall. For here, though buried far beneath the ground, was gloriously spired and quite inspiring *Somnium*, the Palace of the Moon, the like of which was never seen, unless it were in dream. Marbled, enamelled and mosaiced like a precious jewel, it sparkled on a sudden, as if by fullest Moonlight; and I saw what I had written, and I knew I'd written true. For there *is* no other world but dream, and all that others say is real, is *not*.

To write, and write it *true*... that is a thing of wonder, and sublime.

So standing in that fountain-sprinkled court, all paved, I swear, in moonstones, I took soft Cynthia, suddenly clad (I know not how) in merest film, into my arms' embrace, and kissed her as my true beloved. She began to sing a Somniac song; I knew the words as well, though written by I knew not who (yet I suspect Endimion Lee, even though I know full well that, if he had wrote that song, then I had written *him* in turn). And we kissed again, and how she clung, so warm; and more than this, she was my Goddess and my woman both, united in a single lovely form, and she was in my arms and held so close, that somehow we were one and never more to part.

And I never would have let her go, except at last she broke away, and took my hand, and laughing led me on. She led me quite across that court and through another gatehouse, to a further quadrangle yet beyond. And standing there before my wondering eyes were glorious edifices quite unruined: great halls and temples of the lovely Moon, a glitter-sparkled throne-room of the beauteous satellite-queen, and marvellous octagon-towers with oriel-windows crystal-paned, and library-chambers full of glory (for no one ever dreamed the like of Somnium, and all its books are full of glorious Somniac dream, and Diana of the many names and aspects; and all her tales are tolden there, her sweetest stories and her truest loves, her histories and her hymnals, and such vasty epics of the silver-spattered night as old blind Homer would have writ, if ever he had set eye upon the lovely Moon). For Somnium is more than palace, more than temple, more than college, and even more indeed than that strange and mysterious School of Night of cherished memory; for Somnium, exactly as I wrote it, is the outpost of the Moon upon the Earth, the Embassy of Golden Planet Spheres, the Colony of the Sparkling Stars. But most of all, it's of Diana, and all that's lunar, and feminine, and sweet, and loved.

I had written it as combining Tudor palace, and classical acropolis, and nine parts in ten of dream; but having it before my eyes in truth, I knew that it was all of these, and yet it was much *more*. Because it *is* all those things that *cannot* be, and because they cannot be, and *are*, then there is nothing here but *miracle* and *wonder* and everything that sweet *Diana is* and *gives* and *cherishes*.

And Cynthia she turned to me again, and all the film she wore before was now dissolved, and she was naked now except a filigreed pectoral necklace of silver-mounted gemstones, strung mesh-wise from her shoulders to her lovely rounded breasts; the pointed golden crescent it was shining on her brow, and the Moonlight sparkled silver in her eyes. And no more was she just my sweetest Cynthia, but Diana Regina, Goddess-Queen of Somnium, eye-flashing and imperial, lovely-locked and beauteous in her majesty.

Yet more than this, she was Selene, who stands above the all: perfection of perfections, perfected nine times more.

And for I knew not then how long it was at all, it seemed to me that time was quite annihilated; and all the world it rippled then and became but lights that shone out from her eyes. And at the same time I could not look upon such loveliness, while just as much I could not look away. And there was merely lucent shimmering light, and all that light was in Selene, and Selene, she was in every light that ever burned. I knew then that I looked on Goddess, with all her human form shrugged off; and all I thought to see among that light was sweet eternal love. I yearned to lose myself in all her light; but still I was a creature of the wheeling temporal world.

She let me have myself back at the last (I think), though *when* that was, I never was quite sure. And sweet Selene, descended through Diana first, she dressed herself in Cynthia's form once more. Though still she was a light.

And as she stood before me, gleaming oh-so-brightly in her loveliness, I realised we were encaverned then no more, and above us all the silver stars were scattered quite across the infinite sky, and Somnium, that should have been but never was before, threw up its soaring spires and titan turrets in all their glory to heights undreamed since Salmoneus played the ape of Zeus. And then the full Moon sailed swiftly up toward the zenith, silver-gilt and beaming, and we were bathed, the both of us, in an impossible delirium of lovely glowing Moonlight.

And I could do nothing else but fall upon my knees before her, the Empress of Nocturnal Bliss, and kiss her lovely ankles, and surrender everything that ever made me what I am, and worship my dear Cynthia-Selene beyond all measure, for without her I was nothing, and with her I possessed the world.

And I knew then, beyond all doubt, that I, at last, had come back home. Home from the world of lowly men, and mud and mire and matter; and returned again unto the world of lovely lunar angels and she who, bright-eyed and brown-eyed in her high imperial pomp, led them onwards all majestic, and was by far the loveliest of them all.

And Cynthia took my hands and raised me to my feet, and kissed me, and with that simplest kiss made all my world, and me besides, divine.

I do not know how long I held her naked in my arms; or if I ever did. I only know at last I looked again, and once more beheld dear Cynthia human, dressed quite as she had been when first we'd descended the cellar stairs.

We were encaverned once again as well, the Moon no longer in the sky. And Somnium, though builded up as tall as just before, no longer had that sparkle.

'Not quite finished yet,' sweet Cynthia Brown-eyes smilingly remarked, all winsome and all wistful. I was not quite sure to what she did refer: to *Somnium*, my book, or Somnium, that reviving palace, or even then perhaps to both. Or perhaps, indeed, to *me*. She did not give me time to think.

'Now chase me for a kiss,' she giggled next, and dashed away, her lantern held so high. She was as fleet as Atalanta; I had no golden apples. I only caught her at the cellar-door; we'd almost closed it tight behind us, and she'd had to put her lantern down and use both hands to move it. Yet looking back now as I write, I have to think she could have been the quicker. I did not care; I did not think; I'd caught her and demanded my reward. I kissed her then so long and deep I thought I'd die there in her arms. To do so would have been quite sweet.

I had to let her go at last; I had her clutched so close and I was so aroused, I thought that she would notice.

The inn had closed when at the last we rose up from the cellar. Sweet Flora's flowers were gathered round the blazing taproom fire all hugged up in each others' arms and kissing; I thought this was a little odd, and how they laughed to see my wide-eyed stare. But if I thought it rather odd, I also thought it rather sweet. I imagined the whole group of them as sisters; beyond that again as sisters of my own; and then I thought of Lizzie helpless in their cuddling arms and victim of their kisses. It was too much. I had to stop, before I thought of Liz and Cynthia together naked in my bed. My soul was saved, I thought, by Flora, who offered me a mug of hot mulled wine. I drank it at a draft and waited for my head to spin.

I do not quite remember then how many further drafts I drank, or who I kissed, or who sat on my lap; nor, indeed, who played the harpsichord so sweetly and so skilful. Somehow it seemed a plot, to leave me then no time to think of what I'd seen down in the cellar. It worked so well my memory's almost disappeared; though what remains it makes me blush. All I recall is darling girls, and my hands seemed little more than paws; one, I think, I tried hard to undress, but which I do not know; another, I kissed about the ear because it made her shiver; and one, I know, I tried to touch… I simply cannot write down where.

They must have carried me off to bed, and once again undressed me. I hardly dare to think just what those lovely girls they might have done to avenge themselves for what I tried to do to them; fortunately, by then I was in no condition whatsoever to remember anything at all.

I woke this afternoon and wrote once more to Liz; begged her yet again to come and join me, or failing that, at least to write. Oh how I wish that she was here, to dance with me by Moonlight, to kiss me when I'm drunk.

To sleep with me at night.

Without my Liz, this world is best forgotten.

Sunday, 21st October 1803

Last night was so confusing. I know I drank too much, and smoked too much, and kissed too many ladies.

And how I danced, although I know not quite to what. I danced, it seemed, the last dance in the world, whereafter then all time would cease to be.

Some part of me it knows that, being Saturday night, the hall was once again quite crowded, with fiddlers playing jigs, with men in soldiers' uniforms with all the brains of prawns, with thugs and highwaymen who'd rather leap a while with ladies before they skipped a-rope or shot each others' heads off, all come up the hill to dance with Flora's warm-lipped maidens.

Another part knows all those ripe young girls were there with me alone in lovely Cynthia's parlour, and wearing nothing more than pure white petticoats. No other man they wanted then to dance with, nor other man to squeeze and kiss them. And all the music then was gavottes and galliards, all tinkled on the harpsichord. And how we leapt, and how we loved; and how they were so sweet a-prancing. And Cynthia most of all; because I knew that every girl I danced with (call them Flora, Violet, Rose or what you will), all were Cynthia in disguise; and yet she could not hide at all the sweet round softness of her lovely body. I hugged her, oh so tightly.

And yet I also know that (Cynthia perhaps apart) those lovely maids were all outside, full-dressed and dancing in the hall as well.

I did not understand it then; and now I do not either.

I'd wanted to return below and explore some more of Somnium; but Cynthia would not let me. She told me, mock solemn but quite firmly, that if I wished to see those spires again, my writing must be finished first. Besides, she asked, all wreathed in smiles, how could I leave so many lovely ladies unpartnered for a dance? I almost answered that they had partners quite enough there in the hall outside, but still I was confused; besides, a moment later, soft, smiling girls were all around me, offering me their hands and begging loud for dances and for kisses.

I let myself be persuaded. It was not hard at all.

Before too long I was quite drunk, and dancing as if there was no other thing in life. Another drink or two and I added kissing to my world. I told those sweetheart girls I loved them all, both individual and collective. Another glass, and then I said I'd forsake London quite for good, and simply stay with all my lovelies ever more, and kiss them till the world was ended. I glanced around then, and Cynthia looked at me so strangely.

And when I'd drunk a little more, I simply stopped remembering.

I woke this afternoon all afire to pick up pen and paper, to write my story's coda.

And so my little tale of *Somnium*'s quite concluded.

'Why how now, good my lord?' asked young Bartholomew Greene, a browning oak-leaf wind-tossed still and falling past his shoulder.

And Endimion Lee, his head was all a-reel.

He knew he'd been this way before, he knew he'd dreamt a more-than-dream; he hoped that if he closed his eyes, it'd happen all again. And yet he knew it wouldn't; and memory was all he had for now.

He sat a horse by dark-wood Shooters Hill, but now the sky was twilit-bright, and nothing seemed amiss. But everything was gone. A void was in his soul and mind, and only now a little spark, it lingered in his heart. A flame he'd always cherish, called Diana.

And now to think her name was but to think of loss. He cursed the Fates that would not let them love; and then the worst... he cursed himself for never thinking: were the Fates a dream as well? Could they, opening up their love-besmitten eyes, have woken from that prohibition? He did not know, but all the world now seemed to him collapsed into an abyss of deep regret.

For everything was gone.

'Why stop you here, my lord?' continued Greene. 'This hill has all too ill a name.'

Endimion Lee, he raised a hand, and though it seared his soul to say it, said it anyway: 'It's nothing, Bart. A moment's pain, here in the chest, a rising humour setting all my brain awhirl. You see? It's passed away already. So let's be on to Greenwich.

'Besides,' he smiled, 'I know you would not linger here. They say it's fairy-haunted.'

'Then let's be gone!' exclaimed Bart Greene, his voice too loud, his eyes all looking out their corners.

'Aye, perhaps, we should,' Lee told him then, and looked down for to find what rubbed him in his doublet. 'But tell me, Bart, did you ever once, at night, dream dreams you thought so real, you had to think them true? And wake up all amazed, to find it was not so?'

'I never did, my lord! Though once I dreamt of finding pots of money that...'

'No more!' commanded Lee, his voice all shaken, for now he knew just what his hand had found inside his doublet. And knowing that, he could not talk of money, far too base compared to dream. 'Another word before we get to Greenwich, and Bartho' Greene, I'll thrash you for your life. Now ride ahead. I'll catch you 'fore the crossroads.'

His harshness on the moment caused regret, and yet he had to be alone. He drew his hand out from his doublet, looked down upon a jet-black raven's feather; remembered how she'd told him 'keepsake', remembered how he'd called it 'treasure'.

He looked up then to woody Shooters Hill, he saw the lovely Moon arising.

And all his world dissolved in tears.

Monday, 22nd October 1803

Dear Gods and Goddesses of the world beneath the Moon, and all those more above, please help me get this down. I have to write this while I have the chance, and while I can remember.

I have not slept since yesterday afternoon.

As soon as I had finished, I read my final pages to dear Cynthia. She sat upon my knee to hear them; I thought this was so sweet. A charming kiss was my reward when at the last I stopped; by way of celebration, we transformed supper to a feast.

Although I thought I knew already, I had to ask her if she liked my work. She laughed and ruffled up my hair.

I kissed her.

I did not have to mention after that just how I wanted to spend the evening; dear Cynthia started preparing lanterns quite spontaneous. Yet before we descended to the cellar, Flora lined up all her darling maidens, so I could gently hug and kiss them, before we went down to the dark. Flora I embraced last of all, then Cynthia as well, because I could, and just because I wanted to. Even so, this kissing quite confused me.

So arm in arm and hand in hand, then down the stairs we went, my Cynthia and I, and through that ancient door.

I have to hurry on; I'm not quite sure how much longer I can write.

The white marble sculpture now showed Diana in her chariot, whipping up her horses; the curtain wall was fully built, and when we reached the sunken garden, there, below a glowing Moon, we found it full of pure white lilies.

But Somnium itself...

It stood there bright in all its old perfection, quite restored; and oh, it looked so wondrous. And more than this, it was a palace full of lights. Each window shone, and all around the walls were flaring torches set in sconces. Upon the roofs were flags and banners, all whipcracked in a wind that simply was not there. And everything else, it glowed so fine by Moonlight.

We went inside, and then I was so puzzled; for there, somehow arrived ahead of us, were Flora, Violet, Iris and the rest (dear Daisy too, she is a sweet young thing). Hardly dressed at all in gauzy robes, they curtseyed oh so charmingly and called dear Cynthia 'Mistress'; to me they smiled and kept their eyes downcast, I could not understand quite why.

'Sweet girls, I love you all,' I said, and then they looked up all huge-eyed and all a-radiant. And as for Cynthia, I took her in my arms and kissed her; and all her maidens then they gently did applaud.

They brought us, too, great goblets of the finest wine. I cannot quite describe it. If, compared to plain and everyday sack, I'd never tasted strong Falernian; then this was just as much again, for this, I knew, was Moon-wine. A glass, and all my soul it was transported up to heaven. Dear Cynthia hugged me tight and held me up; several days passed by, it seemed to me, before my dizziness did subside. And when it did, I looked on darling Cynthia nude, and oh her eyes, they glowed.

We roamed about then at our leisure, and Somnium palace is a marvel. She took me to the library; it was quite as I had thought it: a place bewondering and bewildering.

For all those books I'd mentioned in my *Somnium* were there: *all* of them, the ones quite real, the ones that might have been, once upon a time, the ones I knew I had made up completely. Even Perkyn of old Hampton's, which I'd added for a joke. Dear Cynthia grinned to see me so confused.

And more than this, she took me to a special shelf, and gave me such a kiss before she'd let me look.

And there, already bound and printed, was my *Somnium*. My journal too, the very one in which I'm writing now, that was there besides.

But there was more.

Another three books of Moon-romance were there upon the shelf as well, all gold-stamped with my name as author: *A String of*

Lustrous Moon-Pearls, Sweet Sister Selena of the Star-Decked Night and *High Diana's Majesty*. And next to these, another dozen journals. And *Miscellanea of the Moon*.

I tried to pick them up (for how I longed to read them) but found I simply could not. Cynthia explained it was because they were not written yet, existing only now as thoughts that might well come to be.

And as I stood there all a-wonder, my eye slid upward to the shelf above, and saw there five thick tomes that bore the name of old Sir Endimion Lee (who I thought I had created); and one of them, of course, it was called *Somnium*. Then glancing down I saw another *Somnium* too, and knew its author was that stranger of the future, 'S'. It begged me quite to read it; and yet somehow I thought I knew its every word already.

I wished so much to linger, for every book around me was a miracle-text and treasure-scripture of the lunar heaven, and all I wanted then was just to sit and kiss dear Cynthia as she read them out to me.

She would not let me stay. Told me all these books could only be read by those who actually lived there, but hoped I'd read them soon.

I did not know quite what she meant. Some part of me it knew I walked in quite impossible worlds; another part thought simply that I dreamed; another said quite plain that I was drunk. Or worse than that, quite mad.

And some part (though I know not whether it was large or small), said all I saw and heard and felt was real.

I stood there all confused. Sweet Cynthia squeezed my hand, and smiled, and led me on.

She led me upward to a soaring tower that made young Severndroog seem midget. I looked down then on all the Somnium I had wrought, its buildings, its sculptures, its gardens and its jewels, and saw them all by glorious Moonlight; and more, I knew the darling woman in my arms, although she called herself mere Cynthia, was dear Diana Regina too. And more, she was my Goddess.

We arrived then at Diana/Cynthia's bedchamber, exactly as I'd written that too, with all its huge round bed. And there were Flora and her darling girls as well, all naked too and all the sweeter for it. I've never seen so many lovely smiles.

I wanted then, of course, to take dear Cynthia straight to bed, and if her charming nymphs they wished to stay and watch, or better yet to join us, then I would be delighted.

So Cynthia Brown-eyes cried out 'Moon mischief!' with a laugh, and all those lovely girls they tickled me. I could not quite believe the way my own invention had come back then to haunt me; but, oh, their little fingers. If there was mischief in that room, it all was with the maidens; and how they were so naughty. All those tickles that I'd hardly dared administer them, they had no compunction now at all in giving back to me.

At last I realised they'd had my clothes off. Then tiny-fingered Cynthia tickled me while all the others held me helpless.

At last I cried surrender; another minute and I knew my heart would fail. It seemed the darling woman had played with me for hours.

She laughed and kissed me then, and called me hero; I was not quite certain why.

They let me dress again before we left the chamber, indeed, they tried to help me; themselves they did not bother.

And so we went downstairs, and slipped out of a back-door at the farthest corner of the palace.

Then Cynthia led me through a rearward garden I'd never thought was there; took me to the palace wall and out a hidden sally-port.

I knew where she was taking me. I did not know quite why. And more, to start, I did not even recognise it.

By day and normal sight, I know it all turfed over; by Moonlight how it sparkled white, all covered up with chalk-chips, mingled up with marble.

Yet there was more now covering up the burial mound besides, for carved memorial slabs lay on its flanks. They were arranged in order.

The latest one read 'Sir Endimion Lee, beloved of the Moon. Taken up above the world and kissed for ever more, 1603.'

And there were others there before.

Guillaume of Eltham. Ælfred of Woolwyche. Lucius Albinus, Londiniensis. Odumnus the Trinovante. Others yet before I just cannot quite remember.

Yet there was space for more to follow. Two slabs were there already, quite uncarved. I thought I knew the names that would appear on both.

Somnium's guardians, all of them; and watchers of the Moon-hill too. Lovers of the Moon, and just as much beloved.

The message was quite plain. Lay down the short and brutal earthly life; rise up to everlasting lunar bliss.

I have to hurry on. There is so little time to write.

As we returned through Somnium's grounds, dear Cynthia said I had to make a choice; and oh it was a hard one.

For she and all her lovely girls were going back at last to Somnium; and Somnium, again, was returning to the Moon. She wished I would go with them. For there, at last, she'd take me in her arms, her bed as well, and rather more than kiss me. And all her lovely nymphkins, they would love me too.

But going, I would leave the world behind.

And worse, in going I would forsake my Liz.

She did not try persuasion.

We came back up the cellar stairs and found The Bull all closed and dusty. No maidens had come back with us; no drinkers sported in the taproom; and all the doors were locked.

I cannot quite say how, but I rather do suspect it has been closed since Jude Brown's execution. But what this means, I simply cannot say.

I'm going with her, of course. Whatever that may cost, I know I have to. The 19th century world to me is as empty as The Bull.

The dawn will be here soon. We cannot stay.

There is a heartbreak pain in this, of course. I mean, my dearest Liz.

But do I have a sister? She has not written; I cannot find her letters. Indeed, I cannot find anything at all now that I am sure I had before I did arrive here.

And yet, in case she *is*, I've written her a letter, to leave here when I'm gone. Indeed, I have to leave it here, for somehow now I find I cannot quite remember even my own address (was it 7, or was it 9?). This journal and my manuscript I'll leave as well; I know they are already there in Somnium, and Cynthia tells me every single thing it must be left behind.

Whether anyone will ever find them, I simply do not know. I am not even sure if they exist at all.

And as for me, I can no longer tell. Perhaps I'm real, or written by another. Perhaps in writing me, he made me real, if only for a short time. Or perhaps I've written him, when he was writing me. I really do not know. Or mayhap he and I, and all the other authors and characters we between us created, all are one somehow: one author, one story; one hero, one Goddess. Endymion and Selene.

Dear Cynthia is smiling at my door, and oh she looks so lovely. I have to put my trust in her, because she is far more than Cynthia. I know she is Diana Regina; and sweet Diana too.

And more, she is Selene, all haloed up with Moonlight.

Primal Goddess; dearest love; perfection of delicious dreams.

I know not what it means to leave, except renunciation. Perhaps I'll die and leave this empty shell behind; or simply turn to Moonlight.

Oh, she glows and beckons.

I know I have to go all naked; but she is naked too, and so we are together in all things. She says I cannot take anything of the earthly.

And now she calls so urgent; I fear I will be left behind.

Dear Liz, if ever you existed in a real world at all, I cannot say how sad I am to leave you. And if you're not, or if you are, dear Cynthia says that I will find you there with me somehow in Somnium; for all my lady-loves will be as one. In that I find my comfort. And yet, my Liz...

I have to go.

I wish that I could take dear Lizzie with me.

Sweet Liz, of all the women here below the Moon, you always meant the most to me, because you are my sister; and more than that, my love. I wish you so much love and happiness.

And if they tell you I am dead, then, darling, do not weep.

For I am gone to heaven in the Moon.

And now farewell.

Oh, Liz, this is so hard.

My sweetest Liz, I loved you.

Steve Moore died suddenly, under a Full Moon, in March 2014. It was always his intention that we should produce a paperback of his novel *Somnium*, which we initially published in 2012. On the occasion of this new edition, we have taken the opportunity to reproduce a short chapbook, *Sketches of Shooters Hill*, originally published by Steve's own Somnium Press, in an edition of 30, and privately distributed to friends. Also included here are photographs from a small tour of the settings featured in his novel, led by the author.

Sketches of Shooters Hill

Just three
With pictures for the hard-of-hearing

The Burial Mound

Probably the oldest, smoothest and lowest man-made structure on Shooters Hill is the burial mound, fenced off with green-painted and rust mouldered council railings, that lies at the junction of Plum Lane and Mayplace Lane (old tracks these, that bear the treasured name of 'Lane') and, on the other side, abuts to Brinklow Crescent (a typically unimaginative estate-builder's name for a road which curves below the hill's crest). Some 75 feet across and perhaps no more than four feet higher than the surrounding ground, the round barrow dates back to the Bronze Age; a survivor for nigh-on four thousand years.

A survivor in more ways than one, for in times gone by there were six Bronze Age burial mounds, all full-Moon round, about this Northern tip of Shooters Hill, where the sleeping dead could look down on the windings of the ever-flowing river; eternal motion passing by, below eternal rest. All the others are gone, destroyed in the 1930s by the same estate-builders who gave us Brinklow crescents too. What influences might have risen up from the soil of the old, offended hill, its entire groundplan, looked down on from above, a sickle of the Moon embodied of the mineral selenite, to make even vandalous destroyers such as these, build and name their roads in crescents?

Even so, our grand survivor has not survived intact, for it was 'dug' by unknown hands at the beginning of the 20th century; and worse, whatever contents may have been found have not merely disappeared, they never were recorded. The scar is there today upon the old one's pate: a slight dip in the centre of the mound, where no amount of refilling and returfing could ever quite restore the original time-smoothed contour.

There were more peaceful days. Until the middle of the 19th century, this northern outcrop of the hill was covered in fields of furze which, flowering, would cover the area in the same golden glory that caused Linnaeus such religious rapture when, a while before and some short way away, he looked back down along old Roman Watling Street to distant London town from Shooters Hill's high eminence, and fell down on his knees to see the floral glow that spread for mile on mile. Then, its brow surrounded by a circlet of leafy trees, the burial mound played host to summer picnics. In 1855 came Tower House, or 'Graham's Folly' as others called it, and the mound was fenced off in its grounds; but Tower House went too, along with all the furze, when Brinklow Crescent came to be. An old oak still accompanies the tumulus, just across Plum Lane; and new trees now, by Mayplace Lane, have replaced the ancient chaplet.

Each year in April, the burial mound erupts daffodils, bluebells and, that quaint contradiction-in-terms, the white bluebell, while round its edges springs the thousand-flowered yarrow. In summer all is grass, periodically and mysteriously mown (for I have never seen the mower); in winter, dormancy and the windblown leaves of oaks.

In China, yarrow grew by tombs as well, and was harvested to make the divination stalks with which the *Book of Changes* was consulted. And if not divinatory, it seems to me there's something quite divine about this ancient tumulus as well. There are no signs, no placards, no inscriptions and no marks; whoever sleeps here, sleeps unknown. I'd wish it were an ancient queen, who rested here beneath the Moon; but some pretty king or local chieftain, ruling here when London was not even thought seems rather more the likely. I doubt I would have liked him, yet to lie in the tomb for millennia, and then to be dug up by the curious, still seems rather sad. Perhaps it does not matter, for ancient

Steve Moore leads a tour of Somnium *locations on 1 April 2012 . Here he points out the Bronze Age burial mound featured in the novel. At Steve's request, his ashes would be scattered here by friends following his death in 2014.*

bones would long ago have mingled with the soil, the essence spread throughout the mound itself.

Not long after I began to interest myself in the mound and its relation to the hill, a charming fantasy occurred to me (or intuition, if you will): that whoever had been reverently buried here, oh so long ago, to become one with the earth, had somehow become the tutelary deity of Shooters Hill as well, and would be still for as long as the mound survived. And so, in all the years that have drifted by since then, whenever I've passed the mound on one of my rambling walks, I've bid good morning to the local God; for to do anything less would seem to lack in courtesy.

The courtesy was returned a few days after I began the practice. One March morning; after a light but recent snow (already melted everywhere else), I approached the mound, 'good morning' on my lips, and found a small snowman awaiting me, perhaps a foot high. A conical heap for a body, a snowball for a head... but that head bristled with a 'hair' of little sticks, or perhaps some ancient cunning-man's antlered headdress made of twigs. I knew the God by sight, and paid him my respects. The following day he'd disappeared, never to be seen again. No further sight was necessary.

Born high up on Shooters Hill myself, when I die I want my ashes scattered on the burial mound, by the light of a lovely full Moon. So just for a moment, I too can become an offering to the local Gods and Goddesses, and merge my essence with the native soil... before all that physically remains of me is blown away and scattered, like oak-leaves on the whirling wind.

21ˢᵗ April 2004, in the evening
The first sight of the New Moon
The Old Moon in the New Moon's arms.

The Post-Box of the Ju-Ju Devil-Worshippers

Where the newer Kinlet road, running from a 1930s estate, joins the older Eaglesfield Road, there is a triple junction. Like crossroads, and perhaps even more so, such a meeting of three roads was always considered a place of power, for here lurked Hecate as Trivia, the Goddess of the Three Ways.

On the corner of this junction stands an unremarkable George VI pillar-box, which in recent years had a commonplace rectangular box attached to its side, in which delivering postmen would store their mail while engaged in different parts of their route. Such added boxes, of course, make the pillar-box rather like a crouching hunchback or, by a curious convergence, a postman carrying a sack of letters; they also provide flat surfaces for graffiti-artists.

Generally, I am no lover of the *graffito*, especially when it merely consists of inscribing a name or call-sign (surely there are more artistic or literary aspirations than this?). However, for a couple of years at the beginning of the 21ˢᵗ century, one face of this rectangular box was decorated with the something rather special: a matchstick-man figure of the Devil, about a foot high. Mere lines his arms and legs and body, a circle for his head and dots his facial features; two little horns upon his head, and in his hand a trident pitchfork. More, it was delineated in white paint with a brush, rather than the usual spray-can. I have no idea who painted it so, young or old, male or female, but I will always regard it as a masterpiece of naïve art, at its most primitive. Perhaps the Devil himself painted it, with a talon dipped in ashes from the fires of hell.

At the time I first came across this delightful piece of art, I was romantically involved with a charming lady from Brazil, in whose company I'd visited Salvador-Bahia, the home of the Candomblé religion. Seeing this 'devil-in-white on pillar-box red', I was immediately struck by the resemblance to Exu, the deity who, in the curious Afro-Catholic iconography of the Candomblé, is usually portrayed as Satan. And Exu is a God of the crossroads and junctions. Not surprisingly, I soon imagined some hidden cult of Afro-Brazilian devil-worshippers, otherwise unknown upon the hill, making ju-ju at the junction and posting off their letters to God-in-Hell-Below.

My favourite Satan is long-gone, presumably removed by local council anti-graffiti squads… though some part of me hankers to think he was such an affront to the local Christians that they, themselves, were moved to have him quietly removed. I miss him every time I walk past, and remember his primitive smirk with great affection.

And how often did I carry my letters the extra half-mile more than usual, simply for the delightful frisson of mailing them in such a gloriously Satanic post-box…

23ʳᵈ April 2004, by Moonlight
With a bottle of Chardonnay.

The Picnic of the Imagination

The southern half of Shooters Hill is covered, almost entirely, with woods, with names varying from the obvious to the strange… Castle Wood, Oxleas Wood, Jackwood… some parts of which are believed to be perhaps 8,000 years old.

In some fifty years of walking the hill, however, I have to say (with considerable disappointment) that never once have I gone 'down in the woods today' (not even 'in disguise') and had the 'big surprise' of coming across the Teddy Bears' Picnic. Indeed, I cannot recall seeing a single Teddy Bear in Shooters Hill woods, either picnicking or otherwise. This has always struck me as being a lamentable failure on the part of the universe to correspond to its description in popular culture.

After all this time, it seems obvious to me that the universe is not about to buck up its ideas on this score, and so it has occurred to me of late that perhaps I might be able to assist it with an 'artistic installation' of my own (or, as I prefer to think of it at other times, a 'wheeze'). The project would be essentially simple, the preparatory work consisting of a few trips to the local charity shops to purchase a number of cheap, no-longer-loved Teddy Bears, some plastic cups and plates, and a tattered umbrella for shelter. Then, with the addition of a bottle of lemonade and a box of fairy-cakes, one would make for the more impenetrable depths of the woods, find a secluded spot in the undergrowth, and set the Teddy Bears a-picnicking… perhaps while singing a certain song and laughing like an escapee from a lunatic asylum. One would, of course, feel obliged to take a number of photographs of this momentous occasion, and to record the entire proceedings in a detailed journal.

Thereafter, return visits would be paid every other day, to record and photograph developments. Would the food and drink have been consumed, or would mysterious hands have provided further provisions? Would certain of the Teddy Bears, released from charity shop imprisonment, have made a break for freedom? Or would others have somehow come to join the party? Would there be signs of riotous, lewd or disorderly behavior? And would, eventually, the entire picnic decamp for another location? How long can Teddy Bears party, after all?

Unfortunately for the development of British Art and the notion of unifying culture and nature, there is a certain person in my life who, at the merest mention of such a project, would immediately throw her hands up in horror and cry: 'Poor Teddies!' After that, I would be endlessly upbraided with even thinking of exposing helpless cuddly toys to the ravages of the weather, of vandals, of foxes, of small boys or, worst of all, of dogs. And so, I fear, this project will, as far as I'm concerned, have to remain nothing more than a 'thought experiment' for the forseeable future.

And yet, having once conjectured it, written it down, and made it 'more nearly real' than it was before, who knows what influences will drift into the mental ether surrounding the hill?

And perhaps, when next I 'go down in the woods today', I may indeed 'be sure of a big surprise'...

26th April 2004, in the evening.
While quite, quite sober.

Overleaf: Steve Moore at the foot of Severndroog Castle in Oxleas Wood,
Shooters Hill.

Afterword: *An Architecture of Dreams*

A few years ago, Hackney hierophant Iain Sinclair was soliciting contributions for his forthcoming anthology *LONDON: City of Disappearances*, a collection themed around people, places or things that had disappeared, were disappearing or would disappear somewhere in London. In response I wrote a thick slab of rich, high-cholesterol prose titled *Unearthing*, an unusual excavation of my oldest, best and strangest friend, Steve Moore. While the South London occultist, author and oriental scholar was not, strictly speaking, disappearing at a more alarming rate than anybody else, he had always seemed to me to be deliberately liminal and ghostly in relation to the solid and shin-bruising world around him. Also, it occurred to me that when his vanishing inevitably happened then a unique, perhaps enormously important, human narrative might go unrecorded and unnoticed in a kind of double-dip deletion. Motivated thus, I set to work upon anatomising my consenting subject with his full co-operation, a dissection carried out without the use of anæsthetic. The resultant work has since become a lavish boxed-set audio recording and equally splendid visual narrative in collaboration with the photographer Mitch Jenkins. It's been performed live in the massive subterranean catacombs beneath Waterloo Station, where the work's real-life protagonist was in attendance as the intimate and sometimes painful details of his mortal journey were paraded before an enthusiastic audience of spectators, and the Moon alone knows where this constantly-expanding multi-media endeavour will end up, as musical, computer game or action movie.

Given this bewildering tide of exposure, I have no wish to reprise the biographic details of *Unearthing* here, save for those related to the pivotal point in the narrative where the emotionally deranged main character decides to write a novel that encapsulates his yearnings, his environment, his dreams and sense of loss; a grand old-school romantic fantasy that he decides will be called *Somnium*.

Dreams and fantasy have been, in retrospect, a major and defining element in my relationship with Steve since its inception, back in the formative days of the British comics and science fiction scenes. There was the fantastic nature of the comic books and the American science fiction paperbacks we both admired, wherein extraordinary dream-like visions were expressed with satisfying frequency. Indeed, many of our early pulp S.F. and comic idols later turned out to have channelled their ideas through Greenwich Village reefers, or from the material provided by their dreams. For instance, there was Steve's great pulp role-model Gardner Fox, a prolific writer in a dozen or more genres with as many pseudonyms who penned the interplanetary romance *Adam Strange* in D.C./National Comics *Mystery in Space*, and who claimed to receive inspiration for his comic book work from another world, transmitted to him in his dreams. Whether Fox himself believed this to be true or whether it was just a brightly coloured and imaginative piece of wrapping paper meant to entertain his readers, it's an indication of the way that the oneiric appeared to pervade the 1960s pop-cultural landscape that surrounded *Somnium*'s eventual author back then, in both his and contemporary society's eventful, pyrotechnic and immensely influential adolescence.

When that adolescence took a psychedelic shift during the decade's later years and through the 1970s, the dreaminess of things became, if anything, more noticeable and pronounced. There were the borderline realities that typified Steve's early work with the then-fledgling *Fortean Times*, and the occasionally mystic or phantasmagoric drifts of our cannabinated conversation. Hours would be spent poring over whatever hallucinatory comic strip visuals one of us, usually Steve, had just discovered, whether that be the glittering stippled drift of Dave Sheridan's *Dealer McDope* or the stupefying vistas of former architect Winsor McCay's turn-of-the-20th-century newspaper strip masterpiece, *Little Nemo in Slumberland*. Dreams were very much on the agenda, and I can remember asking if he'd ever been afflicted by a powerful rushing in the ears when on the edge of sleep, something which I'd experienced intermittently since childhood, only to receive a very detailed and firsthand account of the phenomenon and its relationship to lucid dreaming, the first time I'd heard or understood that term. It was around this time that I began to realise that the waking part of Steve Moore's life, the part I knew, was just the iceberg's tip. There was another life entirely going on below the waterline. It would be some few years before he first began to diligently and methodically record his eerie night-adventures, all his lurid astral slapstick, but the blueprint for his later *Twilight Zone* persona was already firmly tacked in place.

Through the 1980s and the 1990s, reading through Steve's last few weeks of dreams became almost a ritual part of my ongoing weekend visits to his family home on top of Shooters Hill, the neighbourhood itself a curiously sedate and dreamlike realm above the supine spread of London that I had become increasingly familiar with since my first stopover at age 14. Technically, I suppose this could be seen as evidence of occult grooming, but having for some decades had far too much hashish in my system to permit more than fragmentary recall of my own dreams, the opportunity to keep up a vicarious relationship with someone else's midnight idylls, mysteries and nightmares proved both irresistible and rapidly addictive. In the same way that repeated reading of an author's work acquaints one with the quirks and subtle ticks of his or her authorial style, the reading of somebody's dream-life over a protracted period of time makes one familiar with the idiosyncrasies of their unconscious mind, the region of their creativity which they cannot control.

In Steve Moore's case, even a cursory reading of his dreams revealed the workings of a highly structured mind that was exact and scrupulous in ordering its information. The evocative and sometimes creepy names of characters parading on his mental stage, such as the memorable Wilfred Cruel or the inter-dimensional crime cartel known only as 'The Suitcase', seemed to emerge fully formed out of the basement of his mind without the need for conscious literary intervention. In the typed and ring-bound dream-logs there is also a precision when it comes to numerals, providing numbers for imaginary bus routes, or the sums of money needed for the purchase of some non-existent book or artefact from the emporiums of his private underworld. The catalogued nocturnal wanderings potentially afford a fascinating glimpse into a writer's mind: is this the way it works for all of us? Is there some reflex we have learned or had imprinted through those years of unrelenting deadlines and providing creativity to order, something that compels us to immediately furnish all the salient details, names and numbers every time that we invent a place or person, even in our sleep? Or is that just one of Steve Moore's many unique and distinct peculiarities?

Beyond this attention to minutiæ, the recorded night-script also has a signature approach to cast and setting. Other than the various invented characters, the dreams are almost repertory ensemble pieces with the same actors and actresses continually recurring. There's a smattering of past or current friends and work associates, a thriving and continuing clan of ghostly, since-departed family and a rotating roll-call of incongruous celebrities, such as a cat-suit period Diana Rigg or, unexpectedly, a number of contemporary cricketers. The cast is noticeably small, around two dozen faces constantly reiterated, with a similarly striking limitation to the range of dream locations. These consist of streets and landmarks found on Shooters Hill where he has lived in the same home since he was born, a few familiar avenues from the metropolis, the occasional remote city or town that is somehow reachable by a 10-minute walk or bus-ride within the telescoped geography of his dreamscape, and most frequently the house in which the greater part of his existence has been contained. Oh, and an unusual preponderance of railway stations, which made the performance of *Unearthing* he attended in the oracle-cave tunnels under Waterloo doubly apposite.

Here and there are dreams which seem to have an obvious occult overlap, such as some of the many visitations by his patron Greek moon-goddess, Selene. Others provide strange little hints and seemingly hidden puzzles, such as the unusual multi-part false-awakening series of dreams that he had in a single night, commencing with a fragment in which I was visiting his house and insisting upon casting the *I Ching* using a novel method that Steve had, in reality, just been sent in the post. Since I was in fact visiting on the weekend following, when I read this dream I suggested that we repeat it in reality, just to see if anything interesting happened. We acted out the initial dream with close attention to detail, and since Steve couldn't remember what question had been asked of the oracle in the original, we decided with a self-referential postmodern twist to make the query 'What was the reading in the dream?' The answer, after consulting the *I Ching*, turned out to be an almost comically accurate 'playlist' for the various sections of the multi-part dream itself. Perhaps you had to be there.

One of the most notable and incongruous elements to be found in the daily-updated files was the distinctive and curiously consistent chunks of buried architecture that were often being dug up or otherwise unearthed from the Shooters Hill side streets of his nightly imaginings. With their scale and their art nouveau flourishes, these fragments might almost have been the remains of one of Winsor McCay's soaring *Slumberland* cities were it not for the ancient classical touches that marked them as a product of Steve Moore and his great fondness for the beautiful, dead and buried classical world.

Around the commencement of the 21st century, circumstances seemed to have left the Shooters Hill anchorite with only sporadic work and with a certain degree of emotional cumulus clouding up his life and his moods. While the actual sequence of events has been obscured by distance, as far as I recall I'd arrived at Steve's for a weekend visit and had read through his latest slew of dreams on the Friday night of my arrival. I think it was on the Saturday morning following, while we were both out for a brief constitutional walk around the hilltop, that I remarked to Steve on how it seemed odd for him to be without a project when he had such a fantastic amount of imagery, ideas, characters and situations collected up in his couple-of-decades-worth of ring-bound dream-logs.

He didn't dismiss the observation out of hand, as I remember it, but expressed some doubts about how such random and irrational material could be successfully included in any kind of comprehensible narrative. I suggested that perhaps he could come up with some piece of new wave science fiction that might not have been out of place in Michael Moorcock's golden age editorial stint on the remarkable *New Worlds*, perhaps a work with overtones of the early, baroque J.G. Ballard: a man, perhaps a writer, living on Shooters Hill and observing dispassionately as an encroaching breakdown of reality itself spreads out across London, manifesting in episodes taken from incidents in Steve's dream-life. I might even have remarked upon the fact that in my own experience introducing a loop of self-reference into a work tends to produce unusual occult feedback in one's actual life. On our way to the shop off Shrewsbury Lane for cigarette papers and Turkish Delight, it's possible that I droned on about how it's the capacity for self-reference in our own dual-stranded DNA that allows human or animal existence; that maybe self-reference is a key feature in the creation of living systems, whether that be an organism or, conceivably, a manuscript.

Of course, he never listens to me. Apart from anything else, despite his admiration for Moorcock and many of the writers of the *New Worlds* stable, Steve Moore has never really been in his heart a new wave science fiction man and has always had more of an inclination towards the romantic fantasy, from his *Adam Strange* adolescence onwards. When he informed me a few weeks or months later that he'd tentatively started work on what would be his first serious novel, I was unsurprised to learn that no traces of anything that could remotely be called science-fictional were to be found in the new work, and that rather than making his dreams into the content of the novel he intended to make it instead a work about his emotional situation as, in more than one sense of the word, a dreamer. The suggested location of Shooters Hill itself had remained intact, and the main protagonist was still a writer, but that was the point at which any resemblance to anything which I myself might have imagined ended. The working title that he was turning over in his mind and considering was a one-word reference to the chunks of excavated architecture from his dream adventures: *Somnium*.

I read through the work in randomly spaced instalments as it was produced, and began to experience a sense of both wonderment and alarm at where it seemed to be headed. Whether it had been my own suggestion or not, self-reference was clearly playing a large part in the developing narrative. The main protagonist is a 19th century writer in self-exile on the top of Shooters Hill, fleeing from a doomed and forbidden infatuation, drinking and writing his way towards madness while lodging in rooms at the Bull Inn, an establishment just up the road from Steve's place that he walked past every day. Although he'd distanced the prose by a couple of centuries from his own actual times and circumstances, the mood of the early-Victorian protagonist seemed to be in keeping with what I knew to be Steve's developing fondness for the doomed æsthetes of the later Decadent movement, part of his general retreat from involvement in a distasteful present or future. The faintest of warning bells started to tinkle when the book's main character suddenly decides that the best way out of his intractable emotional predicament is to write a fantasy novel set in the same location in which he is currently residing, but transposed to an earlier century. The haunted fictional author, Kit, decides to call his novel *Somnium*.

Uh-oh.

While I might have suggested adding a loop of self-reference to the work, I certainly hadn't been irresponsible enough to suggest introducing further such loops to the narrative. Wouldn't that be likely to create some sort of ontological vortex? Or was that what he was aiming for; a bottomless conceptual maelstrom to fling his scrawny carcass into? Either way, I read on with some trepidation.

This meta-novel, this *Somnium*-within-*Somnium*, takes place upon a phantasmagorical Elizabethan Shooters Hill in keeping with the flesh-and-blood author of *Somnium*'s then-current preoccupation with harpsichord music and the enchanted proto-psychedelic culture of the 16ᵗʰ century. The hero, a Walter Ralegh man of action with the lunar appellation of Endimion Lee, finds himself lost in the amorous intrigues of a moon-palace, the enchanted realm of Diana Regina (a name which neatly compresses that of the classical moon-goddess Diana with the honorific of Elizabeth R., and ends up sounding not dissimilar to 'Diana Rigg'). You might say that he's a 'Prisoner in Fairyland', to borrow from Shooters Hill-born Algernon Blackwood's original title for what would become *Starlight Express*. As I've already remarked in my excavation of Steve Moore's life, *Unearthing*, the resultant adventures are like an inverted version of Aubrey Beardsley's decadent pornographic take upon the Venus and Tannhäuser story, *Under the Hill*, only set on top of the hill and without the fleshy consummation.

Just at the point in the developing tale where I was starting to fear that a rebuffed Endimion Lee would find solace in penning a mediæval romance set on Shooters Hill and entitled *Somnium*, it became apparent that while it was indeed the real-life author's intention to deepen his whirlpool of stories this would not be accomplished by simply reiterating the novel's principal device. Instead, we and the Elizabethan protagonist are introduced to the Library of Somnium and its unending array of liminal never-written dream-tomes. These, as it transpires, contain short decadent pieces such as *This Dull World and the Other*, a prose-poem that Steve had previously written during an idle moment and which, with its style and content, had turned out to fit perfectly within the expanding and unfolding layers of *Somnium*. Moving between these layers, the camera-eye of the prose could pull back in a vertiginous swoop from a fascinating and engrossing self-contained fable, to 16ᵗʰ century Endimion Lee reading it in the Library of Somnium, to the 19ᵗʰ century where Kit Morley is writing all this and starting to suspect that there's another writer, somewhere on Shooters Hill in its future, who is writing him. It may have been around this juncture, as the novel neared its completion and began to enter a process of re-drafts and revisions, that I elected to wait and read the book when it was finished, from beginning to end, to see whether this complex twilight endeavour would stand up to daylight scrutiny.

Finally reading the completed work, being able to perceive the whole of its literary shape, was a revelation. As is usually the case upon stumbling across something of rare originality, the mind tends to flail around looking for comparisons by which to measure it. I could only find two. The first, purely in structural terms, was Jan Potocki's overlooked fantasy *The Saragossa Manuscript* with its hallucinatory maze of stories-within-stories and its mirrored characters and situations. The second, for reasons that are more difficult to articulate, would be the equally neglected *A Voyage to Arcturus* by Steve's near-neighbour from down the hill, Blackheath resident David Lindsay.

For me as a writer, the overwhelming impressions that I have when reading an original work like Lindsay's visionary novel or like Steve Moore's *Somnium* are not un-akin to the impressions that I get from the later James Joyce or the gloriously mad rapture of William Blake: there is awe and there is admiration, but there is also that sense of bewildered amazement when it occurs to you to ask the question 'Why would anybody write this?'. Why would anyone, least of all a professional commercial writer of 30 or 40 years' experience, spend so much time and energy and passion upon a work which, in their heart of hearts, they must have known would only be read and understood and enjoyed by a handful of people, if that? It's clearly a task not undertaken in the hope of reward or acclaim, but most probably with an expectation of baffled dismissal. As to why the author wrote it in the way they did, whether we're talking about Blake or Joyce, about David Lindsay or Steve Moore, the only answer that we end up being left with is 'because they had to.' These are all works of vision that speak from their authors' individual souls, things that had to be said in order to articulate the unique feelings, ideas and perceptions that these writers felt were at the core of their personal being.

They are works of compulsion where their creators, we suspect, had no choice but to do things how they did. It wasn't up to them, it was up to the work itself. This kind of pure writing, perpetrated without lust of result, is without question about as courageous as it gets on this side of the typewriter.

Of course, to comment on *Somnium*'s undoubted bravery and originality is to avoid the question which Steve Moore put to me when he gave me the completed and revised manuscript to read around five years ago now, namely, is it any good? Considering the book's ambition, taking into account the dexterity with which it shifts from the prose style of one era to another, bearing in mind the sheer lusciousness of the language and the dizzying range of ideas, I'd have to reply now in the same way that I did to *Somnium*'s author back then: 'I think it's a masterpiece...'

Given the fact that I'm presently writing this afterword for the first edition, I feel it's more prudent to omit the original ending of my response to this extraordinary novel, which was '...but I don't see how it will ever be published.' It just seemed to me that, from the perspective of a publishing industry increasingly unwilling to blow their budgets on new fiction while there are still celebrity chefs out there who haven't yet given us their autobiographies, *Somnium* was far too weird, exotic and defiantly unfashionable a fish to fry. Its plot, not immediately visible to the untrained eye, is much too peculiar and abstract to sum up in a two-line blockbuster pitch. Its Victorian/ Elizabethan stylings are scholarly and authentic and therefore not in step with the current trend for retro-fitting bygone eras in order to make them more comprehensible and palatable to a contemporary audience. Its capitalised Romanticism is not of the type required by the modern equivalent of the Mills & Boon readership. There's no shopping, there's no sex (for all the lingeringly sustained erotic atmosphere pervading the work), and the intellectual readership who are intelligent enough to appreciate the book are all currently embattled by logic-dodging religious fundamentalists who think the Earth was made around last Tuesday, at least geologically speaking, and are subsequently in no mood to be sympathetic to any species of numinous and archaic fantasy. When I speak of *Somnium* being courageous, this wilful refusal to follow the established conventions of this or any other era is what I'm talking about.

Luckily, the world changes very quickly these days, and my abilities as a Cassandra are clearly pitiful. The apparently ongoing fragmentation of culture, far from being the catastrophe that it originally seemed, seems to have allowed a situation where the giant saurians of mass culture are finding themselves in difficulty while enterprises conceived on a smaller and more mammalian scale are becoming possible, providing a way for even the most outré and marginalised of sensibilities to find their natural audience. I hope this is what happens for *Somnium*. I like the idea of modern readers, however many there turn out to be, being able to stumble by chance upon this unexpectedly deep and exquisitely perfumed pool of prose, to encounter an unlikely conjugation of beautiful language and sensibilities so time-sensitive that they may almost seem alien to the modern ear. I also like the notion that every reader who is willing to entertain this genuinely marvellous fantasy is in a way allowing the buried palace of *Somnium* that lies under Shooters Hill a purchase in their own subconscious mind; could be said to be founding and building that magnificent astral structure, making it more solid and substantial, a mind or a brick at a time.

Somnium is not a novel for our time, or necessarily for any other. It exists in the same timeless, visionary continuum that the work of William Blake or David Lindsay exists in, and it is in my opinion one of the most extreme and unique applications of the imaginative writer's craft that I have ever had the privilege to find myself absorbed in; one of the strangest and most lyrical made-up worlds that I have ever visited. I hope that, having reached this afterword, you will agree and recognise a work and author that have, in Colin Wilson's words, the strength to dream: without leaving your bedroom, which is half a dozen paces from the spot where you were born, to construct such a luminous edifice of narrative, with that narrative itself never venturing more than a few hundred yards from that same bedroom. The strength to insist upon a personal territory of the heart and mind, and then to chart that territory so that other love-wrecked mariners might reach it too.

Dream on.

Alan Moore
Northampton, April 2011

Strange Attractor Press 2017